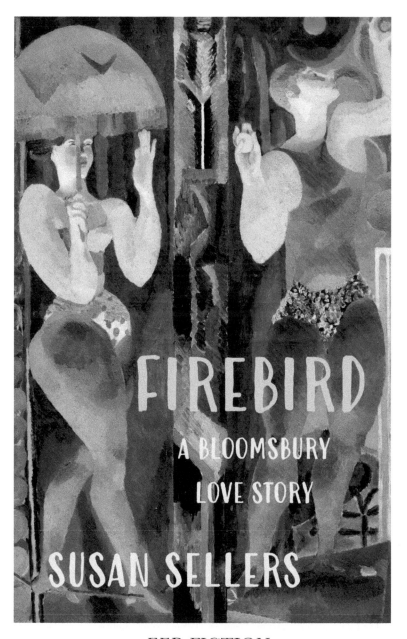

FIREBIRD
A BLOOMSBURY
LOVE STORY

SUSAN SELLERS

EER FICTION
Edward Everett Root, Publishers, Brighton, 2022.

EER FICTION

Edward Everett Root, Publishers, Co. Ltd., Atlas Chambers, 33 West Street, Brighton, Sussex, BN1 2RE, England.

Full details of our overseas agents in America, Australia, Canada, China, Europe, and Japan and how to order our books are given on our website.

www.eerpublishing.com

edwardeverettroot@yahoo.co.uk

Susan Sellers: *Firebird. A Bloomsbury Love Story*

Hardback ISBN 9781913087807

eBook ISBN 9781913087814

First published in England 2022.

Cover image: Duncan Grant, *Juggler and Tightrope Walker*, c.1918-19 (private collection), © The Estate of Duncan Grant / courtesy of Piano Nobile, Robert Travers (Works of Art) Ltd.

Cover by Pageset Limited, High Wycombe.

Book production by Andrew Chapman, PrepareToPublish.Com.

THE AUTHOR

Susan Sellers is Professor of English Literature and Creative Writing at the University of St Andrews. Her first Bloomsbury-inspired novel, *Vanessa and Virginia*, was an editor's pick for *The New York Times* and has been translated into sixteen languages.

For Sue Rabbitt Roff

'dancing... gives you nothing back, no manuscripts to store away, no paintings to show on walls and maybe hang in museums, no poems to be printed and sold, nothing but that single fleeting moment when you feel alive'

— MERCE CUNNINGHAM

'the expected never happens; it is the unexpected always'

— JOHN MAYNARD KEYNES

'how lovely the time was spent with you in the castle'

— LYDIA LOPOKOVA

ACT ONE

'While out hunting, Prince Ivan catches sight of a beautiful bird whose feathers glow as if they are on fire. Captivated, he pursues the Firebird deep into the forest. The Firebird escapes, leaving the Prince a feather and a promise to return should he summon her.'

The curtain rises and the audience settles expectantly. London, in this spring of 1921, is in thrall to the Russian ballet. For weeks now opinion has raged as to whether its bold experiments are expressions of artistic genius or on the contrary barbarian and crude. Yet this is not the controversy that packs the seats of the Palace Theatre despite being blazoned across newspaper headlines. What spurs even those indifferent to ballet to forego rival pleasures and cut short their gossip as the conductor takes his bow are scandalous tales concerning soloist Lydia Lopokova, who tonight resumes her role as Firebird after a mysterious disappearance not even the most zealous journalists can explain.

It is this same Lydia Lopokova who waits in the wings with her partner Prince Ivan, a feather like a scarlet flame trailing from her jeweled headdress. She crosses herself as she hears the low murmurings of the strings, though whether this is because – as she has so endearingly claimed in interviews – she is nervous of disappointing her public after her long absence, or whether it is the mood of foreboding the composer, her lover Igor Stravinsky, instills in these opening bars is impossible to gauge.

Whatever the motive there is no time for her to dwell on Stravinsky now, let alone her dread that despite plans to spend the coming summer together he will never leave his wife, the ailing Katya, or his four children. Nor is there time for Lydia to fret over her own floundering marriage to company manager Randolfo Barocchi and the reason she had to stop dancing and hide herself away. The violins are playing rustling sounds like the stirrings of birds and this is her cue to prepare. She presses up onto the balls of her feet and stretches her arches, windmills each shoulder in turn.

The stage is a darkened forest, the moon a silvery sickle in the jet-black canopy overhead. The trees themselves seem painted in shadow, their forms obscure, their outlines a blur. A hunting horn is heard and the colours shift, first to midnight blue, then deepest Byzantium purple. It is reported of Sergei Diaghilev, the troupe's flamboyant leader, that his maverick talents extend to lighting, and as if to prove this red apples glisten on the still-dusky branches. A harp, its liquid notes sliding in glissando, suggests these apples are as evil as any Eve encountered in Paradise, while the sinister intrusion of a cor anglais confirms our fear that this forest is bewitched.

Lydia has begun counting and at the eerie, tinkling peal of the celeste gathers herself, as if her body is a coil she can compress. Her leap onto the stage is so commanding that she is greeted with none of the applause an adoring public routinely accords a world-famous ballerina. Instead, there is an audible gasp as heads swivel and eyes strain in the attempt to follow her flight. But before we can do more than marvel at her power and apparently effortless grace the spectacle is over, and Prince Ivan, gold-crowned, scarlet-jacketed and sporting a magnificent hunting bow, strays into the forest. This dancer too is a star of the Russian ballet, though the palpable relief when he exits, leaving the scene free for the Firebird to return, highlights it is Lydia people wish to see.

Strings, woodwind and percussion blaze in escalating spirals of sound. A cymbal is struck and Lydia soars centre-stage, convincing all whose gaze is trained on her that her first entrance was not an illusion and she is indeed a magical bird. Such is the impression she creates that many watching are prompted – once the initial thrill subsides – to conjecture that a harness, disguised beneath her costume and connected to a system of wires worked by a team in the wings, must be responsible for her superhuman velocity and height.

The Prince, hiding, spies her, and with a shot from his hunting bow quickly has her in his grasp. The Firebird struggles, torso twisting, wings flailing, in a vain endeavour to escape into the air. Clarinets and horns issue urgent cries of alarm, signaling this is not the romantic pas de deux customary at such moments but a couple locked in deadly combat. The Firebird is courageous, wily, driven by the desperation of the entrapped, and it requires every last ounce of the Prince's strength to hold her. A solo violin sends out a lament and at last the adversaries dance together, as if by acknowledging they are equals there is the glimmering of trust. Now, as the pair circles the stage, their agile, lyrical body-shapes mirror and complement each other. The Prince lifts his prize and she is the Firebird once again, untamed, beguiling, the creature of another world. To a flurry of flutes the Prince sets her down and is recompensed with the gift of a feather. Then, with head erect and beating wings outstretched, the Firebird vanishes, leaving the Prince to stare after her and the audience to wonder how this story will go on.

At a table near a window facing out over a quiet London square, four men, all in early middle age, are lunching together. They have finished their main course which, from the criss-cross of denuded bones congealing in gravy on their plates, looks to have been lamb cutlets, and are waiting for cook to set down pudding, which today is apple pie and custard. They fill the hiatus with conversation that flows easily, as if they are accustomed to spending time in each other's company. Three of the men (the lanky one dressed in suit and tie; the one whose receding hairline flatters his self-image as an intellectual who will yet make his mark; and the one whose perfect features draw comparisons with gods who might be Greek or even Indian) lodge in the house. The fourth – whose exuberant beard froths about his mouth as mischievously as his bespectacled eyes twinkle when, as now, he is conscious of having delivered a witty, well-phrased and probably scurrilous remark – is a regular visitor. It is not only proximity and habit that makes these men so comfortable in each other's company however, nor the bond between two of them forged as members of the same elite club at Cambridge where they studied, nor even the bond between two more as cousins, but the complicated (some would say shocking) sexual liaisons that link them. For three of these men were lovers before they became friends in a triangle which (though not without its inevitable heart-crushing disappointments and bitter rivalries) involved intensities of feeling none of them will forget. The fact that the wife of the fourth is in love with the most beautiful of this trio implicates him in its emotional tangle.

The conversation, as Maynard (in the suit), balding Clive, russet-bearded Lytton and the god-like Duncan wait for pudding, is, as might be expected during a casual luncheon between old friends on an unimportant December day, about none of these things. Instead, they are talking about a new ballet which recently opened at the Alhambra Theatre. This is 'The Sleeping Princess', staged by the legendary Sergei Diaghilev and his Ballets Russes, whose previous dance seasons, including the famous 'Firebird', they have followed with enthusiasm and (while by no means unanimous in their verdicts) admired. Of the four, Duncan is the most effusive in his praise of the new work, perhaps because he is a painter and one of Diaghilev's many innovations has been to commission artists to design his productions with (and this they all agree on) spectacular results. Clive, who has written a book on art as well as an article on the Russian ballet, and Lytton, whose book caused a literary sensation, are less generous. Maynard, who has not yet seen the ballet and is half-preoccupied by the book he himself is currently writing, is content for the most part to listen.

'Diaghilev's "Sleeping Princess" drags ballet back thirty years,' Lytton is grumbling in his high, rasping voice. 'It is pusillanimous and devoid of purpose.'

'Pusillanimous is the word,' Clive affirms. Since there is no sign of pudding, he holds the wine bottle up inquiringly. When Maynard, who seldom drinks during the week, and Lytton, who has delicate health, decline, he pours for Duncan then empties what is left into his own glass. It is an excellent Côte de Beaunes – a present from his lover Mary – and it would be a pity to waste it. 'What was exciting about the Russians,' he continues, swirling his glass and noticing with satisfaction how burgundy-coloured liquid clings to the sides, the sign of a good vintage, 'was precisely their willingness to dispense with the usual confection of pretty feet and prettier skirts and explore the interplay between music and movement. The result might be less immediately pleasing but it elevated ballet to an art.'

'The choice of Tchaikovsky's music was the first in a litany of mistakes,' Lytton groans, 'all the more incomprehensible when one considers the composers Diaghilev has collaborated with. It amounted to little more than saccharine tune-making.' He winces, as if the memory is painful. 'I honestly believed I might be sick.'

Clive nods. 'They say Stravinsky revised it, though it is difficult to see where.'

'The set and costumes were magnificent,' Duncan reminds them. He searches in the pocket of his jacket, paint-spattered despite changing from his smock in his studio nearby before walking the few streets to join the others, and pulls out a notebook and pencil. 'It's rumoured the stage-hands and seamstresses were working sixteen hours a day towards the end to get everything ready for the opening. Even the dresses of the ladies in waiting are hand-embroidered, and that decoration on the Prince's jacket,' he flips open his notebook, sketches a pattern of ornate oak leaves, 'must have been sewn in gold thread.'

'Are there good audiences?' Maynard asks. His voice, in contrast to Lytton's, which has by some been spitefully likened to a squawk, is resonant and musical. 'Must have been an expensive production to mount.'

'Trust you to think of that!' Clive, who is inspecting the label on the now empty bottle and wondering whether the others would consider him overly extravagant if he uncorked another, sniggers.

Maynard lets the remark pass without comment. He does this not because he is unaware of Clive's antagonism towards his career as an economist, which involves him in what all his friends consider an inordinate number of extra commitments (many of which – such as his role as Bursar of King's College in Cambridge where he holds a Fellowship – they deem inappropriate and somehow demeaning for a person who is one of their number), but because it has led to an awkward, mostly tacit competitiveness over money. While Clive has shares in the Bell family coal mines, his bon viveur spending and ad hoc writing career mean his income is rarely what he would wish. Maynard on the other hand has grown increasingly wealthy. Alongside his academic salary, earnings from books and journalism, and payments from various boards and directorships, he has amassed investments which, despite setbacks (most notably in the spring of 1920 when a disastrous decision to buy dollars temporarily threatened to bankrupt him), have made substantial gains. His success as an investor is partly attributable to his encyclopedic knowledge, partly to his perhaps surprising (given his conventional suit and tie) passion for gambling, but also to a rationally derived and strongly held belief that money should not remain idle. This is a view he first formulated during his years as a junior clerk in the London India Office where he was employed immediately after leaving Cambridge, when he became convinced that Indian development would happen more quickly if its populace could be persuaded to invest their spare rupees instead of hoarding them, and it continues to inform not only his economic principles and political allegiances, but his own lifestyle. Indeed, at the current point in time, December 1921, his revenue is such that he has accumulated an enviable collection of both books and modern French paintings, the latter including works by Seurat, Picasso, Matisse, Renoir and Cézanne. And so it is as much out of delicacy towards Clive as a desire to avoid alienating his friends with yet another defence of his career, that when he answers he does so mildly. 'It will damage Diaghilev and everyone involved with the Ballets Russes if the money cannot be recouped. I heard Oswald Stoll advanced first £10,000 then £20,000 so they must be counting on good ticket sales.'

'Audiences have been abysmal.' Clive accedes the point so readily it is as if he has been privy to Maynard's reasoning and is grateful.

'The theatre three-quarters empty,' Duncan, whose own doleful finances are routinely rescued by Maynard in the form of artistic commissions and subsidies, confirms.

Lytton rests his elbows on the table and presses his long fingers together. He too has been a beneficiary of Maynard's money, and though the sales of his wickedly satirical biography *Eminent Victorians* have latterly made this unnecessary, his sense of indebtedness is still raw enough for him to retain a disagreeable feeling of inferiority. He clears his throat. 'Are we to assume the British public is more discerning than we give it credit for?' he wonders, channeling the conversation in a new direction.

'Hardly,' Clive retorts. 'It was the debacle of the opening night. Everything that could go wrong did. The press had a field day.'

'It sounded hilarious,' Duncan interjects still drawing, though his subject is no longer oak leaves but the smoke-grimed boarding houses that can be glimpsed through the silhouettes of bare trees on the opposite side of the square. 'Especially when the Lilac Fairy cast her spell and the creepers that were to grow round the castle got stuck, so the dancer – it was Lydia Lopokova – stood twirling her wand in vain.'

Maynard, whose sense of humour is tickled by Duncan's description, laughs. 'That I should have liked to see.'

''You could go tonight,' Clive points out. 'Though those technical problems were soon dealt with. When I went the set at least operated flawlessly.'

Maynard, impatient for pudding, lifts his gravy-smeared knife and licks it. Lytton and Clive exchange glances. Their friend's uncouth table manners have long been the source of malicious gossip, whenever one of them harbours a grievance against something Maynard has said or done. This was particularly acute during Maynard's affair with Duncan, which ended Lytton's own long love affair with his cousin though it did nothing to alleviate his jealousy. Perhaps because Clive has intuited Maynard's earlier sensitivity towards him, or perhaps because he has no wish to stir up Lytton's animosity, he adds, almost kindly: 'You wouldn't even need to go early. You could buy a ticket at the door.'

Maynard rests his knife back on his plate, shakes his head. 'I've promised myself to forego all indulgences until this book is done. Which it nearly is. Besides, if the production's as bad as you say there seems little point. I've always thought Lydia Lopokova a rotten dancer. She has such a stiff bottom.'

'You liked her well enough in "The Good-Humoured Ladies" to visit her in her dressing room,' Duncan teases. 'I seem to remember she invited you to pinch her calf muscles so you could test their strength.'

8

Maynard grins, picturing the vivacious, undeniably pretty ballerina in her stage make-up, thrusting out her leg to demonstrate her performance had nothing to do with magic but derived entirely from physical stamina, while feeding crusts through the bars of a cage to a yellow canary she addressed affectionately as 'Pimp'. What he remembers most is how she talked almost without stopping, alternately berating her dance partner (whom she considered short and incompetent) and her own choreography – which she insisted was like running miles in sacks of potatoes. Something about the artful way she raised her eyebrows (still painted blue though she was no longer in costume) as she delivered this tirade prompted him to conclude her purpose was to make people laugh. He had been impressed too by the way she spoke, with her Russian inflections and occasionally unexpected or even erroneous word-choice, which lent what she said a strange eloquence reminding him of one of Shakespeare's jocular, perceptive fools. He had found it hard to reconcile his experience of watching the ballet, which from his seat in the auditorium had seemed to him its own magically self-contained world, with this tiny, graceful, roguish woman dressed in a grubby kimono, blowing on a pan of bubbling milk and handing out cups of hot chocolate. 'I'll go,' he concedes, 'before Christmas.'

Cook, her face flushed pink from the oven and climb upstairs, sets an apple pie and jug of custard on the table.

❧

Despite his friends' warning, Maynard is surprised at how empty the auditorium of the Alhambra is. There are the usual balletomanes in the front row, with bouquets of hot-house flowers ready to throw at the feet of the best dancers. In the boxes on either side of the stage are men in evening dress for whom the occasion is a charming preamble to a late supper, their female companions still cocooned in furs against a chill the glittering houselights do little to dispel. The rest of the seats are more sparsely populated, with couples dotted here and there, families preferring ballet to the Christmas shows packing London's theatres, and a group of young men who stride boldly forward from their places at the back as soon as it is clear there will be no more patrons. From the shabbiness of their dress he guesses they are art students, perhaps from the Royal Academy off Piccadilly where Clive's wife Vanessa, now hopelessly in love with Duncan, studied painting with John Singer Sargent. He observes the men under cover of studying his programme, and when a dark-haired twenty-year old with a broad, sympathetic face takes the seat next to his is reminded, agreeably, of his own current lover Sebastian.

He dismisses his momentary regret at Sebastian's absence with the prospect of their spending Christmas together, at the house Lytton rents in Berkshire with his artist friend Dora Carrington and her new husband Ralph, whom he suspects Lytton is in love with. Besides, it is at his instigation that Sebastian is not with him, since he has come to London now his teaching term at Cambridge is over to finish his book: an ambition he has realised this very afternoon. He will need to read it through before sending it to be typed, and there are a few sections that would doubtless benefit from further elaboration, but in the main he is pleased with it. His aim in writing has been to address the criticisms leveled against his first book *The Economic Consequences of the Peace*, in which he exposed what he continues to regard as the debacle of the peace negotiations at the end of the war. He was the senior British Treasury representative at the Paris conference in 1919 and was appalled at its outcome, which not only reneged on agreements reached during the armistice, but demanded reparation payments it was impossible Germany could meet. In his view, instead of promoting harmony amongst nations it laid down conditions that practically guaranteed a second war in Europe. What had made his first book so popular (selling over a hundred thousand copies in twelve languages) were the portraits he drew of the frequently arrogant and dangerously naïve allied negotiators – portraits that included prime-ministers and presidents. Nothing he has witnessed in the three years since it was published has given him cause to revise his conclusion.

To steer his mind away from his book he scrutinizes his programme, and his eyes light on the name of Lydia Lopokova who is dancing tonight. The image he conjured over luncheon of visiting her in her dressing room returns to him, along with the memory of her accepting an invitation to a party he and Clive hosted in their house in Bloomsbury's Gordon Square. He recalls his annoyance at Clive's flirting with Lydia, especially as Clive insisted on speaking French, a language he cannot compete in. Was it after this, he wonders, that he sent her a copy of his book and received in reply a note in her large, sprawling hand, in which she thanked him for his gift with a formality that might have seemed pompous had it not been for her misspellings and the intriguing oddities of her phrasing. After that she disappeared (abandoning the production she was in and no doubt costing Diaghilev and the company a fortune), and there were rumours about her running off with a general from the White Russian Army – a story he always found too romantic to be credible. A far more plausible explanation in his view was that she had become pregnant and retired to have the child, though if that were the cause it is surprising there should have been no mention of it in the papers, which carried stories about her for weeks.

The overture has begun and as the curtain lifts he notes with pleasure that the scene (depicting the interior of a royal palace with dozens of richly dressed guests) is as spectacular as Duncan promised. If his intention in coming tonight was to judge for himself whether this latest offering from the Ballets Russes is as disappointingly retrograde as Clive and Lytton argue, any such objective is quickly relinquished as he becomes engrossed in the tale (familiar to him from childhood visits to the pantomime with his father) of Princess Aurora's christening. When the spurned fairy Carabosse enters with his whiskery face, skeleton hands and long trailing cloak the colour of blood, he remembers the delicious shivers of fear he experienced as a boy. And now it is Lydia herself dancing as the Lilac Fairy, and he watches entranced as she banishes the vengeful Carabosse and transmutes his curse on the infant Aurora into a more benign charm. Her passion captivates him, and so as she circles the stage he is convinced not only of the validity of this make-believe world she inhabits, but that her brave lifting of the curse represents the triumph of good over evil. If he had ever supposed Lydia to be a rotten dancer it is a judgment he overturns now. He has heard it reported that she lacks the technical perfection of fellow soloist Tamara Karsavina, but to his mind she more than compensates with her skill as an actress. She behaves as if everything is happening for the first time, so her movements appear spontaneous and betray no sign of exhaustive rehearsal or being performed before. It is an ability he admires, just as he admired her conversation at their party when Mary, Clive's mistress, piqued by jealousy, eventually took Clive off and he could speak to her alone. What impressed him was that she did not answer his questions in the bored, mechanical manner she might have done given how many times she must reply to such inanities, but as if what he was asking was interesting and fresh.

With hindsight, his decision to go and pay his compliments to Lydia was formed the moment she arrived on stage, though it is only as the Prince reawakens the sleeping Princess that he consciously articulates it to himself. Despite the lusty clapping of the art students and the flower flinging and calls of 'bravo' from the balletomanes, the applause, once the curtain descends and the dancers take their bows, seems too meagre a reward for Lydia's extraordinary performance. As the houselights switch on and the auditorium empties, he heads for her dressing room.

He is uncharacteristically nervous as he approaches her door, not because he is unsure of a welcome — he has met her enough times for a visit to her dressing room to be considered more a mark of politeness than anything out of the ordinary — but because of the emotions the ballet has stirred in him. His new esteem for Lydia (whom he now recognises as an artist of exceptional talent) causes his heart to race and his palms to sweat. He is nervous so rarely that the unfamiliar sensations are strangely intoxicating.

At first, as he hovers in the open doorway, he does not see Lydia. Her room is filled with well-wishers who have hurried backstage for a glimpse of the famous star. He stands his ground until, in a gap, he spies her seated on a stool, wearing the shabby blue kimono he remembers from before. Her hair is pulled into a bun and she is still in her stage make-up, the exaggerated shading round her eyes giving her otherwise symmetrical face a comically lopsided aspect. Lydia herself seems oblivious of her appearance. As he gazes at her, laughing and holding out her hands for her fans to kiss, he is seized once again by the unpalatable memory of Clive monopolizing her attention at their party. He experiences a similar emotion now as a gaggle of balletomanes crowd round her, an emotion which — if it were not for his contentment with Sebastian and the fact he has never physically desired a woman — might trouble him. Instead, he attributes his sentiment to his exasperation that those vying for Lydia's attention do so only so they can boast about it afterwards. His motive, on the other hand, is — what? Though there are a thousand questions he would like to put to her he can scarcely claim, as Clive might with his article on ballet, or Duncan with his painter's understanding, that he has any more compelling reason. Nor can he pretend a genuine involvement with London's Russian émigrés as Clive's sister-in-law Virginia, the wife of his good friend Leonard, could, through her translations of Russian writers into English. No, he is there because Lydia's performance tonight has moved him, and because the few, tantalizingly brief encounters he has had with her in the past have left him curious to know her better.

There is a commotion behind him in the corridor and for a moment he imagines he hears Lady Ottoline Morrell, whose patronage of the arts is well known and who has done much to promote the Ballets Russes during their London seasons. Whoever it is has her back to him, and though she is talking energetically he cannot identify her voice with any certainty over the hubbub of the room. If it is Ottoline, his own chance of an intimate conversation with Lydia must be postponed. He finds pen and paper in his pocket and using the wall as a support writes: 'Please join me for supper at the Savoy when you can, Maynard.' He stops a passing maid and extracts her promise to deliver his message in return for a generous tip. Then he waits as the maid weaves through the throng to Lydia, who reads his note, searches round her, and when she spots him smiles.

§.

How easily Lydia talks to people, Maynard decides, watching her chatter to the waiter at the Savoy as she gives him her coat. He studies her compact figure and graceful movements as she is led between the tables of diners towards him. What draws him is her refreshing, almost childlike eagerness coupled with the physical confidence she has acquired from years of dancing. The former attribute reminds him of Duncan, of whom he remains inordinately fond despite their affair being over, while the latter he wishes he possessed in greater measure himself. Although he can trust himself to speak in front of audiences and, if required, out-argue an opponent, he has never enjoyed being looked at. Indeed, he has often felt – during meetings at his college for example, where the assembled minds are capable of debating for hours – that if only he were a more handsome man he might have won his point more quickly. As he stands to greet her, he is gratified to note several diners interrupt their conversations to conjecture whether this woman he is kissing might be the fêted Russian ballerina.

The waiter fusses over Lydia longer than is necessary, pulling out her chair, opening her menu, shaking out the white folded napkin and laying it across her knee. Maynard is struck by the naturalness with which Lydia accepts these attentions, as if it is incumbent on her to relish them. He compares his own awkward and no doubt haughty reaction and realises she is right, that it is better to show appreciation than to pretend one does not notice or that the service rendered is unimportant. He observes her setting her bag on the floor, wondering how what now seems a perfectly ordinary body, engaged in a commonplace action he might have performed himself, could – only a short time before – have danced so consummately. He should like to know how she is able to leap so high or run on the points of her toes but refrains from asking, not because he is embarrassed (one of the qualities he remembers about Lydia is that she never seems embarrassed), but because he fears if she answers he will not understand. Certainly this is his experience whenever Duncan or Vanessa discuss painting. No matter how clearly they explain an effect to him, he is left with the sense he could no more achieve it himself than he could turn upside down and walk on his hands.

Her bag stowed safely beneath her chair, Lydia places her elbows on the table and rests her chin on her hands. Her hair is scraped back from her face and fastened at her neck in a tight bun, accentuating her broad forehead and surprisingly blue, mercurial eyes. Her nose, which he judges to be as finely sculpted when viewed from the front as those on the statues he and Duncan admired while holidaying in Greece, is, he perceives, dramatically altered when seen from the side. In profile, the tip of her nose curves upwards slightly, so he has the impression as she turns her head that she resembles those flip cartoons he loved as a boy, when by flicking rapidly from one drawing to the next he could change an egg into a bird, or a man into a woman. The transformation in Lydia's case he muses (his thoughts still trained on classical Greece) is between Helen of Troy, whose legendary beauty made her vulnerable, and a robust, mischievous elf. While both figures appeal to him, their combination is irresistible.

'Will you order? Of course it's late and you may no longer be hungry.'

'On the contrary,' Lydia declares, reading her menu. 'I am exceedingly ravenous. When I dance all food in my entrails is stoked into moving so I'm always hollow at end. I should like two of these,' she indicates the sirloin steak, 'but not *bleu*, as the French cook, so it bleeds on plate as if it still belongs to cow. That is not nice to see when you are about to ingest. I prefer my meat like soft leather. Oh,' she adds, skipping to the bottom of the page where the desserts are listed, 'and Chester Pudding, which seems exactly like Lemon Meringue Pie I ate in America except its name is more interesting.' She frowns, assessing whether this intuition is correct, then dismisses the conundrum and beams at Maynard as if she has invented the dishes instead of merely choosing them.

He is struck as on previous occasions by her unconventional English. There is Russian (or what he presumes to be Russian, never having paid the language much attention before) in her pronunciation: in her failure to pronounce the final consonant on a word so his own name is shortened to 'Maynar', or her tendency to place a 'v' where 'w' should be and vice versa. All this he might have anticipated from his limited exchanges with Russians, at fund-raising events for the émigrés fleeing the civil war for example. What startles and delights him more is that her English is peppered with words and phrases which – while her meaning is for the most part clear – are not the usual ones. It reminds him of the word games he excelled at as a boy, played after Sunday lunch at his family home in Cambridge, or with his school friends at Eton. He wonders what his writer friends make of Lydia's linguistic deviations, some of which he suspects she has the knowledge to correct. To his ear, there is an exotic poetry in them.

Her habit of vocalizing whatever comes into her head fascinates him too – as if he is an intimate acquaintance and she is confiding in him. He is accustomed to frank conversations with his friends in Gordon Square where permissiveness has become the rule, but where he sometimes senses that the effect a statement will spark is prized above the need to express it. In consequence discussions can – if left unchecked – become derailed by a requirement to shock, rendering them paradoxically predictable. With Lydia it is different, not because she is averse to impropriety (he gauges she is perfectly capable of relishing scandal), but because there is no premeditation behind her utterances. That he frequently has no idea what she will say next exhilarates him.

The waiter returns to take Lydia's order, though Maynard is disappointed he is too well-trained to register amazement at her gargantuan appetite. He would have preferred the waiter to at least raise his eyebrows at her request for two sirloin steaks followed by pudding.

'Were you at school in St Petersburg?' he quizzes.

'The Imperial Ballet School, with my sister and brother,' she informs him with obvious pride. 'To be excellent dancer you must start when you are very young with classes every day, so we slept at School although our home was nearby. We did not mind,' she continues, as if forestalling his concern, 'since Tsar adored ballet and treated us well.'

She refers to the Tsar almost as if he is alive, he perceives, but before he can comment on this, or speculate on who will succeed Lenin now he is so ill, she has embarked on a topic of her own.

'Girls and boys shared same building though it was engineered so we did not mingle. Even when we danced together we could only touch if step ordained it and never with our eyes. I disobeyed because we girls did not have wombs to become pregnant and nor did boys have the danglings. Several older girls were already expert in sex. There were special passages at Imperial Theatre so we could pass directly to boxes of Grand Dukes.'

He could not be more intrigued if she had come from one of the strange nebulae Edwin Hubble is reported to have observed through his telescope, appearing to confirm the existence of galaxies outside our own. It is a feeling he recalls from their previous encounters: Lydia plunging so quickly into territory he could not have predicted that his mind (usual several steps ahead of any interlocutor) must race to catch her up.

Lydia breaks the bread roll on her side plate into two, spears a pat of butter with her knife and sandwiches it between the halves. The butter has been moulded into the shape of a lucky four-leaf clover.

'There were no girls at my school,' he tells her, emboldened.

Lydia licks crumbs and butter from her fingers. 'So there must have been many boy-boy affairs.'

Again he has the sensation of landing in unexpected terrain. He helps himself to a roll, which he also spreads thickly with butter.

'You are peasant at heart!' she teases, as he – copying her – licks his fingers.

Not all of Lydia's hair has been pulled back from her face. A patch has been cut short above each ear, the bushy tufts contrasting messily with the sleek appearance of the rest. He should like to reach his hand across the table and touch the stubble.

'My grandfather grew dahlias.' He watches her brow furrow in puzzlement. 'Garden flowers,' he clarifies. 'Turned out to be highly lucrative. He made enough money to educate my father.'

'Lopukhov means flower in Russian. In English you call it burdock. The roots are eatable and it has clever manner of distributing seeds. My grandfather dug in fields, but then Tsar freed serfs. Not much changed for my grandfather but he sent his son to army. That was my father's school even if it never taught him to read or write.'

The waiter brings Lydia's steaks, stacked one on top of the other so there is room on her plate for potatoes, a grilled tomato and a serving of mushrooms he does not recall her ordering. The sirloin has been browned at the edges though he is anxious it might not be cooked as Lydia specified. Before he can enquire however she is slicing and chewing as if she has forgotten her request.

'Keynes is English name,' she supposes, her mouth full.

'French. The first Keynes arrived with William the Conqueror, though it wasn't spelled as it is now. He was unusual because after him no one in the family moved far. '

'Pah, all he had to do was cross English Channel!' Lydia spread-eagles her arms as if to demonstrate she could, if required, swim across so small a stretch of water. 'My mother's great-grandfather was engineer who travelled from Scotland to Sweden. His grandson settled in Latvia. This was where my grandmother was born, though she moved to Estonia with her husband. He was brigand and not at all like my mother who prays and goes to church every day.'

Maynard's mind fills with pictures as Lydia talks, first of the Scottish engineer, who, if he calculates the dates correctly, might well have made the journey following the notorious Highland clearances, to the pistol-carrying brigand whom he envisions in a tartan kilt and cap like a character from Walter Scott. He is on the point of asking whether her father remained in the army, but she pre-empts him.

'My father worked as theatre usher,' she reveals, swallowing the last of her steak and scooping up mushrooms.

He glances round the room. Is it his imagination, or have the other diners – predictable and staid only an hour before, an extension of the room's ornamental pillars and fussy drapes – grown livelier since Lydia joined him? 'Your mother was born in Estonia?'

'In Reval, where they speak German. She still prefers it to Russian.' She spears a last tomato, then lets her knife and fork drop to her plate.

'When I was young, our governesses were German,' he volunteers. 'It's the only language apart from English, Latin and Greek I have any proficiency in.'

The waiter reappears with pudding. Lydia stabs the swirls of crisped meringue with her spoon. 'Heaven,' she pronounces, then thrusts the spoon in again. 'Taste,' she commands, holding the sugary confection out towards him, and without a second's hesitation he obeys.

❧

At an easel in front of a window a woman stands painting. Her tall, slender figure is hidden by a dark blue artist's smock she has secured about her waist with a man's striped tie. Her flaxen hair is unpinned but kept away from her face by a scarf patterned with orange, blue and grey rectangles cut from a remnant of fabric she designed herself. The scarf accentuates her English-rose complexion and brooding, sea-grey eyes, which so often strike those who know her as distant or distracted but which for the moment are absorbed in her task.

The view she is transmitting to canvas is the bay of St Tropez, where she has rented a villa for the winter with Duncan whom she loves more than anyone – with the exception of her two boys Julian and Quentin and daughter Angelica. For this is Vanessa, wife of Clive, with whom she has negotiated a surprisingly amicable open marriage, enabling him to continue his long-standing affair with Mary while occupying a significant place in her own life and, crucially, that of their children. The fact that only the elder two are his and Angelica's father is Duncan remains, for the moment, a detail of which even Angelica is ignorant. Certainly it is of little consequence compared to the precarious balancing and sheer hard work required to keep this close-knit group intact. She rests her brush and gazes beyond the terracotta roofs and green olive groves to where the sea, a ribbon of pure azure, shimmers in the distance.

It is characteristic of Vanessa that she should have chosen to paint her view from inside, so that the window – with the horizontal struts that dissect it and the floor-length white curtains that border it – are as much a focal point of her picture as the panorama beyond. Indeed, the interior that frames the composition is rendered more compelling by the presence of a small wooden table on which she has set a vase containing three sunflowers. The table's polished surface reflects the blue of the sky, though not in the same proportions as her painting where the sky is sliced off by the top of the canvas. If this mirroring offers an economical means of conveying the sky's enormity, it is harder to fathom why the full extent of the table legs and half of an adjacent, pink-cushioned cane chair have been included. Vanessa is aware as she considers the mahogany-brown floor on which the table stands that this conjunction of interior and exterior will baffle almost everyone who looks at her painting, leading them to dismiss the result as overly preoccupied with the domestic, or to conclude she cannot be a good artist because she lacks the ability to concentrate single-mindedly on one subject. Unlike her sister Virginia (who has yet to write the books that will confirm her as a genius, and who seems to her sibling worryingly eager for praise) Vanessa finds it straightforward to disregard such thoughts. This is not, as some have cruelly supposed, because she lacks Virginia's driving passion. She is as ambitious for her art as her sister. The difference is she has little interest in the events of the outside world except where they impinge directly on her life. If this was already a trait of her personality as a girl (when almost the only escape from the cloistered family home was a daily walk round nearby Kensington Gardens), it is one the incomprehensible and sickening carnage of four years of war confirmed. What has replaced it is the desire to keep all those who are important near her, even if this necessitates at times an almost superhuman mastery of her feelings.

She mixes ivory, pale lemon, grey onto her palette. The sun has warmed the section of wall between the window frame and curtain, a lightening she plans to convey. It will counteract the heavy block of dark floor which – though necessary to the whole – threatens to draw the eye away from the flowers on the table and the roofs, trees and sea outside the window. She estimates she has an hour, two at most, before the children return hungry for lunch after a morning on the beach with Grace, the young woman she brought with her from England and who is proving a willing and able aid. Duncan has taken his sketchbook to the harbour, and though she is aware this is in part motivated by the hope of meeting a young man he had a conversation with yesterday, this does not unduly alarm her. It is some years since Duncan has had an affair serious enough for her to feel threatened, as she did when he was in love with Bunny Garnett and she was forced to invite Bunny to live with them or risk losing Duncan. Though she is constantly fearful this could happen again, and is too realistic to expect any repetition of the night when Duncan came to her bed and she conceived Angelica, she is content to be in St Tropez where there are few demands and she can spend her days painting. Despite this morning's visit to the harbour and other – mercifully brief – disappearances, Duncan seems as intimately bound to her as it is possible for him to be. As she works lemon into the grey of the wall she feels absorbed, fulfilled, almost serene.

A door slams somewhere in the house. Slowly, as if to delay the moment when she must draw back from the engrossing colours on her canvas, she adds a daub of lemon to the developing texture of the wall. Then she puts her brush and palette down and looks, first at the window with its table and curtained view, then at her picture. It is in this position, arms akimbo, head tilted to one side, that Duncan finds her.

'There.' Vanessa indicates where she has begun to paint the table legs and wooden floor tiles. She waits until Duncan is alongside her and his eyes can follow hers, from the red mahogany of the tiles to the burnt umber of the table and on out through the window. Without his uttering a word she knows he understands not only her quandary but her intention – as if she is able to harness his vision and in the process sharpen her own. She perceives that the problem is not (as she first believed) the preponderance of brown, but her failure to echo this elsewhere. Suddenly she sees that she must first darken the terracotta roofs beyond the window, then perhaps – and the idea comes to her like a bolt of pure happiness – accentuate the ripening brown of the seeded centres of her sunflowers. It is moments like these, she thinks, turning and smiling now at Duncan, that make everything else – the nights she goes to bed alone aching with longing for him, her agony when he embarks on a new affair and she worries this time he will not return – bearable.

Duncan has brought her letters from the post office in town. She glances quickly through the pile, tucking most in her skirt pocket to deal with later. One – from Maynard – she keeps, recognizing immediately his regular, well-spaced lines. She pictures him as she tears the envelope open, his pen moving rapidly over the paper as it races to keep pace with the swift flow of his thoughts. She has often wondered if it is speed that causes him to leave a gap between the last word of a sentence and its full stop, as if this is the place where he draws breath.

'Lydia?' Duncan asks as she reads. He is referring to Maynard's last letters sent just before Christmas, in which he described inviting the Russian ballerina to dinner after watching her dance 'The Sleeping Princess'. What had perplexed them both was Maynard's insistence that he judged Lydia to be perfect in every way. Since he was due to spend the holiday with Sebastian (a liaison he has soothingly characterized as middling and not head over heels), they eventually dismissed his statement as a temporary infatuation – no doubt spurred on by his gullibility for sumptuous theatricals.

'He's in deep,' Vanessa reports, locating Maynard's phrase and quoting it exactly. 'And terrified. Almost beyond rescue.'

Though Duncan stays silent, apparently preoccupied by the blocks of brown on her canvas, Vanessa senses his dismay. He will find it hard if Maynard falls for Lydia, despite it being his own failure to commit that ended their affair. She recalls a conversation with Maynard in which he confessed his distress at Duncan's growing attraction to her younger brother, Adrian. There are, she decides, glancing back over the letter, two types of love: the kind that is never fully extinguished, and the sort that is like the merry-weather face on a clock, appearing only if the sun shines and vanishing forever as soon as the temperature drops. Duncan's feelings for Maynard are as immutable as her own for Duncan, lacerated now by the additional terror that Maynard may be about to transfer his affections to a woman. She is aware Duncan is still reeling from Bunny's marriage to Ray Marshall, which has prompted him to question whether he too must attempt to change. While Vanessa would like nothing more than for this to happen, she does not expect any alteration in their current arrangement, which – while far from ideal – she infinitely prefers to any dishonesty or dissembling.

'Lydia's good fun,' Duncan declares at last, the generous side of his nature reasserting itself. He picks up a brush and adjusts the angles of Vanessa's roofs with brisk, aggressive stabs. 'That night at the Courtaulds' party when she danced on top of the piano! She was so jerky and mechanical, like a doll that had come to life.'

Vanessa contemplates her roofs now clear against the green of trees and fields. 'Whatever it is it won't last,' she promises. 'Maynard knows dozens of clever women, and he's never shown the slightest interest in any of them. Not even that secretary who practically threw herself at him. He'll soon tire of Lydia.'

Her words have the desired effect. Duncan still works on her roofs but with less ferocity, as if painting is no longer a distraction but an activity he enjoys. Though it is unusual for Vanessa to talk at such length, she makes herself continue. 'Clive believes Lydia's incapable of a decent conversation. In his last letter he wrote about a lunch Maynard invited her to in Gordon Square. The discussion turned to happiness and whether it was right to seek personal fulfilment if this came at the expense of the greater good. Just as the debate was at its most intense, Lydia jumped up and demanded they open the window so they could listen to the chatter of starlings perched in a tree outside.'

'Clive has always seemed keen on her,' Duncan remarks, his eyes still trained on the canvas. 'There was that other party, when Clive monopolized her until an irate Mary dragged him away.'

Vanessa locates a rag and wipes her hands as she considers this. Clive's viciousness about Lydia in his letter surprised her too. Though his comments amused and gratified her they struck her as disingenuous: as if he were convincing himself he could have no reason to like Lydia.

'What's clear,' she explains to herself as much as to Duncan, 'is that Lydia is far too hare-brained and flighty to interest a man like Maynard for long.'

'He adores a good joke,' Duncan observes, surveying his alterations. A row of arches drawn along the white wall of the largest building catches his attention and he searches round for paint.

He is wavering, Vanessa recognizes, watching him squeeze red vermillion and burnt ochre onto her palette. He wants the best for Maynard even if this will make him unhappy. 'Anything more than a brief flirtation is preposterous. Imagine Lydia in Cambridge, or at a Treasury dinner where the talk is about politics and finance.' She dabs at a stain on her fingers with the rag. 'It's all very well her living like royalty at the Waldorf, but what happens when she stops dancing – which she'll have to do soon enough. She must be nearly thirty.' She frowns. Her stain requires turps and she scours round for the bottle. 'No, Maynard's letter is a cry for help, and if he can't extricate himself it's up to his friends to save him. How long will he be in India with the Royal Commission?'

'Several weeks. Why?'

'It'll get him away from Lydia, give him chance to reflect.' She hears the front door opening, the sound of children's feet in the hall. Why do they always come in like a stampede of wild beasts, she wonders, pocketing her rag. 'I'll write to Maynard after lunch, advise him to concentrate on India. I'll make it plain none of us judge Lydia to be right for him.'

The moment Madame Lopokova appears in the hotel lobby a porter is at her side, asking if he can whistle her a taxi, and if not whether he can fetch her an umbrella as it is raining. Lydia declines the taxi since she prefers to walk, but conscious she must accept something agrees to the umbrella. She is a favourite with staff at the Waldorf where she has lived since her ballet opened in the autumn, partly because she is famous, partly because her occasional eccentricities (such as bursting into the hotel kitchens and climbing inside one of their recently acquired refrigerators to cool down) adds a dash of excitement to their otherwise humdrum jobs, but mainly because she is willing to chat to them, which they appreciate. The porter she calls Fred hands her an umbrella and opens the door, and she sets off for the Ritz where Maynard Keynes is waiting to have tea with her.

This will be their first meeting since Maynard left London to spend Christmas with friends, and while Lydia is not overly given to introspection (having learned in the course of a life largely spent on tour that events have a way of arranging themselves which no amount of wishful thinking or fretting can alter), she finds herself intrigued by him. He is no dance connoisseur and yet has attended every performance of 'The Sleeping Princess' since the beginning of December except when he has been out of town, often sitting alone in the increasingly empty auditorium. She is curious enough to be tempted out into the cold and wet of a January afternoon when she might have been lounging amongst satin pillows on her comfortable bed at the Waldorf, eating a box of Fuller's cakes and preserving her strength for tonight's show.

The strong leather boots which were one of her first purchases on arriving in London carry her confidently over the puddles as she heads up the Strand. She glances at the brilliantly lit shop windows marveling at all that is on display, and trying not to dwell on the terrible tales of hardship she hears about life back in Russia. Can it be possible? People queuing hours for food in St Petersburg and fuel so scarce wealthy citizens have resorted to burning furniture and even paintings to keep warm. Like many of her compatriots who trained at the Imperial Dance Schools and who travelled to Europe to join Sergei Diaghilev and his Ballets Russes, her view of Lenin and the Bolsheviks is composed of piece-meal scraps (snippets from newspapers, occasional letters from her family in which she suspects the truth is glossed over to spare her feelings, reports from more recent émigrés often received second-hand and doubtless distorted in the telling). The notion that Russia is at war with itself fills her with horror, especially since no one seems able to predict with any accuracy who will win or what will happen when they do. She still finds it hard to believe the Tsar is dead; she danced for him often and still has the brooch he gave her as a schoolgirl for performing Clara in 'The Nutcracker'. She calculates that his son Alexei, whom she trusts is alive and in prison, must be sixteen now, and secretly hopes that one day soon he will succeed his father and champion ballet again.

Though she has received no correspondence from her family for some time and worries her own letters and parcels are not reaching them, she resolves to go shopping again in the morning and – with Fred's able assistance – send a fresh package. She has noticed Fuller's sell fruitcakes in tins to which she plans to add packets of tea, coffee and bars of chocolate, since these will keep fresh even if their delivery is delayed for months. She has reached the end of the Strand now, and as she stops to wait for a gap in the bustle of cars and horse-drawn carriages, she turns her face up to the rain. The sun was shining in St Petersburg the day she kissed her mother goodbye as she boarded the train for Paris with her brother Fedor and the others joining Diaghilev on his summer tour. How she teased her mother for regretting it was not raining since according to the proverb this would guarantee her swift and safe return, promising she would be back before the dancers' summer recess was over and in time to start rehearsals for the autumn season. That, Lydia recalls with a pang, was more than a decade ago, and as the rain spatters her face she is tormented by a fear she may never see Russia again. Certainly it would be madness to return when everything there is in such crisis – even if she had a reason to go back. A crowd has banked up on the pavement behind her, and spying an opening in the traffic at last she leads it across.

She pauses in front of the tall column on Trafalgar Square with its statue of the famous sea captain, surveying the Grecian portico and dome of the National Gallery where her friend Vera Bowen (Russian like herself though married to an Englishman) has taken her. There are children playing tag round the four bronze lions that guard the Square, their governesses gossiping in a huddle beneath open umbrellas near the central fountain. To her right is an organ grinder whose monkey – shivering despite its doll-size coat and hat – dances listlessly to the reedy notes of the barrel organ. From her left comes a sweet roasting smell and she hunts for her purse. She spreads her gloved hands over the glowing coals of the brazier as the seller scoops chestnuts and twists them into a paper cone. Since the few benches and even the flat rim of the fountain are pooled with rainwater, she concludes that the only place to sit is the rounded back of a bronze lion. She grins as she hoists her skirt to mount her beast at a clutch of children, perplexed at witnessing an adult trespass into territory they are sure must be forbidden and which only the bravest among them will attempt. Lydia's chestnuts are hot and burn her tongue but their taste is delicious. She glances round in vain for a clock to check the time and contemplates calling to a passer-by, before deciding it is of no consequence if she misses Maynard. Three girls dressed identically in brown wool coats and Tam O'Shanter hats are playing hopscotch among the puddles, and she watches them as she cracks a second nut. Perhaps it is the memory of her mother the girls' tartan caps invoke that make her chide herself for her lack of consideration and clamber down from her lion. She offers her remaining chestnuts to the children but they are too awestruck by her outlandish behaviour to do more than shake their heads. Instead, she stoops and holds the paper cone out for the monkey, who selects a nut with a tiny, delicate hand. The rest she throws for the pigeons whose greedy, flapping squabbles cause such a hullaballoo it attracts the attention of the gossiping governesses.

Lydia quickens her pace as she walks up the Haymarket towards Piccadilly, anxious now in case she is late and Maynard has another appointment and cannot wait. She likes him, she realises, stepping back from the pavement's edge as a two-tier bus advertising Player's Navy Cut splashes past. She likes his mind, quick and fizzing as a firework, and so crammed with knowledge a conversation with him is an education. At the same time, he never makes her feel inferior but listens seriously to her contributions. He is not a beautiful man – no one would say that he was – but he has kindly, blue-grey eyes accentuated by long lashes and dark eyebrows, and a soft, expressive voice which reminds her of her father. She likes the capable way he takes care of everything, so that whenever she is with him she has the sense she could share her difficulties and he would help resolve them. She remembers their dinner at the Savoy and his full, sensuous lips and thick moustache as she spoon-fed him dessert. His hair combed flat against his scalp draws attention to his vast forehead, and his nose (in contrast to her own, which is snub if viewed from the side) is long and perfectly straight.

At the Ritz, Lydia is shown through an archway to a glass-ceilinged room with brightly lit chandeliers and palm trees in pots. Though all the tables are occupied she spots Maynard easily, seated near a marble pillar. He has the newspaper open in front of him but does not appear to be reading since he notices her at once and waves. She gives the waiter her drenched coat and the umbrella Fred thrust at her, still furled unopened round its pole. Unbuttoning her gloves she pauses for a moment in front of a roaring fire, toasting her bare hands and lifting each foot in turn to dry her boots until her cheeks blaze red and her clothes start to steam. Maynard, taller than she recalls, stands to greet her, and she threads her way between the tables towards him.

'You're soaking,' Maynard remarks as she approaches, holding out a chair. 'Didn't the hotel provide you with an umbrella?'

'They did but I did not open it,' Lydia informs him, 'since it was only light spray and not proper rain pouring from a bucket. Ah,' she corrects herself as she settles opposite him, 'this is expression I learned the other day. In English you compare rain to cats and dogs not buckets, though I cannot discover why.'

'It's perverse of us,' Maynard agrees, 'but there is a reason – not a pleasant one I'm afraid. The idiom harks back to a time when roofs were thatched. Sometimes, during heavy downpours, nesting animals would be flushed out of the straw.'

'This cannot be it,' Lydia protests, wrinkling her nose in disgust. 'In Russian we are literal with our bucket, but from English I was expecting romance!'

'Such as?' Maynard rests his elbows on the table.

'Odin, god of storms, travels with dogs. So they must be signals of rain.'

'A much better explanation. And the cats?'

'Simple. In Russia cats bring luck, but here they are companions of witches. Probably they fall from witches' brooms since they cannot balance so well in wet.'

Maynard chuckles. 'It's good to see you, Loppy. It seems an age since we had dinner.'

'Now there is expression I don't follow, since by "an age" you can only mean two weeks.'

'Exactly. Just think how many days, hours, minutes, seconds that is.'

Lydia folds her arms. She senses Maynard is flirting and is flattered. She joins in his game. 'If that is how you count then it will be vast number. A day has thousands of seconds.'

'Eighty-six thousand and four hundred to be precise. So if we multiply that by – what did you say – fourteen', Maynard does a rapid calculation, 'it comes to one million two hundred and nine thousand six hundred.'

'Oh, Maynar', Lydia exclaims laughing, 'why do you waste time drinking tea with me? You are too clever, managing such giant numbers in your head without even pen to help.'

As if overhearing this mention of tea, the waiter arrives with a silver pot and pours two cups.

'You shouldn't think me so very clever,' Maynard advises once the waiter has gone to fetch sandwiches and cakes. 'Arithmetic requires less skill than almost anything you do on stage. How is the ballet going by the way? Have audiences improved?'

'It was like dancing in mortuary over Christmas. There are

rumours that if more tickets are not sold and soon, Stoll – who put money up – may close down show.'

'That would be a pity,' Maynard acknowledges, 'especially after the work everyone's put in.'

'The work is not so significant. Having no money is.'

'You mean your contracts won't be honoured?'

Lydia shrugs. 'How could they be? But it will be worse if Diaghilev cannot even pay for performances we have danced.'

'But if that happens, how will you live?' Maynard is aghast. He watches Lydia spoon sugar into her tea, impressed at her calmness in the face of such catastrophe.

'Savings, if I have any. I must ask Fred.'

'Fred?'

'Porter at Waldorf. He keeps my money in safe.'

'You bank with a hotel porter? Loppy, this is lunacy!'

'Fred is most trustworthy,' Lydia promises. Though Maynard's concern is gratifying, she cannot help grinning at his incredulous expression.

'It isn't about being trustworthy, but good economics,' he insists. 'In the right bank account your money will grow.'

'This I should like. But I don't know if it's possible since I've no idea how long I'll be in London and my address is hotel.'

'That might cause difficulties,' Maynard concedes. 'Still, a hotel porter.' He spoons sugar into his own teacup as he considers the situation. 'I know what you must do. Let me be your banker – at least while you're in England. I'll place your money where it will earn a generous rate of interest, though of course you can access it whenever you wish.' He leans back, smiling at her now. 'And it will give me the best possible excuse to see you again.'

❧

The doorman at Fortnum and Mason's directs Maynard past counters laden with hot-house fruit, jars of preserves, trays of hand-made chocolates, packets of tea and coffee to a flower stall in the corner, where he stops and gazes about him. Though he told Lydia the truth about his grandfather's horticultural success and its impact on the family fortunes, he is shamefully ignorant when it comes to flowers himself. As a boy growing up in Cambridge, it was his mother, Florence, who took charge of the house and garden, alongside a host of charitable and civic duties that currently include being the city's first woman councillor and serving as a magistrate. Unlike his surgeon brother Geoffrey, whose scientific abilities enabled him to identify any plant with an impressive ease, his own boyhood recollection of their garden is of the stones his mother accumulated and an area of grass where he practised his golf swing in readiness for a round with his father. He stares at the bright splashes of colour on the tiered stands, trying to decide which to choose. Dahlias he recognizes, but though he searches among the red, pink, yellow, orange and even purple blooms he spots nothing the right shape or size. A pretty assistant comes to his rescue, and when he explains the flowers are for the Russian dancer Lydia Lopokova suggests a bouquet of two dozen red roses.

The store is quieter than usual. The last time he visited was in the run-up to Christmas, when it was full of shoppers buying presents. While he waits he sets his briefcase down on the floor. On the wall opposite is a framed poster, proudly announcing that Fortnum's will provision the forthcoming British expedition to climb Mount Everest. The poster has a black-and-white photograph of bearded men in stout boots posing by a canvas tent against a backdrop of snow-covered peaks he identifies as the reconnaissance mission of the previous year. He studies the men's oddly eclectic assortment of hats and weather-beaten faces smiling for the camera. He recalls reading that in order to reach the mountain the team had to trek first through India then Tibet, as the shorter route across Nepal remains closed to foreigners. The memory jolts a realisation that in a few short weeks he will be sailing to Bombay as part of a Royal Commission, a post he rashly accepted in the hope of preserving free trade in India, and which will keep him there for months. The words of Vanessa's letter, sensibly advising him to use his time in India to quell the churning emotions his meetings with Lydia have so unexpectedly stirred, come back to him. He is aware Vanessa wrote responding to his plea for help in disentangling himself from his infatuation, and he trusts that she and Duncan have his best interests at heart. What worries him is that if what Lydia reports and the rumours he hears are true, then the ballet will close prematurely leaving Lydia with no source of income. If this happens, she will disappear from London again and it might be years until she returns.

The Christmas decorations are being dismantled. A young man wields a step ladder into position and removes trails of greenery and scarlet ribbon from an overhead light. He is wearing the same uniform as the doorman but has deposited his cap on the bottom rung of the ladder, exposing a surprisingly unruly mop of blond curls. As he tugs the last strand of ivy free and lets it drop to the floor, he spies Maynard observing him and for the briefest moment holds his gaze. Then he pulls at his left ear and inclines his head in the direction of the door. It is the subtlest of gestures, and yet the meaning is unmistakable. Though it is some years since Maynard has had sex with a complete stranger, the fact that this coded invitation should arise as he is on his way to see Lydia at her hotel reassures him. He turns his mind back to Christmas, which he remembers now as a succession of tranquil days spent with Sebastian at Lytton's house, untroubled by tormenting thoughts of Lydia. The young man clambers down from his perch and tidies the greenery and ribbons into a sack. As he passes Maynard he lets his arm brush lightly against his coat sleeve. Maynard picks up the briefcase containing Lydia's bank papers but makes no attempt to follow. In the past he would have pursued the young man without hesitation. He attributes the fact he does not do so now to the calm plateau he has reached in his relationship with Sebastian.

The assistant has selected his roses and spread them on the counter. She takes a pair of scissors and trims the thorns from their stems. He pictures Lydia in her dressing room surrounded by flowers from admiring fans, and wonders if when he arrives at her hotel his own will appear mundane. He wishes he had chosen a different gift – chocolates perhaps, or perfume – but it is too late to remedy this. The assistant ties his bouquet with a scarlet bow and hands him a card for his message. He finds his pen and considers what to put. This is not the first time he has written to Lydia, but so far their correspondence has been limited to prosaic arrangements or at most an expression of thanks. He has never attempted to communicate any of his complicated feelings for her, though he has wanted to. His reserve is not attributable to any delicate regard for Lydia's husband, since it is clear their marriage is over and any dealings are limited to his role as manager of Diaghilev's company. Nor is it caused by the stories circulating of Lydia's affair with Stravinsky, despite confirmation that the composer visited her in London while arranging Tchaikovsky's music for the ballet. No, his hesitation is because, yet again, he has not the faintest idea what to say. He returns his pen to his pocket and informs the assistant he will not include a card.

His bouquet is ready, sheathed in tissue paper. He pays and picks up his briefcase. The young man with the blonde curls has returned, his sack empty, and manoeuvres his ladder beneath a second ivy garland. This time, as he loosens the foliage and ribbon, he does not look once in Maynard's direction. This is hardly surprising given Maynard's response and the extreme caution that must be exercised. Nevertheless, he finds himself regretting this new indifference, as he should have liked a further sign that his attention was not distasteful to the young man. Now he has his gift and there is nothing left to do except make his way to Lydia's hotel he is starting to feel nervous. He walks back past the displays of fruit and chocolate, towards a counter selling headscarves. Here there is a mirror and for a second he catches sight of his thinning hair and exposed forehead, the nose he has always considered too prominent, the full lips he cannot help thinking rubbery, and grimaces. He holds up his flowers as if to shield his face from view, wishing he had inherited his brother Geoffrey's good looks along with his botanical knowledge.

When a maid ushers Maynard into the bedroom of Lydia Lopokova's suite at the Waldorf Hotel and he finds her sprawled amongst satin pillows, dressed in her kimono, his first impulse is to wonder if he has the right day. Books, newspapers and magazines are strewn on the bedspread beside her: he recognises the cover of *Vogue*, a copy of *The Daily Herald*, an open Russian-English dictionary whose cracked binding and dog-eared pages indicate repeated use. He stares at the spine of the book she is reading and is intrigued to discover it is Shakespeare's complete works.

As if to dispel his fear that she has forgotten their appointment, Lydia jumps up from the bed to greet him. She gives a cry of pleasure as he hands her his roses, rips open the paper and presses the flowers to her nose. She reaches up on tiptoe and with her spare arm inclines his head so she can plant a kiss on each cheek.

'Beautiful', she declares, passing the bouquet to her maid to put in water. 'I am so happy you've come. I have questions about *A Winter's Tale*.'

'I'm sorry,' Maynard gestures vaguely towards the bed. 'You were not expecting me.'

Lydia folds her arms across her chest, cocks her head to one side. Her hair is gathered in the bun he has come to regard as her habitual style, so her facial expressions are instantly visible. She frowns.

'Oh, Maynar', you don't remember? You described play so dazzlingly I've been desperate to read it. I've reached scene where

Antigonus is chased by bear.' She giggles, then is immediately serious again. 'But my heart leaps in my mouth for poor Perdita, left all alone in world. I hope Shakespeare has contrived happy ending for her. Come.'

She links her arm through his and leads him into a second room, which has two sofas and a low table on which has been set a tray of tea.

'You see,' she chides, 'it is you who is wrong. Most certainly was I expecting you.' She throws herself on one of the sofas and gestures he should do the same.

Maynard, still in his coat and carrying his hat, searches round in vain for the maid. There is a stand in the corner, though instead of coats it is hung with two wire cages, one containing a pair of yellow canaries who hop and tweet excitedly at the sound of Lydia's voice, the other a bird with rainbow plumage Maynard cannot identify.

'Don't worry. That one won't object to your coat. He's stuffed – present from Sitwells. Have you been to their house? They have most marvelous ovary.'

Maynard suppresses the desire to laugh, unsure whether Lydia is aware of her mistake or whether (as he often suspects) her word-choice is deliberate and adopted for comic effect. He glances shyly at her, searching for a clue, but she is pouring out tea, her face a study in focused concentration. He wishes the maid would return with the vase of roses. He would prefer to hand his coat and hat to her instead of braving the birds.

'I promised Ethel my magazines while we had tea,' Lydia explains, as if he has voiced his thought out loud. 'She and I share sweet spot for Charlie Chaplin. There is exclusive feature on him.'

Maynard drapes his coat over the back of the sofa and sits facing Lydia. She does not seem at all perturbed that her maid is reneging on her duties, showing him into Lydia's bedroom and then abandoning them entirely. He settles his briefcase by his feet and after a moment's hesitation rests his hat on top of it.

'Chaplin does hilarious impression of Nijinsky's "Afternoon of a Faun".' Lydia stands and sticks out her bottom, rubbing it vigorously and rolling her eyes like a drunkard. 'He sits on cactus and prickles oblige him to dance. But not at all like Nijinsky!' She capers round the sofa, waving her arms as if she has indeed been stung, then chuckles delightedly. This time Maynard joins in. He cannot help it. A phrase he has perhaps overheard from an admirer comparing Lydia's laughter to the popping of champagne corks comes back to him. It is not accurate he decides. The sound is far more irresistible.

'Now,' Lydia insists when they are quiet again, 'you must relate your Christmas holidays. Mine were exceedingly monotonous. Performing to empty seats every night because anyone sensible goes to pantomime.'

'So audiences have not improved? What is the position with Stoll?'

Lydia, who has resumed pouring out tea, pulls a face. 'Diaghilev has persuaded him to cough out more money, but Stoll insists this is last.' She adds sugar and milk then passes Maynard the cup, which has a saucer but no spoon. She has forgotten the strainer too and escaped leaves float on the cloudy brown surface. Maynard wonders if he should point these oversights out before resolving to remain silent. For all he knows it might be a Russian tradition to drink unstirred tea with leaves.

While she prepares her own cup, into which she drops a slice of lemon, Maynard looks about him. There is a fireplace with a rug before it and an oval mirror above the mantelpiece. An oil painting of a river and trees that would cause Duncan and Vanessa to shudder in its dull adherence to convention hangs in a frame on the wall opposite. There are standard lamps in each of the corners though they have not yet been switched on. Unlike the bedroom, which in addition to the disheveled bed had books, newspapers and magazines scattered across the floor; stray garments slung over the back of the single armchair; and so many hats perched on hat boxes he could not believe one woman could wear them all: in this room, the only sign of Lydia's residency apart from the birds is a battered leather trunk protruding from behind one of the sofas.

'My moving-home,' Lydia proclaims, indicating the trunk. 'My companion on so many travels: Paris, New York, Buenos Aires, Lisbon, Madrid.'

'I hope you won't be travelling,' he counters, feeling bolder now Lydia has made it clear she was waiting for him, and indeed has been reading *A Winter's Tale* on his recommendation.

'I hope so too. It isn't good always to journey on hoof.' There is a cherry cake on the tea tray from which Lydia cuts two generous slices. She slides one onto a plate and pushes it across the table for Maynard, then bites into the second herself. 'Though soon you'll go away.'

Her comment startles Maynard. He does not remember mentioning his Indian visit to Lydia. 'Nothing is definite,' he informs her, though this is not strictly true. While his brief is still under negotiation, he has a train ticket to Venice and a berth reserved on a ship there that will take him to Bombay. So far, whenever he has considered the trip, he has regarded it as occurring in a safely distant future, but as he contemplates boarding first the train then the steamer now, it comes home to him how long he will be away. 'I may not go,' he blurts out. 'I've agreed to write for the *Manchester Guardian*, which will be difficult if I'm in India.' This last statement is not a fabrication, though it has not featured as an obstacle before.

'Marvelous!' Lydia swallows the last of her cake and claps her hands . 'You are so clever! How proud I shall be to find your name in newspaper and boast I have drunk tea with you. What is your subject?'

'How we might climb out of our current economic depression. And there is a conference in the spring – in Genoa – I am to report on.' He pauses, trying to determine whether her enthusiasm is genuine or expressed merely out of politeness. If the latter, he will be disappointed but not wholly surprised. He has long been accustomed to the indifference of his friends whenever he discusses the details of his work. He knows his capacity for pouring over figures bewilders Duncan and Vanessa, and that for Clive and Lytton that puzzlement is commingled with a sizeable measure of disdain. His mind loops back to the war, and his friends' disapproval when he accepted a post at the Treasury, instead of declaring himself a pacifist and risking prison as they did. Though they remain grateful his Treasury status helped grant them exemption from the fighting when he gave evidence at their Tribunal, he is aware they consider him complicit in the slaughter. He has tried pointing out that he was powerless to reverse the orders that sent millions of men to their deaths, but that he could and did ensure there was money to provision both Britain and its military – which was not the case in all combatant countries. He glances at Lydia, but instead of boredom or censure she appears engrossed. 'The difficulty,' he confides, encouraged, 'is that I must write in a popular style – or attempt to.'

'This you will do,' Lydia promises, 'because whenever you explain I seize meaning straight away. And my education ended when I left School!'

Maynard smiles. He is on the point of objecting that Lydia is more than capable of understanding anything she chooses without any intervention on his part, when he sneezes. Immediately, she is at his side, fussing in case he is ill and calling for her maid.

'You have chill,' she frets, pressing her hand to his forehead to test his temperature despite his assurance it is nothing. 'Ethel', she addresses the maid who reappears in the doorway, 'bring blanket. We will light fire. And order more hot tea.'

Maynard, who is feeling perfectly well, accepts the blanket from Ethel, then, once the fire has been lit and a fresh tray set on the table, a second cup of tea. He is conscious this response is not entirely honourable, but he is enjoying Lydia's attentions as well as her close proximity too much to stop. Instead of being on the sofa opposite, Lydia is now sitting near enough for him to smell her scent, which has the sweetness of lilies, but also a darker, more exotic note reminiscent of Christmas spice. At last Ethel brings the vase with his roses and stands it on the table. He is satisfied with the result. The florist at Fortnum's has done an excellent job. The room has grown darker as they have talked and while the curtains remain open there is no light now from the street outside. Ethel asks if she should switch on the lamps but Lydia shakes her head and dismisses her, with the invitation to borrow as many magazines as she pleases.

'I love way flames lick and crackle as they burn,' Lydia muses, once Ethel has gone. 'When I was girl my sleeping place was shelf above fire.'

'That doesn't sound very comfortable – or safe,' Maynard observes. He still has the blanket spread over him even though he is not cold. It reminds him of when he was ill with rheumatic fever as a boy and his mother, Florence, cocooned him in eiderdowns. For days she stayed by his bedside and read to him.

'On the contrary,' Lydia advises, 'mine was best place. I did not lie there when fire was raging, but coals stayed red and warmed me all night. I missed it when I had to sleep at School.'

'When was that?'

'I was nine.'

'That is young,' Maynard concedes. 'I only boarded from thirteen. My first two schools were near enough for me to walk home.'

'I lived close too, but once we were accepted at School we were only allowed to leave on Sundays. On condition Tsar did not require us of course – for example to dance at party at Palace.'

How naturally Lydia refers to the Tsar Maynard notices, not for the first time, as if they are personally acquainted. 'Were you happy at school?'

Lydia puffs out her cheeks. 'It was tremendous hard work. To be dancer you must train like mule. This is what people never grasp. Even now, if I don't practice every day I suffer. And if I miss two days, audience suffers.' As if to demonstrate, she raises a leg into the air until her foot is above her head and her toe pointing to the ceiling. 'What about you?' she quizzes, letting her leg fall back to the sofa and tucking it gracefully beneath her.

'I enjoyed the lessons and was on good terms with several of the masters – and I found friends. But there were ugly sides to the school. Boys can be cruel.'

'Oh,' Lydia exclaims, 'girls too!'

'Perhaps,' Maynard persists, 'but at Eton where I was the system almost encouraged jealousy and vindictiveness. It did not help that I was a scholarship boy or that I won prizes, particularly for mathematics. Nor,' he continues, averting his gaze and staring into the fire, 'did my appearance help. Or that I was terrible at sport.'

'Your appearance?'

Maynard taps his nose. 'Too big. My nickname was "Snout".'

To his astonishment, instead of sympathizing Lydia laughs. 'Fiddlesticks! I wish I had such exquisite straight nose.' She leans so he can feel her breath, then turns her head so she is in profile. 'Snub', she pronounces. 'It's why name of ballet was changed. When it was proposed I dance Princess Aurora for certain performances Diaghilev complained no one could judge me a beauty. So it became "The Sleeping Princess". You don't believe me!' she accuses.

'No, I don't,' he confesses, laughing too. 'You are exceptionally beautiful as you very well know! Though it's a good story.'

'Then tomorrow we shall talk to Diaghilev, who will confirm it.' She reaches for cigarettes from the table, flips the lid of the packet open and offers it to Maynard. As he takes one, Lydia seizes his hand. 'Oh, I never noticed before.'

'Cycling accident.' He raises his curled little finger so she can study it better. The room has grown even darker and the only light is from the fire. 'I was twelve. My own fault, I was going too fast. Nothing serious but for some reason this finger never quite recovered.' He is talking for the sake of talking, in the hope that if he does nothing to divert Lydia's attention she will keep hold of his hand.

'You have beautiful nails,' she remarks, stroking his damaged finger. 'My father believed in excellent manicure. So now I never trust men who fail to keep their hands in order.'

'I can't abide bitten nails. The revulsion is so strong that when I am interviewing students for Cambridge I avoid their fingers in case this influences me.'

To his regret, Lydia drops his hand and helps herself to a cigarette.

'But did you always only like boys?' She rummages in her pocket for a match, lights first Maynard's cigarette then her own.

'Yes,' he confirms as they smoke, 'only boys'.

Lydia nods. 'It is same for many men dancers I know. What is harder to imagine – for the sex I mean – is two women. I suppose it all belongs in fingers. And tongue. Did you never experiment with women?'

'Once when I was in Alexandria. I went to a brothel.'

'And?'

For a moment they smoke in silence. Though all he can distinguish of Lydia is her shadowy silhouette, he is acutely aware of her presence. She seems to pulse with an electric energy. He watches the tip of her cigarette glow bright each time she inhales. 'Nothing'.

'Pah!' Lydia tosses the butt of her cigarette into the fire and after a few seconds he follows suit. He would like her to touch him again. No sooner has he formulated this thought and they are clasping hands, and he is caressing not only her palm but her wrist and forearm. Next his fingers are sliding up the silk sleeve of her kimono to the soft flesh of her upper arm, which has the smoothness of butter he reflects, though his analogy is hardly poetic. 'You have lovely arms Loppy,' he murmurs. Lydia shifts so she is staring straight at him, and he studies her face in the firelight, those pale eyes which brim with contagious merriment, but can also convey such sadness he longs to comfort her. His lips brush her cheek then find her mouth, and she is letting him kiss her, and now kissing him back with such fierce passion something stirs in him. When Lydia pulls away to look at him again, her expression is so direct and open that it is not the rejection he always fears at such moments, when his body is most abhorrent to him. On the contrary, her calm, clear gaze is exonerating and inviting.

Slowly, as if allowing him time to stop her should he choose, Lydia moves her hand down his body until she reaches his stiffening sex. 'That woman in Alexandria,' she declares solemnly, 'must not have been right woman.' She begins to massage with firm, unexpectedly sure gestures. Maynard would like to keep his eyes fixed on hers, but discovers he cannot. He leans back and sighs pleasurably.

'You see how nice this feels. We dancers learn to take care of our bodies and the sex is especially recommended. Not over-doing it of course. There was ballerina in South America who had it too much.

But she was nymphomaniac with irritable womb. What?' she demands, as Maynard guffaws with laughter. 'Did I use wrong term? My English is a little wild.'

'No,' he protests, putting both arms round her, 'words should be a little wild. That way, they challenge what we think we know.'

With adroit fingers Lydia unbuttons his trouser-fly.

❧

'Bold,' Vera decides, walking round Lydia's new lodgings and letting her gloved hand touch the distempered walls hung with Vanessa and Duncan's paintings, the bookcase that looks as if it might have been constructed by an amateur, the pale Indian rug on the polished floorboards, the embroidered cushions on the chairs, the green and white chintz curtains. Vera is taller than Lydia, with fashionably bobbed hair. She is still wearing her cloche hat and three-quarter-length coat trimmed with a mink fur collar as the fire has not been lit in the grate. 'Personally I find it unappealing. These Bloomsbury artists strike me as crude and lacking in skill. How long can you stay?'

'These are Vanessa's rooms – she's in St Tropez for the winter painting. Only her children are here as they have school.' As always when Lydia speaks Russian, her words flow easily; though her English is fluent enough for her to say whatever she wishes, the language still feels foreign, like dancing with an unfamiliar partner. 'Maynard is confident Vanessa will keep me as a lodger even after she returns. She has rooms spare.'

'Maynard doesn't live here himself?' Vera walks to the window, her heeled shoes clicking on the wooden floor, and stares out over Gordon Square.

'No, his house is further down. Vanessa's husband Clive has rooms there. Because of his mistress, Mary.'

Vera wheels round. 'Doesn't Vanessa mind?'

'She's in love with Duncan, who of course only likes men.'

Vera studies a painting of a woman in a blue dress reclining on a red sofa. She has on a straw hat and her feet are crossed so the soles of her shoes are visible. Behind her is a set of shelves on which books with coloured spines are piled haphazardly, while next to them a curtain patterned with gaudy crimson flowers and green leaves frames a window. The woman's eyes, which are the same cornflower blue as her dress and too large for her face, gaze unsettlingly at the viewer. 'Vanessa?'

'Painted by Duncan. That's Charleston, where they all lived during the war. Maynard still has his room there. He believes it's what kept him sane.'

'So you like this man?' Vera opens her handbag and brings out a packet of De Reszke cigarettes.

'I do. He feels solid and safe, as if I can lean on him and he won't break in two or disappear.'

Vera retrieves her lighter, which has a watch face inserted into the black and turquoise striped enamel, and holds the flame steady while Lydia lights a cigarette. 'Your husband has left for good?'

'Two weeks ago, before Stoll closed the show and Diaghilev fled. He knew it was coming. As usual he imagined he could help himself to my money but this time I outwitted him. I'd already given Maynard most of what I had to put in a bank. So my bills are paid.'

'And you don't mind?'

'Mind?' Lydia snorts contemptuously. 'On the contrary, good riddance!' She squats on a low stool with a tapestry seat depicting two winged angels brandishing swords. To stave off the chill, she has buttoned a long wool cardigan over her dress and wound a tartan shawl round her shoulders. 'I mean it,' she insists. 'I liked Randolfo at first but that feeling soon wore off. Actually, we should never have been married.'

'Oh?' Vera pulls her coat closer about her.

'Very few people know this,' Lydia drops her voice to a whisper even though they are alone in the room and no one else in the house speaks Russian. 'Randolfo still had a wife.'

'A bigamist? Isn't that illegal?'

'Randolfo's wife was American. They were not together long but problems arose over the paperwork.' A door slams somewhere in the house. 'Adrian, Vanessa's younger brother. He and his wife live in the basement.' She points her toe in the direction of the floor. 'They're training to cure mad people. Admirers of Freud and his talking cure.'

'The lunatic who blames everything on sex? What a family! There's another sister isn't there? Married to that socialist. Harold is always quoting her reviews. What's she like?'

'Virginia?' Lydia strikes a pose by the mantelpiece, her face pulled thin and long. 'She gives the impression she's miles away not listening at all, then crack,' Lydia stamps her heel down hard, 'her words snap like a whip.' She perches back on her stool. 'She's very clever. So I play the joker even harder.'

'She sounds terrifying.' Vera searches for an ashtray. There is a blue ceramic dish with yellow apples on the table which Lydia pushes towards her.

'She is, though she has a sense of humour too. And she's learning Russian. But not as fast as her husband.'

'What will you do?'

'Wait to see what happens. I've written to Diaghilev, reminded him of the plight everyone is in. Fortunately Massine has money for a new season at Covent Garden so I have work.'

'Massine? I heard he was back from South America. What's the new programme?'

'Have you heard of Walter Wanger? He's promoting the movies and wants the Ballets Russes to perform a live interlude.'

'So Massine will be Diaghilev's successor?'

'Not if I have anything to do with it! But until Diaghilev can pay his creditors it's better he remains in Paris.' Lydia knocks the ash from her cigarette into the dish. 'I'm one of the lucky few. Massine can't take everyone.' She glances at Vera, suddenly thoughtful. 'Do you have any openings? I know you're doing Chekhov but why not another ballet too? You understand what's needed in a libretto and your eye for costume and lighting rivals Diaghilev's. Several of the dancers owe money and will soon have nowhere to live. One or two even talk of returning to Russia. Despite everything we hear.'

'The stories are terrible. It's hard to know how to help. What I do is small-scale, unless…' She stubs her cigarette out. 'Your name brings in audiences and attracts sponsors. Perhaps we could stage a ballet together? As partners?'

❧

Maynard sets a full stop at the end of his sentence and relaxes his grip on his pencil. A glance at the clock on the mantelpiece informs him he has been writing for three hours. He shuffles his pages into a tidy stack and calculates his morning word-count. It is a habit that dates back to his schooldays, when he recorded the hours he studied in his diary so as to compare each week's productivity with his previous score. He has long suspected the origins of this practice were the regular work rhythms he learned from home, where his father John (who also taught at Cambridge) wrote his books on logic and political economy, assisted by his mother Florence. Whatever its roots it has become as integral to his routine as checking the cricket score, a game whose leisurely form he admits is grossly inefficient but which he adores nonetheless. Though the morning's word total is pleasing, he is not so foolish as to imagine it is quantity he will be judged on. And yet he reasons, playing devil's advocate (a strategy he successfully adopts in his intellectual endeavours), completing tasks on time is important. His ability to finish all the items in his in-tray before anyone else in the Military Department of the India Office where he was a junior clerk was one of the factors in his recruitment to the Treasury. He raises himself from the couch on which he has been lying and deposits his sheaf of papers and pencil on the floor.

He crosses the room to his college window and watches the King's undergraduates in their black gowns as they hurry, heads bent, against the biting wind that blows, legend has it, unimpeded from the Russian Urals. This term, because of his Indian visit, he has exempted himself from the timetabled interruptions of teaching. He misses the fresh-faced students with their familiar maleness and motley personalities: some shielding shyness with ebullience, others apparently more withdrawn but harbouring a quiet confidence. He enjoys unraveling the flaws in their arguments and their questions, preferring the clever ones whose thinking challenges his own, but always patiently willing to explain points not grasped to those whose interest is genuine. He sits down at his desk. There is still half an hour before luncheon will be served in the wood-paneled dining room with its portraits of former King's Provosts dating back to Henry VI, in which to catch up on his correspondence.

First on his list is Vanessa. It was impossible to fathom her reaction from her brief reply to his request that Lydia should move into Gordon Square. He has not yet confessed that instead of following her advice and using his Indian commission to distance himself from Lydia, he has cancelled the trip and is more deeply involved than ever. He finds Vanessa's letter and rereads it. Is it his fancy, or is there a note of hostility towards Lydia? True, she agrees to rent the two spare rooms, but her agreement is perfunctory, as if instead of sympathizing with her plight now it is clear Diaghilev can pay no one she would prefer Lydia to fend for herself. He retrieves Vanessa's earlier letter in which she urges him to go to India and forget Lydia. Here too, the tone feels forced – as if there is an ulterior motive behind her words she is careful to screen. He appreciates it will have come as a shock to his friends that he has fallen in love with a woman, though he is by no means the first of their circle to do so. Adrian, Vanessa's brother, who had an affair with Duncan, is now married to Karin with a daughter. Yet he does not believe that is it.

He feels certain if it were someone else – one of the young women painters from the Slade perhaps, or a student from one of the women's colleges in Cambridge – Vanessa's reaction would be less severe.

To combat the disagreeable sensation this suspicion provokes, he picks up the letter he received from Lydia that morning. He likes her reaction to his article in the *Manchester Guardian*: 'a magic telescope', she assures him, 'through which I see further and more clearly than before.' Silly to be so susceptible to praise; he is after all nearly forty and has won more than his fair share of prizes. Her endorsement contrasts with the opinion of Clive and Lytton, whom he has heard describe journalism as a bastard art despite writing for newspapers and magazines themselves. He has considered explaining that he hopes the experience will enable him to set out the problems he intends to explore in his next book more lucidly. He has toyed with the idea of reporting the sum he will earn from his assignment but again has not done so, partly so as not to draw attention to his superior financial circumstances, but mainly because he is aware that one ingredient in their scorn is the belief that valuing one's work in monetary terms is intellectually dangerous, like dealing with the devil. This latter attitude is not confined to his Bloomsbury friends since he has encountered it in Cambridge, when confiding to a colleague how lucrative his position on the board of a life insurance company has proved for example. What bemused him was his colleague's nonsensical assumption: not that the payment might compromise his independence, which he could understand, but that the money might dull his scholarly judgment. When, on the other hand, Lydia learned of his guest editorship of the newspaper she raised an arched eyebrow and with an impish grin asked 'how much?'

He glances up. On the wall opposite his desk, above a low bookshelf, are four muses, two male, two female, representing art and science. They were painted by Vanessa and Duncan and he lets his gaze settle first on the woman in the red dress reading from a long scroll of white paper, then on the naked body of the man with his right arm raised as if for emphasis. Though Sebastian was not a model for either of the male nudes Maynard always traces his lover's likeness in the contours of this second figure. He studies the broad shoulders and powerful arms, the muscular torso and prominent sex, the elongated thighs and surprisingly slender feet. Sebastian is not due to arrive at his rooms until teatime, but he is already looking forward to seeing him again.

These past weeks have been hard on Sebastian, and one of his motives for coming to Cambridge now is to reassure him that his current obsession with Lydia does not threaten their relationship, which remains as important to him as ever. He is conscious from Sebastian's letters how impatient and unhappy he has been, and plans this afternoon to make it up to him by proposing an Easter holiday. He would like to take Sebastian back to North Africa, repeating their tour of the previous year, where they can be together openly.

Not that he has encountered any direct antagonism towards his sexual proclivity. On the contrary, first at Eton then at Cambridge and even at the Treasury during the war, there was, if not open acceptance, a tacit acknowledgement that this was his private affair and should consequently be respected. Certainly he has never felt fearful – as others of his persuasion have – of arrest and prosecution. This he attributes to the liberal attitudes of his Bloomsbury friends and to his learned habit of vigilance. Though he has, in the past, been as promiscuous in his liaisons as Duncan, at one time notching up his conquests in his diary with the same proud zeal he reserved for his academic attainments, he has always been alert to the dangers and approached each new situation with caution. Periodically, he worries about Duncan, whose generous nature means he is less circumspect. Still, a month in North Africa, where he and Sebastian will be able to share the same hotel room and even touch in public without risk of imprisonment, will be a healing step for them both.

He turns his focus back to the window. Straight ahead, on the other side of the courtyard, older college buildings frame his view, their leaded glass panes glinting in the wintry sunlight. He has not yet invited Lydia to Cambridge despite being keen to do so. Rarely has he met anyone so eager for information and he rehearses what he might tell her: how a church, several hostels and part of a street had to be cleared to build King's chapel, the limestone for which was hauled a hundred and fifty miles from Yorkshire on ox-drawn carts. He stares at Lydia's handwriting and unpredictable, often ingenious diction. His article, he reads, will doubtless breathe to others as it has to her, inspiring them to put his ideas into practice. Inkblots decorate the edges of her page and he tries to picture her writing it. Perhaps, he conjectures, it was at a rehearsal for her new ballet at Covent Garden, or during a break in the morning practice she undertakes with the same religious dedication Vanessa and Duncan apply to painting. She would, she informs him, like to cosset him in the abundance his article has breathed into her – a formulation he deems worthy of a poet. Her next lines in which she promises she will cover his entire body with flaming kisses leave him tingling with desire. He picks up his pen and writes quickly. He has spent so long deliberating over how to respond to Vanessa that there is barely time to reply to Lydia before he must go down to luncheon. He can hand the letter to the porter on his way to his meeting of the finance committee at two to catch the afternoon post. Then, at four, he will return to his rooms where he will organize tea and a fire and wait for Sebastian.

Lydia lets herself in through the front door of 50 Gordon Square and checks the hall table for a letter from Maynard. She stares at the empty plate painted with a blue Venus on which post is left for the house's occupants before remembering it is Sunday. She has spent the afternoon with dancer friends discussing rumours that Diaghilev is raising funds for a European tour, and a few lines from Maynard would have cheered her. Though she defended Diaghilev for absconding, insisting Stoll's threats left him little choice, she did not have the heart to confess he has not responded to either of her letters. On the contrary, despite her own hopes of a reunion, she encouraged them to accept whatever work they were offered, explaining she had appeared alongside impersonators and even a troupe of performing poodles when she had been down on her luck in America and that it had not harmed her career. The cold in the cramped, mildewed room shared by two of the dancers was so biting not even her present of vodka and Russian cigarettes could stave it off. Buckets stood on the floor to catch drips from the leaking roof and the only place to sit was the mattress on the rusty double bedstead, which − as Lydia observed − at least had the advantage of forcing them to huddle close and pool their body warmth. At one point, a rat ran from behind the rotten skirting which they trapped, before taking pity on the petrified creature, christening it 'Diaghilev' and letting it escape. She wishes Diaghilev had been there to witness how, as the hours passed and they grew hungry, the only food in the dancers' cupboard was a tin of sardines and half a packet of soft biscuits. Lydia traces the border of orange cross-hatching interspersed with blue dots on the rim of the empty post plate and curses, violently, in Russian, glad she is alone in the hall and there is no one to overhear her. She removes her coat and hat, catching sight of herself in the oval mirror that hangs above the table as she does so. She is lucky, she reminds her reflection. Not only is she partnering Massine at Covent Garden, but she has Maynard in her life, arranging accommodation and taking charge of her money. Should she want anything, all she has to do is ask and an envelope of bank notes is left for her. The recollection of how precisely the sardines were halved and even the biscuit crumbs shared merges with harrowing images of the famine in Russia now appearing in all the newspapers. Next Sunday, she resolves, she will invite any of her fellow dancers still in London to Gordon Square, where she will feed them so well their fat will last an entire week.

As she plans a shopping expedition for Beluga caviar and fresh gingerbread, she remembers the conversation with Vera and her suggestion she might use her own connections to sponsor a ballet they could stage themselves. Though Lydia has never run a company she has learned a great deal from her two decades of dancing, and she trusts Vera's theatrical ability and judgment on practical matters. Maynard, she is certain, will provide sound advice and might even put up some of the money. She wonders if Sam Courtauld, the textile millionaire, who is always paying her compliments and asking her to stay, would consider backing them. Perhaps – now Diaghilev's position is clear – she could approach Oswald Stoll herself. She hangs her coat and hat on the stand.

It was a mistake to dwell on the caviar and gingerbread, she thinks as she climbs the stairs. Since there was only one tin of sardines amongst eleven dancers she left this for the others pretending she disliked the fish, so all she has eaten since breakfast is a stale biscuit. She is about to trace her steps and head towards the basement to scavenge for bread and honey when there is a peal of woman's laughter. It appears to come from the direction of the kitchen. She doubts it is Mary, Clive's mistress, who rarely puts in an appearance at number 50, or Vanessa who is still in France. It is definitely not Adrian's wife Karin whose American cadence she would recognize. She supposes it might be Grace, the girl Vanessa has hired to look after her children and who has returned with them from St Tropez so the two eldest can resume school. She prays it will not be the cook, whose accent she finds impenetrable and whose manner gives Lydia the uncomfortable impression her intrusions are ill-timed and too numerous. She pivots on her heel to investigate.

The kitchen is lit with a rosy glow as she pushes open the door. Grace, her brown hair pinned back from her face to reveal her features cut finely as glass, is at the head of the table, pouring cups of hot milk for Vanessa's two youngest children. The dark eyes –

which all Lydia's visitors agree are bewitching – flash a smile as she pulls out an empty chair. The children smile too. She is a favourite with them, not only because of the sweets she dispenses from her pockets and willingness to dance for them, but because she can stand on her hands for longer than either of the boys and lets Angelica thread ribbons through her hair. No sooner has she sat down at the table than the children clamour for a story. She runs through the tales she has already recounted: of skating on the frozen Nevsky near her home in St Petersburg, or how she was driven from her School in a horse-drawn carriage with the blinds pulled down to the Tsar's palace where there was a always a smoking samovar of tea and dishes of hot and cold zakuski. Grace offers her milk but when she admits she would prefer one of Grace's omelettes both women laugh, because last Sunday Lydia devoured no less than three.

'Did I tell you,' she begins, turning to the children as Grace opens cupboard doors for eggs and a pan, 'about the time I was in Portugal during revolution?'

Quentin, who is eleven with disheveled blond hair flopping across his forehead, stares. 'You mean people fighting, with guns?'

'Most certainly I do. They fired at our hotel. We had to push mattress against windows for protection. For three days we did not dare go outside. One dancer, who was away when shooting started, came back to discover her bed pillows riddled with bullets. She retrieved them to make belt.' She pauses to allow the children to absorb these details, watching Grace cut a knob of butter from the dish and let it sizzle in the pan. At number 46 where all the residents eat their meals Grace is almost as much an interloper in the kitchen as Lydia, her role limited to carefully prescribed tasks such as peeling potatoes or washing dishes. But at number 50 and on Sundays, which is the cook's day off, she is undisputed queen, free to do as she pleases. Last Sunday, as she counted the dozen shells Grace had cracked for her three omelettes, Lydia worried the cook might grumble about the quantity of eggs in the same bad-tempered tone she reserved for her shot knees. Grace assured her this was unlikely, since any of the residents from the square with a key could have used them – including Mr Keynes who paid all the servants' wages. When Lydia first heard the cook refer to her knees as 'shot' she was alarmed, until Grace explained it meant the bones had worn thin and not that a gun had been fired.

'What happened then?' Quentin wants to know. 'In Portugal.'

'We performed ballet. Though in square outside so everyone could watch.'

Grace pours the whisked egg and milk into the frothing butter, adds salt and pepper, grates in a helping of cheese. As she tilts the heavy pan to spread the mixture evenly, Lydia reflects how young she is, barely more than a girl herself.

'What about food?' Angelica, who is four and already dressed for bed, demands. 'In the hotel room.' She flicks a finger round the inside of her empty cup to clean it.

'Fortunately I had chocolates, present from King of Spain, and another dancer had smoked sausage. So first day was not so bad.'

'Chocolate and sausage.' Quentin licks his lips, as if testing the combination.

'We had cigarettes too. Except on last day when we had smoked them all. By the time manager knocked on door to announce revolution was over our stomachs growled like wolves.' She places a hand with the fingers pointing upwards on either side of her head to imitate wolf ears.

'A wolf dance!' Angelica pleads, clapping her hands. Grace, who is sliding Lydia's omelette onto a plate, shakes her head.

'This must be eaten hot,' she announces firmly. 'Angelica, you should have been asleep an hour ago. And Quentin, it's time for you to go up as well. Or else what am I to tell your mother when I write to her?'

The children protest, but only mildly. They are tired, and after a few vain attempts to coax Lydia into a wolf dance, Angelica kisses them goodnight. Quentin, who tries to persuade Grace to cook him an omelette too, is slower to leave, but eventually follows his sister.

'Perfect,' Lydia declares tucking into her supper, then translates the word into French. She is helping Grace learn the language so next time she accompanies the family to France she can speak to people.

'Tell me about Vanessa,' she appeals to Grace, when they can no longer hear the children's feet on the stairs. She has devoured her omelette and tears a hunk of bread from the loaf to wipe the buttery traces that remain. The kitchen is warm and she is no hurry to return to her room where there is no one to talk to.

'Mrs Bell? You've met her.'

'Only with other people. Never conversation alone. What's she like?'

'Quiet,' Grace offers after a moment. This is not a question she knows how to reply to. 'What do you want to know?'

Lydia sets her elbows on the table, cradles her chin in her hands. 'Maynar' – Mr Keynes – says she's devoted mother. So why does she stay in France when her children are here?'

'To paint.'

'She has studio upstairs.'

Grace tidies the children's cups and Lydia's plate to a corner of the table. 'She likes the light in the south at this time of year. And in Paris she visits other painters.' She glances at Lydia, still unsure if this is the type of information she means. Lydia nods in encouragement. 'She hates being disturbed if she's painting so I suppose that's another reason why it's easier on her own.'

Lydia considers this. She imagines Vanessa in a room flooded with sunlight, copying a vase of flowers like the one that hangs in the dining room.

'That must be lonely,' she reflects. 'I should not enjoy solitude. Dancers live like bees in hive, especially before performance when everyone is buzzing. We must be careful not to crash into scenery as it moves, or collide with other dancers warming up.'

'Mrs Bell wouldn't like that,' Grace admits. 'Interruptions break her concentration.'

'Well she needn't mind me. I'm only here for sleeping. Except next Sunday when I'll throw huge party.' She gazes sidelong at Grace, an idea forming in her mind. 'Come with the children. There will be Russian general to teach sword-play to boys. And Angelica will be universal darling.' She raises an inquiring eyebrow. 'And I'll invite delivery boy. The one who transforms to beetroot whenever he glimpses you.'

The rain slows to a drizzle and a pale sun bursts through the clouds. Lydia has her arm linked through Vera's, whose tall, stylishly dressed figure contrasts sharply with her own. They form a striking pair as they make their way up Regent Street, sidestepping the puddles and pausing to peer in at shop windows. Londoners have grown accustomed in recent years to the presence of Russians in their city (supporting Russian relief efforts and even in some circles adopting what are perceived to be Russian characteristics such as a greater outpouring of spontaneous emotion than the British temperament allows), yet the sound of the Russian language is still sufficiently exotic to attract attention. Lydia's latest appearance in *Vogue* magazine also causes heads to turn and passers-by to speculate as to whether she might be the celebrated ballerina. That Lydia herself seems oblivious to such stares only intensifies their conjectures. Her failure to acknowledge these tributes is not – as some (feeling themselves snubbed) vindictively suppose – because her fame has made her inured, but because she has no wish to interrupt her conversation with Vera. She is telling her friend about an alarming letter she has received from her sister in St Petersburg, which has confirmed her fear that her family receive little of her correspondence.

'Eugenia thanks me for the ballet shoes but not the gloves and boots I sent at the same time. Or the woollen jackets and shawls. She complains the last news they have of me is a newspaper article announcing 'The Sleeping Princess" – which was months ago. Yet I write at least once a fortnight.'

'It's the censors,' Vera reminds her, steering them round a gaggle of young women emerging from the Café Royal whom she realises have recognized 'Loppy' and in a moment will be pestering for autographs. 'Though in the case of the parcels it was more likely desperation.' She quickens her pace, shepherding Lydia along with her. As she predicted, the women are elbowing each other and searching in their handbags for pens. 'If I were a postal worker in Russia and found warm clothes I could wear or sell,' Vera continues once the skirmish is averted, 'I'd be tempted. I'm surprised the ballet shoes arrived. What else did your sister say?'

'The winter was vicious. The theatre – which by the way is no longer called the Imperial Mariinsky but the State Theatre – so cold the dancers soaked their feet in bowls of ice.' She catches at Vera's sleeve. 'For Eugenia's birthday the company burned flats from an old set to build a fire and feasted on cabbage soup and herrings.'

'Doesn't sound much of a celebration. What about the rest of your family? Is everyone well?'

Though Vera does not mention the epidemic directly, Lydia is aware she is alluding to reports of cholera and typhus spreading from the famine-ravaged countryside to the starving cities. She sighs. It often seems as if the only stories she hears of Russia are of people dying in unimaginable numbers and appalling hardship. 'Eugenia describes piles of rotting rubbish and rats the size of boars. People forced to trade their treasures for bread or a bundle of firewood. What's worse is I'm certain she doesn't tell me half of it.' She stops, suddenly, causing the two men walking a few paces behind to bump into them. 'Sometimes Verochka,' she confesses as the men bow in apology and the pair move on, 'I worry we can't ever return home'.

'But should you like to?' her friend wonders. 'It's been more than a decade since we left and so much has changed, I'm not sure there'll be anything of what we remember to go back to.'

They are approaching Liberty's and to distract her Vera points with her free hand to a display in the window. Lydia grimaces at an ankle-length coat with an over-size collar and turned-back cuffs. 'That mannequin must be twice my height. I could wear the hat,' she volunteers, admiring its broad brim, 'though I might get stuck in doorways!'

'Not that one. The suit next to it.' Vera indicates an India green skirt and drop-waist jacket that has a ribbon of black fur running down the front. 'Green is a good colour on you.'

'The hat might work. And the skirt's not too bunchy.' Lydia admits this in an effort to appease since the purpose of their outing today is to buy her new clothes.

'It'll take more than a new hat to smarten you up,' Vera protests. 'Seriously, if we're going to run a company we have to instill confidence. No one will sponsor us if you turn up in clothes that might have been donated to the Russian Refugees Relief Fund. Think of Diaghilev. He's a genius when it comes to impressing backers.'

'I'll paint a white stripe in my hair, pin orchids to my breast and peer at the world through a monocle. Actually that's not a bad idea. Why don't I just dress as a man? I'm joking,' she promises, catching sight of Vera's face. 'What about that second coat, the navy one at the back? That looks like it should last.'

Vera groans. 'How am I ever to make you fashionable, Lidulechka?'

'I don't need to be that. Only a little well-groomed.'

'The two are indistinguishable.' Vera propels her towards the door, which an attendant in uniform opens for them. 'Come on, you can try on hats too.'

An hour later, the pair occupy a table in a quiet corner of the tea room, their shopping complete, if not to their mutual satisfaction (since there are rather more hats than outfits), at least to the point where both parties feel exonerated: Lydia because she has a hat resembling a French beret with an egret's feather and another that sits like a sideways saucer at a jaunty angle, and Vera because Lydia now possesses a dress and matching jacket suitable for a meeting with Oswald Stoll, whom they have approached for money. The friends are not discussing their purchases however, nor – for the moment – plans for their company, but Vanessa Bell, who has returned to Gordon Square after her stay in France.

'One positive outcome of the work with Massine ending is that I am in the house more,' Lydia is explaining. 'Vanessa and I didn't set off on the right note. I'm always so wild with energy after a performance – I want to smash through things and start again. Vanessa grumbled to Maynard that my noise late at night disturbed her. So now I take care to spend pleasant times with her.'

'What do you talk about?'

'Ballet mostly. Vanessa is very English and doesn't say much – not at all like us Russians, who talk and talk and still have words to spare. I must summon my energetic speaking spirits when I'm with her.'

'Perhaps she enjoys being quiet,' Vera ventures.

Lydia lifts the teapot to pour them a second cup but it is empty. She signals to a passing waitress who nods. 'She never gives the slightest sign of wanting to be peaceful. And some of my chatter arouses her interest. When I gossip about Mary for instance. Her husband Clive's mistress,' she reminds her friend.

The waitress returns with fresh tea. When it has been served and they have helped themselves to lemon and, in Lydia's case, sugar, Vera removes a bundle of papers from her bag and sets them before her friend.

'"Masquerade – a romantic comedy set in eighteenth-century Venice"', Lydia reads. 'Let's hope Stoll stumps up the money. And the Coliseum agrees.'

'Is it definitely all over with Massine?'

'That miserable stick insect! You saw the posters he printed. His name in giant letters and mine squashed in a corner. He was a monster when we took the curtain calls – sweeping past me as if I was invisible. It isn't as if he's especially talented. His choreography for *Togo* was preposterous – full of dangerous dancing traps and so confusing half the audience failed to follow. I'm not surprised all he's got lined up are the music halls.' She leans closer. 'He owes me money. Maynard is instructing his solicitor to write to him.'

'How are things with Maynard?' Vera's tone is deliberately light. Though she is not well acquainted with Lydia's Bloomsbury friends something about them puts her on edge. Once, at a party at the Sitwells, she was given the distinct impression Vanessa and her sister sneered at her account of the improvements she was making to her husband Harold's family home as well as their London residence, which – if her suspicion was accurate – only demonstrates what hypocrites they are. After all most of the group divide their time between two addresses. Maynard strikes her as opinionated and overbearing, though this is a view she takes pains to hide from Lydia. Seldom has she seen her friend so absorbed by a relationship.

'He's in Genoa, writing about a conference for one of his *Manchester Guardian* supplements. Though happily he confines his work to the day so he can spend his evenings in the casino.'

'Gambling?' Vera raises an eyebrow.

'Maynard has a system and always wins.' Lydia blows to cool her tea. 'He arranged a holiday and hired a chauffeur to drive us round London, stopping at all the important places. He's appalled at how little history I know.' While her hands remain clasped round her cup, her eyes implore Vera to approve.

'He's teaching you?'

'He is. I've often regretted not being one of these young women studying at a university. With Maynard I'm catching up on my education. I call him my speaking book. This makes it sound dull but it's the opposite. We played such a prank on the beafeaters at the Tower my sides nearly ruptured.'

'And Sebastian?' Vera probes.

Lydia stares into her tea, frowning. When she looks up again her expression is troubled.

'The night before Maynard caught his train we toasted buns over the fire and he read to me. He has such a beautiful voice, like listening to Shakespeare. I was so happy I kept pinching myself. Then, next morning, when I went across to number 46 for my lunch, I noticed a letter addressed to Sebastian propped on the hall table for the post.' She shakes her head. 'I can't share him.'

'Nor should you.' Vera reaches for her hand. 'You must issue an ultimatum. Maynard has to choose.'

Footsteps crunch on the gravel path. Vanessa, paintbrush in hand, her hair hidden by a paisley scarf, sits back on her haunches and smiles as her sister, Virginia, rests the cane that always accompanies her walks over the Sussex Downs against the open French windows and stamps the mud from her boots. Her thin, angular frame is swathed in a long grey cardigan and she carries a coat over one arm, presumably at Leonard's insistence for the day is warm despite it only being April.

'You look well,' Vanessa remarks as they kiss, noting with relief the bloom the six-mile journey from Rodmell (where Virginia and Leonard have a house) has brought to her sister's cheeks. 'What was the doctors' verdict?'

By way of answer, Virginia studies the assortment of scrubbing brushes, bleach bottles and paint pots at Vanessa's feet. 'The usual,' she replies vaguely, 'Hamill advises one thing, Sainsbury another. Damp?' She points to a fur of greenish-black stains cloaking the wall.

Vanessa nods. 'It's seeped in everywhere this winter. Even in this room, which is south-facing. I don't believe Clive or Maynard visited Charleston once the whole time Duncan and I were in France. I had hoped by coming down on my own I'd be able to work. As it is, my days are spent scraping away mold and battling to restore order in the garden.' She stares disconsolately about her, as if all she surveys is catastrophe and ruin.

Virginia's gaze follows her sister's, but what her eyes take in are Vanessa's hand-printed curtains in turquoise and umber billowing in the slight breeze, a jug of red tulips picked from the garden, the rug designed by Duncan with its geometry of diamonds and squares, an oval mirror retrieved from a French flea-market above the fireplace. She has long admired her sister's genius for transforming wherever she happens to be living into a comfortable home that is at the same time a work of art. Everywhere Virginia looks arresting conjunctions of pattern and colour draw her, or her attention is caught by a beguiling object – often hand-made. Even the coal-box, roughly nailed by Duncan from off-cuts of wood, is decorated with a lute-playing angel as mesmerizing as any she and Leonard discovered in the Italian and Spanish churches they visited on their honeymoon nearly a decade ago. She considers explaining all this to her sister, indicating the way afternoon sunlight pouring through the open windows illuminates the cobalt dots and orange cross-hatching she has stenciled onto the legs of the low table, or how the vivid magenta flowers embroidered onto a lace mat contrast dramatically with the black and white striped porcelain statue of a zebra (a favourite of her nephew Quentin). 'See,' she would like to say, 'how you make everything coalesce, as if the world has suddenly righted itself and my own petty afflictions are eased.' She communicates none of this however, having learned after four decades of a closeness intensified by their mother's death when they were still in their teens, that the most effective route to countering Vanessa's resistance is to press the opposing view.

'*Tum me et te*,' she begins, then regrets the phrase. Her enjoyment of Latin and Greek was never shared by her sister. 'All I've done since arriving in Sussex is clean, garden, paint and bake. The books I packed for review remain largely unread. Yesterday was entirely lost to yellow-washing the earth closet.'

As anticipated, when confronted with this self-image mirrored in her sibling, Vanessa is appalled. 'What about your novel? The one with the young man who dies in the war. Weren't you planning to finish it?'

'"Jacob's Room?"' Now it is Virginia's turn to look perturbed. 'I fear it's nothing but sterile acrobatics. Especially when compared to Joyce's "Ulysses" – which has genius in it, even if the effect is raw – and Katherine Mansfield's new story collection. Not to mention Tom Eliot's book-length poem announced for the autumn – what?' she demands, registering her sister's grin.

'So you've lost your nerve! Come on, you can slay your fears by hearing how few paintings I've finished for this exhibition Roger has organised, while I brew us tea.'

Twenty minutes later, their self-confidence restored thanks to the renewed goading of artistic ambitions that so often occurs when they are together, the sisters recline on canvas deckchairs facing out over the garden, admiring droves of self-seeded blue forget-me-nots beneath the tumbling white blossoms of the apple and pear trees. They have commiserated with each other on the problems of maintaining two households without adequate means, agreed that all three of Vanessa's children (of whom Virginia is exceptionally fond) are thriving, discussed the tense situation in Ireland (Vanessa's reluctance to engage in political matters notwithstanding), and, as they refill their tea-cups and Vanessa spreads the raspberry jam she bottled last summer onto the remaining scone, embark on the perplexing riddle of Maynard's new-found obsession with Lydia.

'It can't last,' Virginia promises, accepting her portion of the scone. Like so many of their friends, she is persuaded that whatever madness has catapulted this ill-assorted and frankly ridiculous couple into being will soon dissipate, releasing Maynard to his multiple career interests and former settled proclivity for loving only men. Even more importantly as far as her sister is concerned, Maynard will retain the prominent place he has held in Vanessa's life since the war, when he spent whatever spare time he could engineer away from the Treasury at Charleston and where he continues to pay for a room. Though Virginia does not share this intimacy with Maynard, often feeling skittish and dull-witted in his presence, and – if she is honest – abhorring his lack of imagination and his gluttony (the latter prompting her to caricature him in her diary recently as a gorged, blubbery seal), she nonetheless prizes his intellect and considers his book on the peace settlement one of the most significant works to have been written on the aftermath of the war. She finds it incomprehensible that such a mind should be infatuated with Lydia, who appears incapable of holding a serious thought in her head or participating in a meaningful conversation. 'Lytton – who is not above gloating at the prospect of Maynard making a fool of himself – can't abide her. Calls her a half-wit with a brain to match those caged canary birds she dotes on. He judges her ignorant and stupid. Apparently, when quizzed for a view on Russia under the Bolsheviks her response was a lewd innuendo.'

'You might say the same of me,' Vanessa admits, 'though perhaps without the lewd innuendo. Immediately I open a newspaper and my head floods with reminders of all I need to do.'

'But you're not contemplating an affair with Maynard. Politics is his world. Once whatever has ensnared him has run its course – which it will – what can he hope to talk to her about if she can't express a sensible opinion on the situation in her own country. No,' she concludes, removing a tin of tobacco and packet of cigarette papers from her cardigan pocket, 'there's too great a divide between them. Maynard's manners can be uncouth, but he's well read and relishes fine language. Lydia's English is riddled with oddities and errors.'

'Which he adores,' Vanessa persists. 'Claims she's a natural poet. Did I mention I invited him to Paris when Duncan and I were there? He replied immediately citing Lydia as the reason he couldn't join us. It wasn't long after her ballet closed. He's never turned down Paris before.' She sets her empty teacup on the grass. 'I'm afraid the situation is grave. Meanwhile we tie ourselves in knots wondering what to do.'

'Leonard reports that Maynard and Sebastian are planning another trip to North Africa.' Virginia spreads a cigarette paper flat on her knee and trickles a line of tobacco onto it. 'So his feelings for Lydia cannot run deep.'

'A trip changes nothing.' Vanessa takes the rolled cigarette and searches her own pockets for matches. 'Maynard's letter was a clear cry for help. Unless we act, he'll find himself saddled with a woman with no means of supporting herself and no prospects. The season with Massine was a flop, even Lydia admits Diaghilev is unlikely to attract fresh sponsors given the extent of his debts, and this company she's planning with Vera Bowen seems doomed to fail. You know Maynard still owes us money?'

'From those lost investments? He'll pay it back. With interest.' Though this is old news, Virginia is concerned to see her normally calm and composed sister so troubled.

'But what if Lydia won't let him? She has extravagant tastes. She was living at the Waldorf before she moved into Gordon Square.' Vanessa strikes a light, draws until the tip of her cigarette smoulders. 'The point is Duncan and I depend on Maynard. Not just to look after our finances. I'd struggle to keep Charleston going without his contribution. And he's good to us in other ways too.'

'Perhaps,' Virginia proposes, distributing a second pinch of tobacco along a fresh oblong of paper and twisting it deftly, 'we all need to try harder with Lydia.'

'That's Duncan's view. He counts Lydia a good sport. Which she is I suppose – though her idea of fun seems very different to ours.' She passes her cigarette so Virginia can light her own. 'The Sunday before I left Angelica failed to appear for breakfast. I found her in bed, eating bread and jam she'd persuaded Grace to give her the night before. Her justification was *oblomovschina* – which apparently means blissful indolence. It's Lydia's influence of course.'

'Still,' Virginia coaxes, suppressing a smile.

'What would we have accomplished if we'd lain in bed all day as girls,' Vanessa bursts out. 'I'd never have been accepted at the Royal Academy and you wouldn't be a published author without all those years of hard graft.'

'It would have dismayed father,' Virginia concedes.

Both sisters fall silent, remembering their father compiling his dictionary in the room above theirs at the family home in Hyde Park Gate. How long the days had seemed to them then, as Vanessa practised her drawing and Virginia read and wrote, punctuated only by a walk at lunchtime and the obligatory ritual of afternoon tea.

'I wish Lydia wouldn't interrupt so much.' Vanessa's tone is gentler, as if she is ashamed of her former harshness. 'She will keep barging in whenever I'm settling down to work. It's the main reason I had to come away. I've reminded her until I'm blue in the face that I need finished canvases for this exhibition, but instead of leaving me in peace she parks herself on a stool and chats away for hours at a stretch. She's like one of those unstoppable trains that erupt in nightmares. No matter how little I say in return she keeps on going – about nonsense. Whatever time I've managed to clear for painting vanishes with nothing achieved.'

'Hideous,' Virginia agrees, gazing at a border of wallflowers, their yellows and russets radiant in the spring sun. 'I can't abide guests turning up unannounced hoping for tea and conversation if I'm intending to write.' She looks sidelong at her sister. 'But are you sure Lydia understood? Or could she have misconstrued your silence and interpreted it as assent. She's not exactly brimming with sensitivity.'

'I can hardly insist,' Vanessa protests, reddening. Though she is reluctant to admit it, she acknowledges the truth in Virginia's analysis. She has always found speaking her mind difficult, especially if the situation is an awkward one. She stares at a sparrow pecking for scone crumbs at her feet. 'Lydia on her own is bad enough, but then there are her endless visitors. She's constantly hosting parties, especially on Sundays when her dancer friends are free. They last most of the day and sometimes all night too. Sunday is when I catch up on chores.'

'Perhaps if Lydia moved in with Maynard?'

'Refuses to. Claims it will destroy her reputation since she and Maynard aren't married.'

Virginia's reply is a peal of laughter. 'Who would have credited it? A woman estranged from her husband, whose affairs if rumour is to be trusted include a Polish Count and Russian General, baulking at impropriety!' She flicks her cigarette stub onto the grass and grinds it with her heel. 'Maynard should take heed or Lydia will make a Tory of him yet. He's always had a conventional streak.'

'I dread him bringing her to Charleston for the summer.' Vanessa tosses her stub after her sister's. 'Imagine her here, disrupting our quiet mornings with the relentless thud of her dance practice so no one else can work. Sabotaging mealtimes and excursions with her antics. Ruining after-dinner conversation with her inane gossip and stupid jokes.' She extinguishes the burning tip of her cigarette with such vehemence she scuffs a patch of bare earth on the grass. 'Everywhere Lydia goes she trails mess and dirt – as if an army of servants exists to wait on her.'

Virginia toys with suggesting Lydia would make a valuable addition to the theatricals that are frequently staged at Charleston, but Vanessa's earnest expression causes her to refrain. She is surprised as well as pleased by her admission that she treasures the debates their circle regularly holds, for it is rare for her sister to contribute. Mostly she sits knitting, her face impassive, so it is impossible to decipher whether she is listening or lost in contemplation. Lydia, with her fidgeting and flightiness, would be an unwelcome interloper on such occasions. Not only would her propensity for uttering out loud whatever random fancy flits through her head prevent any serious investigation of their subject, her presence risked turning the proceedings into a farce. She has witnessed Lydia yawn noisily in boredom, or jump up suddenly and propose a dance. She herself would hate hosting her, should it be a question of her staying at Rodmell. 'What will you do?' she asks, feeling powerless to advise.

'Rent in St Tropez.'

'That's absurd! You always spend the summers here. You can't allow Lydia to force you to change plan.' Virginia is shocked. One of her motivations for coming to Sussex now is in the hope of seeing Vanessa more. She missed her dreadfully during her absences in the autumn and winter. She doubts she could bear it if Vanessa were to return to France for the entire summer.

'Maynard must be reasoned with,' she declares, 'you should write to him. Explain you cannot be expected to accommodate Lydia. This is your house after all.'

Lydia unlocks the door to number 46 and stands for a moment in the hall. She has come straight from the theatre and is in two minds about whether to remove her coat and hat. No doubt she stinks to high heaven, for she has taken to wearing two layers of clothing during rehearsal in an attempt to sweat her body back into shape. She has even bought an additional pair of gloves for this purpose. She drops her coat in a heap and confronts her reflection in the hall mirror, raising her arms to where she can see them and pinching their plump flesh hard. Her hat, which she has ornamented with additional plumes above each ear, she retains for now.

She has no appointment with Maynard until later in the evening, and is aware the sensible course would be to return to her own rooms at number 50, bathe herself and rest. She attributes her reluctance to do this to her fear of bumping into Vanessa, whose hostility towards her seems if anything to have worsened since her recent visit to Charleston. When Lydia first moved in to number 50, she attributed Vanessa's cold-shouldering behaviour to her evident anxiety about her forthcoming exhibition. She devoted her spare time to reassuring Vanessa in the hope this would improve matters, often sitting and talking to her while she painted. Yet no matter how many hilarious anecdotes of near-disastrous performances she recounted (such as the time she was billed alongside a troupe of performing ponies in America and one escaped onto the stage during her solo), none of her efforts to make Vanessa laugh and persuade her all would come right in the end seemed to help. Indeed, Vanessa's stony silences grew grimmer and more prolonged, while her odd, hurtful snubs increased in frequency. Only yesterday, she arrived at number 50 to find the ribbons and laces she had begged from a seamstress at the theatre for Angelica to dress up in left out on the step for the rag-and-bone man to collect.

Lydia straightens her hat feathers. Vanessa's baffling conduct is not the only reason she has preferred coming first to number 46. Her day has been difficult and she is in need of Maynard's wise counsel. She longs to plant herself on his knee and bury her face in his chest while his arms wrap round her. She adores his unfailing ability to offer solutions to whatever problems she brings. Today's rehearsal for the ballet she is devising with Vera did not go badly all things considered, especially now she has hit on a plan for sharing their only male lead amongst their small troupe of women. Her scheme to intersperse solos with short pieces involving unusual combinations of dancers is working, and her decision to adapt routines from existing ballets has reduced the amount of fresh choreography she must invent and the number of new steps they must learn. Of course, her task would be easier still if she had been able to persuade Stoll to book Vera's 'Masquerade' for an eight-week run at the Coliseum as she originally intended, but Stoll – for all his reserved English politeness and punctilious dress – is less gullible and susceptible to being charmed than she supposed. He has refused to invest in their venture without their first proving themselves in this trial run.

Today's tribulations, Lydia acknowledges as she starts up the stairs, are of a more serious nature than the thousand and one obstacles beleaguering a new company operating on a shoe-string. The morning began with Vera haranguing her over her slowness in concocting a sequence that would incorporate all three of their female soloists, accompanied by complaints that she was wasting precious rehearsal time for which they had only a limited budget. When Lydia professed her exhaustion at having to direct as well as dance (for Stoll has insisted she appear in at least half the programme), Vera exploded and accused her of being a frivolous amateur. To this, Lydia countered that Vera lacked understanding since she could not dance herself – at which juncture Vera stormed out, leaving Lydia so distraught she considered abandoning the project and offering herself as a tragic actress. Only when one of the other soloists reminded her Vera was newly pregnant and this was doubtless making her irritable did she recover a little of her equanimity.

Worse even than this argument with Vera is the news she received in the afternoon that Enrico Cecchetti, whom she continues to call 'Maestro' because he taught her as a girl in St Petersburg, is closing the studio he opened when he followed Diaghilev to London and retiring home to Italy. She is fearful that without him the backwards slide in her technique (all the more visible when she performs alongside younger and more recently trained dancers) will accelerate. For though the discipline of regular practice is so ingrained she exercises even on the days Cecchetti is not free, working alone in her room at number 50 is not the same. Like all great teachers, she testifies to no one in particular pausing half way up the stairs, Cecchetti is a genius. His barking orders and fierce tapping cane force her past what she might attempt herself, whilst simultaneously preventing her from achieving a result too quickly (an error she is prone to). As a result, he improves her performance without risk of injury. She is uncertain how she will manage without him.

These thoughts are coursing through her head and she is preparing her translation for Maynard – editing and embellishing to ensure maximum attention and sympathy – when she hears the sound of a woman speaking in his sitting room. The voice is not Vanessa's, nor the mealy-mouthed secretary Maynard occasionally dictates to whom she suspects of habouring a secret crush on him. Disappointed, for she has anticipated having Maynard to herself, she knocks on the door.

Inside, leaning against the unlit fireplace, Maynard is conversing with a woman whose expansive forehead, earnest expression and greying hair parted at the centre and swept back from her face Lydia seems to recognize. The woman is sitting very upright in her chair and dressed in a high-collared blouse which strikes even Lydia's untrained gaze as old-fashioned. A teacup balances on her knee. Maynard looks at Lydia as she comes towards him, but instead of the affectionate welcome she has been expecting, holds out his hand. If this more formal manner of greeting is designed to prevent her from flinging her arms round him and smothering him with kisses, it has the desired effect. Lydia's forward momentum is so abruptly halted she almost loses her balance. Her eyes search Maynard's as she shakes the outstretched hand, but he appears fascinated by the maroon and blue zigzags on the rug. The woman stares at her curiously.

Maynard clears his throat, but before he can utter a word Lydia is talking, apologizing for intruding unannounced and then (as she glances down at her sweat-stained dance tunic) apologizing for this second blunder by embarking on the story of her hellish day. Once started, it is not a tale she feels inclined to leave unfinished, especially since her voice seems the only firm anchor in a situation that both bewilders and frightens her. She describes going to Cecchetti's studio and pleading with him not to leave London, all to no avail. She explains (her voice gathering speed, for Maynard's silence is growing more intolerable by the moment) how her idea inspired by Greek tragedy for a sequence to cast all three of her female leads will flounder unless she can secure more rehearsal time. She is on the point of dramatizing the quarrel with Vera, when he holds out his hand again. This time it is to interrupt her.

'May I', he begins, appearing to recover his composure and addressing his visitor whose forehead and eyes Lydia now identifies from Maynard's own, 'present my mother Mrs Florence Keynes, who has been in London visiting my brother. And this,' he continues with a formality that rips through her like a blade, 'is Vanessa's new lodger, the Russian ballerina Lydia Lopokova.'

The sight of so many paintings stops Lydia in her tracks. The door to Vanessa's room is ajar and curiosity compels her to push it wider. She has come straight from number 46, pleading tiredness and the need to bathe as her excuse for refusing Maynard's grudging offer of tea. She is hurt and confused, and dreads returning to her own part of the house where she will be alone with her fear she is no more than a passing dalliance in Maynard's life. She takes a step into the room. These must be Vanessa's pictures from the South of France, she realises, gazing first at a flotilla of white sailing boats on an emerald sea, then at a sun-dappled vineyard where grapes hang in hazy purple bunches, now at terracotta-roofed houses their windows ablaze with scarlet geraniums. Two of the paintings – a woman in an armchair whose face is featureless and a jug of wild flowers with the background still unfinished – are set on easels, while the rest perch on chairs or the tops of tables or lean against the walls. Since moving into Gordon Square Lydia has grown accustomed to Vanessa's artwork, much of which (like the heavy, lumpen plates they eat their meals on) she finds coarse and ugly. This opinion is confirmed by Vera, who on viewing Vanessa's interior decoration pronounced her devoid of talent and – more alarmingly – taste. In Vera's assessment, Vanessa would do better to devote more attention to her children, whose unruly behaviour she disapproves of. Yet something about all these canvases together arrests Lydia, as if cumulatively they demand greater attention, so colours which at first glance seem ill-chosen or a queer vantage point starts to make sense. She is examining a picture of misshapen apples in a striped dish when she hears footsteps.

'They tempt me to eat,' she declares, with such enthusiasm Vanessa, about to protest at Lydia's intrusion, is disarmed. It has rankled with her for weeks that none of the inhabitants of Gordon Square has noticed the two paintings she recently hung in Maynard's sitting room. Even Maynard (to whom she has in the past confessed her worry that she has neither the time nor the skill to create serious art) has said nothing.

'I've still a great deal to do,' she insists in as careless a tone as she can muster, for after all Lydia's praise scarcely counts. 'The men from the gallery are due at the end of the week.' She stands in front of one of the easels, contemplates the jug of wild flowers. She must finish this before the children reappear from their outing with Grace, so that tomorrow she can continue with her portrait of Virginia. She pulls a smock over her dress and wraps her hair in a scarf, hoping these signs of preparation combined with her reminder about the exhibition will shoo Lydia away.

Lydia, however, heeds none of these signals. Instead, she offers her services, suggesting first she might mix Vanessa's paints, and when this produces no reaction, volunteering to clean her brushes. As if to prove the latter is a task she is familiar with she picks up a large bottle of turps and unstoppers it. 'On tour,' she explains, fishing a paintbrush from a jar and locating a rag, 'there's so little time before a performance everyone, dancers included, must lend hands.' She sloshes turps onto the rag and rubs vigorously at the brush. Drops of the sticky, resinous oil splash onto the floor. Vanessa stifles her desire to beg Lydia to stop. She understands Lydia is being friendly, retrieves a newspaper from a stack by the window and spreads it beneath where she is working. Then she returns to her easel and the jug of flowers.

'I love how your apples float above dish,' Lydia remarks, using the brush to point and spraying an adjacent rug with turps so Vanessa is forced to unfold a second sheet of newspaper. 'It is way Picasso paints. He worked with us in Paris where he married my friend, Olga Kokhlova. For her portrait he positioned her eyes at different levels, like this.' She closes her right eye and draws an imaginary cylinder above her brow with her finger.

'You met Picasso?' Vanessa is intrigued.

'Such a rogue! In sketches he made of me I am plump and ordinary, like banal, well-fed wife. Even when he drew me on horseback for "Parade" I have fat arms and bandy legs.'

Trust Lydia to divert a potentially interesting conversation into one about herself, Vanessa muses, wishing Virginia were there so she could benefit later from her no-doubt scathing analysis. She has not yet acted on her sister's advice and written to Maynard over Charleston, but resolves to put pen to paper this evening. Though Lydia's zeal seems genuine and her eagerness to help well intentioned, this invasion of her work space is intolerable. She spots Lydia discard her turps-sodden brush onto a chair and almost cries out in exasperation. If ever she needed further proof that hosting Lydia for the summer would ruin all her careful plans for painting with Duncan, excursions with the children, and leisurely meals with friends, she has it now. She retrieves the brush from the chair and mops at the cushion with her smock. The clock on the mantelpiece (one of the few childhood mementoes she transported with her siblings to Bloomsbury after their father died) chimes the hour. She resolves on silence as the most effective tactic for ousting Lydia so she can use whatever time remains on her picture.

Lydia, who appears to have forgotten her mission of assisting, squats on a stool to watch. Vanessa is a puzzle to her. She is an imposing presence, with an austere, delicate beauty Lydia compares to a far-away star. Despite Vanessa's evident hostility and the rebuffs she has endured in recent weeks, there are occasions – such as her mention of Picasso a moment ago – when Lydia senses a thaw and hopes they might become friends. She remembers an evening early on when she, Duncan and Vanessa walked back from a party together. They had been drinking and were all tipsy, especially Duncan who could not walk in a straight line and had to be prevented from straying off the pavement into the path of oncoming traffic. To entertain them she had mimicked the antics of drunken droshky drivers in St Petersburg, and when she lamented she had not seen her family in years, Vanessa kissed her in sympathy. As they crossed the communal garden in the middle of Gordon Square, Lydia linked her arms in theirs and led them dancing over the grass. By the time they reached the other side Vanessa was laughing so hard she had to lean against the iron railings to catch her breath. Lydia wishes she could rekindle this bond with Vanessa now. She would like to consult her about Maynard, since by his own admission Vanessa is the only woman amongst his acquaintance whose opinion he values. It has dawned on Lydia that Maynard's reluctance to reveal the nature of their relationship to his mother might be connected to Sebastian, whom she assumes his family has met. Whether this means they acknowledge him as Maynard's lover – and that her own claim to this status is futile – are questions she longs and fears to answer.

She clears her throat, intending to speak about Maynard, but Vanessa's stony countenance prevents her. Though she has not yet added a single mark to her painting, she is staring at it so fiercely it is clear her attention is lost. Lydia relates instead the story of her morning quarrel with Vera, hoping this will gratify Vanessa whom she suspects despises Vera as a wealthy dilettante. Yet not even Lydia's comically exaggerated account of Vera increasing the tempo, until her choreography grew so frenzied the Grecian maidens resembled angry wasps, stirs Vanessa. Only when Lydia names Duncan, who is advising on a solo based on the Scottish reels he learned as a boy, does Vanessa look round.

'Even Vera,' Lydia stresses, 'who will find faults in heaven if ever God lets her in, approves Duncan's designs for my costume. Have you seen his drawing of my jig? He gives me twelve legs to show my kicking heels.' She giggles, relieved to have Vanessa's notice again. 'I am crazy flying octopus.'

Vanessa, who has stopped studying her painting to listen, blanches. Duncan has not shown her his drawing. In itself, this is not unusual, especially if it is only a sketch. Nevertheless, Lydia's description of his involvement in her Scottish reel sounds an ominous chord. Though she has schooled herself to accept there are areas of Duncan's life she will never share, his artistic collaboration remains precious to her. She recognises Duncan's genius as a painter, a consideration that in her estimation outweighs any lesser factor such as whom he has sex with. While she is too honest to deny there have been periods when Duncan's affairs have left her distraught, she has contrived ways to survive them. She is not certain she can do this should Duncan abandon their creative intimacy – particularly if any new confidante has talents she lacks. Despite her exasperation with Lydia, Vanessa is aware she possesses qualities Duncan finds attractive, such as her propensity to play the fool and devil-may-care refusal to plan ahead. These attitudes Vanessa can no more envisage indulging in than she can imagine being without her children. On the contrary, ever since first her mother then her half-sister Stella died and as eldest daughter she became responsible for the family home, it has seemed to her that half her concentration is squandered on accommodating the myriad needs of everyone round her. Lydia, she has discovered, seems not only incapable of managing without multiple attendants, but is willfully insouciant when it comes to money. This might be permissible if Lydia were rich, but strikes Vanessa as foolhardy and even culpable given her current circumstances. It has occurred to her that if Maynard were to cease funding Lydia, she would be forced to leave Gordon Square and chance her luck elsewhere. She recalls a conversation with Mary, at a party Maynard and Clive hosted for the Ballets Russes shortly after the war, when Lydia was still a stranger to them. During a rare exchange of confidences, Mary divulged she was anxious Lydia was bewitching Clive. He had written her a love poem so full of pretentious hyperbole and tortured rhymes Virginia pronounced it a masterpiece. 'A firebird on and off stage,' Mary concluded, 'who'll lure and enchant, before flying away leaving a trail of feathers.'

She glances at Lydia, brooding and miserable on her stool. She wonders if Mary is right and she is heartless – the type who thrives on fresh conquests. She thinks of the letter she must write this evening to Maynard. Though she will remind him of his plea for help, she is under no illusion as to what his reaction will be. He appears more smitten with Lydia than ever.

Hearing a sigh, Lydia turns. She has upset Vanessa with her idiotic chatter, she realises, curbing the impulse to jump up and hug her. Lydia has witnessed how Vanessa settles whenever Duncan is close, and wishes she could ask about their relationship. Duncan's sexual preference for men is no secret. A conversation might not only comfort Vanessa (for Lydia retains a belief in talking as a panacea for most evils), it might also provide a clue to her own distressing triangle with Maynard. Before she can broach the subject however, the flutey notes of a barrel organ penetrate from the street outside.

Vanessa watches Lydia raise the sash window and toss coins from her pockets to the organ-grinder below. Though this interruption is unwelcome, Lydia's face framed by the window interests her and she reaches for a notebook and pencil. She has no money to pay models and might as well put Lydia's intrusion to good use.

'Have you met Maynar's mother?' Lydia wonders as the repeating patterns of the mechanical organ die away. 'Maynar' is giving her tea, but when I knocked he was embarrassed by me. It's why I ran away.'

This admission surprises Vanessa. It cannot be straightforward having an affair with Maynard, she perceives, particularly given his contentment with Sebastian. The similarity with her own situation strikes her. While she has come to accept the sacrifices loving Duncan requires (both for her own sake and for their daughter's), nothing impels Lydia to make the same difficult choice. Relieved, for she has no desire to cause Lydia distress, she sees that in saving Maynard from an infatuation she suspects he already regrets, she might also spare Lydia.

'Forget Maynard,' she blurts out before her courage fails, 'the two of you inhabit different worlds which in the long run can only lead to misery. Better to end now and remain friends.' Then, to forestall whatever protest is forthcoming, she adds: 'You do know Maynard and Sebastian are planning a tour of North Africa together?'

Lydia storms down the stairs of number 50, hurls open the front door and runs the few steps to number 46. Without pausing to consider whether Maynard might still be with his mother, she charges up to his sitting room.

'Is true,' she erupts, too shocked by Vanessa's revelation to knock, 'that you will go to North Africa with Sebastian?' She plants herself in front of the chair where Maynard sits reading. 'Only yesterday we shared every secret of our bodies so I felt certain we were two closest beings in world. You spoke of spending summer holidays together. I even advised Vera this morning she must not count on me for August. Now I uncover you are plotting other arrangements the whole while without single squeak to me so I must learn it from Vanessa.'

Maynard, who has been engrossed in a newspaper article about Gandhi's trial, looks up. Lydia is a few feet from his chair, her fists clenched, looking as if she would like to take a swing at him. He has no doubt she would do it too and that her punch would be decent, for dancing has made her strong. Nor does he doubt that he deserves it. Ever since his mother left to catch her train back to Cambridge he has berated himself for not introducing Lydia as he should. He knows his failure upset Lydia and that it is why she refused his invitation to stay to tea.

'I'm glad you've come back, Loppy. There's a question I've been wanting to ask you. I met my solicitor this morning and outlined your situation. It might take a while, but he can see no impediment to your eventually being free to marry again.' He stands up from his chair then, to Lydia's amazement, bends down on one knee. 'Consequently, I should be honoured if you would consent to becoming Mrs Keynes.'

Maynard deposits the box of Fuller's cakes on Lydia's dressing table. He is disappointed he has missed her, for though her rehearsal was set for ten and it is now almost eleven, he has been harbouring the hope that today might be one of the days when she arrives late. It is the reason he has hurried back from seeing his solicitor, whom he has instructed to write to the first Mrs Barocchi as well as to Lydia's husband informing them of Lydia's intention to divorce. He checks her sitting room and when, as he suspects, it too is empty scribbles a message to leave with the cakes.

He pictures Lydia as he writes, tumbling out of bed at the last possible moment and dressing in whatever garments come to hand, then racing downstairs to plunder left-overs from the kitchen for a late breakfast. When Lydia first described these concoctions he had not believed her, until he witnessed her one morning devouring cold ham from the bone and the remains of a fruit junket. Quite what the cook makes of these outlandish recipes she wisely keeps to herself. He is aware these raids upset Vanessa and did once mention this to Lydia, who responded – brilliantly in his view – by tipping one of the maids to carry a plate of breakfast to her room. Vanessa's decision to end this arrangement on the grounds the supplementary payment would cause tensions among the servants has always seemed to him an error.

Maynard is particularly sorry not to be in time to present Lydia with cakes for this morning's breakfast since the assistant at Fuller's helped him pick out her favourites. Her evident popularity with the staff was such he was tempted to disclose his momentous news, which is that he and Lydia are to marry as soon as her divorce can be settled. Though he has had all night and most of the morning to absorb this marvelous prospect, he cannot desist from replaying their conversation of the previous evening in his head: partly to reassure himself he has remembered it correctly, and partly out of sheer joy at the outcome. He wonders whether Lydia has told Vera or any of the dancers and if she feels as happy about the decision as he does. While he has always considered reason and not emotion to be his guide, the confirmation that Lydia will become a permanent feature in his life gives him such pleasure he can barely stop smiling. He even caught himself twice en route to his solicitor's whistling the tune of a popular love song, surprising a group of nurses leaving the hospital after their night shift and even invoking a grin of recognition from the police constable directing traffic on the Euston Road. The words of the song infiltrate his brain and he tries to decide if, with a little practice, he might sing it to Lydia tonight. After all, few women can be as deserving of the song's title 'Angel Child' as his Loppy.

He adds a few last words to his note, expressing the wish that Lydia as the good fairy might change him into a cake so he can experience the excitement of being gobbled by her. He is crossing the landing when he notices several canvases, parceled in brown paper and tied with string. These must be the paintings for Vanessa's exhibition, waiting for the gallery men to collect them. He has not yet reflected on what might have prompted Vanessa to inform Lydia of his plan to return to North Africa with Sebastian, and though he fears the motive was ill-intentioned, he is in too good a humour to challenge her about this now. On the contrary, he is seized by a desire to tell Vanessa of his engagement to Lydia. Possibly, he anticipates that in so doing he will put an end to the tensions that have arisen since her arrival in Gordon Square. Though it is the case he initially struggled against the feelings Lydia stirred in him, it is many months since he has regarded her presence in his life to be as essential as the oxygen he breathes. Mainly, he longs simply to confide in Vanessa, whom he continues to regard as his closest female friend.

He knocks at the door of Vanessa's room which springs open at his touch. Inside are more parcelled canvases, as well as a number of paintings that have not yet been wrapped including a few that are unfinished. His eye takes in flowers in a partially painted jug and an as yet featureless face that nonetheless reminds him of Virginia. Believing Vanessa cannot be far, he walks to the table by the window and studies an arrangement of vegetables and fruit, noting soiled carrots, apples of varying degrees of ripeness, and even an unpeeled potato of the type Vanessa's children like to turn into faces by inserting buttons for eyes and twigs for hair. There is a damp sheet of old newspaper beside them, one of its corners rearing up like a snake's head. In it, are the severed carrot tops which he understands will have been removed for an aesthetic reason, such as their feathery leaves spoiling the more solid shape of their shanks or the green clashing with that of the apples. If it were left to him he would remove the paper containing the carrot tops, but he knows better than to touch. Once, when he and Duncan were on holiday together, he cleared an apparently random collection of objects from a desk, forcing Duncan to abandon his drawing of them. Instead, he plunges his hands into his pockets and hums 'Angel Child'.

'Congratulations', he begins as Vanessa appears at last, 'there must be twenty-five pictures here.' His remark is prompted by the memory of a conversation in which Vanessa worried she might not have enough new paintings for her exhibition and would have to hang old work to fill the gallery walls. He intends it to be reassuring, but when she does not reply he adds, encouragingly: 'you'll reserve two for me to buy.'

Vanessa sets down the jar of water and clean brushes she is carrying. She has not been expecting Maynard, imagining he would be on his way to Cambridge where his teaching has resumed. She presumes he is here because she is the one who revealed the North Africa expedition to Lydia, and while she does not regret this, she has neither the time nor the appetite for a scene.

She approaches the canvas on her easel. Though all she has accomplished so far are a few outlines to which she has added patches of colour, what she sees pleases her. In the centre are the beginnings of three apples, and as she traces their shapes with her hands she finds herself wondering if Lydia meant what she said about her style evoking Picasso's. While she knows the sensible course would be to continue with the jug of flowers and portrait of Virginia since both are almost complete, they repeat old ideas and if she is honest no longer interest her. The apples, on the other hand, seem to her luminous with possibility.

Maynard, by the window, watches as she works. Despite familiarity with the process through his artist friends, the slow but perceptible transformation of a blank space into a painting fascinates him. He thinks of Charleston where Duncan and Vanessa lived permanently during the war, and how, catching an early train from London one Friday, he arrived to find Vanessa kneeling in front of the bookcase in his room. Though he has forgotten the precise date and hence what newspaper report or more likely uncensored account from those invalided in the fighting might have distressed Vanessa, he remembers her greeting him with such despondency he could think of nothing comforting to say. Instead, he sat wordlessly on the bed, his briefcase with its Treasury papers on the counterpane beside him. At that moment, he had felt keenly the lunacy of expending ever-increasing sums of money and men on a victory he concluded could never justify its cost. He is unsure how long he remained there, or whether he confided any of his misgivings to Vanessa, but he is aware that the quiet calm of her repeated brush strokes as she decorated the grey-painted wood of his bookcase soothed him. When finally she sat back on her heels to survey the effect and asked whether he should like her to colour the spines of his folders yellow, her question seemed more pressing and reasonable than any demand from the War Office.

As if she has been privy to these ruminations about Charleston, Vanessa looks across at Maynard. To her surprise, he appears neither angry nor upset that her disclosure about Sebastian and North Africa has brought his relationship with Lydia to an end. On the contrary, he seems serenely absorbed in the progress of her picture. Could it be, she wonders in alarm, that Lydia and Maynard's affair is not yet over and they have come to a fresh understanding?

Maynard, still buoyed by the knowledge he and Lydia are to marry, catches Vanessa's eye. 'Two paintings,' he repeats. 'Any two — though I must admit I like these apples.' He points to the same picture Lydia admired which has not yet been parcelled for the gallery.

Like a string that has been pulled so tight any further exertion might snap her, Vanessa perches on a chair, letting the wing of the backrest shield her from Maynard's scrutiny. How smug he is, volunteering to purchase two of her paintings when it is obvious he cares nothing for her art. It still rankles that he has failed to comment on the pictures she has hung in his sitting room. That he has expressed no preference as to which of her canvases she is to set aside for him only confirms his indifference. His offer is made out of pity and his assumption that — as happened the last time she exhibited her work — very little of it will sell. She is aware she should be grateful since heaven knows she needs the money, but what she feels is resentment and dislike. She begins to hope his affair with Lydia is not over. They deserve each other.

To rid herself of such thoughts (which she knows are not only unjust but temporary), she repositions herself before her easel.

'I was going to write to you last night,' she tells him, locating a tube of cadmium red and squeezing it onto her palette.

Detecting the edge in her voice, Maynard's impulse to share his news subsides. Vanessa is exhausted, he perceives, her expression the one of forced composure he has learned indicates strain. Given the litany of petty grumbles and complaints Lydia's presence in Gordon Square has generated in recent months, he is sensible of the fresh ructions his engagement will provoke. Though he is optimistic his marriage will eventually resolve these tensions this will not happen instantly. Besides, now is not the moment for a battle. He wants Vanessa's exhibition to be successful. His pledge to buy two of her paintings springs from a genuine desire to facilitate this. He is also not yet ready for his triumphant mood to be spoiled by his friends' disapproval. He should like to enjoy his jubilation a while longer, before the difficult business of extricating Lydia from her marriage and championing her cause against her Bloomsbury detractors starts in earnest. He should also speak to Sebastian. While he suspects from certain remarks Sebastian has let slip it is an outcome he is half expecting, he should not like him to hear from a third party. He owes Sebastian this much.

'About this summer,' Vanessa continues as she streaks the red paint into her apple skins. 'You of course are welcome at Charleston, but I've been talking it over with Clive and we do not feel we can accommodate Lydia.'

Maynard's immediate instinct is to laugh. He is relieved but not surprised that Vanessa did not name Duncan who appears fond of Lydia, while the irony that Clive has been consulted is not lost on him. Though he grasps why Vanessa wishes Clive as the children's father to spend time with them at Charleston, he is mindful that Clive's visits are shorter and more infrequent than Vanessa would like and often include Mary.

'You know how it is there. We have our rhythms.'

'I see no reason why Lydia can't fit in with these.' Despite his earlier promise to himself not to touch the items Vanessa has arranged on the table to paint, he picks up one of the apples. He objects to the insinuation that Lydia will disrupt the pattern they have developed at Charleston, where mornings and most afternoons are reserved for work. It is on the tip of his tongue to remind Vanessa of Lydia's international reputation as a dancer, renown she could not have acquired without considerable discipline. He toys with pointing out that she is far more successful in her chosen field than any of them – and certainly when compared to Vanessa, her sister Virginia or Clive. He desists however, recognizing the cruel inappropriateness of this statement when Vanessa is preparing for her exhibition.

'She does not need, as we do, uninterrupted calm to work,' Vanessa persists. 'She admits herself she thrives when surrounded by people, bustle, noise.'

Maynard turns the apple over in his hand, schooling himself to be reasonable. 'I'm confident if I explained Lydia could find plenty to occupy herself. She's a voracious reader.'

'There's also the question of how she would fit in with the rest of our time.'

Though Vanessa refrains from mentioning the long, earnest discussions that have become such a feature of their gatherings, Maynard understands these are what lie behind her remark. He knows the prevailing view among Clive, Lytton and Virginia is that Lydia has little to contribute intellectually, and that they consider her uneducated, vulgar and brash. He contemplates repeating the more favourable estimations of others of his acquaintance, such as his writer friend Morgan Forster who has proposed recording Lydia's original and thought-provoking observations. It even crosses his mind to remind Vanessa that she rarely produces any illuminating insight during their group conversations, often opting to remain silent.

'Lydia will be an asset to our theatrical evenings,' he suggests instead, steering their debate into less hostile territory, 'and if she cannot already play bowls, I've no doubt she'll pick the game up quickly.'

Vanessa puts down her brush. 'Can you honestly envisage her spending the summer happily with us at Charleston? It would be like introducing a peacock into the garden, all those exotic displays of her tail feathers entirely lost on us sparrows.'

The image is so vivid and stinging Maynard instantly attributes it to her sister. Though he has in the past relished Virginia's scathing and often hilarious verbal portraits of the foibles and follies of others, this confirmation that Lydia and no doubt he himself have become her targets disturbs him. Ever since school he has abhorred people laughing at his expense, and he fears Virginia's brilliance. If Lydia is a peacock, Virginia he likens to a hawk, distantly attentive until suddenly she swoops in on her prey with deadly precision and ferocity. He has no intention of sacrificing his Loppy to her talons.

'As it happens, we've other plans. Lydia is working for much of the summer and in September, when she's free, we've the prospect of a house near Bournemouth. So we shan't be coming to Charleston.' He returns the apple to the table, no longer caring if it is not in its original place.

A light springs on, startling Lydia cocooned in a nest of feathers and fur in the costume store. Vera, who has spent the past twenty minutes searching the rabbit warren of dressing rooms backstage at the Coliseum, takes in Lydia's recumbent form. She is dismayed to see her friend has fallen asleep in the smart green suit they bought to impress potential sponsors. Only Lydia's hat, which has been swapped for a wig and set on one of the papier-mâché heads lining the walls, appears to have escaped unscathed. Vera picks her way between the tightly-packed rails of clothes, the racks of shoes and boxes of labelled accessories until she reaches Lydia's side.

'Bad night?' She moves a donkey mask from the bench Lydia is lying on so she can sit beside her. She knows Lydia's sleep has been plagued by bad dreams recently and is sympathetic. Since discovering she was pregnant, she too has been prone to insomnia.

'Terrible,' Lydia confesses, raising herself onto her elbows and blinking in the sudden glare of the light. 'I dreamt I was on a ship happily dancing when the alarm sounded to evacuate.' She disentangles herself from the crumpled folds of a satin ball gown, a pair of feathered wings and what might be the rest of the donkey costume. 'It reminded me of sailing to America during the war because all at once there were soldiers shooting bullets. One went right through me and though I woke and was still alive, I was too shaken to sleep again.'

'Still no news on the divorce?' Vera places her hands on the now visible swelling in her belly. She has not yet felt the baby move, but the doctor has assured her it will not be long.

'Apparently I've papers stuck in three separate countries.'

'Maynard must have strings he can pull.' Vera watches as her friend swings herself into a sitting position. Remarkably, her suit does not appear too creased. 'Did you see Stoll? What did he say?'

'The usual. He's encouraged by the reviews, but insists he can't for the moment extend the run.' Lydia retrieves a black notebook she has pegged beneath a donkey hoof. The page she opens it at contains a long list of figures, accompanied by underlinings, crossings out and numerous ink blots. On the right, she has written the £900 Stoll has advanced; on the left are her expenses, including the dancers' salaries, Vera's fee for her libretto, design costs and even an unforeseen payment to the Coliseum firemen. Her current deficit when she reaches the bottom of this column is a staggering £177.

'I don't suppose,' she taps the £300 Vera is claiming with her finger, then abandons the thought. She has already attempted to persuade Vera to reduce her charge for 'Masquerade', only to be met with a forceful rebuttal. When she revealed this to Maynard he snorted contemptuously, pointing out that this represented a third of their income from Stoll. Given that Vera and Harold scarcely needed the money, it indicated a flagrant overestimation of Vera's role in the project he could only attribute to greed. He blamed Harold whom he has never trusted and advised Lydia to break with Vera. To cheer her, he quoted from the many favourable reviews she has received for her choreography as well as her dancing, promising noble failure is preferable to cheap success.

Lydia shuts her notebook. Maynard's unwavering belief remains a lifeline, and yet she is aware the rosy future he imagines is naïve. She was able to devise dances for Stoll by drawing on the repertoire already familiar to her. How she might fare if required to create entirely new material is less certain. She also knows Stoll only agreed to her choreographing the ballets on condition she perform in them, and that it is her reputation as a dancer that procures her work. While she hopes she has a few more years left in her dancing bones, the time is approaching when she will no longer draw in the crowds. She reaches beneath the bench for two pairs of ballet shoes she has stowed there and inspects the soles for cracks. In America, where she could earn thousands of dollars in a week, she rarely needed to make her shoes last more than a single performance. How she wishes she had some of that money now. She glances at Vera, who looks too pale and tired to discuss the calamitous state of their finances let alone embark on another skirmish over her exorbitant fee.

'At least you'll have a thrilling event to occupy you over the summer.' She gives Vera's stomach an affectionate pat. 'While I must partner that stingy louse Massine. In towns no one has heard of. Even Maynard refuses to visit me in Harrogate.'

Vera finds smelling salts from her bag. The smell of moth balls is making her nauseous. She would like a glass of water but feels too listless to move. 'What will Maynard do?'

'Write. And travel to Germany. He's advising the government there.' Lydia cannot keep the pride from her voice. The number and importance of Maynard's activities never cease to amaze her.

'Will he spend time at Charleston?'

Lydia removes her hat from the papier-mâché head. She locates the wig she swapped it for and tries it on, stooping to glimpse her reflection in a mirror propped on one of the shelves. 'Do you think Maynard would love me more if I cut my hair short like a boy?' she quizzes. Then, as if to dismiss the question, she replaces the wig with her hat. 'He might go to Charleston. Especially now Vanessa has written assuring me I'm welcome too.'

'I thought you weren't going to accept?'

'I'm not. But Maynard might visit anyway. He sees Vanessa's letter as an overture.'

Vera shifts her position, trying to decide whether a cigarette will help her nausea. 'But your engagement's official?'

'No one believes it will happen. Which may be right given the stalemate with my legal papers.' Lydia retrieves the donkey mask, fondles the long ears. 'My first role at School was a fairy in "Midsummer Night's Dream". How I made my brothers laugh when I explained Titania falls in love with a donkey!' She sits beside Vera, pulling the mask onto her knee. 'I don't understand. I've always been good at making friends. Yet the harder I try with Vanessa, the more she seems to dislike me.'

'She'll come round.' Though Vera has no reason to believe this is true, she is feeling too unwell to reopen the thorny subject of Lydia's precarious relations with Maynard's Bloomsbury friends. 'The fact Vanessa wrote to you proves how unwilling they are to lose Maynard. And Maynard will take your side.'

'Perhaps, though he agrees with Vanessa it would be better if I moved to a different address in Gordon Square.' Lydia settles the donkey mask over her face and brays a loud, rebellious hee-haw. 'At least Maynard and I will be together in September. He's rented a house for an entire month. Right by the sea.'

Coming to the end of his chapter, Maynard turns his book over on his knee and leans back in his deckchair. It is mid-morning and the sand is already hot beneath his bare feet. He adjusts the brim of his straw hat to shade his eyes from the sun and gazes about him. Studland beach, which is flanked at his back by grassy dunes, stretches so far to his left it is impossible to determine where it ends, while on his right it tails into headland tipped by three giant chalk formations known locally as Old Harry rocks. In front of him is the sea, its unending blue broken only by the lacey frill of a wave or an occasional sailboat.

He reaches down and rolls the hems of his trousers higher up his legs. He has not, as most of his party has done since arriving in Studland, changed into a bathing suit and swam, protesting at the coldness of the water and vaunting the superior merits of reading. He pulls his hat-brim lower and surveys his guests, dotted in clusters of two or three across the sand. There is Hubert Henderson, with whom he is editing *The Nation*, talking to his old Cambridge friend Jack Sheppard. Dadie Rylands and Raymond Mortimer, two men he also met at Cambridge, are lounging on towels, smoking. They were the first into the sea this morning, setting off with strong, even strokes until their heads were mere bobbing balls on the horizon.

Maynard looks for Lydia and finds her sitting on a rug with Leonard. He concludes from the lively dance of her hands that she is recounting one of her stories. He also gauges from the attentive manner of Leonard's listening that he is engrossed. Their obvious pleasure in each other's company encourages him. He is aware that despite Vanessa relenting over Charleston, she was relieved when he timed his visit to coincide with Lydia's performances in Harrogate.

He tips his head back and stares up at the sky, letting his thoughts range with the wheeling gulls and shape-shifting flecks of cloud. He is conscious of Lydia's frustration at how many people he has asked to join them in Dorset. He concedes she has right on her side, since he too imagined when planning the holiday they would have more time alone together. As host he has responsibilities, for though the Duke of Hamilton from whom he has rented the house possesses a large and well-trained staff, there are innumerable daily decisions to be made. Only yesterday he upset the smooth running of arrangements by omitting to mention an excursion to Bindon Abbey and cancelling luncheon at short notice. Not for the first time he regretted that Vanessa, with her practical wisdom in domestic matters, had declined his invitation.

His eyes follow a solitary gull swooping for fish. He remembers Vanessa's painting of Studland Beach, finished before the war. In it, a huddle of children plays round a woman standing before a bathing tent. The only other people in the picture are reduced to outlines. He has wondered what prompted Vanessa to depict the scene as she did, but as he contemplates the beach now he starts to perceive it as he supposes Vanessa must: an expanse of white sand bordered by the blue of sea and sky against which human figures scarcely register.

Lydia, he realises as his gaze locates her again, is flirting with Leonard, and as if he is seeing her as well as the beach through Vanessa's eyes he finds himself willing her to stop – not for his sake (it is only Leonard and he has no reason to be jealous) but for her own. He recalls Virginia's warning, as they drank coffee on the terrace after dinner, that Lydia had no right to object if men refused to take her seriously when she persisted in behaving as she did. Later, in his room, Lydia burst into tears, complaining his friends interpreted her actions in the worst possible light while he failed to lift a finger in her defence.

Maynard alters his focus to where Virginia reclines in her deckchair. Though her book is open, it is Lydia she is observing. It occurs to him that exactly as Vanessa uses whatever is at hand for painting, so Virginia might be studying Lydia for her novel. While the broad brim of Lydia's hat prevents him from glimpsing her face, he can picture her expression as she courts Leonard and finds himself fearing for her. Whatever scene Virginia is composing is unlikely to be favourable to Lydia. Her quick-darting mind can be pitiless.

There is a tap on his shoulder and it is Jack, with a question so multi-faceted and absorbing it takes them several minutes to unravel. When at last they have answered it to their mutual satisfaction and he is free to return his attention to the beach, the rug Leonard was sharing with Lydia is empty. Leonard he spots easily, stooping over his wife presumably to ask if there is anything she needs. He searches for Lydia but she is not with his friends. Nor is she walking along the shore or exercising on the sand. He scans the dunes then, more anxiously, the sea. Finally he spies her, resting flat on her back so from a distance it is possible to miss her. Her pose reminds him of their outing to Bindon Abbey, where Thomas Hardy famously imagined his heroine Tess being placed in a sunken grave. The ruined Abbey charmed them and they discussed Henry VIII's suppression of the monasteries, and whether Thomas Cromwell might accurately be considered England's cleverest statesman. Lydia drew a comparison with Russia, where buildings are routinely commandeered by the Bolshevik regime, until a shout announcing the discovery of the grave stopped their debate. It was shallower and narrower than they had anticipated, and as they crowded round Virginia related the episode from the novel. Lydia, for whose benefit she did this, stepped into the opening and lay on the ground, her white-stockinged legs stretched out in front of her and her arms crossed over her chest. She stayed so still Maynard began to believe he might be staring at her corpse, and he had felt a rush of affection – not only for Lydia but all his friends.

The beach, which has been temporarily eclipsed by memories of the Abbey, disappears as two hot, sandy hands blindfold Maynard's eyes.

'At last you have free space!' Ignoring his objection that the deckchair will not hold them both, Lydia plants herself on his lap.

'You were talking very intently to Leonard.'

'I was explaining my riding lesson. Today was the trot which people warned would be horribly bouncy, but if you are experienced ballerina it is no worse than being heaved up and down by incompetent partner.'

'So you're glad to be here,' Maynard chuckles.

'I am. I should like to stay longer on this beach in hot sun with our worries far away.'

'We still have a few days.'

'Then I depart for Johnstons and you to shoot deer. Are you sure I mustn't accompany you? Party may be men only but I could come as faithful hunting dog.' To prove her suitability for this role, she licks his cheek so zealously Maynard pinions her in his arms.

'You caused quite a commotion with the staff,' he murmurs affectionately. 'Poor Loppy – having to learn the hard way that for all our stiff upper lip, the English are aghast if the rules of propriety are flouted.'

A shadow falls across them. It is Hubert waving a newspaper, wanting to discuss politics with Maynard. Reluctantly, Lydia dislodges herself from his knee. She would like to ask Maynard how he learned of the unfortunate incident with the valet, but having been humiliated once this morning is too embarrassed to raise the matter in front of Hubert. She leaves them dissecting the latest development in the conflict between Greece and Albania, pleading a desire to cool her feet in the sea.

Lydia walks a dozen or so paces over the hot sand then looks back. As she expected, Maynard is scrutinizing the paper and listening to Hubert, engrossed in argument over Mussolini. If he has not already forgotten her he soon will. She casts about for fresh company, considering first Dadie and Raymond strolling towards the dunes, then Leonard who has left his wife to her book and is talking to Jack. Everyone it seems is engaged in a conversation or activity with no need of her presence. She speculates, wildly, whether they would notice if she stripped off her clothes and ran naked towards the water.

She contemplates Virginia next, one hand on her book, the other shielding her eyes as she scans the bay. She recalls Virginia's stinging remark in the garden, expressing surprise at her reading Shakespeare in English when her command of the language is so imperfect. Lydia might have abandoned *King Lear* entirely had not Virginia – as if to atone for the hurt – suddenly pointed to where a silvery-blue butterfly fanned its wings in the sun. They watched entranced until the creature took to the air, when Virginia's arm circled her waist and for a moment she had the glorious, inexplicable feeling Virginia was attracted to her.

Dadie and Raymond have paused to greet Virginia who (judging by their laughter) is entertaining the pair with an uproarious tale. The prospect of sharing the joke is too tempting to pass up and Lydia starts towards them. As she approaches, she catches the occasional word. She recognises 'valet', and 'bribe'. The next phrases, which prompt loud guffaws from Dadie and Raymond, are pronounced so bizarrely Lydia cannot decipher them. She quickens her pace, straining to hear, until she realises with a shock it is her own Russian accent Virginia is mimicking. She stops dead in her tracks, certain now that what Virginia is recounting is the story of her period and how she attempted to dispose of her stained undergarment by leaving it to be burned in the drawing room grate.

'So much for the nobility of the Russian soul,' Virginia is concluding to the accompaniment of wild hilarity, 'when it is composed of such swift passions it makes friends and enemies in an instant.'

Wishing a hole would appear before her so she could dive into it, Lydia hurries towards the dunes then along the path that leads to the Duke's estate. By the time she reaches the park she is moving so quickly the gardeners interrupt their grass-cutting to watch. One of them, wiping the sweat from his brow, fears an accident must have befallen one of the guests on the beach and wonders about raising the alarm. Lydia, once she arrives at the house, races up the stairs, leaving a track of sandy footprints in her wake. Inside her room she takes a leather bag from under the bed and stuffs it with a random assortment of items. When it is full she snaps the clasps shut, not caring that there are more clothes hanging in the wardrobe and books on the table. Still in her beach dress she thrusts feet into shoes, thuds the bag down to the hall. Here she instructs the startled butler to ring for a taxi to drive her urgently to the station.

'You told no one you were leaving?' Vera signals to her maid to pour out tea.

'No one,' Lydia assures her. 'I waited for the taxi at the end of the drive then caught the first train here.'

'So what happened?'

'At first it was small things, a glance of disapproval or teasing comment. I couldn't always decide if it was meant. Then we went to Bindon Abbey and Virginia gave a speech about how it features in a novel. Of course she did this for my sake because she assumes I'm too ignorant to have read Thomas Hardy. I'm afraid it brought out my devil.'

'What did you do?'

'I lay in a grave and feigned death! I was a preposterous corpse because I had on my pink jacket, the one trimmed in white fur. I hoped the spectacle might cause Maynard to reflect and appreciate me more. But he was busy talking to Leonard.' She accepts a cup of tea which she gulps thirstily. 'Not for a second did I imagine when we planned the holiday he would invite so many guests. We were almost never alone.'

Vera indicates to her maid to refill Lydia's cup. 'That doesn't sound so terrible. Certainly not a reason to leave.'

'I'm not telling it well. It's hard to explain how it is with Virginia. One evening in the garden, after a taunt at my choice of book, she showed me the butterflies. She knows all their names. One is "Vanessa Atalanta" which is "Red Admiral" in English. I laughed at the idea of Vanessa being an admiral in a red jacket and this made Virginia laugh too. Her arm was round me and, well, I hoped we might become friends.' She slips off her shoes revealing feet still sandy from the beach. 'So when can I kiss baby Nicholas?'

'We'll go to the nursery after tea,' Vera promises. She gestures to the maid to cut the fruitcake then, sensing Lydia will talk more freely if they are alone, dismisses her.

'Now it's just the two of us,' Vera coaxes handing her a plate, 'you must tell me what forced you to get on a train and come here.'

Lydia reaches for a slice of cake. 'The morning was spent on the beach,' she begins. 'I arrived late because of my riding lesson. Virginia was telling a story that had everyone in stitches. I thought what fun it would be to join in, except that as I got close I realised her story was about me. Only she was adding and twisting ingredients so that according to her version I am both a barbarian and a buffoon.' She pauses to swallow mouthfuls of cake then bursts out angrily. 'I never kissed the valet or sobbed at the cook's feet! That was entirely Virginia's invention!' She leans forward to set her cup and plate on the table then, noticing she is still dressed in beach clothes, returns them to her knee as if to disguise her incongruous attire. 'Besides, what does it matter if our *prokladki* are burned in a grate inside the house instead of outside in the garden? If there's a woman in Virginia's next novel who's frivolous and stupid I'll have no doubt at all it's me.'

'Maynard didn't come to your rescue?'

'He was deep in conversation with Hubert, on a different part of the beach. But even if he'd heard, he wouldn't have responded as I wished.'

'And how is that?

'With storm and rage until everything bad is forced into the open! Maynard's ancestors might be French but he's English to his marrow. He doesn't agree that in a quarrel our Russian custom is best, because once the air is clear we have the chance to cry and make up.'

Although Vera is accustomed to the see-saw course of her friend's affair with Maynard, she is struck by Lydia's tone. She has never known her analyse his failings with such clarity before, and nor has she witnessed her so dejected. She wonders whether to change the subject, and if this might be the moment to tiptoe upstairs and peer in at Nicholas' cot. She studies her friend silhouetted by the high windows that look out over the Bowen's Bedfordshire estate, and concludes that for now she will do better to keep Lydia here where they can talk in private.

'You had no other allies?'

'A few. Virginia's husband Leonard was as kind as ever, and I always get on well with Jack Sheppard. He teaches classics in Cambridge with Maynard, but is the opposite of a solemn professor.' She brightens. 'I teased him he might be one part Russian because he loves jokes and silly pranks as much as we do. He'll be sad I've left.'

The maid reappears to inform Vera she is wanted on the telephone. Vera waves her away with a message to the caller she is not at home. 'I presume that will be Maynard, worried by your sudden departure. He'll want to know where you are.'

'Let him worry,' Lydia erupts with such fury the teacup and plate on her knee crash to the floor. 'He's off on his own to Devon on Friday. It seems women aren't welcome at hunting parties.' She piles shards of china haphazardly on the table. 'I even volunteered to go as his dog.'

Vera considers ringing for the maid then decides against it. Lydia's old dress hardly matters and the rest can be dealt with later. 'Is Sebastian one of the party?'

'If not Sebastian, then another.' Lydia kicks at a fragment of plate with her bare feet. 'The stupid thing is Maynard and I are happy together.'

Vera opens a silver cigarette case. 'What will you do? You are of course welcome to stay with us.'

'I've been contemplating returning to Russia.'

Vera starts. She has not expected this. 'As a dancer?'

'I'm not brave enough to perform in workers' clubs for bread to keep me from starving,' Lydia admits. 'The ballet I grew up with barely exists anymore. Did you hear Lenin turned Kschessinska's old home into an office? But I miss my family.' She helps herself to a De Reszke. 'First, I might go to Monte Carlo, find out if that old rogue Diaghilev has any crumbs for me.'

'What about your engagement?' Vera passes Lydia a lighter.

'That's all over. Maynard and I will never be married.'

ACT TWO

'Lured on by evil demons, I am drawn into the heart of the enchanted forest where I gradually lose my way. One by one my hiding places are discovered and destroyed.'

My father grabs my hand as we dart between the trams and horse-drawn carriages that fill St Petersburg's main thoroughfare, our boots rat-a-tatting on the cobbles. We pass hawkers selling fish from barrels they swear are caught fresh from the Neva, and boys beside barrows of onions, beetroots, turnips and potatoes, the mud frozen on their skins. Women with baskets of apples and flower-posies tug at the sleeve of father's coat, but he bats them away with a grin. One, prettier than the rest, her cheeks crimson with cold, tucks a rose under his fur-trimmed collar and he relents and reaches into his pocket. My father is handsome in his usher's cap with his beard trimmed close and the swaggering walk he learned in the army, and when he presses a few kopecks into the girl's outstretched palm she blushes. Under my own coat I am wearing a hand-me-down dress from my sister Eugenia, with new lace flounces to disguise where the fabric has worn. I have kept my hair in papers the whole morning and it jiggles and jumps in fat, bouncing curls as I walk.

We enter the Mariinsky Theatre through a side door, where father introduces me to the woman who will stay with me while he works his shift at the Alexandrinsky Theatre close by. She holds a pair of silver opera glasses with mother-of-pearl handles I hope she will let me look through. I follow her up four flights of stairs to a balcony where people are already seated: families in their church best, black-gowned governesses flapping about their charges like crows. The orchestra is warming up, and though I cannot see the musicians I know from father they are in a darkened recess in front of the stage. My mouth gapes at the gold-painted galleries, at the chandelier spurting out light like an upside down waterfall in the ceiling overhead. I crane for a glimpse of the Imperial crown and am disappointed to discover there are blue drapes pulled across the box beneath, a sign the Tsar will not be attending. Below, on velvet-cushioned chairs, princes and counts in uniform greet each other, accompanied by ladies in exquisite dresses. I study them so I can describe them later to mother, but only have time to note the medals hanging on ribbons from the noblemen's breasts and the glittering jewels of the ladies' tiaras when everyone round me bursts into applause.

A man with a black moustache bows to the audience from a stand near the stage. This is the conductor and as he waves his hands I hear music. I decide then and there that all conductors are magicians. I picture Eugenia and my brother Fedor amongst the dancers waiting behind the closed curtain, despite father explaining they have not been long enough at the Imperial Ballet School to be selected for a role. I try to recall their gossip about their classes when they come home on Sundays, but all I can remember is their nickname for their teachers which is 'Toad'. I wonder if the dancers feel nervous and what they do to prepare. I promise myself that if I were waiting, I should take a deep breath to puff out my chest and not be scared at all.

The curtain rises. Angels in knee-length white tunics hover before a forest, arms curled in graceful arches above their heads. To my amazement they are running on the tips of their toes, as lightly and effortlessly as if this is natural. I cannot fathom how they do it and lean forward for a better view. I consider asking my companion if I can borrow her opera glasses, but she has pressed them to her eyes and I do not dare. A crowned angel enters, her white tunic garlanded with flowers. After a moment in which she stares sadly towards the trees, she wheels round in a sequence of slow circles, her hands rising and falling like birds. My companion rests her glasses on her lap and whispers that the woman is a princess in love, but I am not interested in who she is or the details of her story. All I want is to watch her move. I stand up in the cramped space between the seats so I can copy her. It is fortunate I am little as there is scarcely room. Suddenly, a turbaned man leaps to her side, lifting her so high I gasp. Now she is a flying angel, and as he carries her off through the forest I close my eyes and imagine I am flying too.

Two boys in sailor jackets are fidgeting in the row behind. They are bored and on the lookout for mischief. One finds a packet of raisins he shares with his friend. They spend some minutes cramming their mouths with the fruit when a better plan strikes them. Their game now is to fling handfuls of raisins over the balcony rail, scoring points if anyone is hit. Ordinarily this would amuse me too, but I am annoyed by the distraction and cough to attract the attention of their governess. I am relieved when she scolds them. The stage darkens to reveal a garden and a temple wall. The angels form themselves into two lines, then, tilting forward so their heads almost touch the floor, each raises a leg into the air. I kick up my own leg in imitation, but instead of mirroring their beautiful shapes, I jerk myself sideways and topple to the floor. After this, I do not attempt any more of their steps but watch motionless from my seat.

We wait a long time for father once the performance is over. I do not mind because it is warm in the foyer and my companion lets me chatter. I realize she knows the theatre well because several of the ushers speak to her. I ask if she will take me to meet the dancers but she laughs and tells me this will happen soon enough. It is dark when we set off for home. Father is in a merry mood and buttons up our coats against the falling snow. On the Nevsky Prospect the hawkers and barrow boys have disappeared, moved on by police in the pay of shop owners whose dazzlingly lit windows display tobacco, wine, silk, snuff and chocolate from countries as far away as France, Italy, The Netherlands, England. The women with their baskets are still here, together with a clutch of shivering children in filthy, ill-fitting garments selling mushrooms, but they do not bother us. I answer father's questions about the ballet with an elaborate demonstration despite the bruise I can feel spreading under my curls. When we reach our building I race up the stairs and push open the front door. Mother is sewing in her Scottish cap, and smiles as I hurl myself into her arms.

'So', she asks, helping me out of my snow-damp coat, 'did you enjoy the dancing?'

Before I can answer, father towers over her and plants a kiss on her forehead. She stiffens, and I sense she has smelled the vodka on his breath. She says nothing, only holds out her hand for his coat. As she hangs it with mine by the fire to dry, I see tears shining in her eyes. I assume this is because of the vodka which has made us late, so to prevent the argument I know will follow I plunge straight into an account of the ballet, spicing my description with plenty of detail. I insist it was as breathtaking as the great dome on top of Kazansky Cathedral, as spectacular as the Stroganov Palace, as exhilarating as when I try to outrun the trains leaving Vitebsk Station.

'It was as if all the fairy stories in our book were thrown into a cooking pot and stirred into one'.

Mother takes me onto her lap. I have made her gay again and I am glad. She pats my curls and I wince as her fingers find my bruise. Immediately she is parting my hair, checking for traces of blood.

'How did you fall?'

'I was watching the angels in white dresses,' I tell her, 'kicking up their legs in a line. Like this.' I slip from her knee and grasp the arm of her chair. This time, as my leg flies up, I keep my balance.

'A born dancer', father declares, glancing at mother who ignores him. She takes me back onto her lap and continues to inspect my scalp for cuts. Satisfied at last that I have nothing more than a bump the size of a small quail's egg, she twists me round so I am facing her.

'Lydia, when you saw the dancers, did you think you might like to be one of them?'

I slide a strand of blonde hair that has slipped from her tartan cap back into place.

'No,' I reply, 'I don't want to be an angel in line. I want to be the important angel, the one wearing the crown everyone watches.'

੬

A voice wakes me from my perch above the kitchen fire. It is still early, because the square of the window is dark and my younger brothers Nikolai and Andrei are curled asleep in their blankets. The shelf on which I lie is warm, though the ashes have not yet been raked and the grate stocked with a fresh supply of coals from the scuttle. I prop myself onto my elbows to listen.

'We've discussed it a thousand times,' father is protesting. 'If she is accepted, the School will feed, clothe and teach her for free. Don't you want her to have a good education?'

Mother's response is too low to hear, but when father speaks again I realize they are talking about me.

'Damn it, she could earn twice my salary even as a junior dancer. And if she works hard and does well the figure could be ten times that. The rumour is Mathilde Kschessinska has so many clothes and jewels she can't wear them all, not if she lives to be a hundred. And that's without counting her carriages and houses.'

Again mother's reply is too quiet for me to catch.

'She'd be under the patronage of the Tsar! Surely that's protection enough. Or would you rather she follow in your footsteps and end up a masseuse? Hardly a well-paid profession. Or a particularly reputable one come to that.' Father's tone now is a sneer, and I pray Nikolai and Andrei will stay sleeping a while longer so they do not have to witness this.

'Besides, you know how strict they are at the School. Especially with the girls. Eugenia says they're fined if they so much as glance at a boy. Even when they're dancing together. If they're chosen to perform, they're taken to the theatre in carriages with the blinds drawn down. And always a companion goes with them.'

There is a pause during which I picture father, his black brows knitted in a scowl, struggling to rein in his temper.

'When I explained all the string-pulling needed to get her name on the list you didn't object then.'

'What choice did I have?' For the first time, mother's voice is loud enough to penetrate the wall that separates the living room from the kitchen.

'I can't petition the Alexandrinsky for any more money if that's what you're thinking. I'm already the highest paid usher there.'

I slide off my shelf and pull on my skirt. If this quarrel runs like their others, now is the moment for mother to remind him of all the roubles he squanders on drink. Unless father apologises with promises to abstain, she will move on to cock-fighting and card-games. If she believes we are out of earshot she may even accuse him of worse vices.

'There are your tips,' mother begins.

'I use those to pay back the money we borrowed for Anna's funeral.'

This mention of my dead sister is cruel. I pick at a thread on my skirt, imagining mother straight-backed in her chair, her hands clutching at her prayer book for comfort. She will have reached for this instinctively but it will only enrage father. He considers her church-going obsessive and will point out all she spends on votive candles and donations. As he does, he will grow more abusive and may even strike her, not because he cares about the sums involved which are small, but because her piety scares him. To my relief, he adopts a different line of attack.

'At least she won't be a serf, to be sold, gambled or moved at whim', he counters. This reference to his ancestors is possibly the only one of his stories to contain any truth. It is told, as now, whenever he wishes to gain mother's sympathy. 'Let her attend the audition. You saw how her face lit up when I explained they were willing to consider her.'

'The School has Eugenia, Fedor, and now they want my pretty darling....'.

'She wouldn't have to board right away,' father coaxes. 'She's only eight and could sleep at home for the first year or so. You could walk with her in the morning, and the School would send someone to accompany her once classes are over.'

I hold my breath, willing mother to agree. Instead it is father who speaks again, as if my plea has reached him through the thin partition wall and sparked a fresh idea.

'Thousands of families petition the School every year for a place at the audition. Of the three hundred they see, only twenty are chosen. Think how disappointed she'll be if we don't even let her try.'

&

It is father who stands beside me in the corridor of the Imperial Ballet School as I wait to appear before the Selection Committee. He is talking to another parent, whose pale-faced, long-limbed daughter I eye warily. I am surprised to discover from this conversation that father is on first-name terms with several junior ballerinas from the Mariinsky. The corridor hums with the noisy chatter of children and the more measured tones of their parents or chaperones. Opposite me, a girl in a velvet dress and gleaming new leather shoes bends her knees and points her feet as if she knows how to dance. The realisation she has had lessons makes me hiccup with nerves. I wonder how many of the auditioning children have already learned ballet.

My name is called and an attendant shows us into a vast room, with a wooden floor and a long table on a platform at one end. Sitting on the far side of this table are twenty men and a handful of women, none of whom are smiling. I itch to know who they are, and why the men are in court clothes while the women wear black, but when I whisper my question to father he shushes me. They are so solemn I promise myself that when it is my turn to come before them I will make them all smile. Our attendant leads us first to a smaller table pushed against a side wall, where I am instructed to strip to my chemise so a doctor can examine me. I ask if I must remove my socks, a good luck gift from mother, and am informed I must. When I am ready a nurse lifts me onto the table and measures me with a tape. The doctor, as he approaches, smells of carbolic soap. He has almost no hair. He peers at me through half-spectacles, holding out my arms and even asking me to open my mouth so he can scrutinize my teeth as if I am a horse. Once he has inspected my front, he rotates me and taps at my shoulder blades with his knuckles. The nurse writes his comments in a ledger.

'Small for her age, though well-proportioned, with the exception of the arms which are too plump. The legs are strong and the feet particularly so. Pretty child,' he notes, though it scarcely sounds like a compliment, 'the nose is a little snub but the eyes are good. Blue.'

I am escorted to a second side-table in front of which sits a grey-haired man with a silver-knobbed cane. The attendant finds my name on his list and puts a tick against it. There is another child ahead of me whom I recognize as the girl from the corridor even though she is no longer wearing her velvet dress or her beautiful shoes. I survey the mottled pink of her calves and decide that now we are equal. The grey-haired man pokes at her bare feet with his cane.

'Flat,' he pronounces, and orders the assistant to strike out her name. 'You can go home,' he decrees, without looking up.

I am scared after what I have seen. I make a great effort to stand with my feet arched so the old man will not declare them flat.

'Put your knees together,' he directs as the assistant propels me forward. 'Now straighten your legs.' He lifts a monocle to his eye, squints through it for a moment, nods. Then he waves me away. All that is left is for me to dance before the judges on the platform.

'Remember to turn your feet out', father prompts, as I join a short line of waiting children. From my place, I spot the girl with the flat feet crying by the door. Her father is remonstrating with one of the attendants though I do not think he is listening.

I put on my best smile when it is my turn to stand before the long table, and am cheered when a rosy-cheeked count in a gold-braided jacket smiles back.

'We want you to run,' a woman explains, fingering the pearl necklace at her throat, 'first away from the table, then back again. Can you do that? '

I set off. I understand this is my chance to prove myself. I run as if I am in the park with mother and trying to keep pace with the trains as they leave St Petersburg for the far corners of Russia. I run as if the whole of my future depends on it. In no time at all my hand is on the far wall. I spin round, and gulp in air. Then I run back. This time it is the wind I imagine, whipping up storms in the Baltic so even the great cruise ships in the port are tossed on the waves like spinning tops. Only once I arrive again at the table, panting but triumphant, do I remember father's tip about turning out my feet.

My days at the Imperial Ballet School are like the tartan caps mother wears, an endlessly repeating pattern of stripes and squares. We are woken by a bell and must stand by our beds to be counted. Then we form a line to splash ourselves with cold water from the tap. Maids help us tie alpaca aprons over blue cashmere dresses, fasten white wool stockings, and lace black leather shoes. We say prayers before breakfast where we are counted again and served with a buttered bun and an egg. Conversation is not encouraged in the dining room unless it is for a purpose, such as asking for the salt to be passed or more tea to be poured from the steaming samovar. The first hour of the day is for private study and once this is over we are escorted to a changing room where we substitute starched grey dresses for blue ones, and pink stockings for white. The ballet shoes are made of unbleached cotton and have long ribbons, which must be wound round our ankles and knotted at the right tension. If we are recovering from an injury or illness or have some other reason to fear the practice will be gruelling, we spit on the knot for luck.

The room where we learn ballet has a handrail attached to each wall, and a long mirror in a wooden frame which can be moved to different positions so everyone has a chance to see themselves. In my first year at the School, I made the other girls laugh by pulling silly faces into it whenever I thought I was not being observed, but I no longer do this now I am a full boarder. Our teacher this year is Enrico Cecchetti, who is Italian and whom we address as 'Maestro'. He was once the most famous dancer at the Mariinksy Theatre, and it is rumoured that when the Tsar first watched him perform he decided he must be a demon made from rubber. I do not like Maestro to begin with because all he does is shout at me, until one of the senior girls confides this is a good sign, since he only shouts at pupils he believes have talent. After this, I am proud whenever he bellows at me to keep my chin up or my shoulders down, and treasure his curses as others might praise.

Our morning class lasts two hours. We spend most of it with one hand on the rail, referred to as the barre, rehearsing foot positions and movements like plié and tendu. 'The building bricks of ballet', Maestro calls these. We work first on one side, then swap hands and repeat the sequence on the other. After this we stand in the centre, where we do everything again, but this time without the support of the barre. Sometimes, if Maestro is satisfied with our progress, we are allowed to advance to harder steps like développé or jeté. I like these best of all, especially the jeté, since even Maestro acknowledges I can jump higher than any one else my age. All the words are in French because it was at the court of King Louis XIV of France that ballet was first invented. Some of the girls grumble that we spend too much of our class bending and stretching, but I do not join in their complaints. I can feel my body growing stronger and more flexible, which means that one day soon I will dance like an angel.

If the weather is fine we are allowed into the central courtyard for fifteen minutes after lunch. Our time here is strictly monitored so the boys can take a turn after us, before the bell rings for the start of afternoon school. Everything in our day is contrived so we encounter the boys as little as possible, except when we are required to dance together. At such times we are permitted to touch each other if the steps require it but not to look or speak. Even in the marginally more relaxed atmosphere of the dining room I am not supposed to greet my brother Fedor, though this is a rule I frequently disobey. Fortunately the staff indulge me, since I am still small despite being in my third year. The period in the courtyard is our only reminder that a world exists beyond the School. All the outward-facing windows on the ground floor have frosted glass, and our basement dormitory has no window at all. Talking, though not expressly forbidden while we are outside, is discouraged. We line up once our fifteen minutes are at an end and are recounted.

The afternoons are devoted to the teaching of such subjects as history, geography and mathematics. I practise writing in both the French and Russian alphabets and learn a great many curious facts. These I store up to amuse mother and my younger brothers on my Sundays at home. The Toads push us because the Tsar's dancers must be educated and the reputation of the School is at stake. They are severe but not unfair or cruel. We are never beaten, though punishments are meted out liberally for a list of offences so long I scarcely know them all. My own most common misdemeanours are talking when I am not supposed to and untidiness.

We are counted again before dinner. The remainder of the evening passes in private study, the only variation being music practice or embroidery. I choose music, because it is well known that embroidery is for girls who are unlikely to graduate to the corps de ballet, and who will need a supplementary means of earning their livelihood. My instrument is the piano.

Once we have undressed for the night, we stand before our beds in the vast dormitory. This is ostensibly so we can pray together, though it also makes the task of a final head count easier, since our beds are positioned beneath boards that have our School numbers on them. Usually I fall asleep quickly, tired out by the day, though sometimes I picture myself on stage at the Mariinsky Theatre performing jetés for the Tsar. This is a story I can embellish to my heart's content, so that by the time I reach the part where my name appears with a commendation on the 'Journal of Orders' posted daily in the hall, I am already fast asleep. I have a second story, about running away and joining a circus, which I can resort to if I am feeling downcast, or need to block out the sound of another girl crying. We may not leave our beds without the permission of whichever Toad is responsible for watching us through the night, not even to comfort a homesick friend.

Only during the weekly Friday night visit to the bathhouse, a wooden building in one of the side courts, are we given a measure of freedom. Here the Toads leave us in the care of maids, and we giggle and share secrets amidst the swirling steam without fear of being overheard and reprimanded. We open our hearts to each other as we slather our bodies with soap and then rinse ourselves in the hot water. The bathhouse is where I first learn of the pupil who escaped from the School and ran off with an officer of the Tsar's Horse Guards. The girl who reports the scandal swears it is true, adding it is the reason why we are now counted five times a day. She assures me that if I do not believe her I can read the diary of the illicit love affair for myself because it is scribbled on the back wall of a cupboard. She does not specify which cupboard I should look in and after a few vain attempts to find it I give up. Instead, I save the story to recount to mother on my next visit home, but when I am finally alone with her I change my mind. I sense this is one School story mother will not like.

I am sitting on a bench beside Eugenia in a communal dressing room at the Mariinsky Theatre. I am to appear in tonight's ballet as a raven, a role I have played before. I am already changed into my dark tunic with my cheeks powdered and my shoes correctly tied, and have permission to remain with my sister until the first performance bell rings. Then I am to rejoin the other School pupils chosen to dance as flower girls or pages, until we are delivered to whichever stage-hand has been charged with ensuring we enter our scene at the right moment and from the right side. I spend the time with my sister watching the ballerinas. Several cluster round mirrors applying make-up or arranging each other's hair, while others warm up at a barre at one end. Eugenia is soaking her feet in a bowl of water into which she has tipped a generous dose of Epsom salts. She is in the corps de ballet and has already performed in this afternoon's matinée. She is tired and rests her head against the wall behind us. I stare at her feet which are bruised purple and swollen with lumpy callouses, some of which have bled. Her ripped ballet shoes are next to the bowl.

'You need new ones,' I tell her. 'If you go en pointe in those you'll hurt your feet even more. The stuffing is coming out of the end.'

'This is my third pair this week,' Eugenia moans. 'I've been warned I'm wearing out my shoes too quickly. I won't be allowed new ones tonight.'

'But you can't dance in those. Why don't you buy a pair?' The changing room is crowded and the chatter and bustle make it difficult to talk. I thread my arm round my sister's waist and lean close. 'If I earned 600 roubles a month, I'd have as many shoes as I wanted. I'd spend all my free time shopping and come home laden with parcels. Once I've given mother money,' I add in time, remembering father has another fine for arriving drunk at work, and that Eugenia and Fedor hand mother most of their wages.

'These two ballets are particularly hard.' Eugenia lifts a foot from the cloudy water to demonstrate a series of rapid, staccato movements. 'The shoes scarcely survive a day.' She massages her foot, wincing, before plunging it back into the bowl. 'And we must make ours last a good deal longer than that.'

'What about Madame Pavlova? She's always changing into new shoes.'

'It's all right for Anna Pavlova! She's Maestro Petipa's pet and can request whatever she likes.'

'I don't see why', I say, propelled by a sudden fierce loyalty towards my sister. I lower my voice. 'Did you know she was rejected the first time she auditioned for the School, and wasn't offered a place until she was almost eleven.' It is comforting to think that Eugenia, Fedor and I were all accepted straight away, and before we were nine. 'So she can't be very good.'

Eugenia removes her feet from the water and dries them carefully on a towel. Then she begins the slow process of bandaging, using strips of cotton rag.

'It's true her technique is poor. Her turnout isn't symmetrical and her knees are never quite together. She doesn't have good feet for a dancer. We're the same shoe size though her ankles are weak and her arches too long and too high. But Petipa's word is what counts. He's always altering steps so they suit her better.' She finds a pin, sucks the tip, then stabs it into a blister on her heel. We both watch the pale liquid drain out. 'There's something about her,' Eugenia resumes, returning the pin to the hem of her skirt and padding the blister with cotton. 'When she took over from Kschessinska....' Eugenia glances at me, uncertain how much I know.

'While Kschessinska was pregnant,' I help her.

Eugenia laughs. 'Well, everyone thought she'd been chosen

because she could never be a rival to Kschessinska. Instead audiences loved her. She has this haunting, airy presence on stage, as if she's more spirit than human. She enthralls people.'

I listen, fascinated by my sister's story of this still distant world of solo and prima ballerinas.

'I've heard she packs the end of her shoes with sawdust and glues a wooden block to the sole.'

'I don't know about that, though I have seen her dresser pad her shoe with a strip of leather and flatten out the toe to help her balance.

'Doesn't that damage the shoes?'

'She wouldn't care if it does. Once she has enough flowers and jewels she asks her admirers for shoes. Ordered from Italy. You should see inside her dressing room. She has a basket by the door full of shoes she has discarded. Most barely worn.'

'My mentor, Tamara Karsavina, prefers shoes made from Swiss goatskin,' I confide, relishing this opportunity to share knowledge of my own.

Eugenia does not reply. She is pulling on her stockings, staring miserably at her shoes.

'Let me have them a minute, I've an idea'. Before Eugenia can protest, I tuck them under my arm and am slipping through the tightly packed bodies to the door. In the corridor, dressers with freshly ironed costumes hurry past, while a group of stage-boys manoeuvre a trolley piled high with artificial foliage. No one pays me the slightest attention. I pass two doors and stop in front of a third. I take a deep breath and push it open. At first, all I see are people and vases of flowers on stands. Madame Pavlova is seated in front of a mirror, her back towards me. Her dresser is fitting a band into her hair threaded with silk roses. Next to her a maid holds her costume, while another hovers near a table laid with a jug of lemonade and bowls of chocolate and cherries. A second dresser crouches on the floor working on a pair of shoes. I try to spot if she is fitting them with extra leather when the door opens again, and three women in beaded gowns with lace trains sweep past me into the room. They gather round the ballerina whom they address as 'darling Anna', screening me from her view.

The shoe basket is, as Eugenia described, right by the door. I survey it quickly, calculating it must contain at least thirty pairs. I thrust my hand into their midst and hollow out a space into which I insert Eugenia's worn shoes. Then I filch a pair from the top. Their ribbons are untied but they still have plenty of dancing life left. I hide them under my arm, then change my mind and stuff them down the front of my tunic. This makes me bulge as if I have breasts and I must position one arm across my body to prevent them from sliding out, but it is a good disguise. With my free hand, I arrange the shoes at the top of the basket so it looks as if no one has disturbed them. Then I peep furtively round the dressing room storing every detail of opulence and comfort, before opening the door again. One day, I promise myself as I close it behind me, I will have a dressing room to myself with dishes of chocolate and cherries and visitors arriving in droves to congratulate me. I hear the first performance bell ring and set off down the corridor as fast as my bulky chest will allow.

Eugenia is searching for me when I return to the communal dressing room.

'Quick, I need my shoes.'

With a magician's bow, I pull the stolen pair from my tunic. Eugenia's eyes grow round but there is no time for her to question me. We both hear my name being called.

'No one saw,' I promise, thrusting the shoes into her hand. 'You were right, Anna Pavlova has so many pairs she won't notice.'

It is the holidays and I am helping mother make the cake we will take to church on Easter Sunday. My task is to mind a simmering pan of milk on the stove so it does not boil over. The kitchen is scented with cardamom and vanilla. There is an open jar of honey on the table into which I surreptitiously dip my hand, licking dribbles of golden sweetness as they ooze down my fingers. Mother notices but does not scold. She is glad to have me home again. I am happy too. My School report is better than I feared and I have a surprise stored up. This term, I arranged for earnings from my stage appearances to be paid to me directly instead of being handed to father, and I plan to buy chocolate eggs for my sister and brothers and lilies of the valley for mother.

Nikolai and Andrei are painting eggs that have been hard-boiled. Andrei is too small to reach the table without a chair and his brush has the air of a giant's in his hand. He decorates his eggs with zoo animals, though there is one with the onion domes of Vladimir Church I suspect is for mother. Four of Nikolai's eggs are blood red with only his name drawn on them. These are for the egg rolling competition that will take place tomorrow afternoon on Orekhovaya hill, even though mother has not yet given her consent. I watch him weigh each one in his palm as he assesses its effectiveness in destroying his opponents' eggs. Any he judges too light for such a task he daubs haphazardly with rainbow stripes.

The milk in the pan bubbles and mother warns me not to let it burn. She is measuring out raisins. Traditionally, these are soaked overnight in vodka, but mother will not permit this. Instead, she uses a family recipe from Estonia in which the raisins are dipped in lemon juice and sprinkled with sugar.

'What time will father be home?' I ask.

'Early,' mother answers. 'There's no performance tonight so he'll finish after the matinée.' Though I have heard it all my life, mother's native German comes as a surprise whenever I have been away at School. 'Why?'

'He's going to act the new play for us.'

The milk is frothing up the sides of the pan so I remove it from the heat and blow on it to cool. My reply catches Nikolai's interest.

'Which one?' he wants to know, temporarily suspending his egg-sorting. We all enjoy father's rendition of whatever is appearing on stage at the Alexandrinsky, witnessed from his usher's seat.

'The Merchant of Venice', I inform him, proud I can remember the name. I set the milk pan back on the stove.

'Tolstoy?' Nikolai speculates. Though he deliberately failed his audition to the School by performing like a chained bear, he has no wish to appear inferior when it comes to knowledge.

'Shakespeare,' I correct him. Nikolai looks forlorn. 'He's a good friend of Tolstoy's', I add, to spare his feelings, though I am not entirely sure this is true. I have a sudden suspicion Shakespeare might not be Russian.

'I only know because I had parts in two of his other plays,' I prattle on, moving the discussion in a safer direction. 'In one, a man gets changed into a donkey. The fairy king does it to annoy his queen. The man doesn't realize he's a donkey at first and can't understand why everyone runs away.'

This amuses Nikolai. 'Did the actor wear a mask with big ears?'

'Did he hee-haw like a donkey?' Andrei, who has been listening, pipes up.

I launch into the story of the spell and how funny it is when the fairy queen mistakenly sighs with love for the fat donkey, when mother calls out. I have forgotten all about the milk, which is now boiling furiously and streaming down the sides of the pan.

The cake is finally in the oven, and the painted eggs drying, when the front door opens and there are footsteps.

'Company,' father announces, and men's voices shout 'hello.'

Mother dries her hands on her apron and goes into the hall to greet them. Nikolai and I glance at each other. If father has brought friends home, there will be no sitting round the fire listening to him act out a play.

When mother returns to the kitchen, she is scowling and tight-lipped. Without a word, she takes glasses from the shelf and arranges them on a tray. Nikolai and I watch her.

'Take these into your father,' she instructs, passing me the tray.

In the living room, three men have removed their coats and are warming themselves by the fire. Father has a bottle of vodka which he pours into the glasses.

'Pretty,' one of the men comments, the flaps of his fur ushanka pulled tight over his ears. 'So you're one of Vasili's dancing offspring. I hope tonight you'll dance for us?'

Father is shuffling a pack of cards at the table. 'Careful! She's Imperial Property.' He points to the empty tray. 'Ask your mother for meat pie. With plenty of pickles. I haven't eaten all day.'

I escape back to the others where I relay father's message.

'It's Lent,' mother grumbles when she hears. Although she is a Lutheran and does not enforce the strict fasting observed by the Orthodox Church, she draws the line at meat. She fetches a loaf of bread from the cupboard which she cuts into thick slices. Then she ladles cabbage soup from a saucepan on the stove into four dishes. 'Take them this.'

The men are round the table and a game of cards is underway as I set the tray in their midst. Father advances a bet of fifty kopeks then refills everyone's glass with vodka. Soon, his bottle will be empty and he will be bellowing for Nikolai to run and buy another. I hurry away.

'Are they playing for money?' Mother is grating lemon peel and sighs when I tell her they are. Nikolai takes the empty soup pan and washes it in the bowl. I perch by the table to help Andrei. He is feeling the eggs to test if they are dry. His chubby, child's hands touch each one tenderly, as if he is scared he might break them. No one speaks. Through the wall, we listen to the noisy progress of the card-game.

'What's this?' father roars suddenly. 'Stale bread and cabbage soup when I ordered meat!' A chair scrapes on the floor and a second later the kitchen door is flung open.

'Do you mean to insult our guests?' Father's face is blotched and he sways slightly.

Mother stares at the skin of her lemon as if it is all there is to see. 'I can bring fish,' she offers quietly.

Incredulous, father slaps his thigh. He repeats her German phrase then translates it, pointedly, into Russian. Though he has his back to me, I spot Nikolai stiffen. We both know this lapse into her mother tongue will exasperate father.

Lurching towards the cupboard, father pulls jars and packets out at random. When he does not find what he is hunting for, he slams the door shut.

'What's that smell?' He sniffs the air, heavy with spices and the yeasty warmth of baking.

'Easter cake', I whisper.

'Fine. We'll have that once it's cooked.'

'But,' I begin. My voice trails off. It is never a good idea to remind father of mother's church-going.

'It will be blessed as usual by the priest on Easter morning.' Though mother says this in Russian, in a tone of appeasement, her words have the opposite effect on father. In two bounds, he is at her side, and for a moment I fear he will strike her. Nikolai has the same thought and abandons his saucepan to the bowl. We stand shoulder to shoulder in front of mother. If there is to be a fight, neither of us has the slightest doubt whose part we will take.

Startled by our hostility, Father hesitates. 'I wouldn't care for myself, but there are guests.' His tone is plaintive, cajoling.

'You promised the children a night at home. Without your friends,' mother reminds him.

Father tries one of his special smiles. 'You used to like it when I brought people home. Remember the parties we had in the old days. You made borscht – and pierogi that were light as a feather, everyone said so. When we cleared the table you and I led the dancing.'

'You didn't drink so much then. Or gamble our money away on cards.'

'Our money? I'm the one who shows up at that hell-hole of a theatre and jumps to attention all day.'

'Only you don't,' mother retorts. 'You were nearly sacked for refusing to help that patron pick up his change.'

'It was demeaning, expecting me to kneel and grovel under his seat for a few kopeks.' Father taps his breast as if to indicate the presence of a medal, though he has pawned or sold any decoration he has earned. 'I'm an Honorary Citizen of St Petersburg, don't forget.'

Mother stays silent, resumes grating her lemon.

Realising his words are failing to produce the desired effect, father's gaze travels the room and lands on the painted eggs. 'What's this?' he demands, turning back to mother. 'You lecture me about wasting money, while you let your children spoil perfectly good eggs.' He scoops one up and hurls it to the floor. The shell shatters and the blue-painted trunk of an elephant and a yellow lion's mane skitter at his feet.

Slowly, mother sets the now denuded lemon and grater down on the table. She retrieves her shawl and wraps it round her shoulders, knotting it tight in front. Then she unhooks Andrei's coat from the peg and helps him into it.

As if we are actors who have been given our cue, Nikolai collects mother's prayer book while I find her purse so she has coins for lighting a candle. Then we put on our own coats. We will disappear now, into the safe space of the church, until mother estimates enough time has gone by for father to be calm again. It is how this scene always ends.

'Stop,' father commands, as mother walks past him, the three of us following closely behind. 'I forbid you to go. Your place is here.'

We can still hear his voice as we make our way downstairs to the street door.

I watch from the side of the stage as dancers walk on in twos and threes, pretending to be guests at a party. I spend the minutes waiting for my own entrance by pressing up onto the balls of my feet, keeping my knees together and chest lifted as if I am in morning class. Tonight I am dancing Clara in Tchaikovsky's 'Nutcracker', a role I have been rehearsing for weeks. My dress is sewn with Brussels lace and I have a pink bow in my hair. The soles of my shoes are sticky with resin and the ribbons tied in tight crosses round my ankles. I remember Maestro's advice and take a deep breath. This ballet is important. If I dance well the company will consider me for a place amongst the coryphées once I graduate. The possibility that I might one day emerge from this select group as a soloist or principal is almost too exciting to contemplate. On the way to the theatre, I whispered to Tamara Karsavina how worried I was I might not remember all my steps. 'Little Pet', she soothed, her arm round my shoulder, 'if you forget, invent. Listen to the music and even those who know the choreography will believe the steps have been devised specially for you.'

The régisseur approaches, his assistant carrying the open prompt book. Soon it will be the moment for the children to enter. The régisseur nods and I clasp the hand of the girl beside me. I focus on the music and listen for the flutes' skipping rhythms.

A Christmas tree towers over the stage, decorated with paper chains and toys. There are more toys at the foot of the tree and on each side groups of dancers chatter and greet each other. My eyes adjust quickly to the light as I lead the children into their midst. I am no longer nervous. I have been on stage enough times for it to feel as if this is my natural space. We dance in a ring until the harp slides into glissando when we curtsey and bow to our elders. The boy who plays my brother Fritz is standing too close. He is two years my junior and in awe of me. I cannot extend my arms as I should and elbow him out of the way. This is not a movement we have been taught but the peel of laughter my improvisation produces delights me. The trumpets begin their fanfare. The boys dance this alone and I can stare undetected at the shadowy rows of watching faces. The Tsar is present for tonight's performance though I do not dare look into his box. Instead, I strain for glimpses of the princes and counts seated in order of importance to his left and right. Once the ballet is over, girls from the company will be invited to their boxes, where they will be presented with lavish gifts. If the rumours I have heard are true, a few will then leave with these noblemen for their residencies and only return in time for class in the morning.

The children's parents perform a slow, solemn waltz. I like how they do this, with deliberate, faltering steps as if they are old, even though they are not. I imagine this is what the dancing is like at the Winter Palace whenever the Tsar hosts a ball there. Recently there have been pictures in the newspaper of a party where guests were disguised as historical figures, some wearing costumes hundreds of years old. According to our dresser, whose sister serves in the Imperial household, the Tsarina's robes were so richly embroidered she had difficulty standing and had to remain seated for most of the evening. As the court dance finishes the violas introduce an abrupt change of mood, heightened by low, haunting notes in the trombones. A masked magician appears swirling his cape, and offers Clara a nutcracker doll. I rock the doll in my arms to demonstrate my pleasure, then hold it high above my head as I run backwards en pointe. Petipa was pleased when I did this during practice, but I find it easy and besides if I turn my back the audience can no longer see the doll. The violins play more romantically now and I start the count for my solo. For this, I perform a series of rotations and leaps in a circle the other dancers create for me. The trick is to locate a stabilizing point I can return to so I do not make myself dizzy. I pull up on my ribcage as I execute my first pirouette, ensuring I open out both arm and leg simultaneously. Then it is the jeté which I draw on for momentum. Another pirouette and I am already a quarter of the way round the stage and enjoying myself. It is a routine I have repeated many times, but as I dance it now, dressed as Clara and clutching the nutcracker doll, the steps make sense in a way they did not before. I understand that Clara is showing off and her solo is a means of capturing attention. I push into my feet so I can jump even higher. Then I throw out my chin and cock my head to one side and am rewarded by a shout of 'bravo' and a burst of applause. As I come full circle rose-garlands land at my feet.

In the wings, a dresser helps me into a white nightgown and removes the bow from my hair. Next is the scene in which Clara sits alone under the Christmas tree, crying for her broken nutcracker. I ignore the throbbing in my ankles and calves as I wait. I remind myself that I am Clara, who is charming and graceful and does not have painful legs. Besides, the dance I am about to do is one of my favourites. The magician returns bringing all the toys to life, and a fight breaks out between a garrison of tin soldiers and a band of marauding mice. At first, Clara swoons and faints with fear, actions I perform so well I hear someone mutter 'poor child'. Then, as the battle becomes more desperate and it seems the soldiers will lose, I pluck up my courage and remove my shoe. The stopped horn is my signal to bring it down on the Mouse King's shoulder. In my eagerness, I enter the fray too early and in the hurly-burly drop my weapon. Horrified, I catch hold of the Mouse King's tail, and for a few beats am pulled round after him. There is nothing to do now except follow Tamara's advice. I spin away from the Mouse King then approach him again, this time battering his torso with my fists. I hear the audience cheer and am contemplating jumping onto the Mouse King's back, when to my relief the dancer realises my mistake and falls dramatically to the floor.

In the dressing room during the interval I resign myself to a fine for dropping my shoe and grabbing the Mouse King's tail, but to my surprise no one mentions it. Several of the dancers pat my head as they pass, and when the refreshment trolley arrives I am handed slices of apple and a glass of water into which the server spoons honey. I ask if there are cherries which makes those around me laugh. I sit with my apple and honeyed water and stretch out my feet and legs. They are still throbbing, but the pain feels distant, as if it is in someone else's limbs, not mine. I like being in the dressing room with the corps de ballet, listening to their gossip and watching them prepare, as if we are all part of the same big family. Tonight, the talk is about Alexander, who has been fined for handing out leaflets and his name removed from the performance list. When I wonder what the leaflets are about the girl next to me whispers 'the conditions of working people.' A dancer I recognize as one of my sister's friends joins in.

'Alexander believes it's wrong for company dancers to belong to the Tsar, as if we are his serfs.'

'Sssh,' someone hisses, overhearing us. 'They're threatening to fine anyone who so much as mentions his name.'

In the second half of the ballet, Clara's nutcracker transforms into a handsome prince who takes her to the land of sweets. I become so absorbed in the dancing I forget everything except the music and my next step. The clapping as I make my curtsey at the end is so loud I suspect the stage-boys of striking the thunder board. I cannot carry all the flowers I am given. In the dressing room, I am too excited to stand patiently while my costume is removed and my shoes untied. Messengers appear and some of the girls hurry out. Those who remain pull faces at each other. Then I hear my own name being called. I am to be presented to the Tsar.

Servants part the blue and gold drapes that screen the Imperial box as I approach with a governess. I curtsey as I enter, taking care my knee bends right to the floor. As I lift my head, I see a tall man with a broad forehead, pale skin and blue eyes. The Tsar's hair is a similar colour to father's, though his moustache and beard are lighter. He has surprisingly long ears. His navy coat has a pale blue sash and a collar stitched with gold which stands up stiffly against his neck. The front is decorated with so many medals I am astonished the fabric does not rip under the weight.

A servant holds out a cushion with a velvet box on it.

'For you,' the Tsar says, his voice unexpectedly powerful, 'for your performance tonight'. He acknowledges my curtsey with a nod.

My governess propels me forward with a shove. I open the box and spy a brooch in the shape of a miniature bird. I lift it out and the pearls catch the light.

'Thank you,' I enthuse, attempting to pin it to my dress. 'You couldn't have chosen anything more perfect. I love birds. I'd have cages full of them if the School would let me.' The brooch is snatched from my hand. The governess returns it to its box, which she removes from the cushion. I realise this is what I should have done and am mortified.

'Thank you,' the Tsar echoes, and this time his voice sounds amused.

Only once I am back in the dressing room and can open the box again do I find the note. 'To Lydia', I read, 'a new adornment to our ballet.'

It is a Sunday early in January, the year is 1905. With four girls from my class, I am on my way to the Winter Palace in one of the School's antiquated carriages where later today we will dance at one of the Tsar's private parties. For weeks now the temperature has not risen above freezing, and even inside the closed carriage we mist the air with our breath. We wrap ourselves in the fox fur lining of our regulation cloaks, wishing we had been issued with fur hats instead of black silk bonnets. The carriage blinds are kept drawn to prevent passers-by from staring in and School pupils from seeing out, though there is a tear in the fabric of one through which I glimpse the icy streets. Our governess is young and does not object to our chatter as long as we restrict ourselves to fitting subjects.

We complain about the cold during morning class and in the schoolroom in the afternoons. We outdo each other with tales of shivering in our chilly beds at night, and how when we turn on the tap to wash in the morning there is no water, only a deep growl like a bellyache from the pipe. We are nearly at the Winter Palace when I notice through the rip in the blind that the street is full of people, all heading in the same direction as our carriage.

'At least there'll be hot tea when we arrive,' I declare, remembering the pretty room where we change with its samovar in the corner. 'Last time we had toasted buns.' One of the girls, Elizaveta, has not danced at the Winter Palace before and asks what it is like.

'They sit very near us,' I tell her. 'And do things while we dance.'

Elizaveta's eyes widen. 'What sort of things?'

'People talk and there are servants with trays of refreshments. The men move about. Some of the discussions are so loud you can hear the voices over the music. Once, the Tsarina and one of the Grand Duchesses laughed while Anna Pavlova was dancing her dying swan. They had been speaking about something else and did not realise it was intended to be tragic.' To spare Elizaveta, I do not admit how disconcerting it can be dancing in such close proximity to the Imperial family.

'The Tsar is our patron. He adores ballet,' Elizaveta observes, frowning.

'He does,' I assure her. 'He sends his own envoys all the way to Paris, Brussels and Milan to procure the finest materials for our costumes.' I glance at the governess, suddenly anxious I might be in trouble for reporting gossip. She is playing with the fingers of her glove and her thoughts seem elsewhere. 'Of course,' I continue, 'the Tsar has many pressing matters and can't always be watching ballet. At the moment he has the war with Japan to worry about.' I want to add: 'especially after the defeat at Port Arthur', but do not dare just in case the governess is listening after all and considers my statement to be unpatriotic. The School has banned us from reading any newspaper criticizing the surrender of the Admirals and blockade of the Russian fleet.

The street leading to the square in front of the Winter Palace is now so crowded our carriage is forced almost to a halt. People stream past on both sides. Though the blinds remain drawn we can hear hymns being sung and chants of 'God save the Tsar'.

'Perhaps there's a skating party on the Neva,' Elizaveta suggests. I close my eyes and imagine I am gliding over the frozen river with my sister and brothers. In our races I was always one of the fastest, and with skates on could outpace even Fedor. There are shouts. I snap open my eyes. Whatever is happening in the street no longer sounds like people enjoying themselves. My fingers itch to pull up the blind. Instead, I stuff them deep into the fur of my cloak.

'It might be another strike,' I remark. There has been no electricity for days. From outside comes our driver's voice, explaining who we are and demanding to be let through.

There is a knock. The governess nods consent and I open the carriage door. A soldier peers inside and when he realises we are indeed from the Imperial Ballet School removes his cap. His greatcoat is buttoned against the cold and his rifle slung over his shoulder. He asks where we are headed and when he learns we are to dance at the Winter Palace advises us to wait. Strikers have filled the square with a petition for the Tsar and until there are further orders we will not be able to continue.

We eye each other. Elizaveta worries this will make us late for our performance but I remind her there is still time. Besides, the Tsar will not wish us to dance until he has discussed the petition with the strikers. We hear boots marching in unison over the cobbles and through the open door recognise a unit of the Palace Guard. They have their guns raised in front of them as if they are about to encounter an enemy. Our soldier repeats his directive to remain where we are and hurries to join them.

Almost immediately, there is a second knock on the carriage door. This time it is our driver.

'Excuse me, Miss,' he enquires of our governess, 'should I turn round and return to the School?'

The governess studies her gloved hands as if they might reveal an answer. 'What about the company carriages? Do you know if they are already at the Palace?'

'It's possible,' the driver informs her. 'They left before us.'

'No,' she announces, coming to a decision, 'my instructions are to deliver my pupils to the Winter Palace so they can dance as arranged for their Tsar. You will please drive forward as best you can.'

The driver touches his cap and shuts the door. We hear him encourage the horses. The carriage lurches forward a few paces then stops again. I slump back in my seat and reflect I could be at home, warming my hands by the fire and entertaining mother with stories about my week.

'If we have to wait here for hours,' Elizaveta frets, 'then we will be late.'

I shrug. 'It won't be our fault. They can't fine us.'

'Nor can they begin without us.'

This is true. We are all in the first dance. 'They could find replacements.'

'Who?'

A mischievous notion occurs to me. 'Perhaps the Grand Duchesses? They all have dancing lessons.' I picture the Tsar's daughters, rapped on the ankles by Maestro's cane and forced to practise until the sweat trickles down their bodies. The idea they might perform in our places is so preposterous it makes even our governess smile. I point out that the Grand Duchesses are too fat for ballet when the governess shushes me. Making fun of the Tsar or any member of his household is a fineable offence, she warns me sternly.

All appears quiet outside now and I wonder why we do not move. I shift in my seat and peer out through the tear in the blind. On the pavement, a family huddles round a fire. I observe a mother with a baby in a blanket and two young children crouched by her side. They look hungry and their faces are pinched with cold. The children are not wearing shoes. Suddenly, there is a round of gunfire so loud it makes us start. The horses whinny in fright and we hear the driver's voice calming them. We sit immobilized. There is shouting and more shots. I release the blind not caring how much I am fined.

People pour into the street, running and knocking into each other in their hurry to get away from the square. I spot men carrying icons from their church, women clutching the hands of children. Their expression is one of fear. Two men stagger towards our carriage, half-carrying a third. His coat is open and the shirt beneath streaked scarlet with blood. Recognising the Imperial crest they stop at our window. 'See how the Tsar deals with our grievances,' one of them shouts, 'ordering his Guard to open fire on an innocent crowd.' He turns so the face of the man he is supporting confronts us. There is a gash like a burrowing animal across his forehead and a livid, gaping hole where his right eye should be. Elizaveta screams.

'Return us to the School,' the governess orders, hammering on the wall to attract the driver. 'Quickly.' She snaps shut the blind and fastens it tight with the cord.

Mikhail Fokine, who until recently was a dancer at the Mariinksy, takes over our morning class. It is rumoured he is sympathetic to the plight of the workers and supports their strikes. We have no way of telling if these rumours are true since the circulation of newspapers has been banned. Following the shootings outside the Winter Palace, new regulations have appeared on the School noticeboard forbidding any mention of politics. This does not stop us sharing information in secret whenever an opportunity presents itself. On our last Sunday at home, Fedor confided that the boys had sent their own list of grievances to the Toads and recommended we girls follow suit. I resolve to communicate this in the bathhouse on Friday night, though even here we are aware that the maids stay closer to us than usual, as if they have been instructed to eavesdrop on our conversations and report any deviation from permitted topics. Despite the risk, we discuss the progress of the strikes and whether the Tsar is right to punish the ring-leaders. It is in the bathhouse I learn of the arrest of Elizaveta's father, and how her family has been forced out of their lodgings. She has taken to hiding a handkerchief-sized red flag in the pocket of her apron, which she slips under her pillow at night.

Fokine is handsome and we are all a little love-sick for him. At first, we find his teaching methods strange. He does not sit and watch us as Ceccheti or Petipa do, tapping out the rhythms with their feet or cane. Instead, he stands at the barre, and performs the exercises alongside us. When we move into the centre he charges us not merely to execute the routine, but to visualize the shapes we are creating. He talks to us about Russian folk dance and its powerful expressions of emotion, lamenting the way ballet, with its sterile foreign traditions, has severed itself from these roots.

I enjoy Fokine's classes. I like his reminder that we have arms as well as legs, and his encouragement to use our minds in addition to our bodies. I understand what he means when he urges us to listen not only to the piano or instruments of the orchestra, but to our own, internal pulse. I find his directive to inhabit our steps as if we are actors as well as ballerinas exciting.

One day, as we are completing our barre exercises, Fokine announces a guest. The door opens and a tall, slim woman enters, dressed in a simple white tunic, like those worn by the ancient Greeks. Her hair is not tied in the customary net but flows over her shoulders in a shawl of coppery red. Most astonishing of all her arms and legs are bare.

'Girls,' Fokine calls us to attention. 'Today we are honoured to welcome Isadora Duncan to our School. She is in St Petersburg with her pupils and I am delighted to inform you has agreed to teach you today.'

'Please remove your shoes and stockings,' the woman instructs. Her French, though fluent, rises and falls in a way we are not accustomed to, as if the sounds are unfamiliar in her mouth.

We stare nervously at each other. No one has ever requested this in class before and we are uncertain if it is allowed. When Fokine nods his approval I am the first to sit on the floor and pull the ribbons round my ankles loose.

One by one, we comply. A few of the girls pout a silent protest but I turn my back on them.

'Good,' our visitor praises when everyone is ready. 'Today I am not interested in how high you can raise your leg or how many pirouettes you can accomplish. I know you can all do these things beautifully because you are pupils of the Imperial School and have been trained in them since you were very small.' Her smile as she pauses and looks round the room is mesmerizing, like the luminous, tranquil faces of people praying in church. She stretches out her arms.

'Now your feet are free, I want you to move, in any direction and any manner you please. All I insist on is that you feel whatever you do here,' she places her hand on her breastbone, 'in the solar plexus. This is the seat of the soul and where dancing springs from.'

No one stirs. Even I am not sure how to interpret this command. Laughing, she runs amongst us, tapping lightly on our shoulders whenever she approaches as if she is playing a game of tag. She runs quickly, joyously, like a child. When I feel her hand touch me I set off, attempting to imitate her lightness and grace. She stops by the barre to watch us.

'That's it. No tension, no stiffness, simply let the body move.' She walks to the piano and whispers in the accompanist's ear.

'We will hear watery music,' she explains, 'since this will be the theme of Maestro Fokine's new ballet. I wish you to imagine water as you dance now, how it rushes hither and thither, and finds its own course.'

She extends a slow, rippling arm like a wave over the sea. 'I am picturing the Atlantic Ocean which I crossed when I left America for Europe: its majesty, its mystery, its terrors.' Her arm crooks in a sequence of rapid darts, reminding me of drawings of storms. 'Choose an image of water and allow it to guide you. It might be a fountain, or rain, or the still calm of a lake. It does not matter what you choose, only that it inspires you.'

I hold her words in my head and dream I am a fast-flowing stream, tumbling across grassland and through dense forest until finally I reach the sea. Fokine studies me as I invent. I ignore the girls who signal with their eyes they find this exercise ridiculous and only half-heartedly comply, and dedicate myself to dancing. If this is the coming revolution in ballet then I am a revolutionary. When we are next in the bathhouse I plan to ask Elizaveta where I can buy a red flag.

Spring arrives so late in St Petersburg that it is May before the last of the ice melts on the Neva. Each morning after class I cross the entrance hall of the Mariinsky Theatre and linger in front of the notice board. This is where the management pins commendations and newspaper reviews of current productions, cast lists and rehearsal schedules, the names of those selected for any private performance the Tsar has requested, as well as those who are to represent the company on the summer tour. Today there is an announcement about the final ballet for the current season, typed on thick cream paper embossed with the double-headed gold eagle of the Imperial crest. As is customary, all the important roles are allotted to the principals, and though I hardly bother to skim through these, I read the name of my friend and mentor Tamara Karsavina with pride. She is a rising star in Russia and also famous abroad after appearing in various European capitals the previous summer. This year, she has a contract at the Coliseum in London during the break. I switch my attention to the dancers chosen for small solo roles but my name is not amongst them. I let my eye drop to the last column where the rest of the ensemble is listed and finally discover my name.

I am disappointed. I have been at the Mariinsky for over a year, and though I did well at my graduation and received a good report from the School, I am still only a member of the corps de ballet. I did not mind this at first, enjoying the camaraderie and opportunity to perform on stage every night, but now my invisibility chafes me. I am eager to take on more. For the past six months, I have been paying for extra lessons with my old teacher Maestro Cecchetti in his studio, working on the points I have been criticized for such as my porte de bras. An arm snakes about my waist. I recognize Tamara's light touch and lean against her sweaty warmth. She too has come straight from morning class.

'Congratulations,' I point to her name on the board.

She spins me round and her dark eyes search my face. 'Don't worry, your turn will come.'

'Will it? I don't see how. The only time anyone pays me attention is to tell me off because I am not moving in the same way and at the same moment as all the rest. Do you know, we are even supposed to breathe in unison.' I put my hands on my hips, imitating Petipa. '"The corps de ballet exists only to accentuate the work of the principals. It should never intrude, never be remarked on for its own sake."' I snort indignantly. 'So I must put all my energy into dancing with the express aim of never being seen.'

Tamara smoothes my hair with her hands. 'When are you going to learn to be tidy,' she chides. 'Be patient. Soon you'll be promoted to the coryphée, where you can demonstrate what you're capable of.'

'But that'll take forever,' I wail. 'Honestly, I feel as if my career is progressing backwards. In my last years at School, Fokine chose me for parts – I was Cupid in *Acis*, then the Winter Snowflake in his setting of the *Four Seasons*. I had good notices too.'

'Ah,' Tamara sighs, 'that was before Fokine was considered a dangerous radical. Now the management is terrified in case his interest in peasant dancing conceals a challenge to the authority of the Tsar. Who,' she winks at me, raising her voice to prevent any suspicion on the part of passers-by that we might be engaged in inflammatory gossip, 'is our patron and most liberal benefactor.'

I frown. 'But Fokine has breathed new life into the ballet. The Tsar himself has praised his innovations.'

'Like what?' Tamara demands. 'Deliberately choreographing music that grates on the ear, with rhythms contrived to jar and annoy? Commissioning costumes that reflect the ballet instead of making us look beautiful?

I grin, remembering the row when Fokine refused to let Mathilde Kschessinska appear on stage in her famous diamonds, arguing they were unsuitable for her part.

'Forcing us to take off our pointe shoes and dance barefoot.'

Tamara chuckles. 'Not to mention bare-breasted!'

I screw my face to mimic the disgusted grimaces when several of the older ballerinas learned Fokine had cast them as Arabian slaves and required them to remove their corsets and perform half-naked.

'What about Diaghilev?' I ask, recalling the new assistant manager who included the ballet in his summer tour. 'Can't he speak in Fokine's defence?'

'They distrust Diaghilev even more than they dislike Fokine,' Tamara assures me. 'They are furious because his "Ballets Russes" as he calls them caused a sensation in Paris. Even though the venture lost money, Diaghilev has persuaded his sponsors he can turn Russian culture into the envy of Europe. And for this he has the Tsar's approval.'

I stare at her. What she says makes no sense. 'Surely Diaghilev's success reflects well on the whole company?'

Tamara shakes her head. 'Little Pet, don't you know the world is ruled by jealousy, not reason. Besides, the management is opposed to Diaghilev because he does what they do not: takes an active interest in artistic matters. In their estimation, a manager should be above all that, not dining with composers and deciding which artists will paint the sets.' She drops her voice. 'And they are angry because he's planning a second European tour this summer.'

'With Fokine?'

'And Nijinksy.'

I should have guessed. When I partnered my brother Fedor as Cupid, all the critics talked about was this stubby-legged, long-necked boy who played the lead faun.

'Will the tour be to Paris?'

'Yes. Berlin too I believe. Perhaps Brussels....'

'I do hope I'm chosen!'

'But should you like it? You'd be away from St Petersburg for several weeks.'

I think with a pang of mother then thrust out my chin.

'I'd love it. I hate it when the theatre closes for the season and there's no dancing.' I do not realize until I confess this how much I have been dreading the coming break. Last July, after graduating, I performed for the Tsar at his residence in Krasnoe Selo, but this year the summer stretches ahead with nothing to fill it but father's drinking and the perpetual threat of his violence.

Tamara's perceptive gaze fills with concern.

'Besides,' I add brightly, 'who in their right mind would turn down a chance to visit Paris!'

I work harder than ever. There is no list on the notice board for the dancers who will accompany Diaghilev because his tour is not an official company venture. On the contrary, a reminder is issued that any failure to appear at the end of the summer will be viewed as a serious breach of contract and will result in immediate dismissal. One afternoon, as we are rehearsing on stage, I become conscious of a man watching from one of the empty seats in the auditorium. He is flamboyantly dressed, as if he is to be photographed for a fashion plate for Brizak, and has a flash of silver above his right temple in his otherwise jet black hair. He sits tensed with both hands resting on his cane like he might suddenly pounce. He gives the impression he would make a powerful adversary. I realise at once who it is.

As soon as the rehearsal finishes, I rush down from the stage. Diaghilev is deep in conversation with Fokine and the designer Léon Bakst and ignores me. Undeterred, I tug impulsively at his arm.

'I want to go to Paris with you. You took my sister, Eugenia, last year.' Slowly, the monocle is fixed into position and fierce black eyes assess me. Fearing I will be bawled at for interrupting, I hop nervously from foot to foot. To my relief, he addresses Fokine.

'Name?'

'Lydia Lopukhova. Graduated last year.'

'Competent?'

'More than that.'

Diaghilev grunts. 'She could pass for seventeen. They might like that.' He scowls. 'Give me one reason why I should agree.'

'I can jump as high as Nijinksy,' I blurt out. It is true. My arms may be plump and my porte de bras not as rounded or graceful as Anna Pavlova's, but my feet are better and my legs strong. I smile what I hope is a winning smile. 'Only Nijinsky lands badly, as if he has the hooves of a goat. When I jump my landing is perfect.'

There is a story I like to tell, of how, when we arrived in Paris in the summer of 1910, I stepped from the train and knelt to kiss the station platform. It is a tale I have repeated so often I scarcely know any longer if it is true, but if it is not it should be. Though I could not foresee it at the time, this visit to Europe with Diaghilev and the Ballets Russes was to be a turning point in my life.

I am lodged at the Grand Hôtel, where the bed is so vast I can lie across it sideways and still not reach the edges. It is here I sprawl in the afternoons to rest before a performance, one of the many sausage-shaped bolsters provided as pillows tucked into the small of my back. The hotel is on the Boulevard des Capucines, and through the open window I listen to the clip-clop of horses hooves on the cobbles outside; the noisy thrum of engines and honk of horns from passing motorcars; the voices floating up in a French infused with all the precision and fluidity we were taught at School but could never emulate. For our first week in the capital, I stayed with the other dancers in a boarding house in one of the less expensive neighbourhoods, but then Diaghilev insisted I move into this suite because of the superior impression it creates.

On the table by my bed is a silver pot of hot chocolate. Its smell as I pour is so much richer and more enticing than anything I have tasted in St Petersburg that for a moment I close my eyes in sheer ecstasy. On the coverlet beside me is a bag of pastries I bought on my way back from rehearsal, which I slit open and dunk into the syrupy chocolate. I am hungry and devour the buttery brioches and pain aux raisins with their creamy custard filling in greedy, wolfish mouthfuls.

Also on my bed is a pack of postcards joined to create a paper concertina. I have already sent mother two of these, showing the Eiffel Tower and Arc de Triomphe. I tear off a third, taking care to respect the perforations that attach each card to the next. It has a picture of the Luxembourg Gardens where yesterday I was taken by Diaghilev to be photographed by the press. He has invented a rumour for the benefit of journalists that I am only seventeen, when in reality I will be nineteen this coming October. This is a lie he justifies by insisting it will sell tickets, which will ensure our season here is a success. The newspaper and magazine editors have swallowed his bait as voraciously as fish gobbling bread once winter is over and the Neva finally thaws, and published articles about me as a child prodigy. It is cheering to suppose some of these may reach St Petersburg.

I stare at the fountains on the postcard, and remember the men in pale suits with striped ties playing boules on the gravel; the women with parasols and tiny dogs on leashes strolling amongst the flower borders; boys in sailor suits racing toy yachts on the glassy pond; girls in ribboned straw hats queuing for donkey rides. Magnificent bronzed horses ringed the base of the fountain, and I longed to sit on one and feel the sprays of water splash me. Near the gate of the Luxembourg Gardens, sellers with strings of bobbing balloons and trays of ices vied for our attention, while a white-faced clown in baggy, harlequin trousers turned cartwheels and handed out flyers advertising a Punch and Judy show. Yesterday, I posted mother a card of the Opéra where we are performing, with its classical columns and green roof like a crown topped by gilded figures representing poetry and harmony. I drew an arrow indicating the location of my hotel close-by.

I also sent mother a postcard from Berlin, which was our first stop and where we stayed for two weeks. It was of the Brandenburg Gate through which only members of the royal family may pass. On the back, I described our train journey as we headed south out of Russia, and related how in Germany we were given meat at every meal including breakfast. I imagine mother arranging my cards on the mantelshelf, reading and rereading, tears pricking her eyes. Not once did she dissuade me from joining the tour, despite her reluctance to part with me. She was glad I would visit Europe, and the knowledge that Fedor would be travelling in the same train reassured her I would come to no harm. The fact I will earn as much during these six weeks as I can in a year of dancing at the Mariinsky also helped persuade her. Of course, she hopes I will be sensible and save this money so I have a nest-egg to marry on, but I am not interested in settling down yet. Besides, there are too many things I want to buy.

My rooms are strewn with my purchases, draped over chairs, spilling out of boxes, piled in a precarious heap on my trunk. Every now and then a fan painted by an artist in Montmartre or leather dance shoes moulded to the shape of my feet slip and slither to the floor in a rustle of tissue paper. The maid assigned to my suite would like to tidy my shopping into the empty wardrobe but I will not permit this. I enjoy seeing all my acquisitions on display. When Tamara heard I had spent the three hundred francs Diaghilev paid me for learning a solo part at short notice on a new hat and false curls, she was so cross I feared she might never forgive me. I retorted she had no right to judge until she had inspected the items in question, since I was sure that once she had done this she would agree they were worth every centime. The wig-maker who sold me the curls swore he supplied all the best families in St Petersburg, and declared that by buying from him directly I was economizing on the cost of delivery. In any case, I protested, not everything is for me. I have pocket-knives for Nikolai and Andrei, books for Eugenia and her new husband, a Chantilly lace shawl for mother to wear in church. I continue to extol my virtues as a shopper to the absent Tamara, pointing out all the extras I have acquired gratis in addition to the objects I have spent money on. These include several tablets of soap intended for the train washroom, because I hit on the ingenious idea of preserving the first one I was supplied with in a flannel and using it several times. I even have a bottle of men's cologne from the hotel bathroom left there in case I have a gentleman visitor, which I plan to give father.

My hat has pride of place on the dressing table. It is wide-brimmed and decked with so many feathers it is as if the milliner decided not to deplume the ostrich but glue the bird on top. I have new clothes too, though these are less an extravagance than a necessity given all the parties I am attending. Diaghilev is overjoyed by my socializing and professes I have a natural talent, though I am not certain this is the case since he always has dozens of people he wishes to introduce me to and their questions are invariably the same. They begin by asking politely if I am enjoying Paris, which strikes me as nonsensical since who could not. When they want to know what I like especially I reply the sewage system, because here there is no festering night soil waiting for collection so the streets smell better.

Some are curious about the secrets of Russian ballet, but when I explain it is stretching every muscle until the body screams with pain every day from the age of nine, they laugh and assume I am joking. Once, to prove my point, I offered to show them my feet, but Diaghilev whisked me away before I could remove my shoes and stockings on the pretext he had someone for me to meet, though in fact it was to whisper in my ear that we would do better to keep the mysteries of our art to ourselves. Often, the parties are in brilliantly lit private rooms brimming with potential sponsors Diaghilev is eager to impress, where liveried waiters serve champagne and titbits of food such as a shrimp on a sliver of toast no bigger than a postage stamp, or quails eggs stuffed with caviar to make us Russians feel at home. If I am particularly ravenous I seize the whole tray and sit with it on my knees until I have eaten enough. Occasionally, the parties are in dark, smoky bars and Diaghilev invites composers or designers or painters he wishes to work with. At these gatherings, the discussion inevitably strays to the new style in art, which is not concerned with depicting surface likeness but in conveying a deeper truth. When I enquire what this deeper truth might be I am presented with wildly different answers. One night, I am introduced to my heroine the actress Sarah Bernhardt, but though she is as radiant in real life as she is in the theatre I am disappointed she does not have her pet crocodile in tow.

I bought my hat on impulse after catching sight of it in Le Bon Marché. When it came to clothes I felt less confident about venturing alone into one of the famous Parisian fashion houses, but fortunately several of the other dancers were similarly intimidated so we walked up and down the Rue de La Paix until a door flew open and a woman beckoned us in. Her bell-shaped tunic with sleeves in contrasting colours worn over a chiffon skirt was so fabulously modern we followed her inside. Here, we were offered glasses of mint syrup over crushed ice and dishes of lemon sorbet so we could refresh ourselves after the heat of the street. Jugs of water sprinkled with rose petals were passed round to rinse our hands. Even the air inside the cool, spacious interior smelled expensive, as if an invisible perfumier was hard at work behind one of the many screens creating a cocktail of scents to revive us. Our trepidation at entering such a world-renowned venue dissolved as it became clear the reputation of the Ballets Russes preceded us and we were to be treated as customers of the highest importance. Within minutes we were surrounded by models parading the latest styles, while assistants in black dresses knelt at our feet with drawings and photographs or notebooks in which they sketched designs based on our own ideas. Swatches of fabric were produced and rolls of cloth unfurled so we could compare different shades and textures. Our measurements and preferences were written down, paper patterns cut and pinned to us, and in no time at all we found ourselves the proud possessors of wardrobes with garments for all occasions – as well as several we could not imagine ourselves ever likely to wear. When the boy delivered the boxes containing my finished outfits to the hotel I was impatient to try them. The maid assisted with corsets and buttons, and as soon as I was properly attired I stood in front of the mirror to admire myself. What I saw made me guffaw. My reflection was nothing like the glamorous mannequins in the fashion plates I had taken my inspiration from. When Diaghilev first spotted me in a bunched skirt and fussy, tiered jacket over a blouse with a heavy frill, he teased I was encased in so many layers I might pass for a Russian dumpling. I crossed my arms and retorted that if he cared to examine the labels sewn into the seams, he would discover my layers were none other than the work of Paul Poiret.

I find my pen, write mother's name and our address on the postcard, and stop. So far, I have reported little about my dancing and frown as I consider what I can fit into the space. I recount how I learned two of Tamara's roles so I can cover for her whenever there are clashes with her commitments in London. I am about to plunge into a detailed description of all the steps I had to master in a few short weeks, when I change my mind. If I put all that in, I will not be able to report the most momentous news of all, which is that tonight I am once again to replace Tamara only this time to dance the lead role opposite Nijinksy in Fokine's 'The Firebird'. The realisation I am to do this in less than three hours makes me shiver, though the room is stifling. It is not that I am afraid exactly. The choreography is demanding, especially the leaps and difficult pas de deux, but they are within my capabilities. What worries me is that the improvised charm I have made my forté and which prompted Diaghilev to promote me to principal for his tour is redundant for this part. Tonight, when I go out onto the stage of the Paris Opéra, I must forget I am Lydia Lopukhova and transform myself into a creature capable of breaking the sorcerer Koschei's evil spell. I must become the Firebird, and brave the terrors of the enchanted forest to help Prince Ivan free those who are bewitched. Though the price for this release will be destroying the source of immortality, it is a price I must urge him to pay. If I can convey all this in my dancing, I do not think any role will be denied me.

My taxi pulls up in front of the restaurant and a man sporting a well-oiled moustache to rival even Diaghilev's offers me his arm.

'Josef Mandelkern, at your service,' he introduces himself in fluent Russian, handing the driver a note and waving away the change. 'I hope you're hungry. I have it on the highest authority this is one of Paris' finest restaurants – a city which boasts no shortage of culinary delights.'

I am ushered under an awning, then through the open restaurant door.

'Their signature dish is lobster,' he continues, as we are shown to a table in the corner of a wood-paneled room. 'They remove the flesh, combine it with cognac and cream, then return it to the shell and bake it in the oven. I'm assured it's a taste one remembers all one's life.' A bottle of champagne cools in an ice-bucket and he signals for it to be opened.

'I took the liberty of ordering. Though regrettably they have no Beluga caviar. "What?" I roared when I heard this. "Don't you know that my lunch guest today is none other than Lydia Lopukhova, one of the greatest – no, quite probably the greatest dancer of the Russian Imperial Ballet?"' But there was no procuring the dish no matter how hard I banged my fist or how many francs I promised to pay. So we must content ourselves with the humble oyster until our lobster is ready.'

I put my bag between my feet and sink into the soft upholstered seat. Since dancing for Diaghilev in Europe I have grown accustomed to people praising me. Usually this is because they interpret what I do as miraculous, instead of understanding it is a set of skills acquired over many years. The man opposite is different. Though he has the instantly friendly, solicitous manner I have come to associate with Americans, he has communicated enough in the volley of messages left at my hotel to indicate he is a ballet aficionado. As a result, I am unsure whether to laugh or protest at his excessive flattery.

Our waiter, who wears a buttoned jacket despite the heat, wraps a white cloth over the cork of the champagne bottle and twists it deftly. There is a muffled 'pop' and he pours the frothing liquid into two tulip-shaped glasses. He shakes out the napkin that has been folded into an open fan and lays it across my knee. Though it is early and for the moment there are few other diners I am conscious of my grubby dress and sandals. I have come straight from morning class and the outfit I have changed into is neither grand enough, clean enough, nor sufficiently ironed for my surroundings. A second waiter, attired like the first in a buttoned jacket, approaches our table carrying a tray at shoulder height on the flat of his palm, his tread muffled by thick carpet. He and his colleague address us in quiet, deferential voices, which contrast sharply with the noisy shouting of the cafés and bars where I normally eat. A plate of oysters and lemon halves is set between us. With an easy familiarity, Mandelkern chooses a lemon and squeezes it in his strong fingers, dripping juice liberally over the pearly-grey shellfish. He lifts one of the shells and tips its contents into his mouth, closing his eyes as he swallows. 'Heavenly,' he declares, dabbing his moustache punctiliously with his napkin though there is not a drop of lemon nor a morsel of oyster on it. He raises his glass.

'May I propose a toast, Mademoiselle Lopukhova, to a successful collaboration.'

'Mr Mandelkern,' I interrupt. 'I'm sorry to disappoint, but I've not at all come to the conclusion I wish to dance in America. As you are aware, my leave from the Mariinsky is for the summer only and I am due back in St Petersburg in a few weeks.'

To my surprise my host, who has scarcely stopped talking since meeting my taxi, does not reply. Instead, his eyes shut again, this time to focus on his glass of champagne. Only once it is empty does he open them and look at me.

'Do you realise Lydia – I hope I may call you Lydia and you will call me Josef – that the champagne we drink today – real champagne that is, not the many poor imitations that exist – is in essence exactly the same as when it was first discovered, which by the way was not by a Frenchman but a clever English scientist. Of course there have been refinements in technique since then, but it is still cultivated and manufactured according to practices passed on from master to apprentice across the generations.' He leans forward and I smell his scent of cologne and cigar smoke. 'What I'm offering, Lydia, is a once-in-a-lifetime opportunity to take the champagne of the Imperial Ballet to America.' He sits back, pleased with his analogy, then notices my untouched glass. 'Please, this is from 1901, the last great vintage before harvests were compromised in almost a decade of floods. It would be a crime not to taste it.'

I obey. The champagne is delicious, refreshingly sharp and yet sweet. I drink quickly, forgetting I have a rehearsal this afternoon then a performance this evening and would do well to avoid alcohol. As if reading my mind, Mandelkern selects an oyster.

'Now eat,' he commands, tilting the shell at an angle to my lips. 'Hold the oyster in your mouth then allow it to slide down your throat. Do not attempt to bite or chew.'

I follow his instruction, letting the sea-saltiness and tang of lemon fizz like the champagne on my tongue. A satisfied expression appears on Mandelkern's face.

'I mean to be honest with you, Lydia. The man I work for – Charles Frohman – is one of the most powerful producers in New York City, and he has sent me here with the express intention of hiring you. I have to tell you, Charles Frohman is not a man to take no for an answer.'

The waiter refills our glasses. I gulp mine down and help myself to a second oyster. I am beginning to enjoy myself. It is pleasant being courted, especially when the proposal – that I might break my contract with the Mariinsky and sail to America to dance for a producer I have never met – is too preposterous to consider seriously.

'America,' Mandelkern muses, as if he is recounting a story instead of pressing home his offer, 'is a country proud of its newness and pioneer spirit, while hankering after the traditions and talents of the old world it has left behind. America has nothing resembling the Russian ballet. In truth, most Americans don't have the faintest idea what ballet is. Shouldn't you like to change that, Lydia?' He pauses to sample another oyster, then wipe his moustache. 'There's more. If you accept Mr Frohman's proposition, I guarantee you will be famous.' He pushes the plate of oysters towards me, finds a silver case in his top pocket, removes a cigar and rolls it between his fingers. Immediately, a waiter is at his elbow. Smoke wreathes about him as the cigar is lit.

'Now, permit me to plot what will happen if you return to St Petersburg. Here in Paris, for a few brief weeks while the Tsar retires to his summer residence and the Mariinsky closes, you have danced leading roles, lived in a private suite at the Grand Hôtel, been written about and adulated by the press. Do you imagine this will continue?' He shakes his head, and his features arrange themselves into a look of intense sorrow. 'Allow me to advise you it will not. I am familiar with the formalities and rituals of the Imperial Ballet. You will resume your place in the corps de ballet from whence in time – and on condition you work like a mule and are polite to the right people –

you may eventually progress to the coryphée. Then, after more years of grueling drudgery and more favours – including perhaps becoming the plaything of one of the Grand Dukes – you might be rewarded with a tiny solo.' He sits back, a lawyer confident of winning his case. 'Am I not right?'

My rehearsal and performance forgotten, I drain my glass. For the first time since accepting the lunch invitation, I fear this man with his voice like honey has the power to steer me off course.

'All I've ever wanted,' I blurt out before he can say any more, 'is to dance at the Mariinsky. Now that ambition is within my grasp. What you recommend would mean the end of that dream. You must know we owe five years service once we graduate as a way of repaying the cost of our training. Breaking that contract is a sackable offence.'

Our waiter reappears and clears the empty oyster shells and lemon rinds.

'There are ways round that,' Mandelkern reflects, once the waiter has gone. 'If you do well in America the Mariinsky will take you back. And on your own terms.'

'I admit it's tempting,' I counter, frowning. 'But my mind is made up. I will return to St Petersburg and the company, and next summer, when the theatre shuts again, I will dance in Europe with Diaghilev.'

Mandelkern's eyes narrow.

'Oh Lydia,' he murmurs in a voice heavy with compassion, as if addressing a child he must upset. 'It saddens me to have to inform you this cannot happen. Diaghilev's achievement is almost unprecedented – transporting the splendours of Russian culture and captivating the capitals of Europe. But back in St Petersburg his success provokes envy and suspicion. His ideas are viewed as too avant-garde and there are concerns he does not present the Imperial Ballet in the best light. His arrogance does nothing to alleviate the situation. Even his supporters grow weary of his extravagant demands.' He puffs on his cigar, sending slow, interlocking smoke circles into the air. When he speaks again it is in a half-whisper, though the restaurant is not crowded and no one can overhear us. 'It's rumoured there are plans to oust Diaghilev from the company.' He raises his hand, as if to quash my protest. 'And yes, Fokine too. There are those who long for the Mariinsky to revert to its former ways and resurrect its erstwhile glories – they prize Petipa and his old-fashioned set pieces. This is not a style that suits you.'

I allow the waiter to refill my glass for a third time, though my head spins. If what Josef describes is correct, I have little hope of a glittering future in Russia. I possess neither Pavlova's grace nor Tamara's technical perfection, and without Diaghilev and Fokine to champion me I might remain in the corps de ballet my entire career. I have a sudden, painful memory of Petipa pinching me during morning class and threatening to send me to the kitchen, where he swore my fat cook's arms would be welcomed.

The waiter brings bowls of water for us to rinse our fingers. Mandelkern does this fastidiously, dipping then drying each digit on his napkin, his cigar clamped between his teeth.

'Shall we look at this from another angle?' he suggests, once the bowls are removed. 'How much will you earn next year?' For a second time, he holds up his hand to prevent my answer. 'Please understand, the question is rhetorical. I am already apprised of your salary. In truth, I've made it my business to acquaint myself with the income of everyone who works for the company. Let me observe, simply, that the contract I've been authorized to draw up will pay a thousand roubles more each month you're away than even Anna Pavlova earns in a year at the Mariinsky.'

My head whirls uncontrollably now, though whether from the champagne or Josef's extraordinary claims is impossible to gauge. I ask for a glass of water and think of all I could do with such a sum of money. I picture father, disgraced from his position at the theatre with little likelihood of further employment, our crowded apartment, the hours mother works.

'America is a long way…'. I hesitate. 'How many months would the contract run for?'

'Not many – eight at most. I could arrange for your brother to accompany you if that would make the prospect more palatable. I'm on the lookout for good male dancers.'

I nod, once, as the waiters process towards us, bearing plates concealed under silver domes which they remove with a flourish. Two sizzling, pink-shelled lobsters are revealed.

'So,' Mandelkern concludes, switching role from lawyer to judge as he sums up. 'The only remaining objection is your contract with the Mariinsky.' He tucks his napkin into his collar, his eyes fixed acquisitively on the lobster. 'That is easily solved. They will let you and your brother go. All that's required is to be granted leave of absence. I can write the necessary letters for you.'

A generous measure of brandy is tipped into a copper pan, a match struck and the ignited liquid poured over our plates.

'I'm a great deal older than you Lydia,' Josef continues, once the flames are extinguished. 'And if there is one thing I've learned, it's that life is short. A dancer's life especially so.' He scoops lobster flesh and sauce with his fork and is silent for a moment as he tastes. 'Sublime,' he pronounces, 'lobster, cream, cognac, all that I detect. But there is more.' He closes his eyes again, as if better to savour the ingredients. 'Lemon, shallot, parsley, a little garlic. And of course an excellent fish stock.' He smiles. 'I shall tip the chef and request the recipe.' He pats his mouth with his napkin and I notice how unnaturally white his teeth are. 'Well Lydia,' he resumes, his mood expansive, as if the meal has caused him to forget his mission to hire me, 'do you have a beau?'

Despite my resolution to reveal nothing of my personal life, I feel my cheeks burn.

'Ha, I have found you out! Diaghilev mentioned a Pole. Is it serious?'

When I blush deeper, Mandelkern chuckles.

'Perfect,' he professes, digging his fork back into the lobster. 'We'll concoct a romance, tell the press you're engaged to a Polish count. Who must of course live in a castle.' He slaps the table with his hand. 'Goddamit Lydia, I was wrong when I promised a few minutes ago you'd be famous. I'll go one better. In America I'll turn you into a star. I'll have you in headlines so big they'll be read not only in St Petersburg but the world over.'

❧

After days of staring at nothing but ocean there is land on either side of our boat. I am out on deck where most of the other passengers have gathered too, eager for my first glimpse of America. Crew members in navy blue with flat white hats call out hello as they pass. One asks if I am going to perform my high kicks and I tell him no, not today. Since recovering from the seasickness that kept me locked in my cabin for the first forty-eight hours of our voyage, I have become famous for using the handrail on deck as a barre. The sailors fold their arms in a show of disappointment, but I promise they will be able to watch me dance properly on Broadway and offer them all free tickets. They wonder why I am not with my brother Fedor or Volinine, the dancer Josef has hired to partner me, and I pretend they are below packing even though I suspect they are playing cards and Fedor is celebrating our arrival with a bottle of vodka.

Josef appears at my side and leans his elbows on the rail. He is smoking a cigar and gestures towards a curve of land in the distance.

'The island of Manhattan,' he confirms. 'It's a blur still, but as we get closer you will begin to pick out the skyscrapers. The Metropolitan Life Tower is now the tallest building in the world with fifty floors.'

I squint against the glare and try to imagine what it must be like to live so high up, looking down on birds' nests and tree-tops.

'There,' Josef points again, 'coming into view now. Ellis Island, where thousands of travellers arrive every day in the hope of starting a better life in America. These people are your audience, Lydia. But first we have to make sure they hear of you.'

He turns and runs his eyes over me. His stare is assessing, proprietorial, as if I am an object he owns. Yesterday, after finishing the daily English lesson he insists on since apparently no American speaks either French or Russian, he accompanied me to my cabin and examined the contents of my trunk. Ignoring my protests, he chose several garments and held them up against me. 'Too matronly,' he grumbled, tossing aside a linen suit, before discarding a low-cut dress designed by Poiret himself as 'too sophisticated'. When I complained that the outfit he eventually selected reduced me to a schoolgirl he patted my arm and replied 'precisely'. He discussed with the maid plaiting my hair in braids but I drew the line at this. Once he had decided on my costume he stood me in front of the mirror to practise what he terms my camera mask. I am to regard this in the same way I do the expressions I adopt for my dance roles, such as the dreamy countenance I put on for 'Les Sylphides', or the rascally face of the flirtatious Columbine in 'Carnival'. Josef perched on the bed and barked out instructions, approving particularly of my smile because of the natural gap it reveals between my front teeth. His word for this is winsome.

Josef flicks the still-smouldering stub of his cigar into the churning water, and suggests we return to my cabin so I can rehearse my lines for the press one last time. I am determined not to miss the skyscrapers so declare myself word-perfect thanks to his constant drilling. It is true. Every afternoon, after our English lesson, Josef has dictated phrases for the benefit of journalists which I have memorized. Twice, we have stationed ourselves in a quiet part of the deck where he has fired ludicrous questions designed to prepare me for the American media, often supplying the responses himself. Some of his invented answers are lies but he proposes I treat these as yet another face-mask. What newspapers and magazines crave, he cajoles, is a story, and the best way to prevent editors from creating their own is to provide one. That way we at least retain control. Josef only corrects my mistakes in English when my meaning is unclear. When I quiz him on this he remarks that my errors enhance my Russianness, which the press will find adorable. He encourages me to sprinkle my English with plenty of Russian words and not to worry about my accent.

A man near us, his arms looped about the shoulders of two children, calls out. He lifts each child in turn so they can see above the railing, then kisses the woman beside him. Other passengers follow his gaze and soon everyone is pointing and cheering and shaking hands.

'What is it?' The excitement is infectious and I consider fetching Fedor.

'The Statue of Liberty', Josef proclaims. 'There, to our left. You can just make out her outstretched arm and the gold flames of her torch.'

We must wait for the gangplank once we dock, but even when this has been manoeuvred into position and other people walk down it onto dry land Josef will not let us disembark. By way of explanation he indicates a cluster of men and a handful of women, some holding cameras, waiting by the exit. 'They are expecting Lydia Lopukhova', he informs me, 'whose name by the way they will neither be able to pronounce nor spell. Notice how they follow each young woman with their eyes, trying to deduce "is that her?"' We don't want to spoil their fun by putting an end to their suspense too quickly. Besides, a little anticipation will pique their interest.'

Only as the hurly-burly of those leaving the boat starts to slow will Josef allow us to proceed. He takes my arm as we step onto the gangplank, but instead of waiting for the couple in front taps smartly on the man's shoulder.

'Excuse me, may we come through?' he demands so loudly I start. 'This is Miss Lydia Lopukhova with her colleagues from the Imperial Ballet.'

His announcement causes the stir he intends and soon his message reaches the journalists on the wharf, so that by the time we step onto the dock we are engulfed.

'This way, Miss Lydia,' those with cameras urge, 'that's right. And another.'

I smile and turn my head as Josef has taught to present everyone with a good angle. The shutters click as if they are transmitting dozens of telegraphic messages simultaneously. The interrogation begins.

'Is it true you are a favourite of the Tsar?'

'Is it true you can dance on the tips of your toes?'

'Is it true even Anna Pavlova is jealous of you?'

I trot out my off-by-heart answers, adding embroiderings of my own whenever one occurs to me. The sight of the journalists' pens flying over their notebooks and recording my every word is as heady and gratifying as an outburst of applause while I am dancing. The only question I stumble over is when a woman wonders if I am really sixteen and fresh out of school. This is even younger than Diaghilev's lie about my age, but when I glance across at Josef he shrugs as if to say 'think of it as another role.'

Finally, when Josef senses everyone has enough pictures and quotes for a first article, he intervenes. He puts his arm round me so I am eclipsed by his bulk and addresses the group.

'That's all for today, my friends. We thank you for coming but Miss Lopukhova and her Russian compatriots have travelled a long way and you'll forgive them if I tell you they're exhausted. You'll be able to see them all dance when their show opens at the Palace Theatre in a week's time.' Then, as skillfully as when we met in Paris, he leads me to a waiting taxi already stowed with my luggage.

As he opens the door I turn back to the dispersing journalists.

'Hello New Yorkski,' I shout, and as the taxi pulls away I hear the call repeated all along the wharf.

Through the train window, ripening wheat fields extend as far as the eye can see. On my knee is a postcard and pen but I am not writing. Josef, who occupies the seat next to mine, has disappeared, possibly to the washroom, or else to the restaurant car. He likes to eat a plate of eggs mid-morning fried on one side only. He claims it is the reason he is never travel-sick. In the seat opposite his, my dance partner Volinine has fallen asleep, his finely chiseled features relaxed into softness. Fedor, who is beside him, also has his eyes closed, though I can tell from the way he keeps his head pressed back against the rest that he is awake. He swigs regularly from a bottle of vodka he conceals in a brown paper bag. His drinking, which began on the boat, has increased steadily since our arrival in America, to the point where he scarcely spends a day sober. He is angry that instead of the booking we had been promised in New York, we were forced to perform in a vaudeville-style musical. When I complained about the switch to Josef he replied it could not be helped as the Globe Theatre had offered more money than the Palace. I nudge Fedor and his eyes snap open. I hold up my pen and ask if he has a message for mother. He shakes his head, then lifts his paper bag to his lips and swallows hard.

The photograph on the postcard is of Broadway, though it must have been taken from high up because the street is no bigger than a ribbon: its carts and horses, motorcars and jostling pedestrians reduced to mere dots. It is one of several I bought in New York when it seemed we would serve out the full eight months of our contract at the Globe, repeating the same dull routine night after night as if we were dancing machines. Our boredom must have communicated itself because after six weeks Frohman announced we were to be replaced by a performing bear. We hoped a serious engagement would follow, but instead joined a troupe of variety acts on tour, and are now billed between a female impersonator and a sword-thrower.

I try to recall which cities I have sent mother pictures of since leaving New York, but though I am sure one was of Chicago, I am hazy about the others. The places we have worked in, the dreary hotel rooms where we have stayed, the thousands of miles we have travelled by train, melt into a blur. What I remember are the stages, none of which are designed for ballet, though I cannot let mother know this. My knees have still not recovered from a fall on our opening night at the Globe, where our request to dampen the stage was misunderstood and I slipped on the sodden boards. I wonder which city we will dance in tonight, but instead of the thrill I anticipated when Josef advised us of Frohman's plan and traced our route on a map, I find I no longer care.

In my bag, I have the newspaper cuttings Josef collects assiduously, and I consider posting mother a selection. They all praise me, which she will like. In truth, most journalists treat me as the star Josef vowed America would make me. The reason I have not sent any reviews back home is that very few display any knowledge of ballet. Volinine and Fedor are popular with audiences because they are physically strong, and Fedor is cheered when he crouches low and kicks out his legs as he rotates in a circle for his Cossack dance. I am viewed as a precocious baby who doubtless has wires under my costume to facilitate my leaps. No one pays much attention to what the press refer to as my 'toe-dancing'. Bessie McCoy, whose name appeared in lights at the Globe, swore to reporters she could master the 'trick' after training for just two months in St Petersburg.

'Cheer up,' Fedor urges, mirroring my glum face by wrinkling his brow and drooping his mouth so I smile despite myself. I realise from his flushed cheeks that he is half-way to being drunk, not yet so intoxicated to contemplate hurling himself under the moving train, but enough to recognise how far from home we all are and how different our lives in America have turned out to be from those we imagined. I suppose this is why father drinks, because his life too has not worked out as he wished.

'Perhaps tonight's orchestra will get our pas de deux right,' I suggest, deliberately humming the allegro at funereal speed.

Fedor snorts. 'They won't, but then why should we mind? No one else does.'

I glance round. The rest of the carriage is full of other members of our troupe: a ventriloquist with a dummy named Lester, two juggling brothers, a clog-dancing husband and wife duo, elderly Miss Leonora whose pet poodles walk on their hind legs and pick out letters to spell their names. Fortunately none of them speaks Russian. I tell myself that if they had grasped Fedor's insult, they would have attributed it to his drinking. 'The crazy Russe' they call him, though I suspect this is a label they use for all of us when we are out of earshot. At the start of the tour, Fedor, Volinine and I tried to maintain the high standards we had learned in Russia. We quickly realized that the difficulties we had encountered in New York, where we were at least in one location, were as nothing compared to those of being on the road. Now when we arrive at a destination, it is often only with a few hours to spare, and we rarely have time alone on stage to rehearse. So far all my entreaties to Josef to book practice space have fallen on deaf ears. Frequently, we are unable even to speak to the conductor before appearing, let alone run through our steps with the musicians. If we are not performing we are confined to the cramped interior of a train where practice is impossible. On the first leg of our journey, I asked a group of hula dancers who toured regularly how they managed, but they explained all they needed for their routine to be successful was to sway their hips in their grass skirts and reveal as much flesh as the law allowed. The only other consideration was where to position themselves on stage and this they could estimate from the wings.

Fedor gulps down more vodka. 'At least it's only another four months. Then we can get the hell out of here.'

I lean forward. 'But think what's happened at the Bolshoi in Moscow. They've sacked every dancer who failed to return for the autumn season. Even Volinine.' We look instinctively to where he is sleeping. 'And we've never had a reply to the letters Josef wrote requesting leave of absence. I'm scared the Mariinsky will sack us too.'

'It's a risk.'

'And not the only one. We might not be allowed to leave Russia again. We need the Tsar's permission to travel and he could refuse.'

'I don't care. I'm going back even if I never dance again. And I've done enough travelling to last a lifetime.'

Josef is heading towards us, carrying a plate of sandwiches. They are thickly filled with slices of salt beef and he offers them first to Fedor, then to me. We refuse. Josef's continual eating has become repellent to us.

'I've good news,' he announces unperturbed, as he settles back into his seat. Fedor unwraps his bottle, drinks openly, then passes it to me. I hesitate then copy him. We have spent too many months with Josef to believe he can have any good news unless it concerns making money at our expense.

'We arrive in Oakland later today,' Josef begins, scowling at the sight of the vodka which if reported could land us in trouble. I return the bottle to Fedor so he can hide it. 'Oakland is close to our next venue, San Franciso, where Anna Pavlova is currently appearing with her company. She will greet our train.'

I am astounded. At the Mariinsky, Anna Pavlova is so far above my rank or Fedor's she is unlikely even to have heard of us.

'What's going on?' I demand, suspicious this is yet another of Frohman's schemes.

Instead of answering, Josef bites into a sandwich. 'Delicious,' he pronounces as he chews. 'The beef is succulent, with exactly the right amount of salt.' He removes a freshly laundered handkerchief from his pocket. 'There's a story circulating – of a stand-off between the pair of you. When the press hear you're to meet in Oakland, every journalist within a hundred miles will be there to witness it.' He dabs methodically at his moustache. 'A welcome boost in publicity for all.'

Before I can protest, George, a banjo player who has become a friend, passes by our seats.

'How are you today, Miss Lydie?' He removes an invisible hat and bows low, before elbowing Fedor. 'What's that you're cradling like a newborn?' When Fedor shows him he chuckles and sucks in his breath. 'One helluva headache lurking in there,' he warns cheerily, giving me a wink and continuing up the aisle.

Josef stares after him. 'Scum,' he mutters.

'What exactly is your problem?' Fedor quizzes in Russian. 'Unlike most of the so-called "artistes" on this infernal expedition you've roped us into, George has both talent and skill.'

'I'll tell you what my problem is,' Josef replies, reverting to English again. 'It's having to sit in the same car as niggers.'

'So where do you propose they sit?' I catch hold of Fedor's arm but he brushes my hand away.

Miss Leonora lifts her head from the book she is reading, removes her pince-nez and nods approvingly.

'I'll tell you where they can sit,' Josef continues encouraged, 'in the car with the other animals.'

I stand. Fedor is drunk enough now to start a fight. I shake Volinine awake and signal to him to help me. He puts an arm round Fedor and between us we steer him out of the carriage. We can still hear Josef as we close the door.

'Preferably in the same bolted cages as the monkeys.'

I remove Josef's note from its envelope. It arrived a week ago and if I do not answer soon I risk his turning up here to persuade me to accept his latest proposal in person. In my last letter, I responded to his question about how long I intended to remain away with the words 'for as long as I need'. When he telephoned to object this would not satisfy the press, I reminded him of our agreement. He was to issue a statement explaining I was exhausted after dancing for the best part of a year in a Broadway musical, and needed time to recuperate.

My room smells of the forest, its walls, ceiling and floor made of maple wood the colour of toffee. In addition to the bed, which is oak, there is a washstand with a bowl and jug, a mirror decorated with pine cones, a beech chest with drawers down one side, and a cane rocking chair with two patchwork cushions. There is a patchwork quilt on the bed sewn from so many scraps of fabric it dazzles me. Best of all, the room has two windows, one of which looks out over a garden and apple orchard, the other over trees towards the blue rim of the Catskill mountains. The windows are open and the only sounds that float in are birdsong and the hum of insects.

The boarding house is small, and the other guests are Miss Meadows, a retired schoolteacher, and a mother and four daughters who have recently emigrated from Italy. They will live here where rents are cheap until the girls' father and two elder brothers can earn enough in New York to send for them. Their dream is to establish their own bakery. I consider myself fortunate none of them has heard of me and that the boarding house owners are not inquisitive. Martha, as I am encouraged to call her, is broad-shouldered and capable and a champion of women's rights. She keeps cows and chickens and grows vegetables on a plot of land at the back of the house. It was her husband, Frank, who entered my name in the ledger on my first day. 'Lopukhova,' he puzzled, stumbling over the letters. 'What kind of name is that?' 'Lopokova,' I corrected, pronouncing carefully and adopting the spelling Josef insists Americans find easier. At that moment Martha appeared, her sleeves rolled to her elbows and her hands glistening with soap bubbles from the laundry. 'It's a name like any other,' she reprimanded her husband, smiling at me in welcome, 'just write it in the book.'

I lie on the bed, nestling my head in plump feather pillows. As well as Josef's letter, I have one from Fedor, who is dancing again at the Mariinsky and urges me to come home. I unfold his letter and smooth out the creases. It too has lain unanswered for almost a week. For the hundredth time I mull over Josef's proposition, which is a thousand dollar contract to perform at the Waldorf Astoria Hotel on Park Avenue. I stretch my legs and feet over the rainbow checkerboard of the quilt, as if to test they still function. A year ago, I would have accepted the booking without hesitation, attracted by the money. Now, the prospect repulses me. I have had my belly-fill of staying in hotels where gossip columnists wait to pounce, tipping the bell-boys in the lobby for my room number. I would not care if I was struck off every guest list in America and never had to attend a fashionable gathering again. I have no desire to run en pointe so an audience can ogle me as if I am a freak show. There have been difficult times in America when work has been hard to come by, but I have no immediate financial need. I sent mother money during the long run of 'The Lady of the Slipper', and I have squirrelled away savings. I let my fingers zigzag from one brilliantly coloured square of patchwork quilt to the next. It is a game I play most afternoons, sometimes selecting a particular destination – anything with purple in it for instance, or only landing on fabric that is striped – and sometimes closing my eyes to see where hazard propels me.

My thoughts drift to a bassoon played so high it is unlike any sound I have heard. I visualize a stage with two circles of dancers against a backdrop of blue and green, solid slabs of colour denoting grassland and hills. Interlocking white clouds press down on the dancers, who crouch peasant-like on the ground. For the moment they are all men, their faces swathed in dark beards. They wear belted tunics patterned at the neck, sleeves and hem with bands of red, orange and yellow ochre, motionless as Matryoshka dolls. I hear a discordant oboe, then the strings thrum like drums, as if all the forces that create or destroy life are freshly audible. Awakened, the dancers jump low on flat feet as if bound by the earth's gravitational pull. I imagine how strange it must feel to dance like this with one's energy directed downwards, ignoring the years of training aimed at making us appear to float effortlessly in air – but also how exhilarating.

I have read so many descriptions of the Ballets Russes' 'The Rite of Spring' in Paris that I can run it across the screen of my mind as if it is a movie I am simultaneously taking part in. Its jolting music and alien choreography are all my dancer friends write about. I hear the jeers and protests of a public shocked by a confrontation with its own barbarity when it had been anticipating titillation – a flattering, self-indulgent feast for eye and ear. I picture Nijinsky shouting out the beats from behind the curtain so the dancers can persist with his irregular, syncopated steps despite the uproar. I add Diaghilev, going up on stage to harangue his audience for their conservatism and cowardice. I clench my fists to re-enact the movements of the maidens as they are drawn into the age-old ritual of sacrifice. Josef, who persists in buying all the papers, even those from abroad, showed me the reviews intending to entertain me while I was still performing in New York. He relished each separate condemnation of the ballet's savagery and ugliness. 'Listen to this', he commanded, slapping his thigh in glee, 'it says the dancers stamped like brutes. Diaghilev's obsession with Nijinsky has gone too far. This marks the end of the Ballets Russes.'

I turn onto my side and draw my knees up to my chest, remembering how, when I first met Josef, I was as interested as he is in people's opinion. I kept all the articles he collected in which I, or anyone I knew, was mentioned. As time went on and there were too many to carry with me, I kept only those in which I featured or were printed in what Josef terms 'high reach' publications. Now, I keep almost nothing. I am weary of reading how my favourite American dish is ice cream, or spotting posed photographs of myself paddling barefoot like a child. For every ten column inches written about me, there is scarcely one that does not mention my youth. Josef might have made me a star, but not as an Imperially trained ballerina. I am 'a nimble Russian hoofer', hired as the exotic extra in a Broadway musical, or the new attraction at a hotel nightclub. And yet, I reflect, continuing a conversation I have been having with myself for weeks now, this is hardly Josef's fault. It is thanks to him that I have saved enough money to remain here without working – for months, should I choose.

I return to 'The Rite of Spring', to its thrilling cacophony and violent emotion, and realise how much I have missed being in a company where everyone, from the choreographer to the most menial stage-hand, believes in the work. I force myself to my feet. There is space in my room to exercise, yet all I have attempted since moving here are a few cautious bends. I grip the open window ledge and rise into élevé, but though I feel no pain my mind and body seem disconnected. Even the voices of Cecchetti and Fokine rapping out instructions during morning class, which I used to conjure easily whenever I practised, now seem as distant as home. Mechanically, I move my feet through the five positions, but am unsure if what I am doing is correct or if it is not how to set it right. I rest my free hand on my abdomen, soothing myself with reassurances that all I need is more time and my body will remember – but this leads into territory that is still too painful and I abandon my efforts and fling myself back on the bed.

The truth is I cannot think about what has happened, any more than I know how to resume the career Josef has assembled for me. With each day I spend here that world feels increasingly remote, like a familiar landscape disappearing under snow. Josef has been as kind as he is capable of being, but his touting for fresh engagements shows how little he understands. I can no more dance at the Waldorf Astoria at the end of this month than I can sprout wings and fly back to St Petersburg. Even if my mind were convinced, my body is far from ready.

Josef has understood the need to be discreet. Mother always insisted a woman's reputation, once lost, could never be recovered. When I broke the news Josef stared at me, the ash tip of his cigar glowing red. He asked what I planned to do and I proposed going away, because the same rules apply even in America. He agreed to my request for money, and offered to help find the name of a doctor. What was harder was exacting his pledge that he would concoct no stories for the press, no fairytale fictions of Polish counts and castles. When he complained I would lose ground if we kept silent I lost my temper. 'That ground', I reminded him, 'is me. I'm the one who must deal with this and I'll decide what people hear. Which – until I advise you to the contrary – is precisely nothing.' In the event, my body settled matters for me, and all I had to do was submit to its demands. At least Josef had the tact not to enquire if I was relieved by the outcome.

The other night, once everyone had retired to bed, Martha joined me on the veranda gazing out at the darkening ridge of mountains. For a while she sewed in silence, then, when the light became too dim, set the shirt she was mending aside.

'Do you have a family in Russia?' she asked, her voice sonorous in the twilight.

I cleared my throat and in my halting English told her about mother, Eugenia and my brothers, and how we had all, with the exception of Nikolai, trained with the Imperial Ballet.

'And your father?'

I shook my head. 'He died last year. At almost exactly this time.'

'So the man who came with you in the taxi wasn't your father?'

'That's Josef Mandelkern, my manager,' I replied, smiling at her mistake. 'He often refers to himself as my father though. Foster-father,' I added, remembering how Josef presented himself when we found ourselves embroiled in a court case because of his quarrel with former Bolshoi dancer Mikhail Mordkin. Josef had accused Mordkin of jealousy for excluding me from his 'All-Star Russian Ballet' and the pair had fought on stage, causing a public outcry.

'Is he a good manager?'

'Mostly,' I ventured, then recalled how much Josef's reckless behaviour had cost me. 'At times he reminds me good deal of my father.'

'Oh?'

'My father might have been gifted actor if circumstances were different,' I confided, deciding it would be simpler to change direction than relate how Mordkin had switched programmes at the last moment to showcase another partner, so my fee went unpaid. 'But he never found way to use his talents.'

'It must have made him proud, seeing you use yours.'

'Trouble is, I'm not sure I am.' My response startled me. I had not openly acknowledged my frustration with my dancing career before.

As if to allow time for this thought to settle, Martha reached for a candle. 'It'll keep the mosquitos away,' she promised, shielding the wick with her hand and striking a match. 'I add lemon oil to the wax.' She lodged the candle between us, the soft light bringing her into focus, strong and dependable like the icons people hold up at weddings to ward off evil. 'So what needs to change?'

Memories of father gloating over my achievements and Josef's smugness at my increasing wealth clash and fuse in my mind. 'I did everything required of me at School,' I explained, 'but it was as actor I stood out. One teacher wanted I give up ballet to devote whole of my time to acting.'

'You still could.'

I laughed. 'Not with my rag-bag English!'

'And if you were to return to Russia?'

'Nothing to go back to. I broke my contract. Perhaps if I'd returned when my brother did employment might have been possible, but too much time has now passed. And though I long to see family, I couldn't live at home, especially if I wasn't earning....' I stopped, sensing tears, and for some minutes we sat without speaking, the singing of the cicadas wrapping round us like gauze.

'My father drank all through my childhood,' Martha admitted at length. 'It was my mother who managed everything. With only me and my sisters to help her, she grew our food, tended the house, made our clothes – even nursed my father when he became ill. I learned early on that obstacles can be overcome and women can do anything.'

This revelation was so unexpected I turned to face her.

'If what's stopping you from acting is your English, why not take lessons? I believe Miss Meadows, in the room below yours, was an excellent teacher in her day, and I'm certain she would welcome the extra money. From what I've heard, she used to be something of an actress herself.'

'I can't imagine my manager relishing launch into acting! He grumbles enough about promoting me as dancer.'

'Who mentioned your manager? Perhaps it's time to control your own affairs? You've got through this alone after all.'

It was the first time Martha had alluded to my situation. I braced myself for her interrogation, but instead of questioning me she stood up.

'Women are always being told we're weak, but that's to keep us in our place.' She pinched out the candle flame with her fingers. 'Good night. Time to sleep.'

I did consult Miss Meadows about lessons, and this morning spent two hours in her room working on my English. She reminds me of the Toads at School, severe and exacting but with the well-being of her pupils at heart. The first half-hour was a disaster. I was nervous and all my English words seemed to vanish. After several false starts, in which my tongue stubbornly refused to sound an English 'r', and my ear to distinguish between 'v' and 'w', Miss Meadows ordered me to stop. She directed me to a slim volume on the top shelf of her bookcase she wanted me to pass her. She opened the book, her veined, arthritic hands turning the pages with reverence, then pointed to a passage. I recognized it at once. It was Olga's closing speech from Anton Chekhov's 'Three Sisters', in which she despairs of ever knowing why it is we live and suffer so. I was unaccustomed to seeing the words in any other language than Russian, but their meaning – even in translation – was so familiar I read almost without faltering. When I came to the final: 'If only we could know! If only we could know!', Miss Meadows nodded. She sat with her hands immobile on the quilt that covered her knees despite the sun streaming through the windows, as if allowing the full import of the lines to register. Then she took a notebook she had stowed beside her chair and drew up a timetable. It would, she advised, take many months to improve my English to the level required, but she believed I had talent, and saw no reason why I should not succeed if I applied the same rigour and dedication I did to my dancing.

I take Josef's letter to the table. I know what to say now and tear a sheet from my writing pad. My reply – that I do not wish to accept any more dancing commissions and in future intend only to act – takes no more than a moment to compose. I address the envelope ready for the postman to collect in the morning. My next letter takes longer, since I must recopy it several times. It is to the advertisements section of all the newspapers that review theatre. I announce I am searching for a play, and ask for any suitable scripts to be forwarded care of my manager. Then I write to Fedor with the news that I plan to stay in America a while longer, and reassure him all is well.

❧

The snow in New York is nothing like snow at home. In St Petersburg, when it falls, it does so with passion and no care for economy, coating streets and buildings until it compacts into a solid mass only a shovel and a strong arm will clear. American snow is feeble by comparison, as if it cannot stop being rain. The flakes melt so quickly everything underfoot turns to slush, and when I reach my destination my hat and clothes and boots give the impression I have swum there.

The city is still decorated for Christmas, though the red-robed Father Frosts ringing hand bells and yo-ho-hoing merry tidings have disappeared from street corners. My hotel is next to a toyshop whose windows continue to display model steam-engines and swivel-head dolls but at reduced prices. My suite boasts a private bathroom and an Irish maid named Molly, whose red curls tumbling from her cap remind me of mother. She and I get on famously. She laughed when I complained about the snow in New York, and promised it would soon get cold enough for the lake in Central Park to freeze and for there to be skating. Her appetite for gossip is so insatiable she frequently forgets what she is supposed to be doing. I have asked her to iron my costume for tonight's performance, but instead she is perched on the rim of my bathtub. She dunks the sponge and trickles warm water down my back. I giggle, remembering bath nights at School when we were temporarily released from the Toads' scrutiny and could share our secrets in whispers. Josef advised against this intimacy with Molly, fearing I might reveal a confidence she could leak to the press. I protested Molly would not stoop so low and that our conversations are an excellent opportunity for me to practise my English. Right now, we are talking about the play I am appearing in, which opened a week ago on Broadway.

'You were marvelous, Miss Lydia,' Molly enthuses. 'Even better last night than the first time I saw you. Though you were wonderful then too,' she adds, anxious not to offend, especially since I arranged free tickets. 'Sure, the woman next to me laughed at the way you spoke your lines, as if you were a foreigner, but I explained this is how your character would say them – having only recently returned from a period in Germany.'

'You don't consider it too far-fetched,' I quiz her, accentuating my Russian accent, 'that an American girl from a wealthy family, who's been away in Europe soaking up the new ideas, should fall in love with a chauffeur – only to discover he's the son of a millionaire?'

'I do not,' Molly declares stoutly. 'Besides, it's what every girl wants – to dream a little. And you act it so beautifully. Especially the dancing.'

Instead of cheering me as she intends, her comments depress me. Though the reviews were kind while the play toured the provinces, they have been merciless since we arrived in New York. 'That's all people like,' I sigh, 'my showing off dance steps supposedly learned from a protégé of Isadora Duncan.'

'Not true,' Molly insists. 'The second time I went, I sat next to a reporter who wrote on his pad "LOPOKOVA PRETTY AS A PRINCESS, EVEN IN LONG TROUSERS".' She colours at the memory of the trousers. 'Which won't take me a second to iron. Oh, I nearly forgot, that woman – the one who owns the theatre and coaches you for your role…'.

'Minnie Fiske.' I supply the name.

'That's her,' Molly confirms. 'She telephoned earlier wishing to speak to you.'

'Here?' I am surprised. Normally, Minnie keeps her performance notes until we can go through them at the theatre. 'Did she leave a message?'

'No. Daisy answered the call. When she heard you were out she hung up.'

It is time to get ready. Molly holds open a towel as I climb out of the bath. 'You're so tiny, Miss. Like a child.' She rubs my skin vigorously. 'When my brothers and sisters and I were little, Saturday was bath night. We'd stoke up the fire to heat enough water for the tub, then pile in, one after another, oldest first, baby last. That way we'd all be clean for Mass on Sunday. Like a litter of pink piglets we were – twirling our bodies so different parts of us dried in the flames.'

I like Molly's stories about Ireland and listen as she helps me dress. I know how much she misses her family – especially at this time of year. On Christmas morning, when I presented her with a pair of pendant earrings she had admired, she burst into tears. She could not bear to think of her mother alone at home, now her sisters are all in service and her three brothers fighting in France. She assured me she is not seriously worried because everyone agrees the war will be over soon, but it is hard picturing them sleeping rough and eating heaven knows what instead of sitting down to roast goose and plum pudding. I thanked God as we talked that my own brothers are safe from this war. Josef, who has been following its progress in the papers, reports that Russian losses have been catastrophic, and the Generals are now sending men into battle without weapons or ammunition.

'We should hurry,' I say, pushing thoughts of the war away. 'Or the taxi will be here to take me to the theatre.'

Molly removes my trousers from their hanger and gives them a shake, as if this will rid them of their creases. 'Will you wear the blue or red top tonight? To be sure, blue brings out the colour of your eyes, but on stage red stands out more, especially for those in the cheaper seats at the back.'

I am at the dressing table and Molly is brushing my hair when we hear the knock.

'Come in,' I call, and the door opens. Josef strides into the room in that way he has whenever he is about to make an announcement, shoulders thrust back, head lowered, like a bull preparing to charge.

'I'm not dressed,' I object, more rudely than I intend. 'Can't you wait for me in the lobby?'

Josef signals to Molly to leave us. She glances at me and I shrug.

'I'll be outside,' she promises. 'Shout if you need me.'

'I've just been at the theatre.' There is a tremor in Josef's voice, as if dismissing Molly has sapped his bravura. He rummages in his jacket pocket for his cigar case.

'Well?' I snap, bracing myself for another of his dramas.

He flips open the case and stares at the cigars in their orderly row. 'They've closed the play.'

'Impossible. The curtain goes up in three hours.'

'Not any more.' He rolls a cigar between his fingers to test its texture. It is a gesture I have come to loathe.

'I had a call at my hotel. When the crew arrived at the theatre they found the doors locked and "performance cancelled" signs posted outside. News travelled fast because by the time I got there journalists were sniffing round for a story. It's best you avoid them.'

'I don't understand.' I am no longer angry. All I want is for Josef to account for what I am certain is a mistake, so a solution can be found and the play go ahead as scheduled.

'The reviews have been terrible.'

I wince. 'They've not been particularly complimentary in New York, but we've only been going here a week and the reviews from the tour were ecstatic.'

'The provinces don't count.' Josef searches for a lighter and I pass him the one from my dressing table. It is silver and has a ballerina engraved on the front, a present from an admirer. He studies it for a moment. 'Pretty.'

'A few negative comments can't mean ending the entire run. I spoke to Minnie when the review in *The Herald* appeared and she didn't seem unduly alarmed.'

Josef unscrews the metal match from the lighter then strikes it against the flint. He inserts the tip of his cigar into the flame and puffs, drawing air through the tobacco. Smoke clouds the room.

'Minnie must have changed her mind. Perhaps when Nathan's review came out. Either that, or her husband changed it for her. Those "few negative comments" as you describe them were pretty damning.' He has relaxed now he has delivered his blow, but this has not made him kind. '"Artificial gestures",' he quotes, waving his cigar for emphasis, '"limited emotional range", "a voice so monotonous one begins to hear poetry in the bored shiftings of the audience".'

'This is all your fault,' I storm, getting to my feet. 'You're the one who's meant to be handling the press.'

'That's when I was promoting a *ballerina*.'

'Don't lie,' I warn, handing him an ashtray with the name of the hotel stamped across it, presumably so guests will not steal it. 'You were as exultant as I was when Minnie Fiske and her husband found a play for me. You bought a methuselah of champagne.' I remember Molly, hovering outside the door, and am grateful she speaks no Russian. Our voices will have carried. 'Have I been paid yet?'

'The word is no one will get a penny.'

'What?' This second blow shocks me even more than the first. The names and faces of all those I have worked with on "Just Herself" whirr through my brain, like images on an old-fashioned zoetrope. Lily, my understudy, teaching herself shorthand and typing in case she does not succeed as an actress; Bill, a stage-hand doubling as a prompt, whose wife has just had a baby.

'Cheer up,' Josef urges at last. 'I have one piece of better news.'

'Oh?'

'I've found a producer willing to hire you. As a dancer. It's vaudeville again, but the money's good.'

'Where?'

'Just off Times Square. The Knicker Bocker.'

A hurricane might have swept across the stage of the Metropolitan Opera House, with a full-scale rescue operation underway. To my right, men hammer together a staircase; overhead two more stand atop a scaffold to fasten a silken canopy into place. Yet another unrolls a floor cloth, yelling at anyone in his way to move, followed by a boy with a pot of paint tasked with disguising scuff marks from previous performances. In the still-visible wings, hot irons are run over embroidered capes and feathers arranged on jeweled headdresses, while the prop master counts scimitars and ropes of pearls helped by a band of assistants. I jump out of the path of a cart piled high with Arabian carpets and water pitchers, ostrich fans and gold filigree lamps. From the pit arise random fanfares as instruments are tuned or fingers practise challenging moments in the score. All around me, dancers stretch and chatter noisily.

'Lydia, come and kiss me!' The command soars above the tumult in a tone that expects to be obeyed. I make my way past technicians setting out arc lights to the steps at the side of the stage.

'You could be a Tsar, with that boom in your voice,' I inform Diaghilev as I cross the auditorium, 'you are wasted on ballet!' I fling myself against his bulk and his bear-arms fold round me, lifting me from the floor and crushing me against the orchids in his button-hole.

'You've grown fat,' I tease, when my feet are on the ground again. I reach up and pat the stiffly starched white collar, the monocle dangling from the chain round his neck. So much has happened since I joined the Ballets Russes in Paris all those years ago that it reassures me to find his style of dressing exactly the same.

Diaghilev's heavy-lidded eyes half close and for a moment I fear I have offended him. Then he throws his head back and guffaws.

'And so have you, Lopushka,' he retorts, pinching my waist with stubby, ring-clad fingers. 'I told you eighteen months ago you should have toured South America with us, instead of this soft life of acting and dancing for easy money. Still, a few weeks with Maestro Cecchetti should lick you into shape.'

'He's here?' I glance round, as if my old dance master might appear like a genie from one of the gold filigree lamps.

'He certainly is. Principal character actor. Also in charge of daily class.' Diaghilev's eyes narrow. 'You appreciate I've no big roles for you. Not in New York.'

It is what Josef predicted. When I insisted on meeting Diaghilev anyway he warned that accepting anything less than a solo part would be professional suicide. I refused to listen. 'Diaghilev is a success wherever he tours,' I reminded Josef. 'Besides, I haven't danced – not seriously – for so long I couldn't compete with his latest recruits.'

Diaghilev's attention has returned to the stage and he barks out instructions in Russian and French. A bearded man with black receding hair repeats his orders in English. His translations, though faithful, are liberally seasoned with swear words not present in the original, which make those fluent in all three languages laugh.

'That suits me,' I assure Diaghilev. 'I'm acting in a play at the moment so my time is limited.'

'God's fanny,' the man with the receding hair continues, 'if you lighting men don't get a move on, ruffling American sensitivities will be the least of our worries. It'll be too dark for the audience to see the dancing let alone glimpse any bare tits.' He comes towards me, hand outstretched. 'An honour,' he declares, his dark eyes twinkling. 'I've heard about the mesmerizing Miss Lopokova and I'm humbled to make her acquaintance.' He raises my hand to his lips.

'Randolfo Barocchi, my new manager,' Diaghilev introduces us. 'And these gentlemen,' he indicates a small, seated group, 'represent the Opera House.' He turns to them. 'So what is our verdict? Should we reclaim Miss Lopokova?'

'The play you're currently in…' one queries in English, peering at me through wire-framed spectacles.

'"The Antick",' I help him out. 'About Fourth of July celebrations. I'm girl for most of it then in final scene I'm cowboy. I ride in on billy goat dressed as Pierrot.'

'It's not on Broadway,' the man persists. 'And the ticket prices are what? A dollar and a half? Two? Can't see folks paying the five dollars we'll have to charge.'

I fold my arms across my chest and address Diaghilev directly. 'In St Petersburg, Paris, even London, audiences go to the ballet because they know what ballet is. In this country, for the most part, people don't. Not the kind of ballet you are staging. It will help to include a name Americans are familiar with. I'm proficient in English and you'll need dancers the press can interview.' I point as the arc lights are switched on revealing the sumptuous interior of an exotic pleasure palace. '"Scheherazade" parties might be all the rage in Europe, but this country is prudish about the body still. If you want American women to wear harem pants and lounge on floor cushions, someone they've heard of must show them how.'

'Ha!' Diaghilev beams at me. 'Quite the Impresaria! Randolfo, what is your opinion?'

'That we must not lose such a persuasive and charming person.' Randolfo flashes me a grin.

'So that's settled,' Diaghilev announces, pressing his monocle firmly into his eye as if to fend off any objections the men from the Opera House might make. He links his arm through mine, dropping his voice to a conspiratorial whisper. 'Now, what's this rumour you're engaged to an American?'

I chuckle. I had forgotten how nosey Diaghilev is, especially when it concerns members of his company. 'His name's Heywood Broun, and he's the theatre critic for *The New York Tribune*. We're not strictly engaged though he has asked.'

Randolfo, who has overheard our conversation, interrupts. 'Useful to have an American husband, especially while this absurd war in Europe drags on. Even we Italians haven't been able to resist joining in.'

Diaghilev shudders. 'Warsaw overrun by Germans.'

'And Nijinksy? Is it true he's been arrested?' It is a risk, mentioning Nijinksy, after Diaghilev sacked him for marrying a junior dancer. I only dare because of a report Léonide Massine, whom I remember from School, has replaced Nijinksy both as principal dancer and Diaghilev's lover.

To my relief, Diaghilev is not angry. He draws me to one side.

'It might be possible to bring Nijinksy to America. Negotiations are taking place for his release and King Alfonso – with whom I'm organizing a summer tour later this year – has offered passage on a Spanish ship. If Germany honours its pledge not to attack neutral vessels he'll be safe enough. It amazes me we all somehow sailed the Atlantic without being torpedoed.' He touches his forehead and shoulders in the sign of the cross. 'I scarcely slept a wink the whole time we were at sea remembering the Lusitania.' He surveys the stage. 'Talking of drowning, those imbeciles will bleach the entire set with their lamps if I don't stop them. But it's agreed,' he calls, striding towards the technicians, 'you'll dance for us.'

Randolfo shows me out, entertaining me with funny stories about preparations for the coming production. When we reach the auditorium door he holds it open. 'So what's he like, this Heytree?' he jokes.

'Handsome, intelligent, kind,' I reply, ignoring the deliberate mangling of his name. 'He adores me. What more could a woman wish for?'

'And will you marry him?'

He appears younger in the bright light of the corridor, thirty at most. 'You know how it is. When you're far from home it's easiest simply to go along with things. Until,' I add, noticing how smooth his skin is, as if he bathes every night in oil, 'something occurs to remind you who you are.'

We have reached the foyer where a taxi driver is waiting to take me to the theatre. Randolfo kisses my hand again. 'So there's hope for me.'

❧

It is midnight but the air is still warm against my bare shoulders and arms. We are in Madrid, sitting outside one of the busy restaurants in the Puerta del Sol where candles on the tables illuminate the laughing, animated faces of diners. The square itself is thronged with people: black-frocked matrons gossiping on benches; men squatting on their haunches to play dice; lovers stealing kisses under cover of darkness; children lolling sleepily against their elders. I finish my cigarette and smile at my companion, Igor Stravinsky, who has recently arrived in the city to conduct the Spanish premiere of 'The Firebird'.

'I'm happy,' I announce, flinging my arms wide as if to scoop in the scene before me and hug it close. 'I'm dancing all my old roles with the Ballets Russes, King Alfonso pays our bills, and even Diaghilev appears content. Best of all, we've two months' holiday once we end here before we're due back in America.'

Stravinsky listens, not in the closed way most people do but as a musician might, following the surface meaning of my words as well as their substrata of feeling. His dark eyes bore into me, as if they too are instruments of hearing. His straight black hair is combed flat against his scalp so his face is almost oval, except for his ears which protrude slightly. He has beautiful ears, like the curves on a violin scroll.

'America,' he repeats, placing his knife and fork so precisely across his plate he might have measured the distances with a butler's stick. 'Is that where you plan to spend your life?'

I gaze out into the square. The crowd is starting to thin as children are led away to bed. I watch a mother, no older than I am, lift her already sleeping son to her shoulder, his cheek pressed against hers. 'If I could, I'd go home.'

'Except you can't be sure home exists anymore.'

His matter-of-factness unnerves me. Stravinsky aligns the long points of his fingers, as if in prayer. 'Millions of Russian soldiers dead or captured. The Tsar himself a prisoner. No one knows who's in charge. These are frightening times. Your own family is safe I hope?'

'My youngest brother has just graduated into the Mariinsky.'

Stravinsky leans into the circle of light cast by the candle on our table and smiles.

'What?'

'Half my childhood was spent at the Mariinsky. My father sang in the opera and we had a box.' He folds his napkin into a neat triangle and sets it beside his glass. 'Mother was petrified I'd catch cholera even walking the few streets to the theatre. Do you remember the stench from the cesspools at the back of every building? St Petersburg may have glittered like any other great capital with its art and palaces, but no one dared drink a drop of its water.'

A waiter removes our plates and offers us dessert.

'Food seems plentiful here,' I remark once we have placed our order.

'One of the benefits of keeping out of the war. Though whether Spain can escape its menace entirely is debatable. I hope it can.' Stravinsky leans back from the candlelight so his features once again blur into shadow. 'I like it here. I like how people stay out late, enjoying the cool and each other's company instead of cloistering themselves away behind barred shutters. It caught me off guard to begin with. I travelled on the night train and there was no one at my hotel when I arrived. Even though it was past nine o'clock the staff were still asleep.'

'Is that what made you come? Late nights and the chance to sleep past breakfast.'

'I came because Diaghilev insisted.'

'And you always obey Diaghilev?'

'He pointed out King Alfonso would expect the composer to attend.' His answer is delivered so seriously I realise he has not understood my teasing.

'That would be to distract the King from my Fried Bird performance.' I wag my head and flap my arms in mocking parody of my dance until at last he shares the joke. He is less austere when he laughs and I search for a fresh anecdote to amuse him. 'At least the ballerina I play in your "Petrushka" is meant to be wooden. It will suit me perfectly! Is Diaghilev's story true – that the idea came to you after a night out in St Petersburg, drinking with the droshky drivers and listening to them play their garmoshka?'

'Ah, the garmoshka.' He drums his fingertips to invoke its reedy, fairground sound, then works his arms to pump air into invisible bellows.

'How is Nijinksy?' he wonders, stopping the mime. 'He was sublime as Petrushka.'

'In America with the Ballets Russes, his wife and daughter in tow. Diaghilev staged a grand reunion. The only difficulty was Nijinksy refused to dance until Diaghilev paid him all the money he owed. We were terrified the entire tour would be cancelled.'

The waiter brings our desserts and a dish of ripe peaches. Stravinsky selects one and presses it to his nose.

'So now America adores Nijinsky.'

I dig my spoon into my flan, taste caramel, orange, sweet cream. '*Bien sûr*. But it's also scandalized. Americans like sex as much as the rest of us, only they can't admit they do. Not publicly. When Nijinsky first danced his faun to Debussy's music the audience could hardly have been more outraged if he'd committed murder. After that, he had to pretend he was wistfully dreaming instead of what's in the choreography – masturbating because he lusts after the maidens.' I pause to devour the remainder of my dessert, cleaning the sticky sauce from the plate with my fingers. 'Revealing almost any part of the body creates a rumpus. In Boston, the mayor threatened to close the theatre if a dancer appeared on stage who was not fully clothed.'

Stravinsky caresses the downy skin of his peach. 'I was at the bullfighting with Diaghilev yesterday. He told me he won't return to America.'

'He's always threatening not to sail – ever since a gypsy predicted he'll die at sea.'

'Crossing the Atlantic's dangerous. There've been notices in the papers. If a ship's captured by the enemy, anyone with an allied passport will be taken prisoner.'

'Let's hope we're boarded by our own side!'

'You're not frightened?'

'There were horses on the boat coming over, being transported to the front lines. We could hear them stamping and squealing in terror from below deck. It was enough to alarm the bravest of us. But,' I continue, a new consideration occurring to me, 'who'll take charge of the company if Diaghilev doesn't return?'

'Nijinsky.'

I shake my head, incredulous. 'He has as much organizing ability as a troop of squabbling monkeys.'

'It's what Diaghilev hinted,' Stravinsky comments indifferently. 'Why, would it make a difference as to whether or not you go back?'

I replace my spoon on my plate. I feel suddenly tired, as if the long day of rehearsals followed by tonight's performance has caught up with me. 'I don't have a choice. There's no work in Europe once we finish here. Or in Russia. I've been away too long.'

Stravinsky slices his peach into precisely equal quarters. 'I was in

Lausanne the day I heard the Tsar had abdicated. I'll go back as soon as it's possible. There was a great deal wrong with the old order. Now Russia can start anew.'

'Your wife's Russian isn't she? Does she want to return?'

'Katya is ill, so we must wait.' Stravinsky frowns. 'And your husband?'

I flush. I still find it hard to believe I am married.

'You are newly weds,' Stravinsky persists. 'You must miss him.'

'He does a first-rate impersonation of Diaghilev,' I offer, picturing Randolfo in his tailored American tweed and beige trilby.

'He makes you laugh,' Stravinsky nods approvingly. 'Katya takes care of my soul. Or tries to.'

He waits, as if expecting me to reveal more about Randolfo, but though I am enjoying our conversation and have no wish to keep secrets from him, there is nothing to tell. My mind rifles through the weeks in New York when I was dancing for Diaghilev again and Randolfo became my constant companion, to the months on tour and his suggestion we marry. I saw no reason to refuse him. Unlike Josef, whose interest in me was financial, Randolfo understands my desire to work with the Ballets Russes. Even Heywood, whose marriage proposal I briefly accepted, would have preferred my dancing career to be over so we could, as he phrased it, 'settle down'. Although Randolfo's role in the company is managerial, he fits into its intimate, gossipy ranks as if he were family. 'An Italian passport will enable you to travel as easily as an American one,' Randolfo promised, quashing what he judged to be Heywood's advantage, 'if not more so, since no one in Europe likes Americans. Besides,' he whispered, pulling me close, 'is it not the case Italians are better lovers?'

Only a handful of diners remain. Our waiter removes his apron and lights a cigarette. We pay our bill and head out into the square, where men on low stools are playing guitars. As we approach, a woman begins to sing, her voice powerful and raw, so that even without knowing the words we comprehend her pain. People gather round her, some clapping the rhythm, while others improvise bold, contrasting patterns. Stravinsky touches my arm.

'Notice how they build on the melody, decorating it, altering it, so that what we hear tonight is different from what we might have heard yesterday or will hear tomorrow. At the same time, there's nothing corrupt about their embellishments. We can't follow the meaning because we are foreigners, but we recognize its searing passion and brutal truth.' He slides his hand under my left breast to feel for my heartbeat and leaves it there. 'This is music, spontaneous, with no other aim save to be itself.'

A space opens in front of the musicians and three women step into it, dressed in long crimson skirts. They have combs in their hair and black lace shawls draped over their shoulders. Two attach castanets to their fingers, while the third hoists the ruffle at her hem and sways her hips. Suddenly she stamps down on her heels and executes a sequence of rapid-fire steps on the cobbles. Her free hand and arm undulate in lithe, serpentine rings. I watch entranced. Stravinsky joins in the clapping, smiling whenever he correctly anticipates the downbeat marked by the hammer tap of the woman's heels. Those standing round us nudge each other in approval.

More women break through the crowd, some pulling their men after them. I study how they bend their knees and keep their bodies still, so all the movement is in the lower legs, arms and eyes. I kick up the edge of my skirt and tuck it in my waistband, attempt a few sharp clicks with my heels. Stravinsky encourages me, but I will not let him get away with merely observing. I position his hands on my hips, set mine on his shoulders. We move timidly at first but then with increasing pleasure and abandon, until it no longer matters that the woman sings in a language I do not understand. I sense that what this music expresses is the immutable, sexual yearning of body for body.

It is late when Stravinsky walks me to my hotel. When we reach my room I am reluctant to let him go and invite him inside for a nightcap. As I unlock the door, my marriage to Randolfo seems as distant as if it were someone else it had happened to. I open a bottle of the fortified wine the locals call Jerez.

'You shouldn't always trust Diaghilev,' Stravinsky remarks as I pour. 'Years ago, I saw a ballet at the Mariinsky in which a young dancer played a scheming girl at the carnival. Her name was Columbine and she was sweet and childlike yet also roguish – as if she dealt with the devil. I wrote "Petrushka" because of that girl, not the droshky drivers.'

I laugh, thrust out my chin, and am Columbine again. 'And which of my ballerina selves for "Petrushka" shall you like?' I demand, passing him wine. 'The cruel girl who shuns true love? The vain one tempted by the handsome Moor? The scared one fleeing from the Charlatan? Or the sad girl realising too late what she's lost?'

Stravinsky raises his glass. 'All of them.'

Angry shouts erupt outside my dressing room door. I exchange glances with my dresser, preoccupied with reshaping a pair of feathered wings for tonight's performance. Ever since rejoining the Ballets Russes in America it has been one crisis after another. As director, Nijinsky has proved as capricious and troublesome as the Long Waves that periodically flood the streets of St Petersburg. Only yesterday, as we left Dallas, he strode about the train declaring that since the old hierarchies in Russia have been overturned he was renouncing his place as principal dancer and sharing out his roles. Today, when we arrived in Houston, he darted into a candy store and bought lollipops for the entire company, gleeful as a child. I flop into a chair, not caring that I will crush my net skirt. After months on tour it is crumpled beyond anything my dresser can do to straighten it. I know I should go out into the corridor, help defuse whatever fresh disaster is unfolding, but I shrink from the task. On his worst days, Nijinsky is capable of locking himself in his room and speaking to no one.

There is a knock. I brace myself anticipating Nijinsky, but instead it is Randolfo, wearing his now familiar hang-dog face. I stare at him, this man I have married, with his sunken eyes and weak chin. He is as incapable of solving the current calamity as a pan of warm milk.

'He's gone too far this time,' Randolfo moans, removing a bouquet from the chair opposite mine and sinking into it. 'At least we still have one admirer', he observes, reading the card pinned to the flowers.

It is on the tip of my tongue to enquire if the purpose of his visit is to inspect tributes from my well-wishers, but I refrain. He is here because he hopes I will intervene in whatever the latest drama is. Despite Diaghilev retaining him as manager, Randolfo dare not cross Nijinsky. The problems started in New York, when Nijinsky fell so far behind with the new ballets he was creating the first performances had to be postponed. When they could be postponed no further, they were premiered in such an incomplete state whole sections had to be improvised. The dancers staged a two-day strike, which prompted Nijinsky's wife to claim her husband's career was being sabotaged. Randolfo complained to Diaghilev, who refused to listen on the grounds it is Nijinsky audiences will pay to see.

'Have you wired Diaghilev?' I quiz, referring to the other emergency menacing our tour. 'It's weeks since we've been paid. No one has any money left. We've shared it all out. This includes me, Randolfo. Whatever savings I brought with me are gone.'

Randolfo slumps in his chair, his arms cradling the balding crown of his head, so his voice, when he answers, is muffled. 'Nijinksy refuses to dance "Les Sylphides", which is what's advertised for tonight and what the public is expecting. Scenery, props, lighting, costumes – everything's ready for "Les Sylphides". But Nijinsky objects and insists we perform "Carnival" instead.'

I laugh, I cannot stop myself. Though the seriousness of the situation is not lost on me, Randolfo's aggrieved expression, and the prospect of Nijinksy dressed as a harlequin chasing sylphs across the stage, remind me of my brothers fighting over which pudding mother should cook.

'For heaven's sake,' I fume, when I have caught my breath. 'Where is Nijinsky? In his dressing room?'

'I suppose so,' Randolfo mumbles.

I turn to my dresser. 'Fetch the stage-manager. Tell him to bring his keys.'

While she does this, I contemplate Randolfo. His shoulders are hunched forward, his face buried in his hands. Every now and then he omits a low, self-pitying whimper. I want to slap him.

The stage-manager arrives. I lead him along the corridor to Nijinsky's door, which I open without knocking. When he sees my skirt he complains I am improperly dressed. I ignore him and survey his room. His wig for "Les Sylphides" is on its stand, his long-sleeved shirt with the silk tie and black poet's tunic freshly ironed over a chair. 'Much as I should like to dance Columbine in "Carnival",' I inform him, 'it's not what we've rehearsed.' I indicate his costume. 'Now get changed.'

I shut the door behind me and instruct the stage-manager to lock it, making him swear he will not let Nijinksy out until he is correctly attired for 'Les Sylphides'.

I return to my own dressing room, wondering if we have the resources to stage 'Carnival' on our tour. I do this not to appease Nijinksy but because I should relish dancing Columbine again. Though I have heard nothing from Stravinsky since we said goodbye in Spain, I know from mutual friends he still asks after me. As I open my door, Randolfo springs to his feet.

'It's alright,' I reassure him. 'Just prepare Nijinsky's understudy.' The dresser signals my wings are ready and I stand before her so she can attach them. 'Personally, I wouldn't care if someone else does step in,' I confide to Randolfo. 'Nijinsky might dance like a god but he's the devil himself to partner. Did you notice in our pas de deux yesterday how he removed his hand during the second lift? I was petrified he'd drop me.' I look at my husband, but instead of commiserating he is beaming from ear to ear. He reminds me of father after a quarrel with mother, naively confident life will resume as normal. The comparison makes me cruel.

'It will be wonderful having Diaghilev back in charge.'

Randolfo's smile freezes, as if caught by a camera. 'I thought Diaghilev wouldn't return to America.'

'He won't.' The dresser gives the wires in my wings a final tweak and releases me. I pick up the bouquet from the floor and tear open the wrapping. 'But there's nothing to prevent me joining him in Europe.'

Randolfo's face darkens. He is beginning to sense where this discussion is leading. 'But you can't....'

I release roses and lilies and search for a vase.

'But I can.' The irony that my status as his Italian wife makes my travelling permissible is lost on neither of us.

'You would risk crossing the Atlantic? Now, with all the torpedoes?'

'I'll take my chance.' I set my chin. 'It couldn't be worse than staying here.'

Randolfo leans back in his chair. He knows he is defeated. 'So Diaghilev has a new ballet.'

'About circus artists, selling tickets for their show.' I abandon my hunt for a vase, empty the contents of the waste paper bin onto the floor and arrange the flowers in it. 'Diaghilev swears it will cause a sensation.'

❦

'Well!' I wolf-whistle at Pablo Picasso. 'Diaghilev might have arm-twisted Paris' rich and famous into attending tonight's premiere, but you'll outshine the lot!' I finger the gold trim and sequins on his evening jacket, his immaculate white shirt and perfectly knotted bow tie. 'You must have smiled exceptionally sweetly at one of the dressers. I, on the other hand, have to wear this.' I tug at the blue bodice and hose decorated with white stars he has devised for my role in the ballet. 'I don't care if I dance as a girl or boy, but this makes me look like I have no sex at all.'

'Nonsense.' Picasso clears a space on my dressing table and removes tubes of paint from his pocket. 'You'd be sexy dressed in a postbag!' He squeezes cobalt blue onto his fingers and rubs it over my bare arms, ignoring my screams that he is tickling.

'I'd have preferred a net skirt,' I retort, referring to his front curtain in which we all feature: the librettist Jean Cocteau as a red-suited harlequin; Diaghilev a sailor despite his terror of the sea; me standing on the back of white-winged Pegasus; the composer Erik Satie in a flat hat and cross-garters strumming a guitar.

Picasso's heavy fringe flops over his eyes and he smoothes it back with his hand, streaking his hair blue. He asks if this is my first visit to Paris.

'I was here in 1910,' I tell him. 'It seems a different city. The streets are deserted, the electricity comes and goes, and the bakers no longer sell pastries.'

'It's the war. We're not so far from the fighting.' He applies white to the top of my chest and throat. His touch is sensuous, exploratory, as if the effect he is after will be achieved as much by feeling and instinct as by deliberation and design.

'Nervous?' He takes a step back to assess his work.

'A little. It's a challenging part.'

'But you're not nervous because of the ballet?' He searches for a cloth, fails to find one, wipes his hands on his shirt so it too is stained blue.

'You mean because it isn't what the audience will be expecting: men stomping about in those colossal papier-mâché contraptions you've concocted to the sound of gun shots and foghorns!' I pull out a stool, sit so I am facing him. 'Do you remember what Diaghilev said at the first rehearsal about hoping to do more than entertain? It's why he invited Cocteau for the story line, Erik for the music, you for the costumes and sets. He wants ballet to be taken seriously.'

Picasso screws the tops back on his paints and returns them to his pocket. 'But at best it'll only last a few performances. Even if records are kept, your work will be lost.' Now that his hands are free he gesticulates as he talks, as if sculpting his words out of air.

'If you're anything like other artists I know, finished pictures don't interest you,' I counter. 'All that matters is the one you're working on. And who's to say what an audience will take away with them? Or what they'll pass on to others?'

'Touché!' Picasso's laugh is surprisingly infectious. 'So what will you do next?'

'Diaghilev has been muttering about London, though I doubt he means to cross the Channel while it's being patrolled by German submarines. Even if he manages it, I'm not certain he'll have a part for me. He can hardly bill me as his young protégée anymore. In that sense you're right. A dancer's career is short.'

A stage-hand with a clipboard puts his head round the door. Picasso kisses me affectionately and disappears to join Diaghilev. The overture is beginning as I reach the wings, its brooding strings muted so it is possible to hear the coughs and chatter of the audience as they settle in their seats. I greet my partner, Nicholas Zverev, and we make our way to a gap in the side curtain to prepare our entrance. Across from us Léonide Massine, who has choreographed the ballet, waits too.

The front curtain, with Picasso's cartoon, rises onto a stage glowing with white light, like a cinema screen before the images are projected. The floor cloth is white and as the powerful, thousand-watt lamps Diaghilev has purchased are trained onto it becomes difficult to view directly. Instead, the eye veers away, squinting, dazzled, perplexed. The stage is framed by American-style skyscrapers, their irregular outlines and crooked windows cut out in black and white. At first glance they might be mistaken for ladders so tall their destinations can only be guessed at. They lean, threateningly, as if they might at any moment collapse. Beneath them are two balustrades, one partially engulfed by flames, the other displaying the silhouettes of a woman with a sickle and a horse's head. In a break between the facades a white cloth has been positioned at an angle, its edges patterned with unsubtle curlicues and a harp.

There is an audible gasp as a giant strides onto the stage. He must be ten feet tall and the first impression is of a man with a billboard, though it is strange this should be green and scalloped at the edges like the rough sketch of a cloud. He wears a top hat and his face is half black, half white, with his eyes a circle, and his mouth suggested by a weighty handlebar moustache. A smoking pipe, some three feet long, hangs from what one supposes might be lips, supported by a false arm manipulated from inside the papier-mâché tower. The other arm is the dancer's own and taps a cane noisily enough for it to be heard above the orchestra.

To a fanfare of trumpets, a red and yellow-coated Massine springs onto the stage, his movements halting, as if his limbs are mechanical rather than human and manipulated by strings. His legs and arms act independently, so that his body appears divided from itself. What might have been a series of imposing leaps are fractured by his elbows sticking out at right angles and sharp bends in his ankles and knees.

Between each leap he dances an arabesque with head and torso parallel to the floor, a long Chinaman's pigtail swinging from his red and yellow jester's cap. Though his costume indicates a conjuror he has the white-painted face of a clown. The music switches to circus tunes as the tubas pelt out an oompah beat to the crash of cymbals. Massine arrives centre stage and with an exaggerated gesture raises an invisible object to his lips. His eyes open wide and his cheek muscles flex as if he is about to swallow it. What the object might be is a mystery.

A second giant blunders on, in every way the counterpart of the first except that instead of a pipe glued to his mask-mouth a megaphone is fixed there instead. He holds a board advertising the name of our ballet, 'Parade', and has a flag pole with flags attached to his shoulder. Strapped to his sides are what might be rolled up newspapers, as if he is a newsstand and the papers are for sale. The oompah beat turns into a military march punctuated by the screech of air raid sirens. I clap my hands to my ears to shut out the din.

Flutes and violins play a fast skipping step as a young girl enters, dressed in a white pleated skirt and blue school blazer. She has on knee-length socks and tap shoes, and her loose hair is topped by an oversize Alice bow. There is a clatter of typewriter keys, whose tack-tack-pause, tack-tack-pause she repeats with her feet. Her routine includes the pinwheel turns of ragtime, and a mime sequence inspired by Charlie Chaplin and the melodramatic antics of Pearl White. There is even an escape section based on the sinking of the Titanic, though it seems unlikely anyone in the audience will realise this. Cocteau proposed shouting out explanations but Diaghilev overruled him, arguing it was better for those watching to forge their own connections.

Next is the pantomime horse who performs to no music at all. Although its body, comprised of two dancers disguised in brown sacking, is familiarly comic, its flat, elongated face with pin-dot eyes and colossal teeth is not. But if the face is intended to scare, the creature's movements signal an emotion far more mundane as it embarks on a four-count shuffle, bows awkwardly, then rears so it is standing on two legs. To my surprise the public has grown silent, though whether this is in appreciation, confusion or vexation is impossible to know.

It is our cue and Nicholas hoists me to his shoulder. We are circus acrobats and I take a deep breath as he transports me centre-stage. I balance, release his hand, and swoop my arms over my head as if they are wings and I am a flying bird. I bend my knees and turn out my feet so that when he sets me down I am already in plié. He lifts me again, and this time I twist in a half-circle until I am in a handstand position suspended in mid-air. I have forgotten the soldiers dying on the battlefields, the fuel-shortages and famine in Russia, money worries or where I will go after Paris, and my foolhardy marriage to Randolfo. All that exists are these movements I am making. It does not matter that nothing will survive or even that this may be my last appearance as a ballerina. It is enough to be immersed in this moment of dancing.

The marching music returns for the grand finale though the mood is scarcely one of triumph. Whatever the giants were engaged in has failed and it seems likely the performance they were touting will fail too. Our steps become increasingly frenzied, almost desperate, until with a shudder the pantomime horse collapses. As the curtain comes down, the shouts and whistles from the auditorium erupt into a riot of wild applause and scornful jeers. 'It's sur-real, beyond true!' 'Cowards, you should be fighting at the front!' I gaze up at the box where Diaghilev, Picasso and the others are sitting. 'We've done it,' I want to cheer. 'We've stirred people up, shaken them from their complacency.' As I take my bow I raise my arms to Diaghilev in homage. 'Who gives a fig if they love or loathe our Parade,' I bellow up at him, not caring that my words will be lost in the furore. 'This is what we worked so hard for. This is Art.'

ACT THREE

'The Firebird appears in response to the Prince's summons. She dances, drawing the sorcerer Koschei and his demons along with her until they fall into an exhausted slumber. The Firebird knows that to restore harmony she must destroy the source of Koschei's power. This is the secret of immortality which he has hidden inside a golden casket. As the Prince breaks the casket open Koschei is turned to stone and all those he has bewitched are released. The Prince and Firebird celebrate their freedom with a dance.'

It is spring and the Linden trees that line both sides of the Boulevard Haussmann are in leaf. At a table outside one of the many cafés, Lydia and Vera sit drinking coffee and smoking. They attract curious glances, though not because they are speaking Russian. Paris, like London and Berlin, has grown accustomed to Russian émigrés fleeing first the revolution, then the ravages of civil war and six years of Bolshevik rule. For this is April 1924, and while the increasingly dictatorial Lenin died in January, there is little indication conditions will improve under any of his possible successors. Nor is it the women's appearance that causes heads to swivel and conversations to hush, for though Vera is striking in turquoise velvet and daringly short shingled hair, Lydia has joined her straight from rehearsal and wears a plain cotton pinafore over her dance tunic. What catches the notice of the other café patrons is that Lydia is weeping.

'Cry,' Vera urges her, 'it's a tragedy and you of all people must feel it.'

'Dancers are cursed. And the most talented are cursed hardest of all,' Lydia howls. 'First Tamara, who was kind to me at School and whose technique remains unrivalled, living in a cheap boarding house with scarcely the means to pay her rent. Now Nijinksy – the arms and legs of my heart – failing even to recognise me. Me! When we've partnered each other since we were teenagers.' She wipes her eyes on her sleeve. 'And the curse has landed on me. I feel it in my marrow. Just when it seemed I was happily to become Mrs Keynes and all my worries were behind me.'

Vera, who has travelled to Paris with the express purpose of cheering her friend, opens her beaded evening purse and passes Lydia a handkerchief.

'What happened during Nijinksy's visit?'

'His wife arranged it. The doctors hoped the ballet might rouse him from this terrible depression he's sunk into. But nothing stirred him. Even when I kissed him it was as if I was made out of paper and he could stare right through me.' She lets out a wail so despairing even the waiter, immune to such scenes after thirty years serving at café tables, must clasp his tray with both hands to prevent the glasses of pastis from spilling. 'I didn't always like Nijinsky,' Lydia admits, accepting the handkerchief and blowing her nose, 'his soul is too full of holes. Except when he's on stage. Then his soul fills up and it's as if god himself is dancing.' She pats Vera's arm. 'Thank you for coming.'

'Nonsense,' Vera protests, though she is touched. 'I could hardly leave you to fend alone. That said, dearest Lidulechka, the hotel in the Boulevard Raspail does not seem so awful, and nor do I believe you can be very lonely given how many visitors have flocked to Paris to watch you perform. Little did I dream when I dressed for the gathering at Picasso's studio this evening that the whole of Bloomsbury would be there.'

'Not everyone,' Lydia interrupts. 'Duncan, Clive and Vanessa. And they're not only here for the ballet. Clive's writing about Picasso again.'

The wistful note in her voice does not go undetected, but Vera ignores it. She has spotted Maynard's photograph besides Lydia's bed and attempts to steer their talk into safer terrain. 'I'm to write a review, for *The Nation*. On Massine's new venture so of course I shall feature you. What intrigues me are these rumours of full-scale war between Massine and Diaghilev. Who will win if they're true?'

'No contest. That old Buddha Diaghilev is the victor every time – though actually I should invent a new name for him. Catherine the Great perhaps. He's guilty of monstrous acts – like leaving his dancers in the lurch when he runs out of money – but he knows how to take charge. Unlike Massine or his feeble fop of a sponsor, who might have staged glamorous costume balls but is incapable of producing a ballet. The other night he insisted we sit through an interminable lighting display that looked like a mess of raw eggs, because he wanted to impress the Queen of Romania.' Lydia, warming to her topic, tucks Vera's handkerchief into her cuff. 'On one occasion Diaghilev stationed himself outside the box office and accused Massine of theft, stealing his ideas and artists. I had to bite my tongue not to laugh. Still, it can be galling when Diaghilev's claques disrupt us with their heckling.'

'Massine must have his own claques.'

'He does, but the stingy insect won't pay them properly so their applause gets drowned out.'

'When does Diaghilev's ballet open?'

'Middle of May.'

'And should you prefer to be dancing for Diaghilev?' Vera finds her cigarette case and opens it.

'He wouldn't employ me. Sent word via Walter I've grown too fat.' Lydia selects a De Reszke and pauses to light it. 'He's right. A dancer's career is both cursed and short. It's all over by forty.'

'You're thirty-three,' Vera reminds her. 'And Massine chose you for his leading lady.'

'Sneaky lying devil!' Lydia slams down her fist with such force that the waiter, engaged in stacking their empty coffee cups, jumps back in alarm. 'Lured me with a promise I could name my fee then as soon as I agreed retracted the offer, making out it was all his sponsor's fault in underestimating how much ballet cost.' Her eyes well with tears and she retrieves Vera's handkerchief from her sleeve. 'I've already spent the measly £200 he paid me this month. And he refuses to reimburse for all the new material we must learn. I wouldn't mind if any good came from the extra rehearsals, but he behaves like a bear. And he knows my poor knee is shot.' She massages it tenderly.

Vera orders fresh coffee. She has often listened to Lydia complain about Massine and her returning to this topic now reassures her. Ever since the debacle of Lydia's holiday with Maynard in Dorset, Vera has abandoned her efforts to remain neutral. She is now firmly of the opinion that the affair should end. This latest association with Massine is not only a welcome distraction, it should render Lydia financially solvent again. Vera has been dismayed to learn from one of her friend's chance remarks that Maynard is still supplying her with money.

'You must be pleased with the piece Massine created for you?'

'The one where I dance a jilted lover is not so awful. But "Mercury" is a disaster. It was Cocteau's idea to base it on the Roman god. But then Massine stole Satie from Diaghilev for the music and Cocteau and Satie fell out. Picasso – arch rascal that he is – stepped in and had a field day. At one point three male dancers sit in a bath and pretend to be the graces wearing giant false breasts.' She giggles. 'But that's not the worst. There's also a ballet by that fool of a sponsor which doesn't even have the merit of comedy. He insists on it purely for his vanity.'

The coffees arrive. Lydia stirs sugar into hers and blows on it to cool. She appears calmer and as soon as their bill is paid Vera suggests they should be on their way.

It is only a short walk to Picasso's studio. The front door to the building is propped open by a headless and limbless Grecian statue. There is the hum of people talking as the two women enter the narrow hall. One voice penetrates above the rest. Lydia concentrates for a moment then mouths 'Clive' at Vera. 'Ballet should emulate great art,' they hear, 'not aim to mirror life. It must expose the underlying patterns and energies.'

To their right is a spiral staircase and as they start towards it another voice intervenes. 'Surely it needs to retain a connection to the person or object that inspires it?'

'Vanessa,' Lydia whispers, stopping so abruptly Vera almost collides into her.

'Chin up,' Vera whispers back. 'This is Paris, not Gordon Square. Vanessa's the visitor here.'

'*La voilà*,' Clive proclaims as they come into view, embracing Lydia with such intensity she recoils. 'As you see, we've formed a reception committee on the landing.' He holds out his hand to Vera. '*Enchanté.*'

Vera studies him as they shake hands, taking in the receding auburn hair, the silk cravat instinct tells her has been tied deliberately loosely to give him a bohemian air, the pressed turn-ups on his trousers and sturdy English shoes. Clive keeps her hand longer than he should, perhaps to redeem himself from Lydia's snub. When at last she is released his eyes revert to Lydia, who – Vera is relieved to observe – has shaken off the gloom that has gripped her all afternoon. It is not the first time Vera has witnessed Lydia's chameleon-like transformation from sorrow to joy, an alteration all the more remarkable because it is always sincere. Vera has tried to describe this to her husband Harold, connecting it to her friend's enviable ability to live entirely in the present. This, she speculated, is what gives her dancing dynamism and makes her so magnetic on stage. She watches Lydia now, her arm round the neck of a man with tousled hair and beautiful features she infers must be Duncan. Vanessa (whom she remembers from a party at the Sitwells) is next to him, dressed in a black and yellow check dress with wave-like blue lines and green buttons

There is a shout of recognition from inside the room and a moment later a woman with a heart-shaped face and dark hair hidden beneath a Spanish mantilla is claiming Lydia, covering her face with kisses and talking animatedly in Russian.

'Olga', Lydia confirms. 'We danced together for Diaghilev until she hung up her shoes to marry Pablo.'

They are led past clusters of visitors to a quiet spot by the window. Vera perceives, not without satisfaction, that this leaves Lydia's Bloomsbury neighbours still stranded by the door. There is a cushioned bench beneath the window and Olga sweeps aside the half dozen drawings scattered there before inviting them to sit. For some minutes Vera follows the conversation, listening to news of Olga's three-year old son as well as grumbles about her husband. When their talk moves to unknown acquaintances, she switches her focus to the party. Despite the surprising preponderance of Russian, there is no one Vera feels able to introduce herself to among the motley guests. Instead, she lets her gaze travel the room, which is so full of pictures and unexpected objects it reminds her of being back-stage. She can scarcely count the number of paintings there are so many, some hanging, but most leaning against the walls. Often these are stacked several canvases deep, so that if they are of different heights a curious collage forms. She takes in a woman's head haloed by feathery wings, the tip of an obelisk superimposed on bathers in violently clashing colours.

In addition to finished pictures there are works in progress, some on easels, many resting on furniture. There are even sketches amidst the wine bottles and glasses set on the table for guests. Most of the art Vera supposes to be by Picasso, though some is clearly by other hands. Directly opposite is a sequence of carved wooden face masks she imagines are African. While Vera is not certain she likes what she sees, it intrigues her. She glances at Lydia, still absorbed in her discussion with Olga, and gets up from her seat. The first painting she views is recognisably a guitar, even if its component parts (front with sound hole, fingerboard, strings) are depicted separately, as if the instrument has undergone dissection. Vera picks out what might be the musician's hand and arm, but puzzles over the face. Unless, she conjectures, the viewer must create their own from the jigsaw of shapes.

She looks back to the window, registers the bench is empty. Olga she locates easily, welcoming two new arrivals by the door. Clive and Vanessa have moved to the drinks table; Duncan is flirting with an athletic young man she guesses might be a dancer. There is a second room leading off to the left, but though this is also full of people Lydia is not amongst them. Finally Vera finds her, perched on the rim of a bathtub and staring at a picture of two giantesses striding across sand. They are silhouetted against a radiantly blue sea and sky. The head of one is flung backwards, while the other gazes into the distance. Their clasped hands are raised in a gesture of triumph.

'They look as if they might conquer the world,' Vera remarks, standing beside her friend.

'Don't they. You can almost feel the ground quaking beneath them. They are fearless with no men to trouble them.'

Vera is about to wonder if the pair might be running towards their men, when she realises Lydia is crying.

'Let's go back to the hotel,' she proposes. 'You must be exhausted and you have two performances tomorrow. And Harold will arrive on the night train so I need to be up with the lark.'

At this, Lydia sobs so loudly Vera abandons her attempt to help her to her feet and lead her discretely through the packed rooms.

'You're so lucky to have Harold,' Lydia wails. 'I've no right to wish this, but I should so love Maynard to arrive on the night train too.'

There is a sign on the green rectangle of lawn forbidding anyone who is not a Fellow of King's College to walk there. This Maynard, who is both a Fellow and the College Bursar, ignores. The lawn has been mown in alternating horizontal and vertical lines so straight their intersections give it the air of an outdoor chessboard. Maynard has witnessed the undergraduates playing illicitly on these squares, standing in as chess pieces and sporting armbands to distinguish the warring sides. It has amused him that those captured are instantly redeployed in distracting the porters, who, if the game came to their notice, would be obliged to report the offence.

In a few strides of his long gait Maynard has crossed the grass and is climbing the steps to the Chapel, the stone hollowed in places from the tread of centuries of visitors. Lydia, when she first came to Cambridge, was so moved by the sight of these indentations that she planted her booted feet in them, remaining immobile while Maynard recounted the College's history. She listened attentively as he described how for the first four hundred years only pupils from his old school Eton were offered scholarships, with the special dispensation that they were not required to sit examinations to be awarded a degree. Lydia was wearing a new hat she had decorated with a spray of artificial roses plundered from a dance costume and a silver bell that tinkled continuously. The latter was to remind her to take lungfulls of the gusting Cambridge wind that blew direct from Russia, so she could revivify herself with its air. When Maynard related how the Chapel builders downed tools to protest at the capture of their patron King Henry VI, Lydia – familiar with the Wars of the Roses from one of Maynard's previous English history lessons – gestured to her multi-coloured flowers and claimed this was the reason for her hat. She was, she declared, championing not only the royal rivals with their red and white roses, but all the ordinary men and women caught up in the fighting.

There is a loud swell of organ music as Maynard passes through the wooden screen that divides the Chapel. This was a gift from Henry VIII, and still bears his initials intertwined with those of Anne Boleyn. Lydia relishes the stories of this Henry, whose readiness to execute his wives, ministers and clergy whenever he fell out of love is reminiscent of the Tsars. Maynard takes a seat in the stall reserved for Fellows. As usual at this hour the Chapel is crowded, not only with black-gowned College members but people from the town. He had pointed this out to Lydia, explaining that King's was the only Cambridge College to permit outsiders to join its congregation, a fact of which he is proud. The evening sun streams through the stained-glass windows, patterning the walls and floor with quick-moving, rainbow light. The organ voluntary reaches its climax. Maynard tilts his head and gazes at the famous ceiling, the stone carved as if dozens of fans have been opened so each displays the same extent of its span. When he showed Lydia this she wondered aloud what the fans could be hiding, speculating that since they were in a church it must be deliciously obscene, like dozens of lovers copulating simultaneously. Perhaps because her head was craned backwards and she was unaware of those round her, she had expressed this not in a whisper but distinctly enough for it to be generally audible.

Silence descends on the Chapel. A boy's treble voice, pure and high as if airborne, sings the opening lines of the introit then is joined by others. The Choir enters, preceded by the Dean and Chaplain, and as if at a signal the congregation stands. Maynard observes the choristers in their cassocks, chosen at eight by open audition and educated at the College School. They sing so angelically it is hard to credit these are the same boys he has seen thrashing their opponents on the rugby field, or charming money from tourists by posing in their top hats for photographs while spinning false tales of the town's past. A prayer begins. Out of respect Maynard inclines his head, though he makes no attempt to join in the responses despite knowing the words by heart. He is a regular attendee at Evensong and ready, should this prove necessary, to argue long and hard in its defence. He would, without falsity, contend that the ritual (practised here since the fifteenth century) offers a beneficial opportunity for reflection, as well as a reminder that one's travails and cares are inconsequential if viewed from a sufficiently distant perspective. All this he would assert without any reference to Christian doctrine, and whilst acknowledging the overlaps between his rationale and the justification many would offer for a belief in God. He thinks about all the King's men killed in the war, now honoured in a newly built side chapel. Many of those who enlisted Maynard knew personally, including two fellow Apostles: Rupert Brooke, who died of sepsis on his way to Gallipoli in 1915, and Ferenc Békássy, who joined the Austro-Hungarian army and was killed fighting the Russians in the same year. No one with a clear mind, Maynard concludes as he recites the roll call of names as if it is a private prayer, could subscribe to a God willing to sanction such destruction.

The Choir sings the canticle and Maynard focusses his gaze on the windows, with their vivid portrayals of Biblical scenes. He has heard it reported that the purpose of such depictions was to inform a largely illiterate populace, though he doubts this can have been the case at King's since the scholars would have been able to read. Instead, he surmises, studying two kneeling figures delineated in such detail they seem alive, the motive here can only have been celebration. It is a supposition he connects to yet another Cambridge Apostle, the philosopher George Moore, whose theories are still debated by that select and secret discussion club, including his proposition that what is most valuable is not communion with God but intercourse with one's peers. Maynard is aware this has operated almost as a founding principle amongst those he calls friends, along with an emphasis on the paramount importance of art. He attributes his unwavering concurrence with this latter point to his long-standing admiration for Duncan, though he is also more influenced than he cares to admit by Clive who – while no artist himself – has argued repeatedly art promotes states of thought and feeling that cannot be arrived at through other means. The Dean leads the recitation of the Creed and he turns with the rest of the congregation to face the altar. Maynard would, if pressed, label himself a pragmatist having witnessed first-hand the vanity, prejudice and short sightedness that fueled the war and its aftermath, and yet he cherishes the idealistic hope that if art could be enjoyed more widely good would ensue.

He joins in the hymn, though he has no pretensions about his singing voice. His musings prompt him to remember that his relationship with his London friends is in a parlous state. This astounds him given the main catalyst for the tension has for some months now occupied an uncertain place in his life. While he still sees

Lydia and his solicitor continues to pursue her estranged husband for
a divorce, he is by no means convinced they will marry. Yet this has
not healed the rift in Gordon Square. After his conversation with
Vanessa, in which she told him she would not welcome Lydia for the
summer at Charleston, little has been said between them on the
subject. He is nevertheless aware the view persists that Lydia must not
become a permanent feature of their circle. Lydia herself bears some
responsibility for the animosity, despite her strenuous efforts at
appeasement. It seems there is an inverse equation between Lydia's
attempts to ingratiate herself and a resulting escalation in hostilities,
since her response to rebuttal is often to behave outrageously. The
Dean offers his blessing and the congregation rises. Maynard is glad
Lydia is in Paris and that Vanessa, Clive and Duncan will watch her
perform there. He trusts her collaboration with her old partner
Massine will restore her confidence. He knows she worries she is no
longer the dancer she was. He, for his part, believes she has several
triumphant years ahead of her still, and enough talent to be successful
at whatever she does next. He has read Cyril Beaumont's review of
the ballet she directed with Vera, predicting Lydia's promising future
as a choreographer. The organ plays the final voluntary and he joins
the Dean, Chaplain, Choir and other Fellows in a procession out of
the Chapel.

The porter wishes Maynard a pleasant evening as he enters the
lodge for his post. There is an envelope addressed to him in Lydia's
unmistakable hand, its stamp bearing the naked torsos of sporting
heroes to mark the hosting of the Olympic Games in Paris. Lydia has
inscribed their names on two of these male torsos, encircling both
with a frenzy of asterisks, exclamation marks and the frequently
repeated letter X. Maynard is so eager to read the contents that he
tears it open, instead of waiting as is his custom for the privacy of his
study. Lydia's message is brief but her words thrill him. He is, she
insists, her elixir, without which life is but empty shadow. She misses
him every waking moment and dreams of him at night. She promises
that if he were with her she would kiss every inch of his naked body
with her moist, foxy lips. The porter, unused to Mr Keynes remaining
in the lodge and fearful he might have received unwelcome news,
offers his services. There is a clock above his desk which Maynard
checks, calculating that if he leaves in the next half hour he can catch
the London train and so be in Dover in time for the night ferry.

'Would you ring for a taxi to take me to the station?' he requests.
'I find I am urgently required in Paris.'

&.

Vanessa waits by a table piled with books, newspapers, pens and ink, writing paper, a Kodak camera and open photograph album, her sister's tortoiseshell spectacles and knitting, a tray of spring bulbs for planting. She has always liked this sitting room of Virginia's. Its wooden ceiling beams, earth-coloured floor tiles and the foliage appearing through windows make it seem part of the garden, an effect augmented by pale green walls. Vanessa would like to replicate this blurring of interior and exterior in the studio she dreams of adding to her own house Charleston nearby, creating a space flooded with natural light where she might paint all year round.

At last Virginia appears, huddled in a thick wool cardigan though the weather is mild and the walk from the wooden hut where she writes to the house a short one.

'I lost track of time,' she confesses, kissing Vanessa. 'I wrote nothing for an hour then just as I began to despair words came.'

'The new novel's going well?'

'In fits and starts. I jump one hurdle and flatter myself I can write at full gallop, then some fresh obstacle rears in front of me and my horse shies to a halt. I expect I'm too ambitious.'

'Exactly what you said about "Jacob's Room",' her sister remarks, running her hands over a canvas-work cushion as if looking is not enough and she must feel its pattern with her fingers.

'True,' Virginia admits. 'Though with this one I've always had a strong sense of my central character.' She considers adding that her feelings towards this Clarissa Dalloway, who first surfaced in her writing two decades ago, have altered dramatically since the real-life friend she modeled her on died so tragically. She refrains, not because she wishes to conceal this from Vanessa, but because any attempt to articulate the labyrinthine and largely obscure processes of composition risk fixing the work prematurely and closing off possibilities that might, if explored, prove fertile. 'Would you like to see the orchard before lunch?' she suggests instead. 'The trees are covered in fruit again this year. Not only apples and plums but so many pears we've taken to eating them for breakfast. We've deluged our friends sending parcels. Leonard's baskets when he left for the market in Lewes this morning were so full I feared his bicycle might collapse under the weight.'

They walk along the ash path, through the opening between two flint walls where cordoned pears hang heavy with fruit. Inside the orchard the trees are laden with apples in different states of ripeness, scenting the air and attracting chirruping blackbirds and thrushes. In the long grass buzzing swarms of drunken wasps gorge on fallen fruit. Virginia proudly attributes the abundance of this harvest to Leonard's meticulous care regimen, which frequently requires him to prune in bitter cold or whilst wading ankle-deep in mud. There is a bench in the sun sheltered by one of the walls and the sisters sit on it. They remain for some minutes enjoying the scene in companionable silence.

'I should have brought my paints,' Vanessa sighs.

'You must have fruit enough in the garden at Charleston.'

'We do, but it's peaceful here.' She flexes her hands, her mind casting back to the long, uninterrupted days she and Virginia spent painting and writing together as young women. What futures they had plotted for themselves then. 'Yesterday was entirely lost to Maynard and Lydia. They arrived unannounced declaring they were merely calling in, then stayed for hours. I suspect their motive was to show off Maynard's car.' She balls her hands into fists. 'You wouldn't believe how impossible they are.'

'My mind's still reeling from the horrors of Studland last autumn,' Virginia commiserates, noting Vanessa's sudden melancholy. 'Maynard at breakfast in his leopard-spot dressing gown with Lydia half-naked on his knee, dipping her finger in his egg yolk for Maynard to suck clean.' She glances sideways to confirm this caricature is cheering her sister as she intends. 'Lydia, poker in hand, in the Duke's grand drawing room, triumphantly retrieving her blood-stained knickers from the grate before brandishing them aloft for the world to admire.'

Soothed, Vanessa selects an apple from the grass. 'Still,' she ventures, able to be fair now she has regained her calm, 'we shouldn't be too hard on Lydia. No one would have made a fuss if the blood had come from any other part of her body.'

'So much for the permissive "jazz age",' Virginia muses, recalling the title of an American short story collection. 'It seems one might say or do anything these days – except draw attention to a woman's menses.' Her mind lights on the name of the author – Scott Fitzgerald, she is certain – but since this is unlikely to interest her sister she reverts to the topic of Maynard and Lydia. 'Why were they in Sussex?'

'Viewing Tilton House.' Vanessa bites into her apple. 'Pippin?' she queries.

'We gathered three bushels yesterday just from one tree,' Virginia boasts, choosing a windfall for herself. 'This latest truce can only be temporary. Maynard must tire of Lydia eventually.'

'But will he? Every time it seems their affair is over they find a way to resume. And here they are hunting for a house outside London. Though I swear if they rent in Sussex I shall up sticks to Norfolk.'

As always when her sister threatens to move, Virginia is unnerved. 'There's nothing to bind them. They've no common language, few shared interests and radically different goals. Picture them in ten years' time if they do stay together. Lydia too old to dance but still craving adulation; Maynard unable to write anything of importance and president of so many boards he can talk of nothing but profit and loss.' She stares at her apple, which has been pecked on one side so the flesh is exposed and browning. 'Whichever way you examine it, there's precious little to found a marriage on, and even less to guarantee it will be happy. I suppose a troupe of junior Keynes might secure it.'

'I was under the impression Lydia didn't want children.' Now it is Vanessa's turn to feel alarm. 'She told me once ballerinas dread it more than injury, since they must either give up dancing and get married or contrive a means to support themselves in hiding until after the birth. Unless they rid themselves of the baby in some atrocious way.'

'Maynard and Lydia producing offspring needn't affect you,' Virginia promises, surprised by her sister's reaction.

'Don't you see, it will ruin Duncan's prospects. If it were only marriage to Lydia he might still expect something, but if there are children Maynard is bound to settle everything on them.' She tosses her half-eaten apple into the uncut grass. 'Duncan is Maynard's heir,' she confides.

'And Angelica is Duncan's', Virginia murmurs, understanding at last. Not for the first time she wishes her sister would break her silence, so Angelica might grow up knowing who her father is. She is aware Vanessa is constrained in this by Clive, who fears if his family were to find out it would jeopardise his inheritance. It seems underhand and perilous to maintain the lie indefinitely. 'It can't only be the money,' she conjectures, sensing now is not the moment to raise the issue.

'Of course not. Though I won't pretend I don't lie awake at night worrying, especially with Quentin's school fees to pay in addition to

Julian's. Duncan has no interest in money. He was amazed when I explained Maynard's contribution to Charleston amounted to one third.'

'How does he view the prospect of Maynard and Lydia marrying?'

'As a grim inevitability.' Vanessa swats at a wasp attracted by traces of sugary apple on her fingers. 'He'd prefer us to become friends. He's fond of Lydia.'

'It's possible her divorce suit will fail. It sounds inordinately complicated.'

'There's to be a court case. They were joking about it yesterday – Maynard persuading Lydia to refrain from mouthing obscenities no matter how severely she is provoked. Lydia, on the other hand, seems intent on attending only if she can dress as a man in Maynard's old school blazer and tie. She is contemplating sporting a fake moustache.'

Despite sharing her sister's discomposure over Lydia, Virginia is curious. She has observed how changes of clothes transform people, as well as how men's authority derives more often than not from their robes, medals and other insignia of power. While she has so far witnessed little to endorse Maynard's claim of Lydia's exceptional intelligence, she credits her now for recognizing her marital future will be decided by a male court and for playfully desiring to subvert this.

Vanessa snaps a twig from an overhead branch to wave away the persistent wasp. 'I was remembering the other day how we first got to know Maynard, when we moved to Bloomsbury after father died and Thoby invited his friends on Thursday evenings.' She pronounces their brother's name reverently, as if his death was recent. 'It seemed as I listened to the discussions here was a group determined to live and work as we planned to, without compromise, dishonesty or self-serving.'

Virginia, still mulling Lydia's smart, intrepid scheme of testifying in male attire, speaks up in her defence. 'It takes discipline and dedication to dance well. At least on that score we've no cause for concern. Imagine if Maynard were to hitch himself to a punctilious committee woman who regards art as an indulgence, or worse an opportunity for propaganda.'

'But what Lydia values most are her earnings,' Vanessa counters. 'She's constantly totting up figures in that notebook of hers and informing anyone who'll listen what she is or isn't being paid but should be. It's the same for Maynard's books. I doubt she can quote anything from them with accuracy, but she'll rattle off the tally of copies sold and to which countries.' She picks at the papery, red-gold leaves on her twig. 'I don't mean she isn't serious about ballet, only that her approach is not ours.'

Somewhat to her astonishment, for she not only agrees with her sister but is relishing this rare moment of confidence, Virginia again sides with Lydia. 'It can't have been all plain sailing. At eight she was sent off to train under the Tsar.'

'I don't doubt there've been hindrances,' Vanessa concedes. 'But by her own admission she's been praised and goaded in exactly the right combination from the start. Think how enabling that must be.'

This reflection, comparing Lydia's many engagements and accomplishments with her own difficulties to forge a career as a painter, prompts a different response in her sister. Though Virginia cannot claim to be any more successful (there are still some two hundred copies of her last book gathering dust in the basement in London where she and Leonard house their printing press), what surfaces are her never-quiet doubts that she, a woman, can ever be a writer. How enabling indeed if she could discover a way to silence those doubts. Before she can speculate further on what she might then achieve, Leonard appears through the opening between the walls.

'Lunch,' he proposes, as the sisters rise to greet him.

&

Dressed in her Sunday best and a hat borrowed for the occasion from her new employer, Ruby stands her ground amongst the swarm of journalists and well wishers waiting outside the Registry Office for the married couple to emerge. One of the pressmen, in a rakish trilby, his camera with its flashbulb poised, asks which magazine she writes for. Ruby blushes, not because of his mistaken assumption she is a reporter, but because with his hazel eyes and grin he is handsome. Her reply – that this is her first assignment – strikes her as cunning, since it has been impressed on her she must disclose nothing lest whatever she says find its way into tomorrow's papers. Her honesty pleases her too, for this is indeed her first significant assignment as Miss Lopokova's maid, or Mrs Keynes as she must henceforth call her.

'Mrs Keynes,' she repeats the name to herself. Though it is easier to pronounce than the Russian with its long, bouncing vowels, she likes it less. It seems too plain and ordinary for a woman who has danced on stages all over the world. The handsome reporter in the trilby flips open a notebook, as if he is about to question her. To avoid him, she squeezes past a band of jostling children who have pushed to the front of the crowd for a glimpse of the ballerina, stationing herself on the other side of two women in bath chairs where the view is more restricted and she hopes the reporter will not be tempted to follow. That people should have turned out in such numbers does not surprise her. After all, the new Mrs Keynes is famous, and while Ruby does not suppose many are here on account of the man she is marrying, she is aware he has written books and worked for the government. What has startled her is that only a handful of guests have been invited to attend the short ceremony being held inside the Registry Office. There are the two witnesses – Mr Duncan Grant for Mr Keynes and Mrs Keynes' friend Mrs Vera Bowen – but the only others are Mr Keynes' solicitor, mother, grandmother and sister.

The absence of Mr Keynes' father due to ill health was a blow. Only yesterday Ruby was sent to the post office with a parcel containing remedies for his feet, together with a letter outlining how the remedies were to be administered. She had marveled at these instructions as her mistress wrote them down, while she packed Epsom salts for soaking the feet, honey and garlic to be applied directly to the infected area as both had powerful healing properties, and a bottle of brandy to relieve the agony which, her mistress assured her, was every bit as excruciating as toothache on the toe. When Ruby puzzled over the packet of needles she was informed these were for puncturing the skin so pus could be released, a procedure her mistress had performed many times on herself as well as others. Feet, she explained, are a dancer's brain so one learns to take care of them properly. Ruby was also dispatched to the kitchen to request a batch of biscuits with double the amount of ginger (another efficacious medicine), baked softly since Mr Keynes senior had poor teeth. The cook had raised her eyebrows at this, but since the order came from the woman about to be married to her employer she dutifully increased the proportion of butter and eggs to ensure a more cake-like texture and added an extra teaspoon of powdered ginger.

A policeman posted at the entrance to the Registry Office prevents a woman with a shopping bag from slipping past him. Ruby is glad her mistress has Mrs Keynes senior with her, and that they are fond of each other. Ruby discovered this one afternoon when they were discussing potential wedding outfits. Her mistress confided that while the relationship with her future mother-in-law did not begin well they now had a friendly understanding, especially on the subject of Mr Keynes' health about which they corresponded. Mrs Keynes senior had been impressed by the purchase of a dozen vests from a taylor in Jermyn Street made to her mistress's design, with the aim of reducing the recurrent fevers that periodically grip Mr Keynes since he was ill as a boy. Ruby has heard less about Mr Keynes' grandmother and sister Margaret who are also inside, though his brother Geoffrey, wife and three children have watched her mistress dance at the Coliseum and during a visit to Gordon Square. The latter was the first time Ruby saw her mistress perform, and was amazed at the effortless manner in which she leaped in the air and ran on the tips of her toes in her special shoes. It had concerned Ruby that none of her mistress' family could be present at the ceremony, but was cheered when she learned Mr Keynes' wedding gift was a trip to Russia, where her mistress will be reunited with her mother, sister and brothers after a separation of fifteen years.

The journalist in the trilby has found his way to her side, wondering now about the location of the reception party. Ruby, blocked by the two bath chairs and an increasing swell of people behind her, decides her only recourse is to feign ignorance and pretend she has no idea. Too late, she reflects she might have served her mistress better by picking a plausible venue to throw the journalist off the scent, steering him away from Gordon Square where a party is to be held. It is no secret this is where the couple will live when they are in London, facilitated by the transfer of Mrs Bell and Mr Grant to number 37 – a move that has provoked a level of wrangling and animosity Ruby would not have believed possible amongst those whose conversation frequently turns to the welfare of others. Though more guests have been invited to the party than to the Registry Office, this too will be an unostentatious affair. Ruby imagines further celebrations are planned for the couple's holiday in August at the house they have rented near Lewes, to which Mr Keynes has asked numerous friends. When she suggested this, however, her mistress pulled a face and insisted that half the friends were horrors, including a Cambridge philosopher called Ludwig Wittgenstein to whom it was impossible to say good morning without an interrogation into what you might mean.

Ruby checks the time with the policeman on duty, estimating from his reply that the short ceremony will have started and it can only be a few minutes before the couple appear. When they do it will be her task to step forward and escort her mistress as quickly as possible into one of the waiting taxis. She glances round but there is such a crowd in the street she cannot see to where the cars are parked. Several reporters, including the one in the trilby, seem to reach the same conclusion and ready their cameras. Ruby wishes she had advised her mistress to dress in a cloak since it might have acted as a shield. Even a wide-brimmed hat, such as the pale straw with the pink ribbon Ruby longed for her to wear, would have screened her better than the skull-hugging cloche she eventually settled on. For the hundredth time, Ruby regrets not trying harder to persuade her mistress to choose a different outfit. When she opted for the pleated skirt and matching shirt-top with no decoration except for a single line of buttons, Ruby frowned so disapprovingly her truthful verdict was demanded. She replied (not without trepidation since she was still new to her post) that in her opinion it was the attire of a common secretary – a judgment that caused her mistress to crow with delight. This, she assured Ruby, was exactly the impression she wanted to convey, for it would steer people's minds away from what she described as her scandalous past. In fact, she hoped that since she was a divorcee and so officially a virgin once more, none of the newspapers and magazines would take an interest. What she desired on her wedding day was to become a respectable married woman with a ring on her finger to prove it.

This discussion Ruby reported to the other maids, and together they puzzled over why the new Mrs Keynes should fear publicity so much. She had after all been written about many times, and photographed in a variety of garments including dance costumes which meant that on occasion she was practically naked. So engrossing was this topic that it occupied their shared mealtimes for several days, overshadowing even the cook burning herself on a tray of roasting meat and having to sit with her hand plunged in ice water while smelling salts were fetched and a message sent up to Mrs Bell that luncheon would be late. They had ruminated too over why Mr Keynes' fiancée should set such store by a wedding ring, given that until very recently she had been married without feeling obliged to display one. The matter was resolved when it was realised it would enable her to enroll without embarrassment at the newly opened birth control clinic for married women off the Tottenham Court Road run by Dr. Marie Stopes, whose book *Married Love* they knew from their dusting Mr Keynes had read. The subject of the ring itself troubled them, since Mr Keynes had picked Mr Grant as his witness who was the sweetest of men, but could not be trusted to keep an elephant safe let alone an item as easy to lose as a ring. They had all been relieved when Ruby discovered Mr Keynes intended to carry the ring to the ceremony himself.

At last there is movement from inside the Registry Office as the guests start to surface. First is Mr Keynes's solicitor, followed by his sister, mother and grandmother. As if at a signal the crowd falls silent and all eyes strain forward. Mr Grant is next, uncharacteristically smart in a suit with polished boots, then Mrs Bowen in an exquisite blue and white dress with a matching purse and hat. Finally the couple emerges, Mr Keynes confident and smiling, his bride a few paces behind looking, Ruby is distressed to observe, petrified. The women in the bath chairs notice this too. 'You'd think she was facing a firing squad not getting married', one comments while cameras click and flash, 'as if she's never been photographed by the press before.' The children, who have been promised a ballerina and not some dowdy person who might pass for their governess, complain of being hoodwinked out of their excursion to Regent's Park. Ruby spots the woman with the shopping bag sneak past the distracted policeman and shower the newlyweds in paper confetti. This excites the children though not, Ruby perceives, her mistress who shrinks back even further behind Mr Keynes. The reporters shout out questions, enquiring whether Mrs Keynes will continue working now she is married, and if it is true Mr Keynes has accepted an invitation from Moscow allowing his wife to be reunited with her family. Mr Keynes responds as if he is addressing a lecture hall full of his students, patiently and audibly, while his bride stands stiff and straight as a broom handle, her eyes anxiously sweeping the assembled gathering until they light on Ruby and she mouths a silent plea.

This is the signal. Ruby sidles past the children, engrossed in scooping handfuls of confetti from the pavement. Then, at a nod from Mr Keynes, she is at her mistress's side and holding her arm. As she steers her round the edge of the throng she is aware her mistress is trembling, even though their passage is respected and no one tries to hinder them. By the time they are seated safely in the back of the waiting taxi, Ruby feels as if she has delivered her mistress from torments more terrifying than any conjured by the sorcerer in her Firebird ballet.

Maynard sets his briefcase down in the hall of number 46, removes his hat and jacket and runs a hand through his thinning hair to straighten it. From the floor above he can hear Lydia, crooning one of the new jazz tunes. He empties the loose change and train ticket from Cambridge from his trouser pockets into the dish on the table. The hall smells of lavender which he traces to a box containing two dozen or more bars of soap. Before he can wonder why they might need soap in such quantities, Lydia is speeding down the stairs two at a time and catapulting into his arms.

'You're early,' she exclaims, kissing him so exuberantly he forgets all about the soap. 'I didn't expect you for two more hours at least. How marvelous you shooed away those beautiful boys who revere you as god, while you explain ancient currencies and why government must become smith to nation's money. Or perhaps you thumped hammer at committee, so instead of debating hours whether to spend gift of £100 on books for students or port for Fellows, you taught immediately sensible route which is to halve money and buy both? How are dear Mil and Fil? Is Fil applying garlic bulb as I showed him?'

'You make me sound alarmingly like a Bolshevik!' Maynard chuckles, hugging her. 'But if ever I need a stand-in as Bursar or to lecture I shall send for Mrs Keynes, comfortable in the knowledge that college finances and my students' understanding of economic theory are in capable hands. Mother-in-law and Father-in-law missed you for lunch yesterday, but hope you can join us one Sunday soon. How was your party here? Did you drink the claret I left out for you?'

Lydia looks sheepish. 'I may have warmed wine too close to fire because it bubbled when I poured into glasses,' she admits. 'But no one minded and party was top notch. Lunch ran into tea, which ran into cocktails, which ran into supper I prepared myself, tearing cold chicken from carcass and opening pickle jars. After this we transported furniture to make glorious space for dancing, and when it grew too late for guests to go home for sleeping too. All this produced in me most prodigious idea.' She frees herself from Maynard's embrace and clasps his hand. 'Come and admire.'

As he follows her up the stairs, Maynard takes in Lydia's attire. She has on an old dressing gown and slippers with a scarf round her head, all of which are blotched white. They squeeze past bookcases and chairs stacked on the landing and into the large sitting room. What he sees here causes him to freeze in astonishment. The murals

Vanessa and Duncan hand-painted on the walls have been obliterated in daubs of whitewash.

'My wedding present,' Lydia beams. 'Since finally the old Buddha offers me dance parts again I make new home for my Maynarochka from earnings.' She skips to the window and picks up a swatch of fabric pinned to the sill. 'While you conduct researches for your book I conduct my own. I order this yellow satin for curtains so we'll be cheerful like on summer holidays whenever we sit here. Flowers on satin are violets to symbolize true love.' She taps the floor. 'I've bought carpet blue as sky so we always have tremendous horizon, and I never convert into wife too interested in manicure to discuss dangers of gold standard. I've tracked down perfect candelabra too. Very cheap and the twin of authentic brass when regarded from not too close.' She spots that white from her clothes has transferred to Maynard's trousers. 'And this is not all,' she enthuses, rubbing the material with paint-stained hands and making the marks worse. 'I plan library for you up here, and in basement a barre and mirror where I shall not disturb with my practices.' She abandons her hand cleaning and searches for a rag. 'Also new bathrooms with superior piping. I am serious expert on piping.'

Maynard, still trying to absorb the enormity of the change confronting him, cannot for the moment concentrate on what Lydia is saying about candelabra and bathrooms. His attention is riveted on what is left of Vanessa and Duncan's murals. It is as if a tornado has spun across the walls, leaving white impressions of itself in swirling, irregular splashes. He thinks of the hours Vanessa in particular spent decorating not only this room but so many of those in which he has lived his adult life, finding furniture, sewing curtains, designing carpets and cushions, until almost no surface remains that does not bear her imprint. For some reason, it is his bedroom at Charleston he pictures her in, kneeling by his shelves after receiving news of the losses during the Somme Offensive and asking whether he might not prefer the spines of his folders if she coloured them yellow. He put aside his Treasury papers and they considered the question so intently that for several minutes the terrible slaughter of the war receded. He had felt then that no matter what lunacy or horror erupted in the world here he was with friends who could restore his faith.

Lydia, who has located her brush and is dipping it in a pot of white paint, continues to chatter. 'Of course mine is not such marvelous present as your taking me to St Petersburg, where I will kiss mother for first time since I was teenager, and salute Fedor grown so revered for his choreography and an inspiration to his dancers in these bleak times. Not forgetting my darling Eugenia whose feet always blister and who sensibly adds singing to her repertoire so is now also star of musicals. You will discover what illustrious family I descend from, with exception of naughty Nikolei who might have been dancer but instead is engineer like his grandfather.' She pauses to sweep white across more of the walls. 'Since revolution mother must accept lodgers so I brace myself for home not to be as I remember. Nor,' she reflects, adding one more streak before replenishing her brush, 'can I mention St Petersburg or even Petrograd as it became, but must call it Leningrad and soon I suppose Trotskygrad or more likely Stalingrad since it seems he will win power. When I brood on all Russia has endured I am heartily ashamed as my days by contrast are dipped in chocolate. We shall ferry as much as we can in our luggage. I've already saved soap. You'll complain it weighs heavily but will thank me once we arrive and watch pleasure on faces.'

'That explains the soap,' Maynard murmurs, his eyes still travelling the murals. Lydia, he realises, in the absence of a ladder, has only been able to paint as far as she can reach, so the devastation is restricted to the lower part of the walls.

As if reading his mind, Lydia points with her brush, dripping fresh paint over her hands and dressing gown. 'Next I will stand on chair and do top. Last night I talked to Katya's boyfriend who is stage-hand for Diaghilev and he instructed me in repair of holes.' She smears a length of carefully executed mural with whitewash. 'So that gouge Vanessa dug with her tool when she stole your picture can be smoothed out with paste.' She grins at him. 'I do not believe in marrying me you anticipated catching not only adoring wife and accomplished dancer but skillful decorator too.'

Maynard stares at the excavations in the plaster and the memory of Charleston dissolves. Instead, what he recalls is the recent dispute with Vanessa over the move into number 37, which has included unpleasant disagreements about rent and rates, as well as squabbles as to which possessions she will take and what should remain with Maynard and Lydia. This culminated in a row over a painting Vanessa argued belongs to her and Duncan, despite Maynard quoting date and price of purchase and offering to provide the receipt. Vanessa seemed to accept defeat at this, but the incident unnerved Maynard sufficiently for him to screw the frame to the wall as a precaution. When, after an absence, he found she had returned with a screwdriver to claim it, he banged on her door and demanded its immediate restoration – only to be met with such fierce resistance he had been forced to retreat. For the moment, since he has no key to let himself in to their house, Vanessa and Duncan commandeer the painting, a deed of effrontery and injustice that angers him still.

Lydia, who all this time has focussed on her whitewash, twists round to look at him, suddenly anxious his silence might mask disapproval. 'You do like wedding present?'

By way of answer, Maynard strips off his waistcoat and rolls up the sleeves on his shirt. His trousers he judges to be so splattered as to be beyond redemption. He picks up a paintbrush, slathers it in whitewash, and stretches up to the highest section of wall Lydia has not yet tackled. He experiences a jolt of apprehension as his brush rays the mural white, and his first efforts at erasure are tentative. He has always admired Vanessa and especially Duncan as artists, and is aware what an act of transgression it is that he, of all people, should destroy their work.

'Guess!' Lydia commands, drawing a creature with a long snout, polka dot eyes and outstretched wings in whitewash.

'Flying pig!' Maynard hazards, then, not to be outdone, traces the curve of a head and back. His brush glides easily over the plaster, and while he is under no illusion as to his dearth of talent, he starts to enjoy himself.

'Squirrel,' Lydia shouts out as he devises a sumptuous bushy tail for his beast. Together, they fashion a dog gnawing a bone and a whiskered cat chasing a mouse, followed by a menagerie of cavorting rabbits and a frieze of bubble-blowing fish. Soon every segment of wall that had not previously been whitewashed is teeming with cartoon animals. When there is no more space to cover, Lydia resorts to Maynard's ruined trousers which she patterns with motley stripes, while he, in retaliation, spatters her with paint. Soon they are drenched in whitewash and laughing so helplessly they throw down their brushes.

'What creativity,' Lydia declares, once she has recovered enough to speak. 'Always you announce you are mere wish-to-be-artist, but now I decide you do not tell truth. With this zoo I witness you are endowed with vital courage and the dreaming.'

Maynard wraps his arms round her. 'I like this honeymoon present. Though perhaps we might book professionals to finish off?'

'Honeymoon', Lydia echoes. 'What lovely expression that is. I hope light from such a moon will gladden our train window as we steam towards Russia.'

'You shan't mind the nights in the train then?'

'Pah! You forget I am seasoned traveller. If I had guinea for every night I sleep on train I should be wealthy woman. Main inconvenience is narrow beds, so you must dangle long legs over side. And we cannot so easily lie together.'

'That I shall mind.'

'In ancient Greece,' Lydia informs him proud of her knowledge, 'honeymoon didn't only promise sweet marriage. Honey was exalted as powerful aphrodisiac too. It assisted men's stiffenings and women's moistenings and was spread directly on body to ease the slidings.' She dabs at a smudge of white on Maynard's nose. 'So you must add "sexual sage" to all other experts you procure in marrying me.'

'In Cambridge, whenever one of my students throws out a bold claim, I ask for their evidence,' Maynard retorts. 'Therefore if I am to believe you I shall require immediate proof. Otherwise I will be obliged to deduce this superior sexual prowess you attribute to yourself is no more than an empty boast.'

The three women sitting together in the darkened auditorium of the Chiswick Empire form a striking trio, even amidst the opulent interior designed by the ubiquitous Frank Matcham, who – as tittle-tattle delights in reporting – is responsible not only for building or refurbishing several London theatres, but at least one in towns all over England. While the women might have been less remarkable amongst the crowds flocking to the Empire's popular variety shows, the sparse audience attending today's fare of two Greek plays makes them stand out all the more.

Their arresting appearance is not so much the result of flamboyant attire as the markedly different styles of their dress. The tall one on the left sports a black sombrero that sits oddly with her unfussy, conventional skirt and jacket. The only article of clothing that chimes with her hat is a bold abstract scarf knotted at the throat with which her hand repeatedly fiddles. The woman in the middle is smaller than her companions and wears casual, non-descript garments, topped by a man's woolen waistcoat several sizes too big – presumably an after-thought thrown on in case of cold. The final figure is alone in donning theatre-going garb, if one imagines the scene taking place forty years earlier and that the three have circumvented the need for male chaperones. For while her dress is less full in the skirt than a crinoline would have accomplished and shorter than would then have been permissible, its wasp waist and décolleté neckline combined with dark braids circling each ear are more evocative of Queen Victoria than the simpler lines of female fashion introduced by the war. It is perhaps less mysterious given that this is Berta Ruck (or Mrs Oliver Onions as she must be called since her marriage), for her occupation is the most conservative of the three, beginning promisingly enough at the Slade School of Art followed by Paris, but subsequently that of a popular novelist whose latest offering involving a stolen pearl necklace has sold well on both sides of the Atlantic. Though the diversity in the women's apparel has prompted commentary from the other (mostly male) patrons, what causes consternation is that the smaller one maintains a running and for the most part derisory commentary on the drama by Euripides currently being performed, in a voice loud enough to be heard.

'Soooo doll', Lydia complains, her irritation manifest not only in her volume but in her exaggerated elongation and deliberate switching of vowels.

'Hush,' Virginia pleads, her hand plucking nervously at her scarf. 'You're disturbing people.'

'I only say what is true,' Lydia retorts. 'This should have remained worthy past-time of classics students in Cambridge common room and not be presented on professional stage. Stoll cannot have witnessed it before volunteering his theatre – or else all his marbles are lost. The lead players are not without talent, but where was the hand to channel it? Words bounce off the teeth as if no one has ruminated on meaning, so we do not care straws whether Helen escapes with her Menelaus or is obliged to marry King of Egypt. For example,' she folds her arms across her chest in protest as the actors form a new tableau, 'here are Menelaus and Helen standing wooden in boat, while King on shore rages so feebly we must stuff fists in mouths to prevent laughter and pray for interval.'

The action reaches its climax and the curtain descends. Lydia joins in the clapping despite her attack since (as she explains to her mystified companions) to do otherwise might permit the bad atmosphere to linger.

'Refreshments,' Berta proposes too quickly as the house lights come on and an usherette with a tray of confectionary stations herself in front of the stage. She makes her way along their empty row to the aisle.

Lydia stands and stretches, as if to sit still a moment longer is impossible. With what ease and grace she moves, Virginia notices, her irritation dissipating now Lydia is no longer a source of disruption and embarrassment. She watches her blow a kiss to Jack Sheppard, who gave an opening talk, and who waves cheerily back. To convey her pleasure at this acknowledgment Lydia executes an elaborate curtsey, and Virginia – reminded of Lydia's anecdote of skating on the frozen river in St Petersburg – pictures her in furs gliding effortlessly across an icy Russian landscape. How exhilarating it must be to feel so powerful and liberated in one's body.

'How should you have directed Euripides?' she asks when Lydia has settled back in her seat.

'First grave error was to push chorus into background,' Lydia contends. 'Greek tragedy is like modern ballet, compelling us to look not in single place but several at once. Otherwise we fail to gather all we require to follow.'

The astuteness of this remark catches Virginia off-guard. Is it possible, she conjectures, that Lydia is cleverer than she supposed and this exasperating habit of flitting from one topic to the next, without seeming to consider anything deeply, is a habit? Perhaps even a form of defence? She is aware from other acquaintances such as Samuel Koteliansky, with whom she translated Dostoevsky for her Hogarth Press, that being a Russian émigré in London is not straightforward. For a reason she cannot immediately fathom, it is not Samuel's situation that is uppermost in her mind, nor even that of her husband Leonard who, as a Jew, has his own experiences of being treated as an outsider. Instead, it is the New Zealand writer Katherine Mansfield whose tragic death three years ago from tuberculosis still haunts her. Unlike Lydia, Katherine never downplayed her intelligence but on the contrary allowed it free rein, with the result that her at times acerbic judgments (such as that review in which she accused Virginia of being a decorous, old-fashioned dullard) persist in stinging.

Surprised at receiving no reply, Lydia eyes her keenly. Virginia rouses herself. 'I like your implication that the viewer must be given the freedom to locate for themselves where the significance lies. That freedom is not absolute however, since even according to you there must be a guiding hand.'

'But not in manner of our friend!' With a mischievous grin, Lydia indicates Berta who is waiting in the queue for ices. 'What is doll about her "Pearl Thief" is that good is simply good and bad merely bad. Since good must be victor only amusement for readers is how this can be engineered.'

Again, Virginia is startled by the perceptiveness of this observation. 'So you're saying that here the author's guiding hand distorts and lies instead of allowing life to be as it is, complex and open-ended.'

'Or else,' Lydia chuckles, 'readers demand refund! But art doesn't need to alienate. Diaghilev commissioned provoking material then found ways to appeal to public.' She frowns. 'Why is there no ballet in England? You have strong tradition in literature – art and music have excellent schools – but for dancers it is desert.' She rests back in her seat, her face thoughtful. 'I am not so dim as to believe even strong traditions cannot be broken or shrivel. Ballet – like all else in Russia – has had hard years. I was shocked to grasp consequences when I was home. For artists the only safe thriving is designing government posters and erecting monuments to heroes of revolution.'

There are various strands to this outpouring Virginia should like to pursue. The idea of an English ballet interests her despite her reservations about the art form's potential for decadence. She would also enjoy learning more about Lydia and Maynard's visit to Russia and what life is like under communism – a subject currently much debated given the looming threat of a nationally organised workers' strike. If she is honest, Lydia's family fascinates her too, especially her brother Fedor and what she has gleaned of his ballets that explore natural and political phenomena instead of narrating individual human stories. The strand she settles on is the one that relates most closely to issues preoccupying her in her writing.

'I also like your notion of simultaneity. It's something I've been grappling with myself. How, for instance, to make the past and future resonate in the present moment.' Virginia's hand, which has been still for some minutes, tugs at her scarf. 'The problem, it seems to me, resides in leaving the work open for the reader to enter and move about freely, whilst at the same time providing sufficient scaffolding so it does not collapse. What worries me about ballet is there are so many elements competing for our sensual stimulation. The risk is we drown in a cornucopia of delights and that scaffolding which enables contemplation is lost.'

As if to dispel an undercurrent that has become overly solemn, Lydia claps her hands. 'You English!' she teases. 'Always you distrust impulses and surmise understanding only to happen with head! I agree accumulation of ingredients is shallow route to time-passing and we soon turn nauseous from surfeit. We travel further when we listen to crafted symphony than haphazard cacophony even when cacophony is composed of beautiful sounds. But we travel with heart. And what we gain is knowledge of heart.'

'Ah the Russian soul!' Virginia quips, smiling at Lydia. 'I was wondering when that would enter the equation!'

'It should have entered here,' Lydia retaliates, thrusting her chin forward in defiance, 'so instead of splitting Helen into virtuous captive and betraying phantom she becomes whole woman capable of both.'

'Thus we might love and hate equally,' Virginia concludes with a laugh. 'Perceive the good in the villain and the evil in the judge.'

'That is more compassionate response than your so-superior English sneering at us poor sinners.'

Virginia, remembering the cruel jokes she has frequently fabricated at Lydia's expense, glances away. That she is not the only one of her circle to have exploited and exaggerated Lydia's foibles and eccentricities affords her scant comfort. Nor can she justify herself on the grounds she did this to entertain since it has led to animosity. She is aware how bitterly Vanessa in particular regrets the loss of their former close friendship with Maynard.

'*Ho!*' Lydia, oblivious to the direction Virginia's musings have taken, counters. 'But', she repeats in English despite her confidence this is a Russian word Virginia will comprehend. 'I must reverse your opinion of dance. Words are magical openers – here I concur – but are also treacherous if in fixing meaning they prevent others from existing. Movement by contrast clamours constantly for interpretation.'

Instead of the riposte Lydia expects, Virginia puts an arm round her shoulders. 'If your claim is true, then theatre is the ideal medium since it communicates through language and the body.' Her hand reaches for a stray strand of Lydia's hair, which she winds luxuriously about her fingers. 'You might act yourself.'

'I acted in America,' Lydia reveals encouraged by Virginia's tenderness and this sudden admission of belief in her. 'I was miserable failure on account of excruciation of my accent.' She can feel Virginia's fingers, gently caressing the flesh on her neck where her hair is tied in its customary bun, and lets her eyes close.

'What about plays translated into English, where your pronunciation would not be an obstacle but on the contrary add an authentic note?' Virginia leans closer, so her next thoughts are a murmur in Lydia's ear. 'You could play Nora in Ibsen's "The Doll's House". You'd combine her honesty and subterfuge, bravery and foreboding to perfection. Nora', she continues, her fingers stroking Lydia's cheek, 'in both her own estimation and her husband's is a "doll" – not in your charming sense of "dull" – but because in a society where men are masters women cannot act except by trespass.'

Grateful for this endorsement she might have an acting career in England once she is too old to dance, Lydia smothers Virginia's hand in kisses. Then, as if this is another of those occasions whose spell she must break, she frees herself from her embrace and with a single clap jumps to her feet.

'You shall not guess,' she challenges, 'the promise my mother exhorted when we said farewell. I shall provide clue. It has nothing to do with staying well or usual leaving admonitions.'

Perplexed by this alteration in mood and not a little hurt by Lydia's abrupt curtailing of their intimacy, Virginia shakes her head.

'She urged me to be good wife to my Maynar', which I shall endeavour to be – though not because I must but because I wish.' She spies Berta making her way back towards them and claps again, this time in rapture. 'You are goddess of pure goodness!' she exclaims as Berta distributes her purchases, before giggling and turning to Virginia. 'We missed you, did we not, for verdict on play.'

Lydia's wink as she utters this last pronouncement is delivered with such an expression of conniving merriment that Virginia retracts her earlier resolution to refrain from concocting comic tales at Lydia's expense. She accepts her own ice from Berta and listens to Lydia launch into a discussion of the merits of vanilla over strawberry, chattering nineteen-to-the-dozen for all the world as if Berta is her dearest friend instead of someone she scarcely knows. The elegant, athletic, fur-clad skater Virginia envisioned earlier has disappeared, as has the trapped, disillusioned Nora of Ibsen's play. Gone too is the shrewd critic of Greek drama whose observations absorbed her and the informed, observant traveller to Russia. Who is this Lydia sitting next to her now, Virginia wonders, as the lights darken then brighten again on Odysseus and monstrous Cyclops.

It is snowing as Vanessa closes the front door behind her. Though she is already late, delayed by an altercation with her eldest son Julian, she pauses to look out across Gordon Square, relishing the unfamiliar whiteness and dark silhouettes of the bare trees and garden railings illuminated in the street-light. She would like to go into the garden and walk alone down one of the snow-covered paths. Julian's angry words ricochet round her head and she needs time to compose herself. She is too upset to go directly to the party Maynard and Lydia are hosting. She wishes she could accept Julian's escalating desire for independence as a natural and necessary step to his becoming a young man, but the realisation she must let him find his own way in the world alarms her.

It occurs to her she should have left at the same time as Duncan, or arranged for Clive and Mary to call for her. That way she could have arrived at the Keynes' party in company. As it is, she will be forced to greet Maynard on her own and risk an awkward conversation with him. Relations between them have remained strained ever since their row over Charleston, a state of affairs his marriage has done little to improve. If anything, the quarrels over the separation of their London households have only inflamed matters. She is also fearful of running into Lydia without anyone at her side. Whilst she might reasonably cut an encounter with Maynard short on the grounds he has guests to attend to, Lydia will be deaf to such hints. She will be trapped and bombarded with nonsense until a fresh distraction diverts Lydia.

A couple turn the corner into the square. As they pass under the first of the street lamps Vanessa recognises them and waves.

'You're late too!' Virginia admonishes as she and Leonard approach.

'I was considering playing truant a while longer and taking a turn in the garden,' Vanessa confesses, kissing her.

'Splendid idea! We can send Leonard on ahead to pledge for our imminent arrival. We shall be quite warm,' she coaxes, patting her husband's arm, 'and perfectly safe.'

As if to prove no harm can come to them in the garden, Vanessa produces her key.

'Just one tour,' Virginia pleads. 'And in return you have my solemn promise that when you insist I'm tired and we should leave I won't make the slightest protest.'

Leonard, who has nursed his wife for weeks through a debilitating bout of influenza and who is not at all certain it is wise for her to be out in the cold any longer than is necessary, wraps his scarf tenderly round her shoulders. 'Ten minutes. Or I shall return with a search party.'

The sisters cross the road. There are no lights inside the garden and for some minutes they walk in silence, the only sound their feet on the frozen gravel and in the distance an occasional car.

'Thank you,' Vanessa links her arm through her sister's. 'I doubt I'd have had the courage to face Maynard and Lydia on my own. How was their visit to you in Sussex?'

'Better than anticipated,' Virginia tells her. 'Maynard was less pugnacious than usual, as if marriage and all the suffering he saw in Russia has made him kinder. He's of the view that wealth should be more equally distributed, though not in the brutal, overly controlled manner of Stalin and the Communist Party.' She tucks Leonard's scarf tighter. 'Of course he looked perfectly ridiculous in his Tolstoy blouse and black astrakhan cap, outlining his ideas for pig-rearing at Tilton.'

'So it's true. They'll take Tilton.'

'Their lease runs until the summer. After that, who knows?'

'Maynard's solicitor is bound to arrange it. How did Lydia seem?'

Virginia, aware her attempts to present the Keynes' marriage in a reassuring light are having the opposite effect on her sister, tries satire. 'Hell-bent on playing the good housewife! Prattles on about the best place to buy fish and how she procures the freshest offal by flirting with the butcher. Swears he will rip it straight from the cow in exchange for one of her smiles.'

To Virginia's relief, Vanessa laughs. 'Can this be the Lydia who had to phone me three times to ask how to boil an egg? And for whom hosting a dinner means distributing whatever she stumbles across in the pantry. Joints of meat divided amongst guests with her bare hands. Have you seen what she's done to number 46?'

'I've heard about the new bathrooms and bidet.' She points out a sparrow sheltering in a tree, its feathers fluffed against the cold. 'How's Duncan bearing up?'

'Still feels Lydia's blighted his prospects now she replaces him as Maynard's heir. But he hates arguments. He would like me to make up with them both.'

'And will you?'

'If I can.' They have completed their circuit of the garden. Vanessa swings the gate open. 'I volunteer myself for gossips with Lydia, but always come away with the sense I've been led by the nose down a path I never wanted to take. Even if all I do is listen, I find myself irritated and annoyed to the extent I scarcely know myself. Or rather, I do,' she admits, locking the gate behind them and slipping the key back into her coat, 'but hate and despise what I have become.'

Virginia brushes flakes of wet snow from her sister's hair. 'You always set yourself such impossibly high standards. I'm certain the ill-will you describe and which you deem so despicable is only what us ordinary mortals experience most of the time.' She shivers in the icy chill. 'We should go in. Before Leonard sends out his search party.'

They cross to the door of number 46, still the only one in the square to be painted vermillion red. Inside, they divest themselves of their coats and hats before being shown by a maid into the large sitting room, where clusters of guests stand talking.

Virginia steers them towards where Duncan is engaged in conversation with Lytton. Vanessa veers away, positioning herself in front of one of the freshly painted walls and rubbing her hands over their uniform whiteness, as if she might retrace her obliterated designs by touch.

'Hideous', Virginia shudders, glancing about her. 'One might be forgiven for presuming one had entered a refurbished brothel, with these brash imitation candelabra and florid curtains. If it weren't for the paintings', she indicates the Cézanne, a collection of seven apples she knows Vanessa adores, 'it would be hard to imagine anything more tasteless. And where's all this repulsive furniture from?'

'Auctions mainly. Maynard's always bought books, now he scours the catalogues for furniture too, preferably in lots. Lydia, not to be outdone, returns from every charity sale she's invited to laden with bric-à-brac, gloating she has nine chipped mugs for sixpence or a manicure case with no more than half the instruments missing. The only stipulation is comfort and how little it cost.' She catches Virginia's sleeve. 'You see how ungenerous I become.'

Before Virginia can answer, they hear a theatrical scream pierce the hubbub. As if on cue, Lydia is calling their names and pushing through the assembled guests towards them.

'I was petrified you were not gracing us, since first Duncan then Leonard appear empty-armed.' Lydia plants a hand on each hip, a pantomime scold. 'Then when I hear you have taken turn in snow I long to don boots and join you. But since I am Mrs Keynes and hostess I desist.' She instructs a passing maid to bring two glasses of champagne. 'I only buy one bottle,' she chuckles, no longer cross, 'so it does not bankrupt shopping bill. I save it specially for you.'

How extraordinary Lydia is, Virginia decides, admiring her Regency-style purple silk dress. Despite her outrage at the desecration to her sister's décor, she cannot help admiring Lydia's shameless exuberance. 'What an unusual outfit,' she remarks, fingering the puffed sleeves that reveal Lydia's beautiful arms. 'You might pass for one of Jane Austen's heroines.'

'Antique,' Lydia informs her. 'Except for lace which had to be replaced as mice or moths had made meal of it. I worried it was too sombre so I toned with orange ribbon.' She cups a hand under her bosom to display the trim. 'Is felicitous match?'

This is addressed to Vanessa, who is on the point of confirming orange is indeed a perfect colour complement when the maid returns with the champagne.

'To tip top health,' Lydia toasts, handing them each a glass. 'Now I must abandon you to your devices and hunt out my good friend Vera.' She dives back into the throng of people leaving the two bewildered sisters staring at their champagne.

'Flat', Virginia pronounces, taking a sip.

The maid, Betty, hired in for the party, is unsure whether to follow or stay with the two women muttering about the champagne. Mrs Keynes' maid Ruby recommended her for the work, the two becoming friends after overhearing the greengrocer complain that all three of his daughters were in thrall to the picture palace. Their purchases complete, the pair agreed the picture palace was the perfect place to spend an evening, lost in the love tangles and adventures of others. Betty, to whom Ruby's employer is as exotic as any of the actresses she has watched on screen, remembers her promise to relay every detail to the other servants in her household. She gazes after Mrs Keynes, wondering if her dress can accurately be labeled plum with its bluish sheen, or whether it might be better described as deep lavender.

A woman with striking features Ruby has already identified as Lady Morrell requests a glass of champagne. Since Betty is to serve this only at Mrs Keynes' bidding, she curtseys an apology and hurries after the hostess, who is introducing a woman in a magnificent beaded jacket and handkerchief skirt to two men by the fireplace.

'We come desperate for your opinions,' Lydia petitions Duncan and Lytton. 'We are in dispute over Virginia's novel. I say flighty wife who only notices hats can't be me and even if it is I must not mind.'

Lytton, who has been enjoying his discussion alone with Duncan, scowls at the interruption. He is especially vexed when, adjusting his pince-nez, he realises it is to meet one of the dreadful society women the new Mrs Keynes counts as friends. He registers her fashionably bobbed hair and curiously ragged hemline he deduces is the latest faddish craze. Her gold and jeweled Egyptian bracelet (influenced no doubt by the discovery of Tutankhamun's tomb) must have cost the equivalent of a working man's monthly wage. It concerns him that through his unfortunate marriage these are the people Maynard will live among. Only the other day he was shocked to learn that the Keynes had been guests of honour at a dinner for leading bankers and industrialists. In this context, he supposes he must be relieved their topic is Virginia's novel. 'I assume you mean "Mrs Dalloway"? A book I dubbed a flawed stone.'

'Why shan't you mind if one of its characters is modeled on you?' Duncan asks. Lytton's hostility embarrasses him, but he is also intrigued. It is a subject he has occasionally puzzled over in relation to the people he paints. 'Do you mean you're happy for the artist – Virginia in this case – to make whatever she takes her own?'

'Not exactly', Lydia tells him. 'The artist becomes temporary owner, but only while art is being made. After that it belongs to work. Besides, process of making changes it, like alchemy.' She frowns, searching for a way to explain. 'Even if I attempt to copy another dancer exactly, I cannot do it. My body and way of moving, my thoughts and experience, even my intentions are different. So whatever I take becomes different.' Actually,' she confides, lowering her voice, 'in my opinion Virginia doesn't care enough about her characters for them to acquire independent life.'

'I wouldn't pass that on to Virginia!' Duncan counsels with a grin.

'Tempo of Virginia's brain is allegro but writing speed is andante,' Lydia continues encouraged. 'Maynar' compares modern tendency in novel writing to day-dreaming of nervous wreck. He only likes stories with happy endings. I prefer Virginia's articles, which are so full of her imagination I am lugged forward, understanding despite being lento.' She casts Lytton a sly look. 'You are author she steals from. Your book on Victorians is most exquisite elbow rub of research and invention I've read.'

Duncan, aware from Lytton's softening expression that this no doubt disingenuous flattery has achieved its effect, lets out a guffaw. 'I'd also keep that from Virginia's ears!'

'Why? Failure is as important to artist as success. Though it isn't pleasant to be announcer of failure. Unless one is sadist. Now, I have something I must show my friend.'

She escorts Vera to the basement, where she blows a kiss to the flustered cook and servants in the kitchen. She opens the door to a room at the front of the house, empty except for a large mirror and a barre attached to the wall facing it. The only furniture is a chair and small table by the window. The top of the table is submerged under scrapbooks and newspaper cuttings, pens, scissors, brushes, a pot of glue. More newspapers are stacked beneath the table legs.

Lydia sets her right hand on the barre, mechanically moving her feet through the five positions. Then she smiles at Vera and speaks in Russian. 'Isn't it perfect? I am the happiest woman in London.'

'Despite your hostile neighbours?'

'I think I can charm Lytton.'

'And the two sisters?'

Lydia turns and places her left hand on the barre. 'When you wish your life were different it's easy to be unkind.'

'I noticed Vanessa's husband arrive with a dark-haired woman. Are things still as you described them with Duncan Grant?'

Lydia studies her posture in the mirror, her free arm curved in front of her. 'They are, though I'm not certain that's what makes her unhappy. She and Duncan are like this.' She crosses her fingers.

'Jealousy then? You mentioned Vanessa finds it hard to earn money from her painting.' Vera stops by the table and glances down at the precarious pile of scrapbooks and cuttings. 'Why do cats have whiskers?' she reads aloud.

Judging from her reflection that the line of her neck is wrong, Lydia drops her shoulders. 'She can hardly be jealous since I have no dancing at the moment. In any case, she doesn't care about success in that way. It's one of her virtues. Still,' she tilts her chin, gauges the result in the mirror, 'she doesn't consider a ballerina to be of the same high ranking as an artist. For her a dancer is like a single colour in a painting, valuable but replaceable.'

'What about Mrs Woolf?' Vera shuffles the strewn cuttings aside and opens the first of the scrapbooks. Her eyes skim an article about cows in America mysteriously being milked despite farmers keeping guard.

'Leonard is the kindest of men but he is a worrier, which for Virginia is the same as a too-tight shoe. Not like my Maynard who adores it when I fuss over his aches and chills.' She abandons the barre and stations herself next to Vera, pointing out a letter she has pasted into the scrapbook advocating the extension of women's right to vote so it is equal to men's.

'There was a rumour she was in love with another writer?'

'Vita Sackville-West? She's in Baghdad with her husband. I

suppose they write gloriously passionate letters to each other. Which Virginia probably prefers.' Lydia returns to the barre. 'It makes such a difference, to practise whenever I wish. Soon not even Diaghilev will complain I have no breath or toes and am too fat to be lifted.'

'Will he give you more dance parts?'

'If he doesn't, it shan't be for want of trying. I've eaten no cake or sweets for a fortnight.' Lydia faces herself in the mirror. 'If Diaghilev agrees, I'll dance for a while longer; if he doesn't and nothing else comes my way – perhaps I'll have better luck with a baby.'

'Still nothing?' Vera shuts the scrapbook.

'There were complications, when I was younger. I was warned it might make babies impossible later on.'

'It's too soon to give up hoping.'

Lydia smoothes her skirt so it lies flat. 'I shall mind if it doesn't happen, but not as much as if I could not marry my Maynar'. He's the big walk of my life.' She twists sideways and inspects her profile. 'I do like how this dress makes me taller. Shall we go back up?'

Their husbands are at opposite ends of the sitting room. Vera joins Harold, while Lydia pauses to greet guests. By the time she reaches Maynard, the group he is with has swelled to include Duncan, Lytton, Clive, Mary and Leonard. Virginia is also part of this circle, flanked by Vanessa. Lydia realises they are deliberating whether Maynard should stand for election as the new Provost of King's College. As she takes her place beside him, he slides his arm affectionately round her waist.

'What about Mrs Keynes?' Virginia enquires. 'Presumably it would mean Maynard residing permanently in Cambridge?'

With the exception of Vanessa, who gazes steadfastly at the ground, all eyes turn to Lydia. Even Maynard slackens his hold so he can look at her.

'I believe I make success of Cambridge,' Lydia declares. 'I was quiet at first dinner, fearing clever talk, but with cheese and port I became emboldened to pose question – and received most charming answer.'

'I suspect port was the culprit,' Maynard interjects. 'We're not commonly praised on High Table for our charm.'

'Not to omit the wines accompanying the sole and partridge and dessert,' Virginia ventures, remembering her own dinner at Maynard's college. 'Excellent wines if memory serves for loosening tongues and overcoming inhibitions. And did you volunteer to dance?' she queries, not without malice. She cannot imagine Lydia's propensity to dance whenever she is in company will have impressed the Fellows.

'Not only offer but execute – to noisy applause.' She gives Maynard a conspiratorial wink. 'You won't forget our plan?'

With the air of a schoolboy about to embark on a prank, Maynard co-opts Duncan and Leonard and clears a space for the gramophone in front of the fireplace. Clive, Mary and Lytton drift away.

'I hope he won't be new Provost,' Lydia admits when the three women are alone. 'Not because I shall mind Cambridge. After all, I can be in London when I need and am accustomed to Maynar' being away. But I am not right material for Provost's wife. I know it is polite addressing letters to me now I am Mrs Keynes, but when I attempt reply English words desert and I become gibbering illegitimate.' She claps a horrified hand over her mouth. 'What did I tell you! I shall reduce King's College to laughing horse!'

'If Maynard is elected,' Virginia suggests, touched by this confession, 'he will have a secretary who will be able to write on your behalf.'

'He may not even stand,' Vanessa adds, swayed like her sister by Lydia's honesty. 'It would take him away from writing.'

'You're right,' Lydia concedes, brightening. 'Besides, if I've no dancing I shall require new role. Which reminds me. I've mulled more on English ballet and there's someone here you must meet.'

Betty, who has brought a tray of devilled eggs up from the kitchen, circulates amongst the guests. She does this with trepidation, having sampled one of the broken eggs that could not be presented to visitors. Her mouth is still on fire from the hot Russian mustard Mrs Keynes stirred into the yolks, despite the cook's objection no one would be accustomed to it. Betty spies Mrs Keynes by the window talking to the two women she fetched champagne for, and starts towards them. Then she spots Ruby in their vicinity and switches direction. The cook has emphasized more than once the importance of serving refreshments in different parts of the room.

Instead, Betty targets the men setting up a gramophone by the fireplace. One of them is recounting a story with dramatic gestures. With his lithe body and dark, bewitching eyes he might, Betty conjectures, be a dancer like Mrs Keynes. A film at the picture palace in which the dashing hero falls for a humble flower girl comes back to her, and she drifts into a fantasy that the young man is leading her in a romantic Valse Musette, before upbraiding herself. If she wishes to be employed again in the future she must carry out her duties impeccably. Besides, she is all but invisible in her maid's black dress and starched white apron and cap.

It has grown hot in the room and Betty, blushing now at her foolish daydream, is uncomfortable in her uniform. To her relief, one of the men opens the French window. This is Mr Keynes, whom Betty has heard less about than his wife, though she is aware he is an eminent figure. Before this evening she assumed this meant Mr Keynes was rich, and was flabbergasted when Ruby showed her the house with its inferior paintings and shabby furniture. The apples in the picture above the fireplace for example are nothing like actual fruit and must, in her opinion, be a beginner's work. In her own establishment in nearby Fitzroy Square, it is her task each morning to polish the rosewood dining table and chairs with beeswax, as well as the mahogany cabinets and display cases containing the master's collection of knives and trinket boxes, souvenirs from his colonial service in India. She doubts anything here requires such attention, which must, she concedes, be a blessing for Ruby. The French window now open, she watches Mr Keynes step onto the balcony, his arm round the shoulders of the dark-eyed young man.

Lady Morrell helps herself to an egg. She has a glass of wine in her hand and appears to have forgotten her earlier request. Unlike others who have tasted the dish, the recipe meets with her approval and she reaches for a second. Out of the corner of her eye, Betty detects Mrs Keynes moving towards the French window. She serves a couple speaking a language she supposes might be French or if not Russian, who also relish the eggs. She considers following Mr Keynes and his friend onto the balcony. Lady Morrell hovers near enough to ask again about the champagne, and the prospect of cooler air is enticing. She is on the point of going outside when something happens to hold her back.

The balcony is narrow and Mr Keynes stands close to the young man in the confined space, his arm still about his shoulder. As Betty angles her tray so she can squeeze through the opening to join them, she sees Mr Keynes lean in and plant a lingering, lascivious kiss on the other man's lips. For several seconds, it is as if everything around her falls still and silent, until the slide of the dish across her tray recalls Betty to her senses. She steadies it in time to prevent it crashing to the floor. The crisis averted, she glances about her. No one else appears to have witnessed the scene. The couple talking French, or is it Russian, remain deep in debate, while Lady Morrell has inserted a cigarette into an enameled holder which one of the men assembling the gramophone lights for her. With as much dignity as she can muster, Betty threads her way through the groups of tightly-packed visitors to the door, then down the stairs to the basement, where she breathes in several gulps of air.

Betty is not the only one to have noticed the kiss. Lydia, Virginia and Vanessa glimpsed it too as they neared the French window. Virginia stops dead in her tracks, while Vanessa holds up her hand, as if this gesture might erase what occurred. Only Lydia seems unperturbed. She capers onto the balcony where she blithely chastises the two men.

'There you are, hiding when I am searching high and low!' She seizes their hands and leads them back to where Virginia and Vanessa stand dumbfounded. 'Allow me,' she solicits with mock formality, 'to introduce Fred Ashton, who is not only most darling man but extremely talented dancer and choreographer. And this,' she indicates Virginia, 'is Mrs Woolf, who might help with creating an English ballet. Now I leave you to become excellent acquaintances since my husband and I have important divertissement to prepare.'

With the same dramatic presence as if she were stepping onto the stage at the Coliseum, Lydia propels Maynard into the space cleared for them in front of the fireplace. At her signal, Duncan lowers the arm of the gramophone and winds the handle. Then, as the first notes of music emerge, Lydia calls for silence. 'Dear friends, to celebrate our nuptials we propose for your enjoyment: the "Keynes-Keynes"!'

As if this has been rehearsed many times, Maynard and Lydia face each other and bow. Then, with one arm round her husband's waist and her free hand clasping his, Lydia guides them in a waltz. Though Maynard moves stiffly and his tall frame bends awkwardly as he partners his wife, he executes his part with panache. There is appreciative applause from the audience. Duncan leaves his post at the gramophone and invites Vanessa to dance.

Fred Ashton, his exchange with Virginia interrupted, stations himself at the gramophone and chooses the next record. With a grin, he lowers it onto the turntable and rewinds the handle. The tune that erupts from the bell-shaped horn is faster and livelier than the first. Recognizing it, Lydia wags a chiding finger at Fred. She releases Maynard and hoists the hem of her dress.

Betty, who is watching from the doorway with Ruby, presses up onto her toes. Above the heads, she locates Mrs Keynes, drumming her feet in rapid, intricate patterns and whipping up her skirt so it whirls about her like a wave. With a saucy grin that reminds Betty of her favourite screen comedian Harold Lloyd, she lifts each knee in turn so it is chest height before pointing the toe of her shoe straight outwards.

'The can-can,' Ruby is ecstatic. 'When Mrs Keynes first performed it in London, audiences queued for hours in the hope of a return ticket.'

There are cheers and whistles as Mrs Keynes, whose feet are already moving so quickly Betty can scarcely keep pace with them, begins to revolve in a circle. She does this repeatedly until Betty wonders how she prevents herself from feeling dizzy. Then, to Betty's amazement and the thrill of those already familiar with the dance, she no longer kicks her legs straight out but up, so her toes point at the ceiling.

'Didn't I promise it would be like the picture palace?' Ruby enthuses, glowing with pride at her employer's artistry.

Betty, too transfixed to reply, can only nod.

'What a marvel she is,' Virginia, also enthralled by Lydia's performance, remarks. 'She contrives it so Maynard appears a competent partner.'

Vanessa, whose attention has been diverted by Duncan sketching in his notebook, stares back at the couple. Her sister's observation is correct. Lydia is dancing round Maynard, windmilling his arms like the ribbons on a maypole. Now her face peeps out from behind his back, then from above his head as she vaults onto his shoulders.

'Is it true you'll help her form an English ballet?'

Stung by Vanessa's censorious tone, Virginia is defiant. 'What if I do? We need to find a way to get on. Besides, it's a disgrace we don't have our own ballet.'

Vanessa studies Duncan's swift pencil movements, a rapt expression on his face. Leonard, who has manoeuvred his way through the crowd to his wife's side, is tapping his feet in time to the music. Even Clive and Mary seem entertained by the scene. Only Lytton feigns disapproval, ostentatiously removing his watch from his waistcoat to check the time. 'You're right,' Vanessa concedes, 'it would be better if we could all be friends.'

Lydia demonstrates a sequence of steps then encourages Maynard to repeat them. With the zeal of an over-eager pupil he obliges, unwittingly transforming what he has been shown into ungainly hops and leaps. His endeavours are so idiotic the audience explodes with laughter. Undeterred, his cheeks reddening from the unfamiliar exertion, Maynard places his hands behind his ears and flaps his elbows in a grotesque parody of his wife. He is rewarded with shouts of bravo and rowdy applause. Fred empties the vase of roses from the mantelshelf and throws them at him, and even a smirking Lytton unpins the carnation from his button-hole and tosses it at Maynard. Lydia, pretending to be envious of these accolades, drops onto one knee and stretches her back leg out until it is flat on the floor behind her. Daring Maynard to copy her, she slides her front leg until it too lies flat and she sits in a full split. With a shrug intended to convey the challenge is too simple, Maynard parts his legs and gingerly lowers himself. After only a few inches he stops, grimaces, and turns so his back is facing the audience. Then he lifts the tail of his jacket to reveal a rip in the seat of his trousers.

With a cry of dismay, Vanessa pushes her way to the door and out onto the landing. 'I can't,' she bursts out as Virginia catches up with her. 'I know conciliation is the right path and as I watched Duncan drawing part of me wanted to draw Lydia too. But Duncan will make her mesmerizing, whereas all I see is her monstrous ego. What she seeks is the limelight and she couldn't care less if she reduces Maynard to a fool in the process.' She clutches her sister's arm so tightly it hurts. '*Maynard*,' she repeats, tears running down her cheeks, 'the most brilliant of us all.'

Lydia reaches the top of Firle Beacon and surveys the view. The South Downs stretch out before her, an undulating panorama of open grassland interspersed with wooded copses. She screens her eyes and traces her route up the hillside, over the winding ribbon of road, past hedgerows and fields white with frost to the church spire of Alciston. From here she strains for a glimpse of the roof and chimneys of Tilton House set apart in a ring of leafless trees. She pictures Maynard where she left him in his chair, his green baize writing board on his knee. Like their Victorian bed on iron casters, they bought the chair for its durability and comfort since (as Lydia observed) it was like resting in the arms of an old friend.

On a table at his side, Lydia has prepared a flask of coffee and dish of ginger biscuits so Maynard will not be hungry if she fails to return in time for lunch. She adores the flexible pattern of their days at Tilton, with Maynard working in the morning while she practises dance and plays the piano, followed by a walk together in the afternoon or a trip out in the car. They have fewer visitors than in London and their evenings are spent reading aloud to each other, often poetry or Shakespeare, but also Russian writers such as Chekhov. Once, after laughing helplessly at Maynard's recitation of the dissolute nurse Mrs Gamp in *Martin Chuzzlewit*, Lydia confessed how much she loved being read to. It reminded her of her father re-enacting plays from the theatre where he worked as an usher, which are among her happiest childhood memories. On such occasions, her family listened to the performance together, and for the hour or more it lasted her parents did not argue and a contented peace settled over the household. Maynard returned to Charles Dickens, but the next novel he chose was by Tolstoy, which he handed to Lydia to read with the admission he had last heard it from his mother as a boy.

Though the climb up Firle Beacon has not tired her, Lydia squats on the frozen ground to rest. The hilltop round her is deserted apart from a few hardy sheep, grazing on the patches of green where sun has thawed the grass. Everything else is covered in a white sheen of frost. Her breath mists the air and the icy sensation as it enters her lungs makes her gasp. She feels energized and elated. It has become her habit to return from her walks with ready-made anecdotes to entertain Maynard, and she considers what she might report today. She throws back her head and stares up at the sky, which is sublimely blue despite the cold. She would like to drink in not only the pure air and miraculous sky, but the soft contours of the hillside and farms extending as far as her eye can see. At last she lights on the perfect description. Alone up here, she is sharing a cocktail with God.

The sheep have black faces and when they move they do so in unison, like a corps de ballet. She has ordered beef for Christmas Day as a tribute to Maynard's Sunday lunches with his family, which he still attends whenever he is in Cambridge. Roast beef is a favourite and she has pored over cookery books in search of the best recipe for Yorkshire pudding to complement the meat. Ruby, who has Yorkshire grandparents, has been skeptical about most of the instructions, especially those which stipulate the pudding batter should be divided into patty tins instead of left in a flat pan and placed under the roasting joint so the juices drip into it. In the end, Lydia proposed doubling the quantities and cooking it both ways so they could decide for themselves which method they preferred. Ruby has been dispatched to ask Edgar Weller, their Tilton neighbour, if he will help cut boughs of holly and mistletoe so they can decorate the house, a task she undertook with such embarrassed fluster Lydia gleefully declared she must be in love.

It is the first time she will be alone with Maynard for the holiday and she is determined to spoil him. She is aware he regards Christmas as special despite his lack of religious belief. For weeks she has been accumulating presents, some of which Maynard has been consulted over, others she has acquired on impulse and hidden out of sight. The gifts for her own family in Russia she sent months ago, though she has not yet received confirmation they have arrived. For Vanessa she has a book on gardening which she has secretly read, turning the pages with a handkerchief so her fingers will not grease the paper. For Duncan, she has a sketchbook and a cartoon lampooning the British navy she hopes will remind him of when he and his friends tricked their way as Abyssinian royalty on board a battleship. On first hearing this story, which involved not only Duncan and Adrian Stephen but also Virginia, Lydia professed pride in her association with these dare-devil jokers. Now she is better acquainted, she finds it hard to imagine Virginia in particular participating in such a prank. She supposes she must funnel her subversive energies into her writing. For Vanessa's children, she has envelopes containing sums of money calculated according to age, the smallest amount for Angelica, the largest for Julian. While Maynard approved of this idea, he wondered if money was a little impersonal, so she hid the envelopes for the youngest two in socks stuffed with sweets and Julian's in a box of cigarillos. She has leather driving gloves for Leonard and Virginia since they are contemplating purchasing their first car, and for their dog Pinka (a cocker spaniel she is fond of) a large marrow bone has been added to her Christmas order with the butcher. In the current cold snap, it will keep fresh in the cellar until she can arrange to drive over to Monk's House where the Woolfs are spending the holiday and deliver it in person.

For Maynard, she has so many gifts it has required ingenuity to keep them all a secret. Some, like a new nightshirt, Maynard has already guessed, since she held it up against him whilst insisting he shut his eyes so she could measure she had the correct size. His suggestions as to what it might be were so preposterous she giggled and he, disobeying, peeped. When he saw it was a nightshirt he protested that his existing one, though old, was still perfectly serviceable, at which point Lydia put her foot down. He could not go to bed on Christ's birthday in a moth-infested rag even Ebenezer Scrooge would spurn.

Maynard knows nothing about his main present, for Lydia has locked it inside her trunk and wears the key on a ribbon round her neck. Though this has aroused Maynard's suspicion, he has not been able to prise the key from her, not even when she takes her bath. The present is a doctor's bag she found at a charity sale for Russian refugees, made of soft brown leather with brass clasps. It must have belonged to an émigré doctor, for it had phials inside with Russian labels. It delighted Lydia that these included the same remedy for sore throats concocted from beetroot and vinegar her mother dosed her with as a child. The bag also contained a stethoscope and a small, zipped case containing differently shaped pairs of scissors. Lydia first hid the bag in the kitchen at Gordon Square, then, when Maynard was next in Cambridge, she carried it to St Bartholomew's Hospital where Geoffrey Keynes is a surgeon. Geoffrey invited her into his consulting room anticipating she had come about an illness. She sat opposite him and explained that as Maynard's wife she wished to become proficient in treating not only his periodic fevers, but whatever ailment he might suffer from in the future. He was after all a prominent public figure and she deemed it her role to take first-class care of him. At this, she tipped the contents of the doctor's bag onto Geoffrey's desk and asked if he could provide a list of what else she might need, and if he might demonstrate how she should use the stethoscope.

So far, Lydia has received only the vaguest of hints as to what Maynard's present to her might be. He has introduced into their conversations questions she suspects have been clues, though if they were she has not been able to puzzle them out. Indeed, several were so mysterious she fancies they were framed with the intention of putting her off the scent, such as whether she prefers living in the city or the country, and whether she would be happier surrounded by people or animals. She removes a bar of chocolate from her coat pocket and tears open the wrapper. Despite promising Diaghilev she will lose more weight, she wolfs it down hungrily, hoping her climb and the walk back will cancel out the calories. One of the oddest questions Maynard put to her is how she feels about the close proximity between the house they are renting at Tilton and Vanessa at Charleston. There was an earnestness to his tone and so she replied, honestly, that while she finds Vanessa difficult to fathom, it was no different from their living arrangements in London to which she has become accustomed. She added that she was pleased for Maynard since he had spent so much time at Charleston. Besides, they had been in Sussex nearly a week without visiting Charleston or being visited in turn. She could readily envisage how they might spend months here without seeing anyone.

Lydia presumed Maynard would drop the subject after this, but to her astonishment he returned to it the following day, this time in relation to Virginia and Leonard. He reminded her that while the Woolf's house at Rodmell was further away than Charleston, it was still only a relatively short drive. Baffled, Lydia answered that she thought the distance ideal since Maynard and Leonard had work to do on *The Nation* together. It would also provide a pretext for her to offer insights on the Russian point of view for an article Virginia is writing. Then, to lighten the mood, which in her estimation had grown overly serious, she quipped that she hoped Virginia might model another fictional character on her, presenting her this time as a full-blooded Russian. To facilitate this, she planned to dress in a tunic and trousers on their next visit to the Woolfs. This way, Lydia reasoned, flirting with Maynard now, her sex would be ambiguous and Virginia could choose to feature her as a woman or a man.

Crouching in the chill has made her stiff and she stamps her feet to get her blood circulating. A lone owl, driven to hunt during daylight hours, swoops the crest of the beacon. Despite its vast wingspan it barely makes a sound as it glides past. Lydia stretches out her arms in imitation, wondering whether the movements she has been rehearsing to dance the Firebird again are too frenzied, and whether her interpretation might have more beauty and majesty if she copied this stillness. She had not expected Diaghilev to want her for the Firebird, and while his invitation thrills her she is also terrified. She is hardly the same ballerina as when she first performed the role in London all those years ago.

She starts back down the hill, pushing her hands into her pockets for warmth, though now she is walking again she is no longer cold. The winters here are nothing like those she remembers from home. This morning, before setting out, she pulled potatoes from the vegetable bed, breaking up the solid ground with her bare hands. Maynard discovered her kneeling there and offered her his gloves. Lydia, invoking her peasant origins, indicated the pair tucked into her belt, wagging their dangling rubber fingers at him and nicknaming them her udders. Maynard asked what she would cultivate if the garden were hers. Peas and beans, she replied without hesitation, and cherry trees and moon daisies so she could fill the house with their flowers in the summer. 'No dahlias,' Maynard noted, pretending disappointment, to which she responded she would leave these to him since his ancestor was the expert. At this, Maynard confided that though his grandfather was a celebrated gardener, he lacked proficiency himself. His sole contribution at Charleston had been to weed the gravel paths with his penknife, an occupation he had found curiously satisfying. Lydia sat back on her heels and grinned. There was, she pointed out, more than enough room at Tilton to create a maze of gravel paths should he wish to pursue that pleasure here. For her part, she was looking forward to lying naked in the shrubbery as soon as the sun shone. The currant bushes were so dense they would camouflage her from any Charleston visitors.

The potatoes she has stowed in the pantry so they can be peeled and cut for boiling. She was amazed at how quickly she accumulated enough for their meal. She recalls the clean smell of the earth and its grainy texture as she sifted it between her fingers. There were carrots in a row next to the potatoes. At first, she tried to harvest these by tugging at their leaves, but the stems tore and the orange shanks snapped before she could prise them free. She had more success when she dug into the soil with her nails. The long, spindly roots at the tip of each carrot fascinated her. She pictured them burrowing invisibly beneath her, like the roots of trees extending many feet underground while their trunk and high branches command our focus. She attempted to convey her happiness to Maynard, comparing herself to a plant finally able to put down roots. Unusually, her metaphor unraveled and she grew tongue-tied and shy. To deflect Maynard's notice, she pressed him on his dream of pig rearing, attributing his choice of animal to the superior intelligence of pigs. When he surmised she had this from one of her newspaper cuttings, she flung handfuls of frozen leaves at him. Since they only had the lease on Tilton until the summer, she suggested adopting cats and dogs instead since they would be simpler to transport. They could hardly keep pigs in Gordon Square, much as the idea appealed to her.

Tilton House, once Lydia is sufficiently close to distinguish it through the trees, looks exactly as a home should: solid enough to withstand any storm and at the same time welcoming, a place where occupants can be at ease. There is a pleasing symmetry of windows, while the tiled roof sits a little too low – as if the house has swapped the hat that best suits it for one that will shield it from the elements. Lydia enters by the back door and changes boots for slippers. Then she unbuttons her coat and unwinds the scarves from her head and neck. For most of her walk she has visualized Maynard writing in his chair, so is caught off guard to discover him in the sitting room stoking a roaring fire. The table on which she left coffee and biscuits has been reset with a teapot, teacups, a plate of thickly sliced bread, a butter dish and a jar of Leonard's honey.

'You not only received but deciphered prayers,' Lydia exclaims. 'I was so ravenous clambering back down hillside I almost ate berries in hedgerow. Even though I couldn't be sure if they were poisonous.' She spots the neat stack of pages covered in Maynard's handwriting. 'Did you finish chapter? I was hurling energetic vibrations for luminary cogitation from beacon top.'

'Chapter not only finished, but the next two plotted.' Maynard picks up the teapot, which in the absence of a cosy he has wrapped in newspaper to keep warm. 'No doubt aided by your transmissions. Whenever I've writing to do I should come here. Work that would take weeks in Cambridge or London seems to get accomplished in a morning. Not only accomplished, but turns out better than predicted.'

'So you prove your own theory', Lydia teases as he hands her a cup of tea. 'Predictions are pointless'.

'Not exactly pointless.' Maynard skewers a slice of bread onto the toasting fork and holds it over the fire. 'Though it's almost always what's not been predicted that occurs.'

They watch the bread turn gold. When it is ready, Maynard slides it onto a plate and spreads it with butter. Then he passes it to Lydia with the honey jar.

'Certainly I did not predict I should be waited on so royally,' Lydia sighs, spooning honey. 'From now on I cease all frets over meals and consult you as superior oracle.'

'I'm afraid my prowess ends at tea. Probably because the main ingredient apart from tea leaves and bread is a good fire. It relaxes me, gazing into the flames after working hard all day.'

'*Oblomovschina*,' Lydia chuckles triumphant. 'I shall make you proficient in essential Russian art of doing nothing!' She bites into her toast, closing her eyes to savour the taste. 'Now my mind is empty except for bliss of flavour.'

'I fear I've a long way to go before I reach your heights. My mind is permanently working. Even when I wish it would stop.' Maynard spikes a second slice of bread onto the toasting fork. 'The post came while you were out.'

'Any letters from Russia? I am eager to hear if Christmas gifts arrived.'

'Nothing I'm afraid. But there was some good news. At least, I hope you'll judge it good news. I was intending to save it for Christmas Day, but for various reasons it seems better to tell you now. In case it isn't what you want.'

Lydia stops eating to stare at him. 'What is it?' she asks in alarm.

Maynard wedges the toasting fork between coals in the scuttle and locates a brown envelope amongst his sheaf of writing notes. 'It's from Lord Gage's solicitor. The terms I offered for Tilton on a long lease have finally been accepted. So this house is ours for as long as we wish.'

Applause thunders after Lydia as she exits the stage at the Lyceum and starts towards her dressing room. She is carrying several bouquets, one entirely of orchids, Diaghilev's signature flower. He has written a single word in his cursive hand on the card pinned to the front: 'Bravissima'. She had looked up at his box as his tribute was delivered and he blew her a kiss, the quarrels that have punctuated their long association forgotten in shared triumph. She took her bow with Serge Lifar, her Prince in tonight's restaging of the 'Firebird', whom many are already tipping as the new Nijinsky. The audience rose to their feet to express delight at his virtuosic talent, yet when he stepped back leaving Lydia centre-stage it was clear from the tumultuous shouting of her name she was the one people adored. For some minutes she remained alone, smiling in gratitude and appreciation, while she was presented with so many flowers she could not hold them all. Her decision to direct them to her fellow dancers elicited even more ecstatic cheering from her admirers. At last she held out her free hand in invitation first to Serge, then to the rest of the company, so her final curtsey was made collectively. She lifted her head as the curtain came down and caught sight of Maynard, clapping so hard his hands moved in a blur.

Halfway down the corridor she spies a pair of dressers, heading to the wings to help Koschei and his demons remove their cumbersome masks. Still gripped by the same rush of affection she had felt on stage for everyone involved in the ballet, she beams as they approach. 'Bravissima' she wants to praise these shy young women in her turn. Instead, she thrusts lilies and carnations into their arms.

Lydia has a reason to be grateful to her dressers. She knew, when Diaghilev suggested she reprise her role of Firebird, that he was engaging her as a crowd-pleaser and not because he considered her the best dancer. Despite all her efforts to maintain her daily practice routine and keep an eye on her weight, she is aware she is not in the same league as Diaghilev's latest protégés. She has jested to Maynard that while her muscles seem hell-bent on shrinking into lazy slackness, her stomach and liver have quadrupled in size. It was nevertheless only when she tried on her costume – a short, tight scarlet tutu – that her unsuitability for the part was made blindingly clear. In front of the assembled cast Diaghilev declared she looked more like a plumped chicken ready for carving than the magical, ethereal Firebird. Lydia could not deny the charge and fled the rehearsal in tears. The dressers came to her rescue, helping her design a looser, more flattering tunic with a belt of fabric feathers to disguise her fleshy hips, while the older women loaned her their breast supports.

Her door is ajar and once inside Lydia gives her personal dresser Diaghilev's orchids. A number of bouquets have been sent to her room, including a magnificent display of red roses from Maynard. He has attached a card, confessing that the first time he bought her roses he had not known what message to send. Now he confronts the opposite difficulty, which is that the small rectangle of paper provided for the purpose is not big enough to do justice to Lydia's innumerable qualities, or his pride in her achievements, or his unparalleled happiness that she is his wife. He has addressed the envelope 'To the Firebird', which he initially spelled 'Friedbird' in honour of the running joke between them, and then firmly crossed out.

Lydia perches on her stool and instructs her dresser to admit no one for ten minutes. She has learned that if she starts talking to people too quickly after a performance, their necessarily different impressions will invade and even obliterate hers. She needs time alone to lodge her experience in her memory while everything is vivid and fresh. Otherwise, as with dreams, she will be unable to recall the details later with any accuracy.

A jug of lemonade and dishes of chocolates and cherries have been placed on her dressing table. Lydia glances in the mirror, but perhaps because she still has on her headdress and make-up her reflection reveals nothing back. She eats a cherry and is a girl again, dressed in a raven's costume with powdered cheeks and waiting on a bench in one of the communal dressing rooms at the Mariinsky. Her sister is next to her, soaking her bruised and bleeding feet in a bowl of

Epsom salts. She watches her younger self disappear unnoticed into
Anna Pavlova's dressing room and swap Eugenia's worn out shoes for
a more serviceable pair, marveling at the leading dancer's accolades
and luxury.

She slips on her old kimono. In her head, she hears a flurry of
flutes as the Firebird grants Prince Ivan a feather before vanishing
from the stage. Whenever she replays this scene she pictures her
friend Tamara Karsavina from School in the role of Firebird. It was
Tamara she turned to for advice when she accepted the part, visiting
her in her lodgings and listing on her fingers all the steps in the
choreography she struggled over. Tamara listened patiently to her
worries and when she finished told her to shut her eyes. She bid her
slowly raise her arms, not as Lydia but as a bird. Stiffly at first, but
then with increasing conviction, Lydia obeyed. 'Little Pet', Tamara
encouraged, 'the audience isn't interested in technical perfection.
They want you to show them the Firebird and this you will do. You
have great generosity as a performer. When you dance you invite the
audience to dance with you.' At this, Tamara ordered her to freeze
and open her eyes. 'See', she gestured, tracing the curve at her wrist
and split fan of her fingers, 'your hands have discovered the Firebird.
Now all you need do is transfer this to the rest of Lydia.'

There is a knock, a distinctive double rap, which is the signal she
has devised with Maynard. Her dresser unwinds the shimmering silk
of her turban, tidies her hair and moistens a flannel. Lydia cools her
neck and brow then nods for her husband to be allowed in.

'You were spell-binding,' Maynard promises, kissing her. 'As I was
certain you would be.'

'It's true I heave immense sigh of relief. Even if I'm proposed no
more parts and only dance at home in future, I'm glad to end on high
note and not crash out like antique has-been.'

'Little chance of that,' Maynard chuckles. 'I must have passed two
dozen reporters clamouring for an interview with you. It was all the
ushers could do to persuade them to let you change first. Soon there'll
be stampedes of doting fans and a riot of greedy pressmen jostling to
congratulate you.' He sits beside her in the only other chair. 'I've been
thinking about this article Virginia's writing on the cinema. It's all
very well taking photographs, but why not film the ballet? That way it
will be preserved for posterity.'

'Diaghilev would never agree. People have tried persuading him
but he always refuses.' She swivels round on her stool so she is facing
Maynard. 'He's right. Ballet isn't like other arts which can be enjoyed

again and again. Even if record is kept of choreography, it must be reborn from scratch. Ballet exists only in moment it is happening, in way all strands interact. So it changes each time. A film would try to fix it, which would be lie.' She pours out lemonade. 'It's story of Firebird. To be free we must become mortal.' She offers Maynard the dish of chocolates then pops one into her mouth. 'Which is not sad moral since it teaches us to relish present.'

There are voices and the scuffle of feet in the corridor outside. They hear a knock, quickly succeeded by others. Maynard smiles at Lydia who smiles back. She crosses herself and squares her shoulders. Then, with a wink at her husband, she instructs her dresser to open the door.

CAST LIST

The Bloomsbury Group was a loose friendship alliance of thinkers and artists. They are associated with innovations in art and literature, with pacifism, liberalism and free-thinking, especially in relation to sexuality and women's rights. The group had its origins in a philosophical discussion club known as the 'Apostles' at Cambridge University where several male members studied, and took its name from the London district of Bloomsbury where most members subsequently lived.

Bell, Clive (1881-1964) was a British art critic and a member of the Bloomsbury Group. In his 1914 book *Art* Bell helped pioneer the move to abstraction, coining the term 'significant form' to explore how non-mimetic representation can kindle our aesthetic response. He married Vanessa Stephen in 1907 and they had two sons, **Julian Bell** (1908-1937, killed as a volunteer ambulance driver in the Spanish Civil War) and the art historian and potter **Quentin Bell** (1910-1996). Although his marriage to Vanessa was over by the outbreak of the First World War, they remained close and Bell gave his name to Vanessa's daughter, the painter and writer **Angelica Garnett** (1918-2012). During the period in which *Firebird* is set, Bell was involved in an affair with the British art patron and artist's model **Mary Hutchinson** (née Barnes, 1889-1977).

. . .

Bell, Vanessa (née Stephen, 1879-1961) was a British artist and interior designer and a member of the Bloomsbury Group. It was her decision to move to the London district of Bloomsbury in 1904 with her sister Virginia (see Woolf, Virginia) and brothers **Thoby Stephen** (1880-1906, died from typhoid) and psychoanalyst **Adrian Stephen** (1883-1948), which gave the Bloomsbury Group their name. She studied at the Royal Academy from 1901-1904 and her prolific oeuvre includes paintings such as 'Studland Beach' (1912), 'Interior with a Table, St Tropez' (1921), radical faceless portraits of her sister Virginia and many still lifes which feature or inform elements here. At the start of the First World War Vanessa moved to Charleston farmhouse on the Sussex Coast, and subsequently divided her time between Bloomsbury and Charleston, punctuated from 1921 on with long periods in the South of France. She married Clive Bell in 1907 and they had two sons (see Bell, Clive above). She had a brief affair with the British art critic, historian and painter **Roger Fry** (1866-1934) who, like Bell, remained a close friend, but her lasting love was for Duncan Grant with whom she had a daughter.

Bowen, Vera (née Polianov, ?-1967) was a Russian librettist and theatre designer. She met her second husband the wealthy British Middle Eastern scholar **Harold Bowen** (1896-1959) during her staging of Anton Chekhov's *Three Sisters* in 1920, the text of which he translated.

Diaghilev, Sergei (1872-1929) was a promoter of Russian art. He is commonly acknowledged to have revolutionized ballet by integrating the ideals and innovations of other art forms including music, painting and drama. He founded the **Ballets Russes** in 1909, touring with them to Europe and America. In the same year, he commissioned Igor Stravinsky to write a score for a new full-length ballet 'Firebird', followed by further commissions for 'Petrushka' in 1911 and the 'Rite of Spring' in 1913, the opening night of which provoked a riot. The British dance critic **Cyril Beaumont** (1891-1976) was an important advocate for the Ballets Russes in Britain.

Grant, Duncan (1885-1978) was a British artist and designer and member of the Bloomsbury Group. As a boy he lived with his aunt, the British women's rights campaigner Lady Jane Strachey (née Grant, 1840-1928) and cousins. Unlike other male members of the Bloomsbury Group he did not go to Cambridge University, but studied at the Westminster School of Art, then in Italy and Paris, before taking up residence in Bloomsbury. Grant first met Vanessa Bell in 1905. He had affairs with his cousin (see Strachey, Lytton), with Maynard Keynes, with Adrian Stephen (see Bell, Vanessa) and British writer **David ('Bunny') Garnett** (1892-1981). His lasting close relationship was with Vanessa Bell and he was father to her daughter Angelica, who in 1942 married Garnett. Grant's prolific oeuvre includes the painting 'Vanessa Bell' (1917) of her reclining in a blue dress on a red sofa described here.

Higgens, Grace (née Germany, 1903-1983) was appointed by Vanessa Bell to be housemaid in Gordon Square, Bloomsbury in June 1920. She went on to become the housekeeper at Charleston farmhouse until retiring in 1971. An archive of Higgens' diaries, letters and photographs spanning her long association with the Bloomsbury Group is held by the British Library.

Henderson, Sir Hubert (1890-1952) was a British economist. In 1923 Maynard Keynes formed a company to purchase the British weekly *Nation and Athenaeum*, which he persuaded Henderson to resign his lectureship at Cambridge University to edit.

Keynes, John Maynard (1883-1946) was an influential British economist and a member of the Bloomsbury Group. His father **John Neville Keynes** (1852-1949) lectured at Cambridge University and his mother **Florence Ada Keynes** (1861-1958) became Cambridge's first woman councillor, alderman then mayor, as well as one of Britain's first female magistrates. Keynes' brother **Sir Geoffrey Keynes** (1887-1982) was a surgeon and literary scholar and his sister was the social welfare worker **Margaret Hill** (née Keynes, 1885-1970). Keynes was educated at Eton and won a scholarship in mathematics and classics to King's College, University of Cambridge where he was later a Fellow. As a student he was recruited to the Cambridge 'Apostles' (see Bloomsbury Group), where discussion was fuelled by Cambridge philosopher **G.E. Moore**

(1873-1958), prompting Keynes to conclude that life's aims 'were love, the creation and enjoyment of aesthetic experience and the pursuit of knowledge. Of these love came a long way first.' After graduating he joined the civil service and was posted to the India Office, but the job bored him and in 1908 he secured a lectureship in economics at Cambridge University. His 1913 book *Indian Currency and Finance* ensured Keynes a place on the British government's Royal Commission on Indian finance. From January 1915 Keynes was employed by the Treasury to assist with financing the British war effort. His experiences at the Paris Peace Conference in 1918 informed his best-selling book *The Economic Consequences of the Peace* published in December 1919, which contained controversial portraits and proposals, including the setting-up of a credit fund open to all war-participants and the creation of a free European trade union. In 1921 he edited a series of supplements for the *Manchester Guardian* on European economic construction. He was a successful investor, though early speculations in foreign currency in 1919-20 proved temporarily disastrous not only for himself but for his Bloomsbury friends. Amongst his numerous affairs with men those with Duncan Grant and British sociologist **Sebastian Sprott** (1897-1971) were the most important. He married Lydia Lopokova in August 1925. He was a campaigner for reform in the law against homosexuality and for women's rights, serving as vice-chair for the Marie Stopes Society in 1932 (see Stopes, Marie). He became seriously ill with a heart condition in 1937 and was devotedly nursed by Lopokova until his death in 1946. Despite recurring illness, he was appointed a consultative council to the Treasury during the Second World War and represented Britain at the Bretton Woods Conference in July 1944, tasked with rebuilding post-war international finance. He also served as a director of the Bank of England. He was an advocate for the proposals of British Liberal politician Lord William Beveridge (1879-1963), resulting in the creation of the post-war British Welfare State and National Health Service. Keynes became Chair of the Committee for the Encouragement of Music and the Arts in 1941 which led to the establishment of the British Arts Council. He was given a hereditary peerage in 1942 with the title 'Baron Keynes of Tilton'.

Lopokova, Lydia (née Lopukhova later Lady Keynes, 1892-1981) was a Russian dancer. She trained at the Imperial Ballet School in St

Petersburg under such teachers as **Enrico Cecchetti** (1850-1928), **Marius Petipa** (1818-1910) and **Mikhail Fokine** (1880-1942), and where she met dancers such as **Tamara Karsarvina** (1885-1978), **Mathilde Kschessinska** (1872-1971), **Anna Pavlova** (1881-1931) and **Isadora Duncan** (1877-1927) who all feature here. Her brother **Fedor Lopukhov** (1886-1973), sister **Eugenia** (1884-1943) and brother **Andrei** (1898-1947) were also dancers; Fedor went on to become a distinguished choreographer and director. Her father, **Vasili Lopukhov** (?-1912) was an usher at the Imperial Alexandrinsky Theatre in St Petersburg, and her mother **Constanza** (née Douglas, 1860-1942) was of Swedish-Scottish descent. Lopokova had many dance partners, those who figure here are the Russians **Léonide Massine** (1896-1979), **Vaslav Nijinsky** (1890-1950), Alexandre Volinine (see Mandelkern, Josef), **Mikhail Mordkin** (1880-1944), **Nicholas Zverez** (1888-1965) and **Serge Lifar** (1905-1986). In 1910 Lopokova and her brother Fedor were included in Diaghilev's second summer tour to Europe with the Ballets Russes, after which the siblings departed for America (see Mandelkern, Josef). After an affair with Igor Stravinksy and American journalist **Heywood Broun** (1888-1939), Lopokova married Diaghilev's Italian manager **Randolfo Barocchi** (1885-?) in 1916, who remained married to an American singer Mary Hargreaves. After filing for divorce, Lopokova married Maynard Keynes in August 1925. In the early 1930s, together with British dancer, choreographer and director **Sir Frederick Ashton** (1904-1988), Lopokova became a leading figure in the newly created Camargo Society for the promotion of British dance.

Mandelkern, Josef was a Russian émigré and theatrical agent whose clients included the Broadway theatrical producer **Charles Frohman** (1860-1915), responsible for inviting Lopokova, her brother Fedor and her dance partner **Alexandre Volinine** (1882-1955) to New York in 1910.

Fiske, Minnie (née Davy, 1864?-1932) was an American actress, playwright and director. Together with her husband the theatrical manager Harrison Grey Fiske (1861-1942), she directed 'The Young Idea' in which Lopokova starred in 1914.

· · ·

Morrell, Lady Ottoline (née Cavendish-Bentinck, 1873-1938) was a British promoter of the arts who, from 1907, held weekly parties at her home in Bloomsbury. During the First World War she moved with her husband to Garsington Manor in Oxfordshire, which became a refuge for artists and those refusing military enlistment on moral grounds.

Mortimer, Raymond (1895-1980) was a British writer on literature and art. He moved to Bloomsbury in 1924 and in the same year began an affair with British diplomat and politician Harold Nicholson (1886-1968), husband of Vita Sackville-West (see Woolf, Virginia).

Picasso, Pablo (1881-1973) was a Spanish painter, sculptor, print-maker, ceramicist and set designer, who is widely acknowledged as revolutionizing art in the twentieth century. In 1917 he designed the sets and costumes for 'Parade', choreographed by Léonide Massine (see Lopokova) for the Ballets Russes, with a libretto by French writer and filmmaker **Jean Cocteau** (1889-1963) and music by French composer and pianist **Erik Satie** (1866-1925). One of those appearing in 'Parade' was the Russian dancer **Olga Khokhlova** (1891-1955) whom Picasso married in 1918.

Ruck, Berta (1878-1978) was a British popular writer, publishing serials, journalism and for much of her long career between one and three novels a year, the majority involving a Cinderella-like romance.

Rylands, George ('Dadie') (1902-1999) was a British literary scholar with particular interests in the theatre and a Fellow of King's College, University of Cambridge (see Keynes, Maynard).

Sheppard, Sir John ('Jack') (1881-1968) was a British classical scholar and Fellow of King's College, University of Cambridge (see Keynes, Maynard).

· · ·

The Sitwells were British writers: Dame Edith Sitwell (1887-1964), Sir Osbert Sitwell (1892-1969) and Sir Sacheverell Sitwell (1897-1988). There is a striking portrait 'The Sitwell Family' (1900) by the Italian-born painter **John Singer Sargent** (1856-1925), who taught Vanessa Bell at the Royal Academy.

Stoll, Sir Oswald (1866-1942) was an Australian-born theatre entrepreneur. He opened the London Coliseum in 1904 to present high-quality variety performance, including ballet. In 1920 he founded Stoll Picture Productions and became a leading maker and distributor of British cinema. He was a notable philanthropist and in 1919 was knighted for his charitable donations.

Stopes, Marie (1880-1958) was a British sexologist and advocate of birth control. Her 1918 guide *Married Love* was a best-seller and in 1921 she set up her first birth control and mothers' clinic.

Strachey, Lytton (1880-1932) was a British biographer and reviewer and a member of the Bloomsbury Group. His 1918 book *Eminent Victorians* heralded a new form of English biography in which truth is acknowledged to be fragmentary and in which the biographer's freedom is paramount. In 1917 Strachey moved to Mill House at Tidmarsh in Berkshire with British painter **Dora Carrington** (1893-1932), where they were joined by First World War veteran **Ralph Partridge** (1894-1960, awarded the Military Cross with bar and the Croix de Guerre) with whom Strachey fell in love and whom Carrington married. Carrington and Partridge worked for the Hogarth Press (see Woolf, Virginia), as for a short time did Lopokova.

Stravinsky, Igor (1882-1971) was a Russian composer widely credited with influencing a new, modernist direction in music. In 1909 Sergei Diaghilev commissioned him to write the score for his new full-length ballet 'Firebird' (see Diaghilev, Sergei).

· · ·

Weller, Ruby began working as Lopokova's maid in Gordon Square, Bloomsbury in 1923. She married **Edgar Weller**, the Keynes' Tilton neighbour, in 1925 and remained a close companion to Lopokova.

Woolf, Leonard (1880-1969) was a British author and publisher and a member of the Bloomsbury Group. In 1899 he won a classics scholarship to Trinity College, University of Cambridge where he met other members of the group. After graduating he joined the colonial civil service in Ceylon, becoming the youngest assistant governor – an experience he described as his anti-imperial education and wrote about in his 1913 novel *The Village in the Jungle*. He married Virginia Stephen in 1912 and together they founded the Hogarth Press (see Woolf, Virginia). In 1919 the couple bought Monk's House near Charleston (see Bell, Vanessa), subsequently dividing their time between London and Sussex. Woolf served as secretary to the Labour Party's advisory committees on international and imperial questions from 1919 to 1945, and was literary editor of the *Nation and Athenaeum* from 1923 to 1930 (see Henderson, Hubert).

Woolf, Virginia (née Stephen, 1882-1941) was a British author and publisher, sister to Vanessa Bell and member of the Bloomsbury Group. She is regarded as one of the most important writers of the twentieth century pioneering a new modernist form for the novel and, with the publication of *A Room of One's Own* in 1929, as a champion for women's emancipation. Her father **Sir Leslie Stephen** (1832-1904) was a founding editor of the *Dictionary of National Biography*. She published the novels *Jacob's Room* in 1922 and *Mrs Dalloway* in 1925 referenced here. She was a prolific reviewer, essayist, letter-writer and diarist. She married in 1912 (see Woolf, Leonard) and had affairs with a number of women, including fellow British writer and gardener **Vita Sackville-West** (1892-1962) whom she met in 1922. With her husband she founded the Hogarth Press, publishing authors such as the American poet **T S ('Tom') Eliot** (1888-1965), the New Zealand short-story writer **Katherine Mansfield** (1888-1923), the British novelist **E M (Morgan) Forster** (1879-1970) and declining to publish *Ulysses* by Irish writer **James Joyce** (1882-1941) as it was longer than their early hand press could accommodate. They commissioned an English translation of the works of **Sigmund Freud** (1856-1939) and, in conjunction with Russian émigré **Samuel**

Koteliansky (1880-1955), translations of Russian authors including **Fyodor Dostoevsky** (1821-1881), **Leo Tolstoy** (1828-1910) and Maxim Gorky's *Reminiscences of Chekhov* (**Anton Chekhov**, 1860-1904).

ACKNOWLEDGMENTS

As with any project of long duration, this one had a number of starting points and involved multiple strands. I am indebted to an old friend for enthusing about the exhibition 'Diaghilev and the Golden Age of the Ballets Russes, 1909-1929' at the Victoria and Albert Museum in London, and for prompting engrossing discussion about the unlikely marriage between one of the ballerinas and the economist John Maynard Keynes. I would have made little headway with Lydia Lopokova had it not been for the generosity and willingness of dancers to answer questions, to allow me to watch them work, to share the compulsions that propel them and the challenges they confront. As always, conversations with fellow researchers and writers were crucial during the long period of gestation and composition, and I would like to thank the many experts who responded to emails or met to talk about such divergent topics as Keynesian economic theory, Russian history, the Bloomsbury Group, the First World War, Music Hall in America, the legal situation with regard to homosexuality in Britain in the first decades of the twentieth century, Flamenco, women's fashion and more. I am especially grateful to the late Mark Hayes for advising on John Maynard Keynes, to Claire Davison for setting me right on the Russian language, to Mark Hussey for sharing thoughts ahead of the publication of his biography of Clive Bell, to Sandra Smith for advice on both dancing and writing, and to colleagues at St Andrews University including John Burnside, Lesley Glaister, Gill Plain, Jane

Stabler and Emma Sutton. Any errors are of course my own. My English publisher, John Spiers, has been everything an author could wish for. Robert Travers at Piano Nobile not only replied to my query about Duncan Grant's 1918-1919 painting 'Juggler and Tightrope Walker' but was able to arrange permission so that I might reproduce it courtesy of Duncan Grant's Estate. Embarking on a book necessarily affects those we live alongside, and I would like to register here my appreciation for the understanding and involvement of my husband Jeremy Thurlow and son Ben. Finally, I owe an immense debt to my agent Jenny Brown, whose enthusiasm, support and belief in this project have been a life-line.

Today more than ever, where precisely to draw the line between 'truth' and 'in(ter)vention' is a matter of intense and crucial debate. It has been my goal in telling this story to pay tribute to those who have inspired it, to which end I have not consciously introduced any element for which there is not already a suggestion in what is known of the lives. Most of my evidence has come from reading the words of those who feature here – perhaps most importantly the letters Keynes and Lopokova wrote to each other, a selection of which has been published by Polly Hill and Richard Keynes as *Lydia and Maynard: The Letters of Lydia Lopokova and John Maynard Keynes*. In addition to the letters, The Modern Archive Centre at King's College Cambridge holds a full collection of Keynes' papers and a separate collection relating to Lopokova. I am hugely grateful to the Provost and Fellows of King's College, to Peter Jones, to the College Archivist and all those who work at the Archive Centre for allowing me the extraordinary privilege of sifting through boxes of handwritten correspondence and notes, professional and family photographs, personal scrapbooks, ballet programmes and so much more. Amongst the vast array of published materials, I found Milo Keynes' *Lydia Lopokova* with its first-hand testimonies and the two volumes of Virginia Woolf's diaries covering the periods 1920-24 and 1925-30 particularly helpful. There can be delightful serendipity even within the most rigorous research methodology, an example being the lucky discovery of Berta Ruck's letter to Quentin Bell detailing a theatre outing at which Lopokova was present. Crucially, my research was enhanced by excellent biographies: Judith Mackrell's *Bloomsbury Ballerina* and Robert Skidelsky's *John Maynard Keynes 1883-1946: Economist, Philosopher, Statesmen* – the latter leavened by Richard Davenport-Hines' *Universal Man: The Seven Lives of John Maynard Keynes*.

Of course fiction involves elements such as imagination and empathy in addition to research; it is my hope that in writing a novel I will encourage readers to discover more about the real-life sources which animate this most unusual and enduring of love stories.

Susan Sellers

Lightning Source UK Ltd.
Milton Keynes UK
UKHW022147290322
400788UK00001B/2